THE LAST BATTLE

Now it was the screens of the Earth-machines that flamed in defense. As at the one command, they darted suddenly toward the ship each attacked—nearer—then the watchers from a distance saw them disappear, and the screens back of Earth went suddenly blank.

Half an hour later, nine thousand six hundred and thirty-three titanic ships moved majestically on.

They swept over Earth in a great line, a line that reached from pole to pole, and from each the pale green beams reached down, and all life beneath them was swept out of existence. . . .

—from "The Last Evolution"
by John W. Campbell, Jr.

Fawcett Crest Books
edited by Isaac Asimov, Martin Harry Greenberg,
and Charles G. Waugh:

☐ CATASTROPHES!   24425 $2.50

☐ THE SEVEN CARDINAL VIRTUES OF SCIENCE
   FICTION   24440 $2.50

☐ THE SEVEN DEADLY SINS OF SCIENCE
   FICTION   24349 $2.50

☐ SPACE MAIL VOLUME II   24481 $2.50

And edited by Isaac Asimov, Martin Harry Greenberg,
and Joseph D. Olander:

☐ THE FUTURE I   24366 $2.50

☐ THE FUTURE IN QUESTION   24266 $2.50

☐ SPACE MAIL   24312 $2.50

SPACE MAIL
Volume II

Edited by
**Isaac Asimov,
Martin Harry Greenberg,
and Charles G. Waugh**

Introduction by Isaac Asimov

FAWCETT CREST • NEW YORK

SPACE MAIL VOLUME II

Published by Fawcett Crest Books, CBS Educational and
Professional Publishing, a division of CBS Inc.

ISBN: 0-449-24481-4

Printed in the United States of America

First Fawcett Crest printing: January 1982

10   9   8   7   6   5   4   3   2   1

CONTENTS

General Reader
Anywhere

Dear G. R.,

We are all curious to one extent or another. We all want to know.

Strictly speaking, "curiosity" refers, particularly, to the desire to know what we ought not to know; to poking into something that is "not our business."

Someone who asks to see the sales data for the previous week isn't being curious if he is the sales manager of the company involved; he is merely doing his job. If he is a casual passerby, however, he is being curious. Worse than that, he is "nosy." The figures are none of his business and he doesn't get to see them. In fact, if we are in charge of the material, we are highly indignant over nosiness and are likely to speculate on the possibility of calling the cops if he is bigger than we are, or of handing him one in the snoot if he is smaller.

On the occasions when we are victimized by such curious people, we are likely to have the virtuous feeling that we ourselves are not nosy; that we do not thrust ourselves in where we have no business being.

Would you like to bet on that?

Suppose that you are composing yourself to sleep in a hotel

room, and suddenly notice on the night table a loose printed sheet. You might glance at it casually. It could be a notice from the hotel, a sheet of advertising, even a loose page from a book. We are not at all likely to be interested. We either ignore it or throw it away.

But suppose that sheet of paper is handwritten and turns out to be a personal letter from John to Mary, or vice versa. The chances of its being the least bit interesting are virtually zero, if only because most people have nothing interesting to say, yet you know you would read it—every word—postponing sleep to do so.

It is possible the letter might contain steamy passages of love and passion, but it's much more likely it would not. The absence of the lurid wouldn't matter, however. Even if the letter was one of those "Aunt Hester is feeling poorly these days but sends her love and hopes you are well" types, you would still read on.

Why? Exactly because the letter is none of your business. It was written for one pair of eyes only, and yours are not the pair. You have the privilege of eavesdropping on words not meant for you, and can you resist that?

You know you can't.

When a good story is told in the form of letters or other personal memoranda, therefore, it rouses our interest doubly. The story is exciting in itself; but the air of the invaded personal is a delightful added titillation. It was no surprise, then, that when we presented a collection of such stories, it did very well. So well did it do, in fact, that the shrewd and businesslike people at Fawcett demanded a second volume.

And here it is. Enjoy, G. R., enjoy.

Sincerely,
Isaac Asimov

DIARIES

EXTRACTS FROM ADAM'S DIARY
by Mark Twain

Mark Twain (Samuel L. Clemens, 1835–1910) should not need an introduction for anyone who reads English. Yet, few people realize just how much excellent science fiction and fantasy he wrote during his long career. His famous *A Connecticut Yankee in King Arthur's Court* (1889) is just the tip of the iceberg, because he also wrote many sf and fantasy short stories, which are presently being collected in book form. "Extracts from Adam's Diary" is one of the best of these works—we wonder what kind of tales he would be spinning if he was alive today!

EXTRACTS FROM ADAM'S DIARY

Monday.—This new creature with the long hair is a good deal in the way. It is always hanging around and following me about. I don't like this; I am not used to company. I wish it would stay with the other animals. . . . Cloudy to-day, wind in the east; think we shall have rain. . . . *We?* Where did I get that word?—I remember now—the new creature uses it.

TUESDAY.—Been examining the great waterfall. It is the finest thing on the estate, I think. The new creature calls it Niagara Falls—why, I am sure I do not know. Says it *looks* like Niagara Falls. That is not a reason, it is mere waywardness and imbecility. I get no chance to name anything myself. The new creature names everything that comes along, before I can get in a protest. And always that same pretext is offered—it *looks* like the thing. There is the dodo, for instance. Says the moment one looks at it one sees at a glance that it "looks like a dodo." It will have to keep that name, no doubt. It wearies me to fret about it, and it does no good, anyway. Dodo! It looks no more like a dodo than I do.

WEDNESDAY.—Built me a shelter against the rain, but could not have it to myself in peace. The new creature intruded. When I tried to put it out it shed water out of the holes it looks with, and wiped it away with the back of its paws, and made a noise such as some of the other animals make when they are in distress. I wish it would not talk; it is always talking. That sounds like a cheap fling at the poor creature, a slur; but I do not mean it so. I have never heard the human voice before, and any new and strange sound intruding itself here upon the solemn hush of these dreaming solitudes offends my ear and seems a false note. And this new sound is so close to me; it is right at my shoulder, right at my ear, first on one side and then on the other, and I am used only to sounds that are more or less distant from me.

FRIDAY.—The naming goes recklessly on, in spite of anything I can do. I had a very good name for the estate, and it was musical and pretty—GARDEN OF EDEN. Privately, I continue to call it that, but not any longer publicly. The new creature says it is all woods and rocks and scenery, and therefore has no resemblance to a garden. Says it *looks* like a park, and does not look like anything *but* a park. Consequently, without consulting me, it has been new-named—NIAGARA FALLS PARK. This is sufficiently high-handed, it seems to me. And already there is a sign up:

KEEP OFF
THE GRASS

My life is not as happy as it was.

SATURDAY.—The new creature eats too much fruit. We are going to run short, most likely. "We" again—that is *its* word; mine, too, now, from hearing it so much. Good deal of fog this morning. I do not go out in the fog myself. The new creature does. It goes out in all weathers, and stumps right in with its muddy feet. And talks. It used to be so pleasant and quiet here.

SUNDAY.—Pulled through. This day is getting to be more and more trying. It was selected and set apart last November as a day of rest. I had already six of them per week before. This morning found the new creature trying to clod apples out of that forbidden tree.

MONDAY.—The new creature says its name is Eve. That is all right, I have no objections. Says it is to call it by, when I want it to come. I said it was superfluous, then. The word evidently raised me in its respect; and indeed it is a large, good word and will bear repetition. It says it is not an It, it is a She. This is probably doubtful; yet it is all one to me; what she is were nothing to me if she would but go by herself and not talk.

TUESDAY.—She has littered the whole estate with execrable names and offensive signs:

THIS WAY TO THE WHIRLPOOL.
THIS WAY TO GOAT ISLAND.
CAVE OF THE WINDS THIS WAY.

She says this park would make a tidy summer resort if there was any custom for it. Summer resort—another invention of hers—just words, without any meaning. What is a summer resort? But it is best not to ask her, she has such a rage for explaining.

FRIDAY.—She has taken to beseeching me to stop going over the Falls. What harm does it do? Says it makes her shudder. I wonder why; I have always done it—always liked the plunge, and the excitement and the coolness. I supposed it was what the Falls were for. They have no other use that I can see, and they must have been made for something. She says they were only made for scenery—like the rhinoceros and the mastodon.

I went over the Falls in a barrel—not satisfactory to her. Went over in a tub—still not satisfactory. Swam the Whirlpool and the Rapids in a fig-leaf suit. It got much damaged. Hence, tedious complaints about my extravagance. I am too much hampered here. What I need is a change of scene.

SATURDAY.—I escaped last Tuesday night, and traveled two days, and built me another shelter in a secluded place, and obliterated my tracks as well as I could, but she hunted me out by means of a beast which she has tamed and calls a wolf, and came making that pitiful noise again, and shedding that water out of the places she looks with. I was obliged to return with her, but will presently emigrate again when occasion offers. She engages herself in many foolish things; among others, to study out why the animals called lions and tigers live on grass and flowers, when, as she says, the sort of teeth they wear would indicate that they were intended to eat each other. This is foolish, because to do that would be to kill each other, and that would introduce what, as I understand it, is called "death"; and death, as I have been told, has not yet entered the Park. Which is a pity, on some accounts.

SUNDAY.—Pulled through.

MONDAY.—I believe I see what the week is for: it is to give time to rest up from the weariness of Sunday. It seems a good idea. . . . She has been climbing that tree again. Clodded her out of it. She said nobody was looking. Seems to consider that a sufficient justification for chancing any dangerous thing. Told her that. The word justification moved her admiration— and envy, too, I thought. It is a good word.

TUESDAY.—She told me she was made out of a rib taken from my body. This is at least doubtful, if not more than that. I have not missed any rib. . . . She is in much trouble about the buzzard; says grass does not agree with it; is afraid she can't raise it; thinks it was intended to live on decayed flesh. The buzzard must get along the best it can with what it is provided. We cannot overturn the whole scheme to accommodate the buzzard.

SATURDAY.—She fell in the pond yesterday when she was looking at herself in it, which she is always doing. She nearly strangled, and said it was most uncomfortable. This made her sorry for the creatures which live in there, which she calls fish, for she continues to fasten names on to things that don't need them and don't come when they are called by them, which is a matter of no consequence to her, she is such a numskull, anyway; so she got a lot of them out and brought them in last night and put them in my bed to keep warm, but I have noticed them now and then all day and I don't see that they are any happier there than they were before, only quieter. When night comes I shall throw them outdoors. I will not sleep with them again, for I find them clammy and unpleasant to lie among when a person hasn't anything on.

SUNDAY.—Pulled through.

TUESDAY.—She has taken up with a snake now. The other animals are glad, for she was always experimenting with them and bothering them; and I am glad because the snake talks, and this enables me to get a rest.

FRIDAY.—She says the snake advises her to try the fruit of that tree, and says the result will be a great and fine and noble education. I told her there would be another result, too—it would introduce death into the world. That was a mistake—it had been better to keep the remark to myself; it only gave her an idea—she could save the sick buzzard, and furnish fresh meat to the despondent lions and tigers. I advised her to keep away from the tree. She said she wouldn't. I foresee trouble. Will emigrate.

WEDNESDAY.—I have had a variegated time. I escaped last night, and rode a horse all night as fast as he could go, hoping to get clear out of the Park and hide in some other country before the trouble should begin; but it was not to be. About an hour after sun-up, as I was riding through a flowery plain where thousands of animals were grazing, slumbering, or playing with each other, according to their wont, all of a sudden they broke into a tempest of frightful noises, and in one moment the plain was a frantic commotion and every beast was destroying its neighbor. I knew what it meant— Eve had eaten that fruit, and death was come into the world. . . . The tigers ate my horse, paying no attention when I ordered them to desist, and they would have eaten me if I had stayed—which I didn't, but went away in much haste. . . . I found this place, outside the Park, and was fairly comfortable for a few days, but she has found me out. Found me out, and has named the place Tonawanda—says it *looks* like that. In fact I was not sorry she came, for there are but meagre pickings here, and she brought some of those apples. I was obliged to eat them, I was so hungry. It was against my principles, but I find that principles have no real force except when one is well fed. . . . She came curtained in boughs and bunches of leaves, and when I asked her what she meant by such nonsense, and snatched them away and threw them down, she tittered and blushed. I had never seen a person titter and blush before, and to me it seemed unbecoming and idiotic. She said I would soon know how it was myself. This was correct. Hungry as I was, I laid down the apple half-eaten— certainly the best one I ever saw, considering the lateness of the season—and arrayed myself in the discarded boughs and branches, and then spoke to her with some severity and ordered her to go and get some more and not make such a spectacle of herself. She did it, and after this we crept down to where the wild-beast battle had been, and collected some skins, and I made her patch together a couple of suits proper for public occasions. They are uncomfortable, it is true, but stylish, and that is the main point about clothes. . . . I find she is a good deal of a companion. I see I should be lonesome and depressed without her, now that I have lost my property. Another thing, she says it is ordered that we work for our living hereafter. She will be useful. I will superintend.

TEN DAYS LATER.—She accuses *me* of being the cause of our disaster! She says, with apparent sincerity and truth, that the Serpent assured her that the forbidden fruit was not apples, it was chestnuts. I said I was innocent,then, for I had not eaten any chestnuts. She said the Serpent informed her that "chestnut" was a figurative term meaning an aged and mouldy joke. I turned pale at that, for I have made many jokes to pass the weary time, and some of them could have been of that sort, though I had honestly supposed that they were new when I made them. She asked me if I had made one just at the time of the catastrophe. I was obliged to admit that I had made one to myself, though not aloud. It was this. I was thinking about the Falls, and I said to myself, "How wonderful it is to see that vast body of water tumble down there!" Then in an instant a bright thought flashed into my head, and I let it fly, saying, "It would be a deal more wonderful to see it tumble *up* there!"—and I was just about to kill myself with laughing at it when all nature broke loose in war and death and I had to flee for my life. "There," she said, with triumph, "that is just it; the Serpent mentioned that very jest, and called it the First Chestnut, and said it was coeval with the creation." Alas, I am indeed to blame. Would that I were not witty; oh, that I had never had that radiant thought!

NEXT YEAR. We have named it Cain. She caught it while I was up country trapping on the North Shore of the Erie; caught it in the timber a couple of miles from our dug-out—or it might have been four, she isn't certain which. It resembles us in some ways, and may be a relation. That is what she thinks, but this is an error, in my judgment. The difference in size warrants the conclusion that it is a different and new kind of animal—a fish, perhaps, though when I put it in the water to see, it sank, and she plunged in and snatched it out before there was opportunity for the experiment to determine the matter.I still think it is a fish, but she is indifferent about what it is, and will not let me have it to try. I do not understand this. The coming of the creature seems to have changed her whole nature and made her unreasonable about experiments. She thinks more of it than she does of any of the other animals, but is not able to explain why. Her mind is disordered—everything shows it. Sometimes she carries the fish in her arms half the night when it complains and wants to get to the water. At such times the water comes out of the places in her face that she looks out of, and she pats the fish on the back and makes soft sounds with her mouth to soothe it, and betrays sorrow and solicitude in a hundred ways. I have never seen her do like this with any other fish, and it troubles me greatly. She used to carry the young tigers around so, and play with them, before we lost our property, but it was only play; she never took on about them like this when their dinner disagreed with them.

SUNDAY.—She doesn't work, Sundays, but lies around all tired out, and likes to have the fish wallow over her; and she makes fool noises to amuse it, and pretends to chew its paws, and that makes it laugh. I have not seen a fish before that could laugh. This makes me doubt. . . . I have come to like Sunday myself. Superintending all the week tires a body so. There ought to be more Sundays. In the old days they were tough, but now they come handy.

WEDNESDAY.—It isn't a fish. I cannot quite make out what it is. It makes curious devilish noises when not satisfied, and says "goo-goo" when it is. It is not one of us, for it doesn't walk; it is not a bird, for it doesn't fly; it is not a frog, for it doesn't hop; it is not a snake, for it doesn't crawl; I feel sure it is not a fish, though I cannot get a chance to find out whether it can swim or not. It merely lies around, and mostly on its back, with its feet up. I have not seen any other animal do that before. I said I believed it was an enigma; but she only admired the word without understanding it. In my judgment it is either an enigma or some kind of a bug. If it dies, I will take it apart and see what its arrangements are. I never had a thing perplex me so.

THREE MONTHS LATER.—The perplexity augments instead of diminishing. I sleep but little. It has ceased from lying around, and goes about on its four legs now. Yet it differs from the other four-legged animals, in that its front legs are unusually short, consequently this causes the main part of its person to stick up uncomfortably high in the air, and this is not attractive. It is built much as we are, but its method of traveling shows that it is not of our breed. The short front legs and long hind ones indicate that it is of the kangaroo family, but it is a marked variation of the species, since the true kangaroo hops, whereas this one never does. Still it is a curious and interesting variety, and has not been catalogued before. As I discovered it, I have felt justified in securing the credit of the discovery by attaching my name to it, and hence have called it *Kangaroorum Adamiensis.* . . . It must have been a young one when it came, for it has grown exceedingly since. It must be five times as big, now, as it was then, and when discontented it is able to make from twenty-two to thirty-eight times the noise it made at first. Coercion does not modify this, but has the contrary effect. For this reason I discontinued the system. She reconciles it by persuasion, and by giving it things which she had previously told it she wouldn't give it. As already observed, I was not at home when it first came, and she told me she found it in the woods. It seems odd that it should be the only one, yet it must be so, for I have worn myself out these many weeks trying to find another one to add to my collection, and for this one to play with; for surely then it would be quieter and we could tame it more easily. But I find none, nor any vestige of any; and strangest of all, no tracks. It has to live on the ground, it cannot help itself; therefore, how does it get about without leaving a track? I have set a dozen traps, but they do no good. I catch all small animals except that one; animals that merely go into the trap out of curiosity, I think, to see what the milk is there for. They never drink it.

THREE MONTHS LATER.—The Kangaroo still continues to grow, which is very strange and perplexing. I never knew one to be so long getting its growth. It has fur on its head now; not like kangaroo fur, but exactly like our hair except that it is much finer and softer, and instead of being black is red. I am like to lose my mind over the capricious and harassing developments of this unclassifiable zoological freak. If I could catch another one—but that is hopeless; it is a new variety, and the only sample; this is plain. But I caught a true kangaroo and brought it in, thinking that this one, being lonesome, would rather have that for company than have no kin at all, or any animal it could feel a nearness to or get sympathy from in its forlorn condition here among strangers who do not know its ways or habits, or what to do to make it feel that it is among friends; but it was a mistake—it went into such fits at the sight of the kangaroo that I was convinced it had never seen one before. I pity the poor noisy little animal, but there is nothing I can do to make it happy. If I could tame it—but that is out of the question; the more I try the worse I seem to make it. It grieves me to the heart to see it in its little storms of sorrow and passion. I wanted to let it go, but she wouldn't hear of it. That seemed cruel and not like her; and yet she may be right. It might be lonelier than ever; for since I cannot find another one, how could *it*?

FIVE MONTHS LATER.—It is not a kangaroo. No, for it supports itself by holding to her finger, and thus goes a few steps on its hind legs, and then falls down. It is probably some kind of a bear; and yet it has no tail—as yet—and no fur, except on its head. It still keeps on growing—that is a curious circumstance, for bears get their growth earlier than this. Bears are dangerous—since our catastrophe—and I shall not be satisfied to have this one prowling about the place much longer without a muzzle on. I have offered to get her a kangaroo if she would let this one go, but it did no good—she is determined to run us into all sorts of foolish risks, I think. She was not like this before she lost her mind.

A FORTNIGHT LATER.—I examined its mouth. There is no danger yet: it has only one tooth. It has no tail yet. It makes more noise now than it ever did before—and mainly at night.

I have moved out. But I shall go over, mornings, to breakfast, and see if it has more teeth. If it gets a mouthful of teeth it will be time for it to go, tail or no tail, for a bear does not need a tail in order to be dangerous.

FOUR MONTHS LATER.—I have been off hunting and fishing a month, up in the region that she calls Buffalo; I don't know why, unless it is because there are not any buffaloes there. Meantime the bear has learned to paddle around all by itself on its hind legs, and says "poppa" and "momma." It is certainly a new species. This resemblance to words may be purely accidental, of course, and may have no purpose or meaning; but even in that case it is still extraordinary, and is a thing which no other bear can do. This imitation of speech, taken together with general absence of fur and entire absence of tail, sufficiently indicates that this is a new kind of bear. The further study of it will be exceedingly interesting. Meantime I will go off on a far expedition among the forests of the north and make an exhaustive search. There must certainly be another one somewhere, and this one will be less dangerous when it has company of its own species. I will go straightway; but I will muzzle this one first.

THREE MONTHS LATER.—It has been a weary, weary hunt, yet I have had no success. In the meantime, without stirring from the home estate, she has caught another one! I never saw such luck. I might have hunted these woods a hundred years, I never would have run across that thing.

NEXT DAY.—I have been comparing the new one with the old one, and it is perfectly plain that they are the same breed. I was going to stuff one of them for my collection, but she is prejudiced against it for some reason or other; so I have relinquished the idea, though I think it is a mistake. It would be an irreparable loss to science if they should get away. The old one is tamer than it was and can laugh and talk like the parrot, having learned this, no doubt, from being with the parrot so much, and having the imitative faculty in a highly developed degree. I shall be astonished if it turns out to be a new kind of parrot; and yet I ought not to be astonished, for it has already been everything else it could think of since those first days when it was a fish. The new one is as ugly now as the old one was at first; has the same sulphur-and-raw-meat complexion and the same singular head without any fur on it. She calls it Abel.

TEN YEARS LATER.—They are *boys;* we found it out long ago. It was their coming in that small, immature shape that puzzled us; we were not used to it. There are some girls now. Abel is a good boy, but if Cain had stayed a bear it would have improved him. After all these years, I see that I was mistaken about Eve in the beginning; it is better to live outside the Garden with her than inside it without her. At first I thought she talked too much; but now I should be sorry to have that voice fall silent and pass out of my life. Blessed be the chestnut that brought us near together and taught me to know the goodness of her heart and the sweetness of her spirit!

EVE'S DIARY

TRANSLATED FROM THE ORIGINAL

SATURDAY.—I am almost a whole day old, now. I arrived yesterday. That is as it seems to me. And it must be so, for if there was a day-before-yesterday I was not there when it happened, or I should remember it. It could be, of course, that it did happen, and that I was not noticing. Very well; I will be very watchful, now, and if any day-before-yesterdays happen I will make a note of it. It will be best to start right and not let the record get confused, for some instinct tells me that these details are going to be important to the historian some day. For I feel like an experiment, I feel exactly like an experiment; it would be impossible for a person to feel more like an experiment than I do, and so I am coming to feel convinced that that is what I *am*—an experiment; just an experiment, and nothing more.

Then if I am an experiment, am I the whole of it? No, I think not; I think the rest of it is part of it. I am the main part of it, but I think the rest of it has its share in the matter. Is my position assured, or do I have to watch it and take care of it? The latter, perhaps. Some instinct tells me that eternal vigilance is the price of supremacy. [That is a good phrase, I think, for one so young.]

Everything looks better to-day than it did yesterday. In the rush of finishing up yesterday, the mountains were left in a ragged condition, and some of the plains were so cluttered with rubbish and remnants that the aspects were quite distressing. Noble and beautiful works of art should not be subjected to haste; and this majestic new world is indeed a most noble and beautiful work. And certainly marvelously near to being perfect, notwithstanding the shortness of the time. There are too many stars in some places and not enough in others, but that can be remedied presently, no doubt. The moon got loose last night, and slid down and fell out of the scheme—a very great loss; it breaks my heart to think of it. There isn't another thing among the ornaments and decorations that is comparable to it for beauty and finish. It should have been fastened better. If we can only get it back again—

But of course there is no telling where it went to. And besides, whoever gets it will hide it; I know it because I would do it myself. I believe I can be honest in all other matters, but I already begin to realize that the core and centre of my nature is love of the beautiful, a passion for the beautiful, and that it would not be safe to trust me with a moon that belonged to another person and that person didn't know I had it. I could give up a moon that I found in the daytime, because I should be afraid some one was looking; but if I found it in the dark, I am sure I should find some kind of an excuse for not saying anything about it. For I do love moons, they are so pretty and so romantic. I wish we had five or six; I would never go to bed; I should never get tired lying on the moss-bank and looking up at them.

Stars are good, too. I wish I could get some to put in my hair. But I suppose I never can. You would be surprised to find how far off they are, for they do not look it. When they first showed, last night, I tried to knock some down with a pole, but it didn't reach, which astonished me; then I tried clods till I was all tired out, but I never got one. It was because I am left-handed and cannot throw good. Even when I aimed at the one I wasn't after I couldn't hit the other one, though I did make some close shots, for I saw the black blot of the clod sail right into the midst of the golden clusters forty or fifty times, just barely missing them, and if I could have held out a little longer maybe I could have got one. So I cried a little, which was natural, I suppose, for one of my age, and after I was rested I got a basket and started for a place on the extreme rim of the circle, where the stars were close to the ground and I could get them with my hands, which would be better, anyway, because I could gather them tenderly then, and not break them. But it was farther than I thought, and at last I had to give it up; I was so tired I couldn't drag my feet another step; and besides, they were sore and hurt me very much.

I couldn't get back home; it was too far and turning cold; but I found some tigers and nestled in among them and was most adorably comfortable, and their breath was sweet and pleasant, because they live on strawberries. I had never seen a tiger before, but I knew them in a minute by the stripes. If I could have one of those skins, it would make a lovely gown.

To-day I am getting better ideas about distances. I was so eager to get hold of every pretty thing that I giddily grabbed for it, sometimes when it was too far off, and sometimes when it was but six inches away but seemed a foot—alas, with thorns between! I learned a lesson; also I made an axiom, all out of my own head—my very first one: *The scratched Experiment shuns the thorn*. I think it is a very good one for one so young.

I followed the other Experiment around, yesterday afternoon, at a distance, to see what it might be for, if I could. But I was not able to make out. I think it is a man. I had never seen a man, but it looked like one, and I feel sure that that is what it is. I realize that I feel more curiosity about it than about any of the other reptiles. If it is a reptile, and I suppose it is; for it has frowsy hair and blue eyes, and looks like a reptile. It has no hips; it tapers like a carrot; when it stands, it spreads itself apart like a derrick; so I think it is a reptile, though it may be architecture.

I was afraid of it at first, and started to run every time it turned around, for I thought it was going to chase me; but by-and-by I found it was only trying to get away, so after that I was not timid any more, but tracked it along, several hours, about twenty yards behind, which made it nervous and unhappy. At last it was a good deal worried, and climbed a tree. I waited a good while, then gave it up and went home.

To-day the same thing over. I've got it up the tree again.

SUNDAY.—It is up there yet. Resting, apparently. But that is a subterfuge: Sunday isn't the day of rest; Saturday is appointed for that. It looks to me like a creature that is more interested in resting than in anything else. It would tire me to rest so much. It tires me just to sit around and watch the tree. I do wonder what it is for; I never see it do anything.

They returned the moon last night, and I was *so* happy! I think it is very honest of them. It slid down and fell off again, but I was not distressed; there is no need to worry when one has that kind of neighbors; they will fetch it back. I wish I could do something to show my appreciation. I would like to send them some stars, for we have more than we can use. I mean I, not we, for I can see that the reptile cares nothing for such things.

It has low tastes, and is not kind. When I went there yesterday evening in the gloaming it had crept down and was trying to catch the little speckled fishes that play in the pool, and I had to clod it to make it go up the tree again and let them alone. I wonder if *that* is what it is for? Hasn't it any heart? Hasn't it any compassion for those little creatures? Can it be that it was designed and manufactured for such ungentle work? It has the look of it. One of the clods took it back of the ear, and it used language. It gave me a thrill, for it was the first time I had ever heard speech, except my own. I did not understand the words, but they seemed expressive.

When I found it could talk I felt a new interest in it, for I love to talk; I talk, all day, and in my sleep, too, and I am very interesting, but if I had another to talk to I could be twice as interesting and would never stop, if desired.

If this reptile is a man, it isn't an *it*, is it? That wouldn't be grammatical, would it? I think it would be *he*. I think so. In that case one would parse it thus: nominative, *he;* dative, *him;* possessive, *his'n*. Well, I will consider it a man and call it he until it turns out to be something else. This will be handier than having so many uncertainties.

NEXT WEEK SUNDAY.—All the week I tagged around after him and tried to get acquainted. I had to do the talking, because he was shy, but I didn't mind it. He seemed pleased to have me around, and I used the sociable "we" a good deal, because it seemed to flatter him to be included.

WEDNESDAY.—We are getting along very well indeed, now, and getting better acquainted. He does not try to avoid me any more, which is a good sign, and shows that he likes to have me with him. That pleases me, and I study to be useful to him in every way I can, so as to increase his regard. During the last day or two I have taken all the work of naming things off his hands, and this has been a great relief to him, for he has no gift in that line, and is evidently very grateful. He can't think of a rational name to save him, but I do not let him see that I am aware of his defect. Whenever a new creature comes along I name it before he has time to expose himself by an awkward silence. In this way I have saved him many embarrassments. I have no defect like his. The minute I set eyes on an animal I know what it is. I don't have to reflect a moment; the right name comes out instantly, just as if it were an inspiration, as no doubt it is, for I am sure it wasn't in me half a minute before. I seem to know just by the shape of the creature and the way it acts what animal it is.

When the dodo came along he thought it was a wild-cat—I saw it in his eye. But I saved him. And I was careful not to do it in a way that could hurt his pride. I just spoke up in a quite natural way of pleased surprise, and not as if I was dreaming of conveying information, and said, "Well, I do declare, if there isn't the dodo!" I explained—without seeming to be explaining—how I knew it for a dodo, and although I thought maybe he was a little piqued that I knew the creature when he didn't, it was quite evident that he admired me. That was very agreeable, and I thought of it more than once with gratification before I slept. How little a thing can make us happy when we feel that we have earned it.

THURSDAY.—My first sorrow. Yesterday he avoided me and seemed to wish I would not talk to him. I could not believe it, and thought there was some mistake, for I loved to be with him, and loved to hear him talk, and so how could it be that he could feel unkind towards me when I had not done anything? But at last it seemed true, so I went away and sat lonely in the place where I first saw him the morning that we were made and I did not know what he was and was indifferent about him; but now it was a mournful place, and every little thing spoke of him, and my heart was very sore. I did not know why very clearly, for it was a new feeling; I had not experienced it before, and it was all a mystery, and I could not make it out.

But when night came I could not bear the lonesomeness, and went to the new shelter which he has built, to ask him what I had done that was wrong and how I could mend it and get back his kindness again; but he put me out in the rain, and it was my first sorrow.

SUNDAY.—It is pleasant again, now, and I am happy; but those were heavy days; I do not think of them when I can help it.

I tried to get him some of those apples, but I cannot learn to throw straight. I failed, but I think the good intention pleased him. They are forbidden, and he says I shall come to harm; but so I come to harm through pleasing him, why shall I care for that harm?

MONDAY.—This morning I told him my name, hoping it would interest him. But he did not care for it. It is strange. If he should tell me his name, I would care. I think it would be pleasanter in my ears than any other sound.

He talks very little. Perhaps it is because he is not bright, and is sensitive about it and wishes to conceal it. It is such a pity that he should feel so, for brightness is nothing; it is in the heart that the values lie. I wish I could make him understand that a loving good heart is riches, and riches enough, and that without it intellect is poverty.

Although he talks so little he has quite a considerable vocabulary. This morning he used a surprisingly good word. He evidently recognized, himself, that it was a good one, for he worked it in twice afterwards, casually. It was not good casual art, still it showed that he possesses a certain quality of perception. Without a doubt that seed can be made to grow, if cultivated.

Where did he get that word? I do not think I have ever used it.

No, he took no interest in my name. I tried to hide my disappointment, but I suppose I did not succeed. I went away and sat on the moss-bank with my feet in the water. It is where I go when I hunger for companionship, some one to look at, some one to talk to. It is not enough—that lovely white body painted there in the pool—but it is something, and something is better than utter loneliness. It talks when I talk; it is sad when I am sad; it comforts me with its sympathy; it says, "Do not be downhearted, you poor friendless girl; I will be your friend." It *is* a good friend to me, and my only one; it is my sister.

That first time that she forsook me! ah, I shall never forget that—never, never. My heart was lead in my body! I said, "She was all I had, and now she is gone!" In my despair I said, "Break, my heart; I cannot bear my life any more!" and hid my face in my hands, and there was no solace for me. And when I took them away, after a little, there she was again, white and shining and beautiful, and I sprang into her arms!

That was perfect happiness; I had known happiness before, but it was not like this, which was ecstasy. I never doubted her afterwards. Sometimes she stayed away—maybe an hour, maybe almost the whole day, but I waited and did not doubt; I said, "She is busy, or she is gone a journey, but she will come." And it was so: she always did. At night she would not come if it was dark, for she was a timid little thing; but if there was a moon she would come. I am not afraid of the dark, but she is younger than I am; she was born after I was. Many and many are the visits I have paid her; she is my comfort and my refuge when my life is hard—and it is mainly that.

TUESDAY.—All the morning I was at work improving the estate; and I purposely kept away from him in the hope that he would get lonely and come. But he did not.

At noon I stopped for the day and took my recreation by flitting all about with the bees and the butterflies and revelling in the flowers, those beautiful creatures that catch the smile of God out of the sky and preserve it! I gathered them, and made them into wreaths and garlands and clothed myself in them while I ate my luncheon—apples, of course; then I sat in the shade and wished and waited. But he did not come.

But no matter. Nothing would have come of it, for he does not care for flowers. He calls them rubbish, and cannot tell one from another, and thinks it is superior to feel like that. He does not care for me, he does not care for flowers, he does not care for the painted sky at eventide—is there anything he does care for, except building shacks to coop himself up in from the good clean rain, and thumping the melons, and sampling the grapes, and fingering the fruit on the trees, to see how those properties are coming along?

I laid a dry stick on the ground and tried to bore a hole in it with another one, in order to carry out a scheme that I had, and soon I got an awful fright. A thin, transparent bluish film rose out of the hole, and I dropped everything and ran! I thought it was a spirit, and I *was* so frightened! But I looked back, and it was not coming; so I leaned against a rock and rested and panted, and let my limbs go on trembling until they got steady again; then I crept warily back, alert, watching, and ready to fly if there was occasion; and when I was come near, I parted the branches of a rose-bush and peeped through—wishing the man was about, I was looking so cunning and pretty—but the sprite was gone. I went there, and there was a pinch of delicate pink dust in the hole. I put my finger in, to feel it, and said *ouch!* and took it out again. It was a cruel pain. I put my finger in my mouth; and by standing first on one foot and then the other, and grunting, I presently eased my misery; then I was full of interest, and began to examine.

I was curious to know what the pink dust was. Suddenly the name of it occurred to me, though I had never heard of it before. It was *fire!* I was as certain of it as a person could be of anything in the world. So without hesitation I named it that—fire.

I had created something that didn't exist before; I had added a new thing to the world's uncountable properties; I realized this, and was proud of my achievement, and was going to run and find him and tell him about it, thinking to raise myself in his esteem—but I reflected, and did not do it. No—he would not care for it. He would ask what it was good for, and what could I answer? for if it was not *good* for something, but only beautiful, merely beautiful—

So I sighed, and did not go. For it wasn't good for anything; it could not build a shack, it could not improve melons, it could not hurry a fruit crop; it was useless, it was a foolishness and a vanity; he would despise it and say cutting words. But to me it was not despicable; I said, "Oh, you fire, I love you, you dainty pink creature, for you are *beautiful*—and that is enough!" and was going to gather it to my breast. But refrained. Then I made another maxim out of my own head, though it was so nearly like the first one that I was afraid it was only a plagiarism. *"The burnt Experiment shuns the fire."*

I wrought again; and when I had made a good deal of fire-dust I emptied it into a handful of dry brown grass, intending to carry it home and keep it always and play with it; but the wind struck it and it sprayed up and spat out at me fiercely, and I dropped it and ran. When I looked back the blue spirit was towering up and stretching and rolling away like a cloud, and instantly I thought of the name of it—*smoke!* —though, upon my word, I had never heard of smoke before.

Soon, brilliant yellow-and-red flares shot up through the smoke, and I named them in an instant—*flames!*—and I was right, too, though these were the very first flames that had ever been in the world. They climbed the trees, they flashed splendidly in and out of the vast and increasing volume of tumbling smoke, and I had to clap my hands and laugh and dance in my rapture, it was so new and strange and so wonderful and so beautiful!

He came running, and stopped and gazed, and said not a word for many minutes. Then he asked what it was. Ah, it was too bad that he should ask such a direct question. I had to answer it, of course, and I did. I said it was fire. If it annoyed him that I should know and he must ask, that was not my fault; I had no desire to annoy him. After a pause he asked:

"How did it come?"

Another direct question, and it also had to have a direct answer.

"I made it."

The fire was travelling farther and farther off. He went to the edge of the burned place and stood looking down, and said:

"What are these?"

"Fire-coals."

He picked up one to examine it, but changed his mind and put it down again. Then he went away. *Nothing* interests him.

But I was interested. There were ashes, gray and soft and delicate and pretty—I knew what they were at once. And the embers; I knew the embers, too. I found my apples, and raked them out, and was glad; for I am very young and my appetite is active. But I was disappointed; they were all burst open and spoiled. Spoiled apparently; but it was not so; they were better than raw ones. Fire is beautiful; some day it will be useful, I think.

FRIDAY.—I saw him again, for a moment, last Monday at nightfall, but only for a moment. I was hoping he would praise me for trying to improve the estate, for I had meant well and had worked hard. But he was not pleased, and turned away and left me. He was also displeased on another account: I tried once more to persuade him to stop going over the Falls. That was because the fire had revealed to me a new passion—quite new, and distinctly different from love, grief, and those others which I had already discovered—*fear*. And it is horrible!—I wish I had never discovered it; it gives me dark moments, it spoils my happiness, it makes me shiver and tremble and shudder. But I could not persuade him, for he has not discovered fear yet, and so he could not understand me.

Extract from Adam's Diary

Perhaps I ought to remember that she is very young, a mere girl, and make allowances. She is all interest, eagerness, vivacity, the world is to her a charm, a wonder, a mystery, a joy; she can't speak for delight when she finds a new flower, she must pet it and caress it and smell it and talk to it, and pour out endearing names upon it. And she is color-mad:

brown rocks, yellow sand, gray moss, green foliage, blue sky;
the pearl of the dawn, the purple shadows on the mountains,
the golden islands floating in crimson seas at sunset, the
pallid moon sailing through the shredded cloud-rack, the
star-jewels glittering in the wastes of space—none of them is of
any practical value, so far as I can see, but because they have
color and majesty, that is enough for her, and she loses her
mind over them. If she could quiet down and keep still a
couple of minutes at a time, it would be a reposeful spectacle.
In that case I think I could enjoy looking at her; indeed I am
sure I could, for I am coming to realize that she is a quite
remarkably comely creature—lithe, slender, trim, rounded,
shapely, nimble, graceful; and once when she was standing
marble-white and sun-drenched on a bowlder, with her young
head tilted back and her hand shading her eyes, watching the
flight of a bird in the sky, I recognized that she was beautiful.

Monday noon.—If there is anything on the planet that she
is not interested in it is not in my list. There are animals
that I am indifferent to, but it is not so with her. She has no
discrimination, she takes to all of them, she thinks they are all
treasures, every new one is welcome.

When the mighty brontosaurus came striding into camp,
she regarded it as an acquisition. I considered it a calamity;
that is a good sample of the lack of harmony that prevails
in our views of things. She wanted to domesticate it, I wanted
to make it a present of the homestead and move out. She
believed it could be tamed by kind treatment and would be a
good pet; I said a pet twenty-one feet high and eighty-four feet
long would be no proper thing to have about the place, because,
even with the best intentions and without meaning any harm,
it could sit down on the house and mash it, for any one could
see by the look of its eye that it was absent-minded.

Still, her heart was set upon having that monster, and she
couldn't give it up. She thought we could start a dairy with it,
and wanted me to help her milk it; but I wouldn't; it was too
risky. The sex wasn't right, and we hadn't any ladder anyway.
Then she wanted to ride it, and look at the scenery. Thirty or
forty feet of its tail was lying on the ground, like a fallen tree,
and she thought she could climb it, but she was mistaken;

*when she got to the steep place it was too slick and down she
came, and would have hurt herself but for me.*

*Was she satisfied now? No. Nothing ever satisfies her but
demonstration; untested theories are not in her line, and she
won't have them. It is the right spirit, I concede it; it attracts
me; I feel the influence of it; if I were with her more I think I
should take it up myself. Well, she had one theory remaining
about this colossus: she thought that if we could tame him and
make him friendly we could stand him in the river and use
him for a bridge. It turned out that he was already plenty tame
enough—at least as far as she was concerned—so she tried her
theory, but it failed: every time she got him properly placed in
the river and went ashore to cross over on him, he came out and
followed her around like a pet mountain. Like the other
animals. They all do that.*

Friday.—Tuesday—Wednesday—Thursday—and to-day: all
without seeing him. It is a long time to be alone; still, it is
better to be alone than unwelcome.

I *had* to have company—I was made for it, I think—so I
made friends with the animals. They are just charming, and
they have the kindest disposition and the politest ways; they
never look sour, they never let you feel that you are intruding, they smile at you and wag their tail, if they've got one,
and they are always ready for a romp or an excursion or
anything you want to propose. I think they are perfect
gentlemen. All these days we have had such good times, and
it hasn't been lonesome for me, ever. Lonesome! No, I should
say not. Why, there's always a swarm of them around—
sometimes as much as four or five acres—you can't count
them; and when you stand on a rock in the midst and look out
over the furry expanse it is so mottled and splashed and gay
with color and frisking sheen and sun-flash, and so rippled
with stripes, that you might think it was a lake, only you
know it isn't; and there's storms of sociable birds, and hurri-
canes of whirring wings; and when the sun strikes all that
feathery commotion, you have a blazing up of all the colors
you can think of, enough to put your eyes out.

We have made long excursions, and I have seen a great

deal of the world; almost all of it, I think; and so I am the first traveller, and the only one. When we are on the march, it is an imposing sight—there's nothing like it anywhere. For comfort I ride a tiger or a leopard, because it is soft and has a round back that fits me, and because they are such pretty animals; but for long distance or for scenery I ride this elephant. He hoists me up with his trunk, but I can get off myself; when we are ready to camp, he sits and I slide down the back way.

The birds and animals are all friendly to each other, and there are no disputes about anything. They all talk, and they all talk to me, but it must be a foreign language, for I cannot make out a word they say; yet they often understand me when I talk back, particularly the dog and the elephant. It makes me ashamed. It shows that they are brighter than I am, and are therefore my superiors. It annoys me, for I want to be the principal Experiment myself—and I intend to be, too.

I have learned a number of things, and am educated, now, but I wasn't at first. I was ignorant at first. At first it used to vex me because, with all my watching, I was never smart enough to be around when the water was running up-hill; but now I do not mind it. I have experimented and experimented until now I know it never does run up-hill, except in the dark. I know it does in the dark, because the pool never goes dry; which it would, of course, if the water didn't come back in the night. It is best to prove things by actual experiment; then you *know;* whereas if you depend on guessing and supposing and conjecturing, you will never get educated.

Some things you *can't* find out; but you will never know you can't by guessing and supposing: no, you have to be patient and go on experimenting until you find out that you can't find out. And it is delightful to have it that way, it makes the world so interesting. If there wasn't anything to find out, it would be dull. Even trying to find out and not finding out is just as interesting as trying to find out and finding out, and I don't know but more so. The secret of the water was a treasure until I *got* it; then the excitement all went away, and I recognized a sense of loss.

By experiment I know that wood swims, and dry leaves and feathers, and plenty of other things; therefore by all that cumulative evidence you know that a rock will swim; but you have to put up with simply knowing it, for there isn't any way to prove it—up to now. But I shall find a way—then *that* excitement will go. Such things make me sad; because by-and-by when I have found out everything there won't be any more excitements, and I do love excitements so! The other night I couldn't sleep for thinking about it.

At first I couldn't make out what I was made for, but now I think it was to search out the secrets of this wonderful world and be happy and thank the Giver of it all for devising it. I think there are many things to learn yet—I hope so; and by economizing and not hurrying too fast I think they will last weeks and weeks. I hope so. When you cast up a feather it sails away on the air and goes out of sight; then you throw up a clod and it doesn't. It comes down, every time. I have tried it and tried it, and it is always so. I wonder why it is? Of course it *doesn't* come down, but why should it *seem* to? I suppose it is an optical illusion. I mean, one of them is. I don't know which one. It may be the feather, it may be the clod; I can't prove which it is, I can only demonstrate that one or the other is a fake, and let a person take his choice.

By watching, I know that the stars are not going to last. I have seen some of the best ones melt and run down the sky. Since one can melt, they can all melt; since they can all melt, they can all melt the same night. That sorrow will come—I know it. I mean to sit up every night and look at them as long as I can keep awake; and I will impress those sparkling fields on my memory, so that by-and-by when they are taken away I can by my fancy restore those lovely myriads to the black sky and make them sparkle again, and double them by the blur of my tears.

AFTER THE FALL

When I look back, the Garden is a dream to me. It was beautiful, surpassingly beautiful, enchantingly beautiful; and now it is lost, and I shall not see it any more.

The Garden is lost, but I have found *him,* and am content. He loves me as well as he can; I love him with all the strength of my passionate nature, and this, I think, is proper to my youth and sex. If I ask myself why I love him, I find I do not know, and do not really much care to know; so I suppose that this kind of love is not a product of reasoning and statistics, like one's love for other reptiles and animals. I think that this must be so. I love certain birds because of their song; but I do not love Adam on account of his singing—no, it is not that; the more he sings the more I do not get reconciled to it. Yet I ask him to sing, because I wish to learn to like everything he is interested in. I am sure I can learn, because at first I could not stand it, but now I can. It sours the milk, but it doesn't matter, I can get used to that kind of milk.

It is not on account of his brightness that I love him—no, it is not that. He is not to blame for his brightness, such as it is, for he did not make it himself; he is as God made him, and that is sufficient. There was a wise purpose in it, *that* I know. In time it will develop, though I think it will not be sudden; and besides, there is no hurry, he is well enough just as he is.

It is not on account of his gracious and considerate ways and his delicacy that I love him. No, he has lacks in these regards, but he is well enough just so, and is improving.

It is not on account of his industry that I love him—no, it is not that. I think he has it in him, and I do not know why he conceals it from me. It is my only pain. Otherwise he is frank and open with me now. I am sure he keeps nothing from me but this. It grieves me that he should have a secret from me, and sometimes it spoils my sleep, thinking of it, but I will put it out of my mind; it shall not trouble my happiness, which is otherwise full to overflowing.

It is not on account of his education that I love him—no, it is not that. He is self-educated, and does really know a multitude of things, but they are not so.

It is not on account of his chivalry that I love him—no, it is not that. He told on me, but I do not blame him; it is a peculiarity of sex, I think, and he did not make his sex. Of course I would not have told on him, I would have perished first; but that is a peculiarity of sex, too, and I do not take credit for it, for I did not make my sex.

Then why is it that I love him? *Merely because he is masculine,* I think.

At bottom he is good, and I love him for that, but I could love him without it. If he should beat me and abuse me, I should go on loving him. I know it. It is a matter of sex, I think.

He is strong and handsome, and I love him for that, and I admire him and am proud of him, but I could love him without those qualities. If he were plain, I should love him; if he were a wreck, I should love him; and I would work for him, and slave over him, and pray for him, and watch by his bedside until I died.

Yes, I think I love him merely because he is *mine* and is *masculine.* There is no other reason, I suppose. And so I think it is as I first said: that this kind of love is not a product of reasonings and statistics. It just *comes*—none knows whence—and cannot explain itself. And doesn't need to.

It is what I think. But I am only a girl, and the first that has examined this matter, and it may turn out that in my ignorance and inexperience I have not got it right.

FORTY YEARS LATER

It is my prayer, it is my longing, that we may pass from this life together—a longing which shall never perish from the earth, but shall have place in the heart of every wife that loves, until the end of time; and it shall be called by my name.

But if one of us must go first, it is my prayer that it shall be I; for he is strong, I am weak, I am not so necessary to him as he is to me—life without him would not be life; how could I endure it? This prayer is also immortal, and will not cease from being offered up while my race continues. I am the first wife; and in the last wife I shall be repeated.

AT EVE'S GRAVE

Adam: Wheresoever she was, *there* was Eden.

ASPIC'S MYSTERY
by Arsen Darnay

Arsen Darnay first appeared on the science fiction scene in the mid-1970s with a batch of memorable stories, including "The Splendid Freedom" and "Gut in Hell" (both 1974). His interesting post-holocaust novel *A Hostage for Hinterland* (1976) was expanded from his 1975 *Galaxy* story "Helium."

ASPIC'S MYSTERY

November 19, 2310. I began this diary five years ago to fight boredom and that loneliness which old age imposes. But now I note, musing over this sheaf of paper, that my writings constitute the first and only consecutive record of life in Plutonium. The realization came upon me like a flash just moments ago, and I felt a stir of excitement and hope which by rights belongs to younger men. I couldn't help musing, my eyes on the deserted Pilgrim's Camp far below, that this record might be used by someone else in some future effort to restore the Priesthood to its ancient glory. Needless to say, the record, as it stands, provides all too little information, and if I'm to achieve a posthumous "restoration," I'll have to augment my own narrow observations about the daily life of an aging archivist with some historical perspectives. Furthermore, I should quote the most pertinent portions of the Golden Age documentation in my possession. Then, and only then, a pious and energetic monk of the future might have enough to go on. I have in mind nothing less than reconstruction of Aspic's Mystery—however improbable and optimistic that might sound. And I have in mind, by inference, the proud expulsion of the revisionist rabble that today rules over the Order.

This project awes me to some extent. I am not much of a diarist, much less an historian, and my feebleness suggests that I shouldn't tackle what might turn out to be an arduous

work. On the other hand, who among the surviving brothers
has my skill and my resources? I'm afraid that none can do
what I can do—although each of us old-timers longs for the
past and would gladly bring it back again. Thus I'm left with
the duty, the obligation, to try my hand.

I shall start on the project tomorrow. By then I hope to be
refreshed by communion with Godbod. Now the hunger gnaws
me and the thought of prolonged labor makes me fearful. But
I shall do one thing at once—give a general context thus far
omitted from this diary.

I am Hamsters Dugout, a Plutonium Priest aged seventy-
five. Plutonium is a monastic foundation with origins in the
Golden Age—obscure and mysterious origins, as I shall try to
make plain. Our monastic fortress, a proud construction of
seven pods, the highest (Vigilance) having eighteen levels, is
situated near the settlement of Perpetual in Shashtuk Country or, as the Old Order would have called it, New Mexico.
Today a mere five hundred brothers occupy a small portion of
Plutonium, most of them of the revisionist persuasion, that is
to say they believe in clothing Godbod round about with an
abominable metal. Once this great foundation resounded
with the sound of 5,000 monks, each of them a true believer,
hungry and thirsty for Godbod's proximity, ever anxious to
hold His Substance near. Only a handful of us still survive,
and when we're gone the past will die forever—unless, as I
pray and hope, a pious monk can be found who, reading this
legacy, will set about to restore the past.

November 22, 2310. I have begun to do my research. Our
origins are almost completely lost. What little I know of
Plutonium's past comes in an ancient folder. The folder had
been preserved in a very large Old Order box made of
extremely thick metal. It has a door with a circular lock, but
the lock has no provisions for a key. Marks on the outside
reveal many attempts to get at the treasure within the box,
all of them failures. In my day, however, rust had eaten
through one of the walls, a fact that I discovered by accident
some years ago. Several layers of wall had been eroded, and
with a little help from an iron bar, I enlarged that opening

enough to shine a light inside. Then, by a succession of peeks and groping reaches, I found and extracted the folder, the only item within. I tore the brittle paper as I pulled out the thing and, upon closer examination, found that it was a collection of papers.

More precisely put, it was a file of miscellany, a forgotten file, an occasional file. In other words, it appears to have been the record kept by a busy man who forgot its existence for long periods of time; or else it was a partial file containing only items of some special significance; or else a secret folder, with items of less sensitivity being stored elsewhere.

I characterize the file in such detail to indicate its limitations. It's not unlike a single bone of some fabulous creature—enough to hint that a beast once lived but not enough to say whether it flew or swam. Whatever the nature of the folder, it seems to have survived the Holocaustic War only because it had been kept inside its metal box. The box itself, according to a tradition passed down from archivist to archivist, had been found far from here, in a gully. Scavengers, apparently, had dragged it away and dropped it from a height, without success. It fell to me to extract the nut from its hard shell, something that now, in retrospect, I find luminous with hopeful significance.

November 25, 2310. This morning I rose long before dawn and tiptoed from my narrow nook filled with an intuition of impending success. The coiling hallways of Plutonium, the deserted chambers on both sides, reminded me how still it was. The fortress is an empty shell. When I came to the monastery, a mere boy of fifteen, this Holy Interface brimmed with life. I recall my first vision of the proud giant against the horizon, its seven pods reaching for the sky. Bright pennants cracked at pod tips. Smoke rose from the Pilgrims' Camp on the western frontage, the same one I can now survey from my narrow window. Long lines of peasants waited to deliver tithes at the Gift Corrals. I felt Godbod's ineffable presence and hurried toward the steaming moats, elated. I had found my paradise.

This morning Plutonium was empty and sad. Nevertheless, bent on my personal satisfaction, I was glad of it, glad that the revisionist rabble is so lazy, glad that they sleep late into the day. I hoped that I would reach my objective, and thanks to Godbod I finally did.

Last night, before the rabble had departed the caverns, I had surreptitiously stuffed a soot-darkened rag into the lock of the entry to Cavern A. This morning, to my endless delight, I found that the door had failed to lock, much as I had intended. It yielded to my old man's groaning push. I entered, looked about, a catch in my throat. From the walls glowed phosphorescent paint. The double row of familiar vats and tanks extended into deeper murk. The heat was exhilarating. I stood there thinking of the olden days when thousands filled these caverns every morning. I remembered the deep longing in the chants we used to low, the holy words spoken at the altar, the distribution of hot rocks which we'd hug and kiss before they were collected again, the joyful restoration of our happiness.

I was so lost in thought, a notion suddenly made me start. What if the rabble discovered my unauthorized visitation! They would drag me away and lecture me about my own good, about the New Theology. I quickly hid myself behind a tank and, like a child seeking its mother's safety, I embraced its girth. But this tank had already been encased in accordance with the heretical doctrine. The heavy, softish metal was cold. Godbod had been shrouded, and I felt nothing at all.

I moved deeper into the cavern, stealthily, on tiptoe. At last I found tanks, vats, and pits not yet covered by the Abomination. Godbod boiled and bubbled inside them, invisible to me but not intangible. The radiation penetrated my ancient skin and bones. I fell into a trance-like exaltation that lasted for a timeless moment. I don't know how long I stood there. But suddenly the flicker of torches in motion brought me rudely back. I caught a glimpse of the revisionist rabble come to do its unholy work. The monks wore metal plates over chest, arms, and thighs. Their heads were stuck in oblong tubes pierced for eyes and mouth. They resembled ghosts and goblins. I hid myself until they passed, caught by a feeling of pity for these men who wished themselves protected from Godbod's touch—a touch I cannot taste enough. Then, reluctantly, I moved away.

Now I feel the wonderful contentment which comes from contact with Grace Divine. The biting hunger in my innards is satisfied. I can set to work with unwonted energy.

Today I wish to introduce the documents and to give a general summary of Plutonium's history. I shall begin with a note about language.

When in the year 2006 the Holocaustic War left earth empty and charred, filling the sky with dust that still obscures the sun, not everything was lost. I've been on fourteen excursions into the land as a sweeper, looking for hidden Godbod. And each time I have brought back some item of interest I'd found in now deserted ruins. One of these was a dictionary dated 1919. I have often wished that it had been a later edition. Then again I've blessed what treasure I had. Between the year 1919 and 2006 (much as between the latter and today), the meaning of many words had changed. This presents a problem in the interpretation of my documents, which I'll illustrate with a discussion of the word "brain."

In the 1970s, the period when my records begin, Old Order people evidently meant something other with that word than we do now. "Brain," to us, is the substance in the skull where thoughts are made. We share that interpretation with the people of 1919 but not with the people of the 1970s. I have sets of other writings, not related to the Priesthood, mere bits and snippets without much context, that mention such things as "brainwashing," "brain drain," and "brainstorm." I gather from this that to the men of the late 20th century "brain" stood for some kind of liquid, possibly a very large body of water, perhaps even the ocean which encircles earth (as hinted by the use of the word "storm"). But the meaning of that word did not stand still. It continued to evolve.

Thus, for instance, I found some years ago (or perhaps someone brought it to me, knowing my interest in antiquities) a narrow strip of paper not unlike some I have in the folder. The strip is dated 2005. Most of its contents deal with people or places called "China" and "USSR," but there is a clear reference to "brain-missiles." Checking my 1919 dictionary, I've discovered that a missile is something thrown, flung, hurled. A *brain*-missile is quite incomprehensible to me and will remain so until fortune gives me a later dictionary, something I can barely hope to see at my advanced age.

This introduction will remind my future reader that much of what I have to say about the origins of Plutonium is based on my interpretation of texts that are hopelessly obscure. The texts extend in time from 1974 to 2006. And even if I had the complete file, I am afraid the language would remain a formidable hurdle. I am consoled by the hope that this pious monk for whose eyes this record is intended will have access to better words of reference, will understand the ancient documents more clearly than I, and will revise our history in light of new research.

The origins of the brotherhood must be sought in documents. It is my opinion that we began soon after 1974. By 2006 a tremendous story of Godbod had been accumulated at this site, suggesting a very large Priesthood and thousands upon thousands of yearly sweeps. Thirty-some-odd years are barely long enough to gather so much Grace. Therefore I am certain that the Priesthood began soon after the idea first surfaced in the first of the documents I shall present. From some date in the 1970s until this day, the brotherhood has existed with one brief hiatus, and because of that gap, no oral tradition exists to augment the fragments in my folder. The Holocaustic War seems to have scattered the brotherhood. But thanks to the unutterable mediations of Aspic's Mystery, monks congregated at this spot as if beckoned by an invisible finger. They set to work and built the current fortress over a period of a hundred years, raising its seven pods over the caverns where the Golden Age had hidden its stores of Godbod.

Aspic's Mystery was clearly the heart and center of our cult. Its development is Master Aspic's great contribution. Its destruction must be the cause for the steep decline in our numbers and the loss of our support.

The Mystery was destroyed forty years ago under puzzling circumstances which I hope to relate. At the time few of us understood how crucial Mystery was for our well-being. The effect of its obliteration wasn't felt for sixteen years. Then, suddenly, novices stopped coming to Plutonium.

I have spent much time pondering that fact. Nevertheless, I almost hesitate to offer the best explanation I have. Novices entered the monastery at age fifteen, more or less. If one adds another year, roughly, it might be concluded that men *conceived* before the destruction were still drawn to our gates. But men *conceived* thereafter no longer felt the urge. Such an explanation exceeds the bounds of belief. It would mean that a mystery could influence a man before his birth. Once I had thought that novices were brought to us by special radiations sent out by the Mystery, a kind of call. After it had been destroyed and novices still came, I changed my mind. But when they stopped coming after sixteen years, I fell to wondering again. Now, of course, it might be.

November 26, 2310. I was interrupted yesterday by one of our younger monks. His entrance rattled me badly, I'm afraid, as witness that wild scratch mark and the unsightly blot of ink on the page. Visitors to my isolated nook are so rare, the sudden motion of someone behind me is enough to make me jump. I am extremely hard of hearing. Knocking on the door won't rouse me.

My visitor was a young revisionist, a bright-eyed enthusiast; I guessed at once that he had come to look at my picture books. These are items I found on my ninth sweep; they show scenes of the Golden Age and much exercise the younger monks. He shouted at me for a long time before I understood his real intent. (Visits embarrass me. I'm forced to squint at my guests, head inclined, a hand cupped behind my ear. I compulsively go "Eh? Eh?" when I don't understand. I know how ridiculous I must appear to them. Old age should have reconciled me to the ridicule I think I detect behind my back. But some things are never cured.)

At last I understood the monk. He wanted to borrow one of my books, the one with the buildings.

I shook my head with stern determination. The picture books had never—until yesterday—left my nook. But yesterday I loaned him the thickest and largest of my treasures. Seeing my initial refusal, he pulled from his pocket a small bottle filled with Godbod sludge wrapped in that abominable metal. No doubt he could see the light rise in my eye. I took the stuff and gave him the book. He left and I removed the metal, flung it with disgust across the room. I held in my hand one of those little containers we used to take on sweeps with us—unable, unlike this revisionist rabble, to leave Plutonium for any length of time without a bit of Godbod to satisfy our innate needs.

Now that bottle is safely lodged over my heart, beneath my fraying suit. I need no longer lurk about the caverns, hoping to find an open door. But I'll probably never see that book again.

After the monk left I gave myself over to the enjoyments of Godbod while my thoughts turned on the youth of today. They are touched by a new, rebellious spirit. They claim that men have discovered again the "principles" that made Old Order mysteries work. This young man had recently returned from Californica with a report about a tower that touches the sky. He hasn't seen it with his eyes, but friends of friends report . . .! Inside it, supposedly, mysteries hum and sing again. Whether the story is true or false, that Tower bends the minds of simple youths. They speak about a "resurrection." I agree with Jimsons Hare, another old man like myself. Hare believes we have degenerated. We are a mongrel breed and won't succeed in bringing back the Golden Age.

Today I shall copy the first set of documents. I have neglected this task too long already. The ancient pages are extremely brittle and faded. Some are broken along the places where they had been folded. Entire lines of writing are consequently illegible. Other pieces in the folder are written on paper so thin they remind me of the skin of onions. Unless I transfer the words, they will not last more than another year or two.

The first record consists of four large sheets and one small one. The small one (first of a series in the folder and unusually well preserved) was evidently used to transmit the others. All the items are held together by a small bit of bent metal. The large sheets are obliterated so that almost nothing is legible with the exception of two passages. One of the legible passages is underlined:

. . . long-lived. Strontium 90 and cesium 137 both have approximately 30-year half-lives; there is so much of them within . . . substance, plutonium 239 . . . fantastically long half-life . . . will have to be contained for at least 250,000 years . . .

The second legible portion, slightly better than the first:

. . . question that intrigues . . . seriously proposed that society create a new kind of "priesthood' to watch over the waste, much as medieval monks watched over mankind's written history . . . somehow insulated from the rise and fall of nations through the centuries. Other scientists think the solution lies not so much in recruiting but . . . making a storage vault that . . .

Legible on the bottom of one of the pages, in handwriting, are the words "Dennis Farney, Smithsonian Magazine."

The smaller sheet transmitting the pages is headed by the words "Interoffice Memorandum" and "Future Now, Consultants in Science and Technology." The text is as follows:

Dear Teddy [Teddy is Theodore Aspic, our Master Aspic.] *Here's another one on rad waste disposal. Check that far-out notion on p. 24. Turn you on? Why don't you try to sell the idea to those dunderheads at AEC. Better yet, to that new Contingency Group at Commerce. If anyone can sell it, you can. Might be worth 100K in a feasibility study. I know it's nutty, but you ought to see this overhead. BJ 6/24/74*

I shall have neither the time nor the energy to analyze each of these documents, line by line, as they deserve it. Rather, I shall leave that work to the monk of the future, who'll still have the youth I've spent. I shall make two points and let the matter rest.

It is clear from the above that in the year 1974 the words "plutonium" and "priesthood" were already linked in a "proposal" by "Scientists." Thus we can establish a point of origin for the Order.

Second, the "priesthood" would be created to watch over "waste." The use of that word is highly instructive. My dictionary defines waste as "refuse, offal, garbage, trash, unwanted residue"—the very opposite of that precious substance, Godbod. From this I infer that even in those ancient days men were jealous in the service of the Holy Interface. The word "waste" was clearly a code name to hide the real meaning from the uninitiated. This practice is carried forward and elaborated on in later records.

December 10, 2310. For a number of days I have been in the clutches of the revisionist rabble and couldn't return to these secret labors. My age would excuse me from work, but I consented to do the chores the Abbot thrust upon me. I exult in my little bottle and don't wish to draw undue attention to myself.

I have been drawing maps. The mongrel breed needs maps for an excursion.

In my day we went about the earth without such bits of paper. We knew where we were. We always knew Plutonium's position. The new monks know nothing about that fire in the gut which gave us such a precise sense of orientation. These men could get lost. And to prevent such a deplorable situation, I have been scratching away with pen and brush.

I returned moments ago from the gates of God Pod where all of us had gathered to see the expedition off. Two weeks ago a monk returned after a two-year journey to the east. He had been sent to find more of that abominable metal my brethren use to hide Godbod. A good supply of the metal had been found near Plutonium buried underground, panels and sheets of it made in the Golden Age. But that store has been consumed. Now the monk brought news of ancient mines located in Mokan Country where the Miss-A-Sip flows. Fifty brothers left today to work the mines. They will stay in Mokan for some years, digging ore and smelting the metal. The Abbot plans to organize a transport column which will leave in the spring to bring the first yield of metal back. I wish him luck. The Order is dirt poor. We no longer hold the sons of Shashtuk Country in the ineffable thrall of Godbod. The tithes trickle, no longer flow. The Abbot will have trouble finding horses.

Drawing those maps has no doubt loaded me with sin. Indirectly I have helped the rabble after all. Will Godbod leave me now that I have lent a hand to the forging of His chains? Pious monk of the future, you and only you can cleanse my shame.

Let me resume by presenting two documents without comment. I cannot glean their meaning, but perhaps the future will:

June 19, 1975

Mr. John Clark, Chief
Contingency Planning Section
Office of Energy Analysis
Department of Commerce
Washington, D. C. 20419

Dear John:
I am pleased to submit herewith five (5) copies of our revised proposal titled "The Feasibility of a Permanent Hereditary (or Quasi-Hereditary) Cadre for Long-Term Institutional Supervision of Hi-Rad Wastes."

Please note the changes in the scope of work (and also on the general flow-diagram PERTing the tasks). We've overhauled the sections on Ritualistics and Ceremonial quite a bit. I know you still don't like the religious flavor of parts of this study, but frankly I cannot escape the thought that real permanence cannot be achieved without a little mumbo-jumbo. We cannot rely on good will and a sense of duty alone . . . however detestable, a kind of compulsion is nec . . . They should want to be near the stuff, to seek it out . . . And . . . through.

I, like you, would prefer some kind of mechanistic solution. I've considered the notion of robots, but if this idea is ever going to be implemented, we can't wait . . . cybernetics . . .

and hope the changes will go a long ways toward meeting your objections.

. . . would consider hiring a psychic, astrologer, or someone with that kind of background. Parapsychology, whatever you might think of it, is emerging as a potential tool. The Russians are said to be using . . .

The rest is missing, apparently because the paper tore at the crease. The next document, equally obscure, is one of those well-preserved pieces of "Interoffice Memorandum," although the message on this one is written by hand.

Teddy—Clark called me. Why me? Foaming at the mouth. Said you didn't change a goddamned thing. Wants me to know he resents the way you use political pressures to get this thing funded!!! Can you give him a call? Smooth the feathers? BJ

I shall pass over two other fragments that intervene between these and the next longer record. Both are narrow columns of printing on grayish paper with ragged edges. Only the bold lettering at the top is legible. The first one says: ERDA SWALLOWS AEC; NEW AGENCY TO LEAD ON ENERGY. The second: DEMO BY INTERIOR WOULD DUMP A-WASTE ON RESERVATION. In smaller letters: *Chief of Shashtuk Tribe to Appeal Decision.*

I cite the last item merely because it identifies Shashtuk Country, the first such mention in the documentary record. Before the Holocaustic War, as I've already stated, this region was called New Mexico. And the nearest settlement—now grown much smaller with the falling off of pilgrimages—had the name Perpetual. To my knowledge the term "Shashtuk Country" was never employed with reference to this area in the Golden Age—suggesting again that possibly a code was used, comprehensible to the Priesthood (or those engaged in planning its establishment) and no one else.

Dinner is behind me now, and I am back again. There is still light enough to write, if not to read. I shall spend my time describing Aspic's Mystery as it was in my day.

Before it was destroyed, the Mystery was housed beneath the roof of Vigilance Pod, the central and highest of Plutonium's seven. It was an aggregate of many smaller mysteries. The only visible portion consisted of four strange baskets of thin metal which were placed on the roof, one pointing in each direction of the sky. I had always thought that those strange dishes sent out those radiations I've mentioned before, that inaudible call youngsters in puberty felt as a hunger or a thirst in the gut.

Unlike my fellow brothers, I was lifted up into the hierarchy at a relatively early age. From childhood on I have been blessed by skill in penmanship and letters, and when the Holy Writ, hung on chains in our prayer chambers, had begun to fade after the passage of centuries, I was set to work renewing the books.

Despite my status as a hierarch, I was never permitted to see the rest of the Mystery. Only the highest-ranking monks— the Abbot and his closest advisors—were permitted inside the rooms that housed it. Nevertheless, like any other brother, I sought to learn something about it. I questioned the plutojacks assigned to guard the access corridors, picked up this and that in conversation, listened to old men's speculations. Immediately before the vandalism took place, the brotherhood swarmed. We were trying to recover the Prophet (also called the "needle," "the talking Godbod," and other things besides). But after the failure of that expedition, we all came back again, and then I too joined the long snake of brothers shuffling forward slowly to see the destruction. But what I saw gave me no more information than I had heard in the past. The Agents of Damnation had smashed everything. Fire had done the rest.

The stories had it that the Mystery consisted of three rooms. Each room was named, as follows: Power, Signal Acquisition, and Conditioning. The monks used to talk mostly about Power. In that room, so the rumors went, was a dense mass of Godbod more powerful in its emanations than anything in our caverns. Only the Abbot could enter Power (or so the brothers speculated), and that explained why abbots had so brief a life. Godbod's love called them to an early bliss.

(Let me here inject a note on age. For reasons unknown to me, Godbod has neglected me—perhaps so that I might witness our fate and record it for posterity. In the old days few men survived their 30th year. I did—and it was my shame. Holy sickness has always passed me by. And to confound my miseries, I was never blessed with sores. I chafed under this cruel judgment so long now that it no longers hurts. I see it as part of His design.)

My own interest in Mystery centered on Signal Acquisition— perhaps because it was an open room with tables in the center and a wall on which lights glowed. A "signal!" is a message. "Acquisition" means to get, obtain. What message was obtained in that odd room? What were those lights flickering behind tiny panes of glass? None of the brothers knew or cared. But I'm a man with mystic leanings and drawn to the ineffable. The murkier the better. I would probably be disappointed if I learned the answer. Sometimes I think the quest is all.

I had hoped to record tonight all manner of stories about the Mystery. But the light is failing. I see the sun as a streak of rust on the horizon. The page is a dim gray beneath my hand. I can't go on although I've yet to describe Conditioning. Let me do that before I turn in: All the monks who claimed to know agreed that it was the smallest of the rooms and filled entirely by tightly coiled tubes. They resembled a nest of snakes. Opaque, silvery snakes, one on another, intertwined. "Conditioning" is not a word in my dictionary.

December 25, 2310. Birthday of Superstar. It is a sign of our declining power that this cult is spreading all over Shashtuk Country. It's a testimony of our dying shame that the Abbot and his revisionist rabble have consented to take part in the festivities now unfolding down below. The people have gathered despite the bone-chilling wind and the heavy drifts of snow. They trample all over the Pilgrims' Camp, or what is left of it. Several bonfires have been lit. And the Priesthood of Plutonium is down below serving hot wine from cauldrons. Jimsons Hare told me this morning over bread that our blessed Abbot hopes to win the people's favor by his heretical participation in the cult festival. He serves the peasants wine so that they'll lend him horses in the spring. *Lead*. That's the name of the heavy metal the Abbot wants to fetch from faraway Mokan. Hare told me he'd heard them use the word. I looked it up in my dictionary—and found it, to my surprise. I refused to join the celebration. And now I refuse to watch them any further. But I am too upset to concentrate on composition. Instead I shall copy some more documents and comment on them later.

Trip Report
Organization: National Science
Foundation, RANN Project
Date: February 19, 1976
Person(s) Visited: Dr. Nathaniel Wakethorn

Purpose of this trip was to get a reading from Nat on the Trans-biological Heredity Concept. I went with some trepidations, wondering how Nat would react to such a notion. He thinks Future Now *is filled with kooks, but it seems that since our success with synthetic neurons he has warmed up a little. Nevertheless, I expected him to go right through the roof if I so much as whispered the word "reincarnation" in those hallowed halls. So I approached the matter obliquely. Nat was a little puzzled at f . . .*

. . . totally unexpected reaction. Later, over lunch, he told me about his brother's death in a . . . last summer. (We worked with Fred Wakethorn when he was with the State of New York.) Nat told me about some "strange" things that had happened in the wake of that accident. (A fairly standard pattern: a medium, materializations, cold patches of air in his living room, etc. I sent a summary to Cam Templar to plug into the data bank.) The upshot is that Nat was not only . . . but also . . . suggestions.

. . . most notably the suggestion that we should explore the analogy of neutrinos. His idea is that failure to detect the "soul" may be a consequence of . . . of funding prospects. Which is extremely encouraging. The only string attached, if I read Nat right, is that we've got to plug in Professor Stump as

*a consultant. (Stump is at North Carolina, a physicist who's
been bitten by the occult recently.)*

My general assessment . . . as a subcontract.

                                                    T.J. Aspic III

I can't go on. They are singing down below, and the
Priesthood is singing along. I can't hear them, of course, but I
see their mouths opening and closing in concert. What has
become of you, Plutonium!

December 26, 2310. The cursed festival continues, but
fortunately it has moved out of sight. People and Priesthood
have journeyed to Perpetual. Jimsons Hare tells me that
three oxen will be roasted there tonight in honor of the
Superstar. I shall have time and leisure to relate the story of
Mystery's destruction. But first a brief comment about the
foregoing document.

I have read and reread it several times. Among all the
records left us from the Golden Age, this one excites and
puzzles me most. I understand it less than many of the
others, and yet, and yet . . .

To put it as simply as possible, I have the strongest of
intuitions that this "trip report" marks the start of Master
Aspic's labors on the Mystery. I infer this from the phrase
"trans-biological heredity." "Trans" means beyond. "Biological" means something that pertains to biology or the science
of life. Hence the body? Heredity, of course, is a word we also
use. But I am most interested in what "heredity" implies,
namely the "getting," the "obtaining" of something from our
parents. Getting, obtaining . . .? Doesn't that suggest the
phrase "Signal Acquisition?" I wonder.

. . . But to translate: "Beyond-body acquisition?" What is
acquired beyond the body? The love of Godbod's unutterable
emanations? I leave it to you, monk of the future, to decipher
this "signal."

As I will show later, there are other records which seem to
be referring to the Mystery. One of them, for instance,
mentions some strange object called a "psychotron," which

might well have been a technical term or code word meaning the Mystery. Despite such other hints in my fragments, I continue to believe that the last document is the crucial one and holds the secret.

The Mystery's destruction was linked directly with one of the most glorious and yet most tragic episodes in the Order's history—discovery of the Prophet.

The Holocaustic War left behind it many a great crater, some filled with water, some of them dry. I have seen a good many myself. Monks who left the fortress on a sweep liked these huge concavities. Godbod's Spirit hovered over their waters or over their brittle, glassy dirt. Sometimes we found rocks that brimmed with His divine Life, and those we brought back to place in the caverns. Sometimes we found nothing. But craters were wonderful camping places nonetheless.

Forty years ago a group of sweepers saw a swampy lake in the distance somewhere in Texahoma. They discovered later that it wasn't a crater, but they went to its shores nevertheless, thinking it one. As they drew nearer, all of them felt that unspeakable tingling in the gut, and they covered the last stretch at a run. But in their feverish search around the lake's periphery, they discovered nothing at all. Godbod radiated his presence but couldn't be seen. At last the leader of the sweep pulled off his suit and jumped into the water. A growing excitement led him directly to the spot. Less than the width of a hand below the surface, resting on a hammock of swamp vegetation, lay the Prophet.

By any measure, it was the greatest and most miraculous discovery of Godbod ever made. I've never seen it with my eyes, but its image is imprinted on my brain as if I had been there myself.

The Prophet was long and slender—the length of four men laying head to foot, the thickness of two men standing back to back. It had a dull, silvery sheen, a tubular form, a pointed tip. All those who'd stood in its vicinity or had helped in its aborted trip home swore that some power oozed through its hull—a power stronger than any they'd ever felt before. But that was only part of the story.

The Prophet could speak. I don't know how it spoke—it had no mouth. But its voice was heard the moment they moved it. They moved it many weeks later when a large party from Plutonium had arrived at last with carts and oxen. Then it began to speak and held forth incessantly—but in a strange and frightening way . . . like old village women troubled in the head . . . like someone touched by fever. It also spoke with an oddly distorted inflection, like a stranger from the North who lives where the ice starts.

The Prophet has also puzzled me much, but on that subject I have reached a conclusion. Godbod Himself must have been inside that hull or, more precisely, Godbod's Spirit. His voice had warned of impending disaster. But no one listened to the Prophet. The Hierarchy gloried in the find. They went forth to get the needle shouting their luck to one and sundry, in every village and presidency along the way. It is no wonder, then, that disaster struck Plutonium and that our Abbot roasts oxen in Perpetual with devotees of Superstar.

I must defer relating those events. My inkwell is dry. I have an abundant supply of sootblack, but I can't get vinegar until they all return.

March 18, 2311. I have been ill— and gloriously happy. Godbod has heard me at last. Shortly after I made that last entry, a sore appeared above my eye, the left one, and spread to cover my forehead. Another sprang up on my wrist and ate its way forward to cover my fingers. I couldn't lift a pen. Now the sores have dried out, shriveled. But in my guts I feel the end approaching. I have little time left—but time enough, I think, to finish this labor. He has preserved me for this work. His finger has touched me, gently warning of the end. But He shall let me finish. I'm sure.

I must be quick and set to work. I must hurry and finish before the Abbot's men return with their cargo of abomination loaded on horses bought with heresy. I shall lie down on this cot and pass away to Godbod's bliss before that *lead* is mounted over every crack and fissure of Plutonium and His awesome emanations are bottled up forever. No! Not forever. Only until that pious monk, so rich in widsom I don't possess, finds these pages and sets to work recreating Aspic's Mystery.

Now that I am in a hurry, I shall choose only four documents to copy before they disintegrate. I may not have time for more. Then I shall go on to finish the story of the Prophet, and how the Hierarchy's bragging brought about its loss. I should be done before the month has passed.

Here, first, another note from that unidentified BJ to Master Aspic. My file contains several more which I shall not copy. This is the last of the series:

Teddy—You've got to get to someone in ERDA or DOD about Prof. Stump. I know damn well he deserves the Nobel Prize. But he'll just have to do without it. This stuff is dynamite. I know we're legally clean. You can't very well brainwash something that isn't there. Particle conditioning doesn't violate anybody's civil rights. But strict legality is one thing, public opinion another. If Stump writes up his findings, it won't be long before the cat's out of the bag. And this is no time to let cats out—the Chinese thing, all that. This is the worst possible time to inject an irrelevant issue into diplomatic discussions. Get someone to sit on Stump. He's got to keep his mouth shut. If DOD can't do it, I'll personally drown that s.o.b. in his bubble chamber or whatever the hell he uses. Please get on it right away. BJ 2/2/2004.

I copy this "memorandum" because it contains the word "conditioning." It appears in this document and nowhere else. Yet I am certain that this word refers to one of the rooms in Mystery, the one with the coiling snakes.

Next comes a very puzzling, suggestive document. I have copied others of its type already: gray, narrow pieces of paper. But this one is affixed to the center of a larger sheet. It says:

Phoenix (AP). Chief Bull, leader of the Shashtuk Indians, accused federal officials here of operating what he dubbed a "spirit-catcher" at the nuke-waste complex near Perpetual, NM. Preston Richards, Regional ERDA Administrator, refused comment. An ERDA spokesman labelled Bull's charge "preposterous mysticism."

* * *

Next to the narrow strip of paper, written into the blank space by hand, is the following comment: "How the hell does *he* know!"

I think I know, vaguely, darkly, what Chief Bull might have had in mind with that phrase "spirit-catcher." It has the same ring, the same feeling, as "signal acquisition." Is spirit a signal? A message? Did Master Aspic's Mystery capture and record Godbod's voice, transmitting it to the pious? That might be an explanation. But the puzzle won't be solved until my future, pious monk understands the word "conditioning."

Finally, the last two items in my scant pile of papers from the past. There are two separate pages from a larger work the rest of which is missing. Here we find a reference to a "psychotron," which I take to mean the Mystery.

-15-

volunteers. The rooms used by the control group were carefully shielded to prevent entrance of all measurable electro- as well as psycho-magnetic radiation. Intercourse was achieved no more than once by each couple. Impregnation occurred in 85% of instances (236 incidents) where couples occupied unshielded cubicles (Blocks A, C, E, and G). The results are highly significant (p < 3 × 10⁻⁹, i.e. odds against chance occurrence three thousand million to one). By contrast, couples in shielded cubicles (Blocks B, D, F, and H) achieved 2 impregnations during the entire course of the experiment, traceable to a shielding failure in Block E. Based on Schoenbaum and Bastur, a value of 12.9 impregnations had been predicted for both groups before experiments commenced.

Experimental results dealing with the origin of the psychons active in the impregnations are uncertain because tracking equipment between the psychotron and the cubicles malfunctioned during 17% of elapsed time. However, high probability exists that a preponderant number of the psychons originated in the psychotron.

DESCRIPTION OF THE PHYSICAL LAYOUT. All blocks

were located in a circular pattern precisely 800m from the periphery of the psychotron. Those on the eastern periphery were equipped with special panels to

-29-

were simultaneously monitored, with teams assigned to each operating room and intensive care unit within an 80km radius of the psychotron.

The results indicate a psychotron efficiency of 58%, i.e. the psychotron captured 58% of the psychons with masculine predisposition released by known incidents of mortality within a time-band of 19 min. following termination of vital functions.

March 30, 2311. Flames of insight have licked my feeble brain in the last few days. Now that I have strung them up like beads on a chain, these documents, together with my recollections, appear to give a new insight—an insight I've never had before—and still don't really have. It trembles on the edge of my awareness, almost . . . just almost . . . But then it's gone again.

A warm wind blows outside. I have opened my window to feel the spring. Outside the world renews itself. Pregnant odors recall that sense of adventure we always felt this time of year, getting ready for the sweep. But the sweep itself is obsolete. Nowadays, alas, we sweep for *lead.* I am too old and feeble even to sit, much less to walk. But time runs out and I must finish.

I left the Prophet in its lake and recalled the triumphal march to fetch, to get, obtain, acquire it. I said that the Hierarchy's braggery ultimately spelled our doom.

A future monk may find it difficult to understand how much things have changed in Plutonium. Today the Priesthood tells the people that it exists to serve *them.* The Abbot hasn't said it in so many words (perhaps in deference to old men like myself), but he has implied that the brotherhood exists to *protect* the people *from* Godbod! Blasphemies are piled on blasphemies. Those few novices who come to us come to serve "society." They flute in mellow tones about the "resurrection" and dream of towers in Californica. They lack all religious passion, fervor. Their eyes don't turn up in their sockets when Godbod's wondrous vibrations bite the bone. They are hollow men, mere wraiths compared to the giants of the past.

In the Prophet's day it was all different. We rode the peak of power. *We* served Godbod and the *people* served us. Most families hereabouts had sons in the fortress. We claimed one of two. And the people fed their own. Our reputation reached into all corners of the earth, and many presidencies were jealous of our might.

I well recall stories told by Master Nose. In my time he was the monk who interrogated new novices and returning sweepers, and he got his name because he had a "nose" for enemy agents. Nose told me that not a week passed without an attempt at penetration. The Agents of Damnation tried to enter this Holy Interface with theft in mind. No presidency worthy of the name could exist without its Godbod shrine, heavily guarded against monkish attack. And they sought us out looking for Substance.

(Most of those shrines, I'm happy to report, contained nothing more than lifeless rocks or, at best, a little bottle or two, of the type I treasure above my heart, taken from murdered sweepers.)

Against this background, it is understandable that the Hierarchy's triumphal march should have aroused the presidencies to action. Had our ranking monks been careful, had they brought the Prophet home beneath a cloak of secrecy, the Mystery might still be running beneath the roof of Vigilance. But it didn't turn out that way.

To this day it is not known who organized the armed attack on our caravan or how, simultaneously, the Agents of Damnation entered Plutonium right under the nose of Master Nose. But on that day of shame, July 31, 2271, two events occurred, no doubt carefully coordinated.

Despite the years, the scene is still fresh in my memories. It happened at bread time in the early morning. In those days we used to fill ten eating halls arranged around the girth of

Viligance Pod, and even then there was no room for tables.
We sat on narrow benches while monks passed up and down
between us with baskets. Only the Abbot and his closest
masters sat at a table on a platform in Sludgelove Hall. I was
present at the time, munching bread and a piece of tarrot.
Voices rumbled in low contentment as we ate. We had just
come from the caverns after morning service. Suddenly a
man burst in. He was haggard and bloodstained. He ran
between the monks and stopped at the Abbot's table. In the
sudden hush the man's entry had occasioned, we saw him
lean low over the table. The Abbot had inclined his head
forward to hear the message. Then the Abbot lurched back in
his seat, pale as a piece of paper. After a moment he turned to
the Chief Theologian and whispered in his turn. Then all of
them rose and left the table empty. They took the haggard
man along.

We milled around, aroused, disturbed, for quite a spell.
Then the danger-whistles blew, all of them at once, and in a
body we ran—pushing, trampling, clawing our way—down to
the caverns.

It happened while we were down there, listening to the
Abbot. The Abbot told us a mass of soldiers had overwhelmed
our glorious caravan and had made off with the Prophet. We
growled with rage down there while the Abbot further aroused
our battle ardor with a proud harangue. Then we collected
bits of Godbod and picked up clubs from the weapons room.
Thus we swarmed out of Plutonium, prepared for war.

Meanwhile the Agents of Damnation were busy below the
roof with ax and firebrand. They knew full well how we'd
react to their treacherous deed.

We were less than an hour's march from the fortress when
word came of the Mystery's destruction. The news went
through our ranks like a knife. We continued on, urged
forward by the Abbot, but the spirit had left us. We never
caught the thieves. The Prophet disappeared. Years later I
heard stories that it had been set up far to the north of here,
where the ice starts, in a shrine where oracles are sold. I
could never confirm the story, and by that time the brotherhood had begun its fast decline.

* * *

I feel myself close to the end. Moments ago I rose from my
cot and stared out through my window at the landscape. It
still has a wintry look, but deep in the earth one can almost
sense the thundering rumble of new energies. Jimsons Hare
tells me that a caravan of rabble is on its way back from
Mokan Country bringing *lead*. To cover Godbod altogether.
To shield the mongrels of this day of degeneration from His
unmentionable touch. It is a caravan of shame. I hope to be
with Godbod when it arrives.

BARNEY
by Will Stanton

Will Stanton is a name that should be more familiar to
readers of science fiction and fantasy. However, like other
writers who wrote only short fiction (and in his case *very*
short fiction) he has been sadly neglected, and richly deserves
a wider audience. During the 1950s and 1960s he produced
about a dozen gems for the science fiction magazines, almost
all in *The Magazine of Fantasy and Science Fiction*, including such wonderful stories as "Dodger Fan," "The Gumdrop
Kid," "You Are With It!," "The Last Present," and, of course
"Barney."

BARNEY

August 30th. We are alone on the island now, Barney and I. It was something of a jolt to have to sack Tayloe after all these years, but I had no alternative. The petty vandalisms I could have forgiven, but when he tried to poison Barney out of simple malice, he was standing in the way of scientific progress. That I cannot condone.

I can only believe the attempt was made while under the influence of alcohol, it was so clumsy. The poison container was overturned and a trail of powder led to Barney's dish. Tayloe's defense was of the flimsiest. He denied it. Who else then?

September 2nd. I am taking a calmer view of the Tayloe affair. The monastic life here must have become too much for him. That, and the abandonment of his precious guinea pigs. He insisted to the last that they were better suited than Barney to my experiments. They were more his speed, I'm afraid. He was an earnest and willing worker, but something of a clod, poor fellow.

At last I have complete freedom to carry on my work without the mute reproaches of Tayloe. I can only ascribe his violent antagonism toward Barney to jealousy. And now that he has gone, how much happier Barney appears to be! I have given him complete run of the place, and what sport it is to observe how his newly awakened intellectual curiosity carries him about. After only two weeks of glutamic acid treatments, he has become interested in my library, dragging the books from the shelves, and going over them page by page. I am certain he knows there is some knowledge to be gained from them had he but the key.

September 8th. For the past two days I have had to keep Barney confined and how he hates it. I am afraid that when my experiments are completed I shall have to do away with Barney. Ridiculous as it may sound there is still the possibility that he might be able to communicate his intelligence to others of his kind. However small the chance may be, the risk is too great to ignore. Fortunately there is, in the basement, a vault built with the idea of keeping vermin out and it will serve equally well to keep Barney in.

September 9th. Apparently I have spoken too soon. This morning I let him out to frisk around a bit before commencing a new series of tests. After a quick survey of the room he returned to his cage, sprang up on the door handle, removed the key with his teeth, and before I could stop him, he was out the window. By the time I reached the yard I spied him on the coping of the well, and I arrived on the spot only in time to hear the key splash into the water below.

I own I am somewhat embarrassed. It is the only key. The door is locked. Some valuable papers are in separate compartments inside the vault. Fortunately, although the well is over forty feet deep, there are only a few feet of water in the bottom, so the retrieving of the key does not present an insurmountable obstacle. But I must admit Barney has won the first round.

September 10th. I have had a rather shaking experience, and once more in a minor clash with Barney I have come off second best. In this instance I will admit he played the hero's role and may even have saved my life.

In order to facilitate my descent into the well I knotted a length of three-quarter-inch rope at one-foot intervals to make a rude ladder. I reached the bottom easily enough, but after only a few minutes of groping for the key, my flash-light gave out and I returned to the surface. A few feet from the top I heard excited squeaks from Barney, and upon obtaining ground level I observed that the rope was almost completely severed. Apparently it had chafed against the edge of the masonry and the little fellow perceiving my plight had been doing his utmost to warn me.

I have now replaced that section of rope and arranged some old sacking beneath it to prevent a recurrence of the accident. I have replenished the batteries in my flashlight and am now prepared for the final descent. These few moments I have taken off to give myself a breathing spell and to bring my journal up to date. Perhaps I should fix myself a sandwich as I may be down there longer than seems likely at the moment.

September 11th. Poor Barney is dead an soon I shell be the same. He was a wonderful ratt and life without him is knot worth livving. If anybody reeds this please do not disturb anything on the island but leeve it like it is as a shryn to Barney, espechilly the old well. Do not look for my body as I will caste myself into the see. You mite bring a couple of young ratts an leeve them as a living memorial to Barney. Females—no males. I sprayned my wrist is why this is written so bad. This is my laste will. Do what I say an don't come back or disturb anything after you bring the young ratts like I said. Just females.

Goodby

EVENING PRIMROSE
by John Collier

The late (1901–1980) John Collier was a master of the short fantasy, especially those with unexpected endings. In spite of the fact that he won the first International Fantasy Award in 1951 (the IFA was the direct predecessor of the Hugo Award) for his wonderful collection *Fancies And Goodnights*, and enjoyed some "mainstream" attention, he is still relatively unknown to many contemporary fantasy readers. Other outstanding books include *His Monkey Wife* (1931) and *The Best of John Collier* (1975).

EVENING PRIMROSE

In a pad of Highlife Bond,
bought by
Miss Sadie Brodribb
at Bracey's
for 25c

February 21

Today I made my decision. I would turn my back for good and
all upon the *bourgeois* world that hates a poet. I would leave,
get out, break away—

And I have done it. I am free! Free as the mote that dances
in the sunbeam! Free as a house-fly crossing first-class in the
Queen Mary! Free as my verse! Free as the food I shall eat,
the paper I write upon, the lamb's-wool-lined softly slithering
slippers I shall wear.

This morning I had not so much as a car-fare. Now I am
here, on velvet. You are itching to learn of this haven: you
would like to organize trips here, spoil it, send your relations-
in-law, perhaps even come yourself. After all, this journal
will hardly fall into your hands till I am dead. I'll tell you.

I am at Bracey's Giant Emporium, as happy as a mouse in
the middle of an immense cheese, and the world shall know
me no more.

Merrily, merrily shall I live now, secure behind a towering

pile of carpets, in a corner-nook which I propose to line with
eiderdowns, angora vestments, and the Cleopatraean tops in
pillows I shall be cozy.

I nipped into this sanctuary late this afternoon, and soon
heard the dying footfalls of closing time. From now on, my
only effort will be to dodge the night-watchman. Poets can
dodge.

I have already made my first mouse-like exploration. I
tiptoed as far as the stationery department, and, timid,
darted back with only these writing materials, the poet's first
need. Now I shall lay them aside, and seek other necessities:
food, wine, the soft furniture of my couch, and a natty
smoking-jacket. This place stimulates me. I shall write here.

Dawn, next day

I suppose no one in the world was ever more astonished and
overwhelmed than I have been tonight. It is unbelievable.
Yet I believe it. How interesting life is when things get like
that!

I crept out, as I said I would, and found the great shop in
mingled light and gloom. The central well was half illumi-
nated; the circling galleries towered in a pansy Piranesi of
toppling light and shade. The spidery stairways and flying
bridges had passed from purpose into fantasy. Silks and
velvets glimmered like ghosts, a hundred pantie-clad models
offered simpers and embraces to the desert air. Rings, clips,
and bracelets glittered frostily in a desolate absence of Honey
and Daddy.

Creeping along the transverse aisles, which were in deeper
darkness, I felt like a wandering thought in the dreaming
brain of a chorus girl down on her luck. Only, of course, their
brains are not so big as Bracey's Giant Emporium. And there
was no man there.

None, that is, except the night-watchman. I had forgotten
him. A regular thudding, which might almost have been that
of my own heart, suddenly burst upon me loudly, from
outside, only a few feet away. Quick as a flash I seized a
costly wrap, flung it about my shoulders, and stood stock-
still.

I was successful. He passed me, jingling his little machine on its chain, humming his little tune, his eyes scaled with refractions of the blaring day. "Go, worldling!" I whispered, and permitted myself a soundless laugh.

It froze on my lips. My heart faltered. A new fear seized me. I was afraid to move. I was afraid to look round. I felt I was being watched, by something that could see right through me. This was a very different feeling from the ordinary emergency caused by the very ordinary night-watchman. My conscious impulse was the obvious one, to glance behind me. But my eyes knew better. I remained absolutely petrified, staring straight ahead.

My eyes were trying to tell me something that my brain refused to believe. They made their point. I was looking straight into another pair of eyes, human eyes, but large, flat, luminous. I have seen such eyes among the nocturnal creatures, which creep out under the artificial blue moonlight in the zoo.

The owner was only a dozen feet away from me. The watchman had passed between us, nearer him than me. Yet he had not been seen. I must have been looking straight at him for several minutes at a stretch. I had not seen him either.

He was half reclining against a high dais, a platform for the exhibition of shawls and mantillas. One of these brushed his shoulder: its folds concealed perhaps his ear, his shoulder, and a little of his right side. He was clad in dim but large-patterned Shetland tweeds of the latest cut, suede shoes, a shirt of a rather broad *motif* in olive, pink, and gray. He was as pale as a creature found under a stone. His long thin arms ended in hands that hung floatingly, more like trailing, transparent fins, or wisps of chiffon, than ordinary hands.

He spoke. His voice was not a voice, a mere whistling under the tongue. "Not bad, for a beginner!"

I grasped that he was complimenting me, rather satirically, on my concealment under the wrap. I stuttered. I said, "I'm sorry. I didn't know anyone else lived here." I noticed, even as I spoke, that I was imitating his own whistling sibilant utterance.

"Oh, yes," he said. "*We* live here. It's delightful."

"We?"

"Yes, all of us. Look."

We were near the edge of the first gallery. He swept his long hand round, indicating the whole well of the shop. I looked. I saw nothing. I could hear nothing, except the watchman's thudding step receding infinitely far along some basement aisle.

"Don't you see?"

You know the sensation one has, peering into the half-light of a vivarium? One sees bark, pebbles, a few leaves, nothing more. And then, suddenly, a stone breathes—it is a toad; there is a chameleon, another, a coiled adder, a mantis among the leaves. The whole case seems crepitant with life. Perhaps the whole world is. One glances at one's sleeve, one's feet.

So it was with the shop. I looked, and it was empty. I looked, and there was an old lady, clambering out from behind the monstrous clock. There were three girls, elderly *ingénues*, incredibly emaciated, simpering at the entrance of the perfumery. Their hair was a fine floss, pale as gossamer. Equally brittle and colorless was a man with the appearance of a colonel of southern extraction, who stood regarding me while he caressed moustachios that would have done credit to a crystal shrimp. A chintzy woman, possibly of literary tastes, swam forward from the curtains and drapes.

They came thick about me, fluttering, whistling, like a waving of gauze in the wind. Their eyes were wide and flatly bright. I saw there was no color to the iris.

"How raw he looks!"

"A detective! Send for the Dark Men!"

"I'm not a detective. I am a poet. I have renounced the world."

"He is a poet. He has come over to us. Mr. Roscoe found him."

"He admires us."

"He must meet Mrs. Vanderpant."

I was taken to meet Mrs. Vanderpant: she proved to be the Grand Old Lady of the store, almost entirely transparent.

"So you are a poet, Mr. Snell? You will find inspiration here. I am quite the oldest inhabitant. Three mergers and a complete rebuilding, but they didn't get rid of me!"

"Tell how you went out by daylight, dear Mrs. Vanderpant, and nearly got bought for Whistler's *Mother*."

"That was in pre-war days. I was more robust then. But at the cash desk they suddenly remembered there was no frame. And when they came back to look at me—"

"—She was gone."

Their laughter was like the stridulation of the ghosts of grasshoppers.

"Where is Ella? Where is my broth?"

"She is bringing it, Mrs. Vanderpant. It will come."

"Terrible little creature! She is our foundling, Mr. Snell. She is not quite our sort."

"Is that so, Mrs. Vanderpant? Dear, dear!"

"I lived alone here, Mr. Snell, ever since the terrible times in the eighties. I was a young girl then, a beauty, they said, and poor Papa lost his money. Bracey's meant a lot to a young girl, in the New York of those days, Mr. Snell. It seemed to me terrible that I should not be able to come here in the ordinary way. So I came here for good. I was quite alarmed when others began to come in, after the crash of 1907. But it was the dear Judge, the Colonel, Mrs. Bilbee—"

I bowed. I was being introduced.

"Mrs. Bilbee writes plays. And of a very old Philadelphia family. You will find us quite *nice* here, Mr. Snell."

"I feel it a great privilege, Mrs. Vanderpant."

"And of course, all our dear *young* people came in '29. *Their* poor papas jumped from skyscrapers."

I did a great deal of bowing and whistling. The introductions took a long time. Who would have thought so many people lived in Bracey's?

"And here at last is Ella with my broth."

It was then I noticed that the young people were not so young after all, in spite of their smiles, their little ways, their *ingénue* dress. Ella was in her teens. Clad only in something from the shop-soiled counter, she nevertheless had the appearance of a living flower in a French cemetery, or a mermaid among polyps.

"Come, you stupid thing!"

"Mrs. Vanderpant is waiting."

Her pallor was not like theirs, not like the pallor of something that glistens or scuttles when you turn over a stone. Hers was that of a pearl.

Ella! Pearl of this remotest, most fantastic cave! Little mermaid, brushed over, pressed down by objects of a deadlier white—tentacles—! I can write no more.

February 28

Well, I am rapidly becoming used to my new and half-lit world, to my strange company. I am learning the intricate laws of silence and camouflage which dominate the apparently casual strollings and gatherings of the midnight clan. How they detest the night-watchman, whose existence imposses these laws on their idle festivals!

"Odious, vulgar creature! He reeks of the coarse sun!"

Actually, he is quite a personable young man, very young for a night-watchman. But they would like to tear him to pieces.

They are very pleasant to me, though. They are pleased that a poet should have come among them. Yet I cannot like them entirely. My blood is a little chilled by the uncanny ease with which even the old ladies can clamber spider-like from balcony to balcony. Or is it because they are unkind to Ella?

Yesterday we had a bridge party. Tonight Mrs. Bilbee's little play, *Love in Shadowland*, is going to be presented. Would you believe it?—another colony, from Wanamaker's, is coming over *en masse* to attend. Apparently people live in all stores. This visit is considered a great honor: there is an intense snobbery in these creatures. They speak with horror of a social outcast who left a high-class Madison Avenue establishment, and now leads a wallowing, beachcomberish life in a delicatessen. And they relate with tragic emotion the story of the man in Altman's, who conceived such a passion

for a model plaid dressing jacket that he emerged and wrested
it from the hands of a purchaser. It seems that all the Altman
colony, dreading an investigation, were forced to remove
beyond the social pale, into a five-and-dime. Well, I must get
ready to attend the play.

March 1

I have found an opportunity to speak to Ella. I dared not
before: here one has a sense always of pale eyes secretly
watching. But last night, at the play, I developed a fit of
hiccups. I was somewhat sternly told to go and secrete myself
in the basement, among the garbage cans, where the watchman never comes.

There, in the rat-haunted darkness, I heard a stifled sob.
"What's that? Is it you? Is it Ella? What ails you, child? Why
do you cry?"

"They wouldn't even let me see the play."

"Is that all? Let me console you."

"I am so unhappy."

She told me her tragic little story. What do you think?
When she was a child, a little tiny child of only six, she
strayed away and fell asleep behind a counter, while her
mother tried on a new hat. When she woke, the store was in
darkness.

"And I cried, and they all came round, and took hold of me.
'She will tell, if we let her go,' they said. Some said, 'Call in
the Dark Men.' 'Let her stay here,' said Mrs. Vanderpant.
'She will make me a nice little maid.'"

"Who are these Dark Men, Ella? They spoke of them when
I came here."

"Don't you know? Oh, it's horrible! It's horrible!"

"Tell me, Ella. Let us share it."

She trembled. "You know the morticians, 'Journey's End,'
who go to houses when people die?"

"Yes, Ella."

"Well, in that shop, just like here, and at Gimbel's, and at
Bloomingdale's, there are people living, people like these."

"How disgusting! But what can they live upon, Ella, in a
funeral home?"

"Don't ask me! Dead people are sent there, to be embalmed. Oh, they are terrible creatures! Even the people here are terrified of them. But if anyone dies, or if some poor burglar breaks in, and sees these people, and might tell—"

"Yes? Go on."

"Then they send for the others, the Dark Men."

"Good heavens!"

"Yes, and they put the body in the surgical department—or the burglar, all tied up, if it's a burglar—and they send for these others, and then they all hide, and in they come, these others—Oh! they're like pieces of blackness. I saw them once. It was terrible."

"And then?"

"They go in, to where the dead person is, or the poor burglar. And they have wax there—and all sorts of things. And when they're gone there's just one of these wax models left, on the table. And then our people put a frock on it, or a bathing suit, and they mix it up with all the others, and nobody ever knows."

"But aren't they heavier than the others, these wax models? You would think they'd be heavier."

"No. They're not heavier. I think there's a lot of them—gone."

"Oh dear! So they were going to do that to you, when you were a little child?"

"Yes, only Mrs. Vanderpant said I was to be her maid."

"I don't like these people, Ella."

"Nor do I. I wish I could see a bird."

"Why don't you go into the pet-shop?"

"It wouldn't be the same. I want to see it on a twig, with leaves."

"Ella, let us meet often. Let us creep away down here and meet. I will tell you about birds, and twigs and leaves."

March 10
"Ella, I love you."

I said it to her just like that. We have met many times. I have dreamt of her by day. I have not even kept up my journal. Verse has been out of the question.

"Ella, I love you. Let us move into the trousseau department. Don't look so dismayed, darling. If you like, we will go right away from here. We will live in the refreshment rooms in Central Park. There are thousands of birds there."

"Don't, Charles, don't."

"But I love you with all my heart."

"You mustn't."

"But I find I must. I can't help it. Ella, you don't love another?"

She wept a little. "Oh, Charles, I do."

"Love another, Ella? One of these? I thought you dreaded them all. It must be Roscoe. He is the only one that's any way human. We talk of art, life, and such things. And he has stolen your heart!"

"No, Charles, no. He's just like the rest, really. I hate them all. They make me shudder."

"Who is it, then?"

"It's him."

"Who?"

"The night-watchman."

"Impossible!"

"No. He smells of the sun."

"Oh, Ella, you have broken my heart."

"Be my friend, though."

"I will. I'll be your brother. How did you fall in love with him?"

"Oh, Charles, it was so wonderful. I was thinking of birds, and I was careless. Don't tell on me, Charles, they'll punish me."

"No. No. Go on."

"I was careless, and there he was, coming round the corner. And there was no place for me, I had this blue frock on. There were only some wax models in their underthings."

"Please go on."

"I couldn't help it, Charles. I slipped off my dress, and stood still."

"I see."

"And he stopped just by me, Charles. And he looked at me. And he touched my cheek."

"Did he notice nothing?"

"No. It was cold. But Charles, he said—he said—'Say, honey, I wish they made 'em like you on Eighth Avenue.' Charles, wasn't that a lovely thing to say?"

"Personally, I should have said Park Avenue."

"Oh, Charles, don't get like these people here. Sometimes I think you're getting like them. It doesn't matter what street, Charles; it was a lovely thing to say."

"Yes, but my heart's broken. And what can you do about him? Ella, he belongs to another world."

"Yes, Charles, Eighth Avenue. I want to go there. Charles, are you truly my friend?"

"I'm your brother, only my heart's broken."

"I'll tell you. I will. I'm going to stand there again. So he'll see me."

"And then?"

"Perhaps he'll speak to me again."

"My dearest Ella, you are torturing yourself. You are making it worse."

"No, Charles. Because I shall answer him. He will take me away."

"Ella, I can't bear it."

"Ssh! There is someone coming. I shall see birds, flowers growing. They're coming. You must go."

March 13

The last three days have been torture. This evening I broke. Roscoe (he was my first acquaintance) came in. There has always been a sort of hesitant sympathy between us.

He said, "You're looking seedy, old fellow. Why don't you go over to Wanamaker's for some skiing?"

His kindness compelled a frank response. "It's deeper than that, Roscoe. I'm done for. I can't eat, I can't sleep. I can't write, man, I can't ever write."

"What is it? Day starvation?"

"Roscoe—it's love."

"Not one of the staff, Charles, or the customers? That's absolutely forbidden."

"No, it's not that, Roscoe. But just as hopeless."

"My dear old fellow, I can't bear to see you like this. Let me help you. Let me share your trouble."

Then it all came out. It burst out. I trusted him. I think I trusted him. I really think I had no intention of betraying Ella, of spoiling her escape, of keeping her here till her heart turned towards me. If I had, it was subconscious. I swear it.

But I told him all. All. He was sympathetic, but I detected a sly reserve in his sympathy. "You will respect my confidence, Roscoe? This is to be a secret between us."

"As secret as the grave, old chap."

And he must have gone straight to Mrs. Vanderpant. This evening the atmosphere has changed. People flicker to and fro, smiling nervously, horribly, with a sort of frightened sadistic exaltation. When I speak to them they answer evasively, fidget, and disappear. An informal dance has been called off. I cannot find Ella. I will creep out. I will look for her again.

Later

Heaven! It has happened. I went in desperation to the manager's office, whose glass front overlooks the whole shop. I watched till midnight. Then I saw a little group of them, like ants bearing a victim. They were carrying Ella. They took her to the surgical department. They took other things.

And, coming back here, I was passed by a flittering, whispering horde of them, glancing over their shoulders in a thrilled ecstasy of panic, making for their hiding places. I, too, hid myself. How can I describe the dark inhuman creatures that passed me, silent as shadows? They went there—where Ella is.

What can I do? There is only one thing. I will find the watchman. I will tell him. He and I will save her. And if we are overpowered—Well, I will leave this on a counter. Tomorrow, if we live, I can recover it.

If not, look in the windows. Look for three new figures: two men, one rather sensitive-looking, and a girl. She has blue eyes, like periwinkle flowers, and her upper lip is lifted a little.

Look for us.

Smoke them out! Obliterate them! Avenge us!

VIEW FROM A HEIGHT
by Joan D. Vinge

The winner of the 1978 Hugo Award for "Eyes of Amber,"
Joan D. Vinge became a leading writer in science fiction with
her first story, the haunting and beautiful "Tin Soldier"
(1974). She has produced an impressive body of first-rate
science fiction and fantasy since that first appearance, including an impressive novel, *The Snow Queen* (1980), which won the
Hugo in 1981. One of her great strengths is her ability to handle
point-of-view, a talent well illustrated in the following story.

VIEW FROM A HEIGHT

SATURDAY, THE 7TH

I want to know why those pages were missing! How am I supposed to keep up with my research if they leave out pages—?

(Long sighing noise.)

Listen to yourself, Emmylou: You're listening to the sound of fear. It was an oversight, you know that. Nobody did it to you on purpose. Relax, you're getting Fortnight Fever. Tomorrow you'll get the pages, and an apology too, if Harvey Weems knows what's good for him.

But still, five whole pages; and the table of contents. How could you miss *five* pages? And the table of contents.

How do I know there hasn't been a coup? The Northwest's finally taken over completely, and they're censoring the media—And like the Man without a Country, everything they send me from now on is going to have holes cut in it.

In *Science?*

Or maybe Weems has decided to drive me insane—?

Oh, my God . . . it would be a short trip. Look at me. I don't have any fingernails left.

("Arrwk. Hello, beautiful. Hello? Hello?")

("Ozymandias! Get out out of my hair, you devil." *Laughter.* "Polly want a cracker? Here . . . gently! That's a boy.")

It's beautiful when he flies. I never get tired of watching him, or looking at him, even after twenty years. Twenty years . . . What did the psittacidae do, to win the right to wear a rainbow as their plumage? Although the way we've hunted them for it, you could say it was a mixed blessing. Like some other things.

Twenty years. How strange it sounds to hear those words, and know they're true. There are gray hairs when I look in the mirror. Wrinkles starting. And Weems is bald! Bald as an egg, and all squinty behind his spectacles. How did we get that way, without noticing it? Time is both longer and shorter than you think, and usually all at once.

Twelve days is a long time to wait for somebody to return your call. Twenty years is a long time gone. But I feel somehow as though it was only last week that I left home. I keep the circuits clean, going over them and over them, showing those mental home movies until I could almost step across, sometimes, into that other reality. But then I always look down, and there's that tremendous abyss full of space and time, and I realize I can't, again. You can't go home again.

Especially when you're almost one thousand astronomical units out in space. Almost there, the first rung of the ladder. Next Thursday is the day. Oh, that bottle of champagne that's been waiting for so long. Oh, the parallax view! I have the equal of the best astronomical equipment in all of near-Earth space at my command, and a view of the universe that no one has ever had before; and using them has made me the only astrophysicist ever to win a Ph.D. in deep space. Talk about your field work.

Strange to think that if the Forward Observatory had massed less than its thousand-plus tons, I would have been replaced by a machine. But because the installation is so large, I in my infinite human flexibility, even with my infinite human appetite, become the most efficient legal tender. And the farther out I get the more important my own ability to judge what happens, and respond to it, becomes. The first—and maybe the last—manned interstellar probe, on a one-way journey into infinity . . . into a universe unobscured by our own system's gases and dust . . . equipped with eyes that see everything from gamma to ultra-long wavelengths, and ears that listen to the music of the spheres.

And Emmylou Stewart, the captive audience. Adrift on a star . . . if you hold with the idea that all the bits of inert junk drifting through space, no matter how small, have star potential. Dark stars, with brilliance in their secret hearts, only kept back from letting it shine by Fate, which denied them the critical mass to reach their kindling point.

Speak of kindling: the laser beam just arrived to give me my daily boost, moving me a little faster, so I'll reach a little deeper into the universe. Blue sky at bedtime; I always was a night person. I'm sure they didn't design the solar sail to filter light like the sky . . . but I'm glad it happened to work out that way. Sky-blue was always my passion—the color, texture, fluid purity of it. This color isn't exactly right; but it doesn't matter, because I can't remember how any more. This sky is a sun-catcher. A big blue parasol. But so was the original, from where I used to stand. The sky is a blue parasol . . . did anyone ever say that before, I wonder? If anyone knows, speak up—

Is anyone even listening. Will anyone ever be?

("Who cares, anyway? Come on, Ozzie—climb aboard. Let's drop down to the observation porch while I do my meditation, and try to remember what days were like.")

Weems, damn it, I want satisfaction!

SUNDAY, THE 8TH

That idiot. That intolerable moron—how could he do that to me? After all this time, wouldn't you think he'd know me better than that? To keep me waiting for twelve days, wondering and afraid: twelve days of all the possible stupid paranoias I could weave with my idle hands and mind, making myself miserable, asking for trouble—

And then giving it to me. God, he must be some kind of sadist! If I could only reach him, and hurt him the way I've hurt these past hours—

Except that I know the news wasn't his fault, and that he didn't mean to hurt me . . . and so I can't even ease my pain by projecting it onto him.

I don't know what I would have done if his image hadn't been six days stale when it got here. What would I have done, if he'd been in earshot when I was listening; what would I have said? Maybe no more than I did say.

What can you say, when you realize you've thrown your whole life away?

He sat there behind his faded blotter, twiddling his pen, picking up his souvenir moon rocks and laying them down— looking for all the world like a man with a time bomb in his desk drawer—and said, "Now don't worry, Emmylou. There's no problem . . ." Went on saying it, one way or another, for five minutes; until I was shouting, "What's *wrong*, damn it?"

"I thought you'd never even notice the few pages . . ." with that sidling smile of his. And while I'm muttering, "I may have been in solitary confinement for twenty years, Harvey, but it hasn't turned my brain to mush," he said,

"So maybe I'd better explain, first—" and the look on his face; oh, the look on his face. "There's been a biomed break-through. If you were here on Earth, you . . . well, your body's immune responses could be . . . made normal . . ." And then he looked down, as though he could really see the look on my own face.

Made normal. Made normal. It's all I can hear. I was born with no natural immunities. No defense against disease. No help for it. No. *No, no, no*; that's all I ever heard, all my life on Earth. Through the plastic walls of my sealed room; through the helmet of my sealed suit . . . And now it's all changed. They could cure me. But I can't go home. I knew this could happen; I knew it had to happen someday. But I chose to ignore that fact, and now it's too late to do anything about it.

Then why can't I forget that I could have been f-free . . .

. . . I didn't answer Weems today. Screw Weems. There's nothing to say. Nothing at all.

I'm so tired.

MONDAY, THE 9TH

Couldn't sleep. It kept playing over and over in my mind . . . . Finally took some pills. Slept all day, feel like hell. Stupid. And it didn't go away. It was waiting for me, still waiting, when I woke up.

It isn't fair—!

I don't feel like talking about it.

TUESDAY, THE 10TH

Tuesday, already. I haven't done a thing for two days. I haven't even started to check out the relay beacon, and that damn thing has to be dropped off this week. I don't have any strength; I can't seem to move, I just sit. But I have to get back to work. Have to . . .

Instead I read the printout of the article today. Hoping I'd find a flaw! If that isn't the greatest irony of my entire life. For two decades I prayed that somebody would find a cure for me. And for two more decades I didn't care. Am I going to spend the next two decades hating it, now that it's been found?

No . . . hating myself. I could have been free, they could have cured me; if only I'd stayed on Earth. If only I'd been patient. But now it's too late . . . by twenty *years*.

I want to go home. I want to go home. . . . But you can't go home again. Did I really say that, so blithely, so recently? *You* can't: You, Emmylou Stewart. You are in prison, just like you have always been in prison.

It's all come back to me so strongly. Why me? Why must I be the ultimate victim—In all my life I've never smelled the sea wind, or plucked berries from a bush and eaten them, right there! Or felt my parents' kisses against my skin, or a man's body. . . . Because to me they were all deadly things.

I remember when I was a little girl, and we still lived in Victoria—I was just three or four, just at the brink of understanding that I was the only prisoner in my world. I remember watching my father sit polishing his shoes in the morning, before he left for the museum. And me smiling, so deviously, "Daddy . . . I'll help you do that, if you let me come out—"

And he came to the wall of my bubble and put his arms into the hugging gloves, and said, so gently, "No." And then he began to cry. And I began to cry too, because I didn't know why I'd made him unhappy. . . .

And all the children at school, with their "spaceman" jokes, pointing at the freak; all the years of insensitive people asking the same stupid questions every time I tried to go out anywhere . . . worst of all, the ones who weren't stupid, or insensitive. Like Jeffrey . . . no, I will not think of Jeffrey! I couldn't let myself think about him then. I could never afford to get close to a man, because I'd never be able to touch him. . . .

And now it's too late. Was I controlling my fate, when I volunteered for this one-way trip? Or was I just running away from a life where I was always helpless; helpless to escape the things I hated, helpless to embrace the things I loved.

I pretended this was different, and important . . . but was that really what I believed? No! I just wanted to crawl into a hole I couldn't get out of, because I was so afraid.

So afraid that one day I would unseal my plastic walls, or take off my helmet and my suit; walk out freely to breathe the air, or wade in a stream, or touch flesh against flesh . . . and die of it.

So now I've walled myself into this hermetically sealed tomb for a living death. A perfectly sterile environment, in which my body will not even decay when I die. Never having really lived, I shall never really die, dust to dust. A perfectly sterile environment; in every sense of the word.

I often stand looking at my body in the mirror after I take a shower. Hazel eyes, brown hair in thick waves with hardly any gray . . . and a good figure; not exactly stacked, but not unattractive. And no one has ever seen it that way but me. Last night I had the Dream again . . . I haven't had it for such a long time . . . this time I was sitting on a carved wooden beast in the park beside the Provincial Museum in Victoria; but not as a child in my suit. As a college girl, in white shorts and a bright cotton shirt, feeling the sun on my shoulders, and—Jeffrey's arms around my waist. . . . We stroll along the bayside hand in hand, under the Victorian lamp posts with their bright hanging flower-baskets, and everything I do is fresh and spontaneous and full of the moment. But always, always, just when he holds me in his arms at last, just as I'm about to . . . I wake up.

When we die, do we wake out of reality at last, and all our

dreams come true? When I die . . . I will be carried on and on into the timeless depths of uncharted space in this computerized tomb, unmourned and unremembered. In time all the atmosphere will seep away; and my fair corpse, lying like Snow White's in inviolate sleep, will be sucked dry of moisture, until it is nothing but a mummified parchment of shriveled leather and bulging bones. . . .

("Hello? Hello, baby? Good night. Yes, no, maybe. . . . Awk. Food time!")

("Oh, Ozymandias! Yes, yes, I know . . . I haven't fed you, I'm sorry. I know, I know . . .")

(Clinks and rattles.)

Why am I so selfish? Just because I can't eat, I expect him to fast, too. . . . No. I just forgot.

He doesn't understand, but he knows something's wrong; he climbs the lamp pole like some tripodal bem, using both feet and his beak, and stares at me with that glass-beady bird's eye, stares and stares and mumbles things. Like a lunatic! Until I can hardly stand not to shut him in a cupboard, or something. But then he sidles along my shoulder and kisses me—such a tender caress against my cheek, with that hooked prehensile beak that could crush a walnut like a grape—to let me know that he's worried, and he cares. And I stroke his feathers to thank him, and tell him that it's all right . . . but it's not. And he knows it.

Does he ever resent his life? Would he, if he could? Stolen away from his own kind, raised in a sterile bubble to be a caged bird for a caged human. . . .

I'm only a bird in a gilded cage. I want to go home.

WEDNESDAY, THE 11TH

Why am I keeping this journal? Do I really believe that sometime some alien being will find this, or some starship from Earth's glorious future will catch up to me . . . glorious future, hell. Stupid, selfish, short-sighted fools. They ripped the guts out of the space program after they sent me away, no one will ever follow me now. I'll be lucky if they don't declare me dead and forget about me.

As if anyone would care what a woman all alone on a

lumbering space probe thought about day after day for decades, anyway. What monstrous conceit.

I did lubricate the bearings on the big scope today. I did that much. I did it so that I could turn it back toward Earth ... toward the sun ... toward the whole damn system. Because I can't even see it, all crammed into the space of two moon diameters, even Pluto; and too dim and small and far away below me for my naked eyes, anyway. Even the sun is no more than a gaudy star that doesn't even make me squint. So I looked for them with the scope. . . .

Isn't it funny how when you're a child you see all those drawings and models of the solar system with big, lumpy planets and golden wakes streaming around the sun. Somehow you never get over expecting it to look that way in person. And here I am, one thousand astronomical units north of the solar pole, gazing down from a great height ... and it doesn't look that way at all. It doesn't look like anything; even through the scope. One great blot of light, and all the pale tiny diamond chips of planets and moons around it, barely distinguishable from half a hundred undistinguished stars trapped in the same arc of blackness. So meaningless, so insignificant ... so disappointing.

Five hours I spent, today, listening to my journal, looking back and trying to find—something, I don't know, something I suddenly don't have anymore.

I had it at the start. I was disgusting; Pollyanna Grad-student skipping and singing through the rooms of my very own observatory. It seemed like heaven, and a lifetime spent in it couldn't possibly be long enough for all that I was going to accomplish, and discover. I'd never be bored, no, not me. . . .

And there was so much to learn about the potential of this place, before I got out to where it supposedly would matter, and there would be new things to turn my wonderful extended senses toward ... while I could still communicate easily with my dear mentor Dr. Weems, and the world. (Who'd ever have thought when the lecherous old goat was my thesis advisor at Harvard, and making jokes to his other grad students about "the lengths some women will go to to protect their virginity," that we would have to spend a lifetime together.)

There was Ozymandias's first word . . . and my first birthday in space, and my first anniversary . . . and my doctoral degree at last, printed out by the computer with scrolls made of little x's and taped up on the wall. . . .

Then day and night and day and night, beating me black and blue with blue and black . . . my fifth anniversary, my eighth, my decade. I crossed the magnetopause, to become truly the first voyager in interstellar space . . . but by then there was no one left to *talk* to anymore, to really share the experience with. Even the radio and television broadcasts drifting out from Earth were diffuse and rare; there were fewer and fewer contacts with the reality outside. The plodding routines, the stupefying boredom—until sometimes I stood screaming down the halls just for something new; listening to the echoes that no one else would ever hear, and pretending they'd come to call; trying so hard to believe there was something to hear that wasn't *my* voice, *my* echo, or Ozymandias making a mockery of it.

(*"Hell, beautiful. That's a crock. Hello. hello?"*)

(*"Ozymandias, get* away *from me—"*)

But always I had that underlying belief in my mission: that I was here for a purpose, for more than my own selfish reasons, or NASA's (or whatever the hell they call it now), but for Humanity, and Science. Through meditation I learned the real value of inner silence, and thought that by creating an inner peace I had reached equilibrium with the outer silences. I thought that meditation had disciplined me, I was in touch with my self and with the soul of the cosmos. . . . But I haven't been able to meditate since—it happened. The inner silence fills up with my own anger screaming at me, until I can't remember what peace sounds like.

And what have I really discovered, so far? Almost nothing. Nothing worth wasting my analysis or all my fine theories— or my freedom—on. Space is even emptier than anyone dreamed, you could count on both hands the bits of cold dust or worldlet I've passed in all this time, lost souls falling helplessly through near-perfect vacuum . . . all of us together. With my absurdly long astronomical tape measure I have fixed precisely the distance to NGC 2419 and a few other features, and from that made new estimates about a few more distant ones. But I have not detected a miniature black hole insatiably vacuuming up the vacuum; I have not pierced the invisible clouds that shroud the ultra-long wavelengths like fog; I have not discovered that life exists beyond the Earth in even the most tentative way. Looking back at the solar system I see nothing to show definitively that we even exist, any more. All I hear any more when I scan is electro-magnetic noise, no coherent thought. Only Weems every twelfth night, like the last man alive. . . . Christ, I still haven't answered him.

Why bother? Let him sweat. Why bother with any of it. Why waste my precious time.

Oh, my precious time. . . . Half a lifetime left that could have been mine, on Earth.

Twenty years—I came through them all all right. I thought I was safe. And after twenty years, my facade of discipline and self-control falls apart at a touch. What a self-deluded hypocrite I've been. Do you know that I said the sky was like a blue parasol eighteen years ago? And probably said it again fifteen years ago, and ten, and five—

Tomorrow I pass 1000 AUs.

THURSDAY, THE 12TH

I burned out the scope, I burned out the scope. I left it pointing toward the Earth, and when the laser came on for the night it shone right down the scope's throat and burned it out. I'm so ashamed. . . . Did I do it on purpose, subconsciously?

("*Goodnight starlight. Arrk. Good night. Good . . .*")

("Damn it, I want to hear another human voice—!")

(*Echoing, "voice, voice, voice voice . . ."*)

When I found out what I'd done I ran away. I ran and ran through the halls. . . . But I only ran in a circle: This observatory, my prison, myself . . . I can't escape. I'll always come back in the end, to this green-walled room with its desk and its terminals, its cupboards crammed with a hundred thousand dozens of everything, toilet paper and magnetic tape and oxygen tanks. . . .And I can tell you exactly how many steps it is to my bedroom or how long it took me to crochet the afghan on the bed . . . how long I've sat in the dark and silence, setting up an exposure program or listening for the feeble pulse of a radio galaxy two billion light-years away. There will never be anything different, or anything more.

When I finally came back here, there was a message waiting. Weems, grinning out at me half-bombed from the screen—"Congratulations," he cried, "on this historic occasion! Emmylou, we're having a little celebration here at the lab; mind if we join you in yours, one thousand astronomical units from home—?" I've never seen him drunk. They really must have meant to do something nice for me, planning it all six days ahead. . . .

To celebrate I shouted obscenities I didn't even know I knew at him, until my voice was broken and my throat was raw.

Then I sat at my desk for a long time with my jackknife lying open in my hand. Not wanting to die—I've always been too afraid of death for that—but wanting to hurt myself. I wanted to make a fresh hurt, to take my attention off the terrible thing that is sucking me into myself like an imploding star. Or maybe just to punish myself, I don't know. But I considered the possibility of actually cutting myself quite calmly; while some separate part of me looked on in horror. I even pressed the knife against my flesh . . . and then I stopped and put it away. It hurts too much.

I can't go on like this. I have duties, obligations, and I can't face them. What would I do without the emergency auto-mechs? . . . But it's the rest of my life, and they can't go on doing my job for me forever—

Later.

I just had a visitor. Strange as that sounds. Stranger yet—it was Donald Duck. I picked up half of a children's cartoon show today, the first coherent piece of nondirectional, unbeamed television broadcast I've recorded in months. And I don't think I've ever been happier to see anyone in my life.

What a nice surprise, so glad you could drop by. . . .Ozyman-
dias loves him; he hangs upside down from his swing under
the cabinet with a cracker in one foot, cackling away and
saying, "Give us a kiss, *smack-smack-smack*". . . . We watched
it three times. I even smiled, for a while; until I remembered
myself. It helps. Maybe I'll watch it again until bedtime.

FRIDAY, THE 13TH

Friday the Thirteenth. Amusing. Poor Friday the Thirteenth, what did it ever do to deserve its reputation? Even if
it had any power to make my life miserable, it couldn't hold a
candle to the rest of this week. It seems like an eternity since
last weekend.

I repaired the scope today; replaced the burnt-out parts.
Had to suit up and go outside for part of the work . . . I
haven't done any outside maintenance for quite a while. Odd
how both exhilarating and terrifying it always is when I first
step out of the airlock, utterly alone, into space. You're
entirely on your own, so far away from any possibility of help,
so far away from anything at all. And at that moment you
doubt yourself, suddenly, terribly . . . just for a moment.

But then you drag your umbilical out behind you and clank
along the hull in your magnetized boots that feel so reassur-
ingly like lead ballast. You turn on the lights and look for the
trouble, find it and get to work; it doesn't bother you any
more. . . . When your life seems to have torn loose and be
drifting free, it creates a kind of sea anchor to work with your
hands; whether it's doing some mindless routine chore or the
most intricate of repairs.

There was a moment of panic, when I actually saw charred
wires and melted metal, when I imagined the damage was so
bad that I couldn't repair it again. It looked so final,
so—masterful. I clung there by my feet and whimpered and
clenched my hands inside my gloves, like a great shining
baby, for a while. But then I pulled myself down and began to
pry here and unscrew there and twist a component free . . .
and little by little I replaced everything. One step at a time;
the way we get through life.

By the time I'd finished I felt quite calm, for the first time in days; the thing that's been trying to choke me to death this past week seemed to falter a little at my demonstration of competence. I've been breathing easier since then; but I still don't have much strength, I used up all I had just overcoming my own inertia.

But I shut off the lights and hiked around the hull for a while, afterwards—I couldn't face going back inside just then: Looking at the black convex dish of the solar sail I'm embedded in, up at the radio antenna's smaller dish occluding stars as the observatory's cylinder wheels endlessly at the hub of the spinning parasol. . . .

That made me dizzy, and so I looked out into the starfields that lie on every side. Even with my own poor, unaugmented senses there's so much more to see out here, unimpeded by atmosphere or dust, undominated by any sun's glare. The brilliance of the Milky Way, the depths of star and nebula and farthest galaxy breathlessly suspended . . . as I am. The realization that I'm lost for eternity in an uncharted sea.

Strangely, although that thought aroused a very powerful emotion when it struck me, it wasn't a negative one at all: It was from another scale of values entirely; like the universe itself. It was as if the universe itself stretched out its finger to touch me. And in touching me, singling me out, it only heightened my awareness of my own insignificance.

That was somehow very comforting. When you confront the absolute indifference of magnitudes and vistas so overwhelming, the swollen ego of your self-important suffering is diminished. . . .

And I remembered one of the things that was always so important to me about space—that here *any*one has to put on a spacesuit before they step outside. We're all aliens, no one better equipped to survive than another. I am as normal as anyone else, out here.

I must hold onto that thought.

SATURDAY, THE 14TH

There is a reason for my being here. There is a reason.

I was able to meditate earlier today. Not in the old way, the usual way, by emptying my mind. Rather by letting the questions fill up the space, not fighting them; letting them merge with my memories of all that's gone before. I put on music, that great mnemonic stimulator; letting the images that each tape evoked free-associate and interact.

And in the end I could believe again that my being here was the result of a free choice. No one force me into this. My motives for volunteering were entirely my own. And I was given this position because NASA believed that I was more likely to be successful in it than anyone else they could have chosen.

It doesn't matter that some of my motives happened to be unresolved fear or wanting to escape from things I couldn't cope with. It really doesn't matter. Sometimes retreat is the only alternative to destruction, and only a madman can't recognize the truth of that. Only a madman. . . . Is there anyone "sane" on Earth who isn't secretly a fugitive from something unbearable somewhere in their life? And yet they function normally.

If they ran, they ran toward something, too, not just away. And so did I. I had already chosen a career as an astrophysicist before I ever dreamed of being a part of this project. I could have become a medical researcher instead, worked on my own to find a cure for my condition. I could have grown up hating the whole idea of space and "spacemen," stumbling through life in my damned ugly sterile suit. . . .

But I remember when I was six years old, the first time I saw a film of suited astronauts at work in space . . . they looked just like me! And no one was laughing. How could I help but love space, then?

(And how could I help but love Jeffrey, with his night-black hair, and his blue flightsuit with the starry patch on the shoulder. Poor Jeffrey, poor Jeffrey, who never even realized his own dream of space before they cut the program out from under him. . . .I will not talk about Jeffrey. I will not.)

Yes, I could have stayed on Earth, and waited for a cure! I knew even then there would have to be one, someday. It was both easier and hárder to choose space, instead of staying.

And I think the thing that really decided me was that those people had faith enough in me and my abilities to believe that I could run this observatory and my own life smoothly for as long as I lived. Billions of dollars and a thousand tons of equipment resting on me; like Atlas holding up his world.

Even Atlas tried to get rid of his burden; because no matter how vital his function was, the responsibility was still a burden to him. But he took his burden back again too, didn't he; for better or worse. . . .

I worked today. I worked my butt off getting caught up on a week's worth of data processing and maintenance, and I'm still not finished. Discovered while I was at it that Ozymandias had used those missing five pages just like the daily news: crapped all over them. My sentiments exactly! I laughed and laughed.

I think I may live.

SUNDAY, THE 15TH

The clouds have parted.

That's not rhetorical—among my fresh processed data is a series of photo reconstructions in the ultra-long wavelengths. And there's a gap in the obscuring gas up ahead of me, a break in the clouds that extends thirty or forty light-years. Maybe fifty! Fantastic. What a view. What a view I have from here of everything, with my infinitely extended vision: of the way ahead, of the passing scene—or looking back toward Earth.

Looking back. I'll never stop looking back, and wishing it could have been different. That at least there could have been two of me, one to be here, one who could have been normal, back on Earth; so that I wouldn't have to be forever torn in two by regrets—

("*Hello. What's up, doc? Avast!*")

("Hey, watch it! If you drink, don't fly.")

Damn bird. . . . If I'm getting maudlin, it's because I had a party today. Drank a whole bottle of champagne. Yes, I had *the* party . . . we did, Ozymandias and I. Our private 1000 AU celebration. Better late than never, I guess. At least we did have something concrete to celebrate—the photos. And if the celebration wasn't quite as merry as it could have been, still I guess it will probably seem like it was when I look back on it from the next one, at 2000 AUs. They'll be coming faster now, the celebrations. I may even live to celebrate 8000. What the hell, I'll shoot for 10,000—

After we finished the champagne ... Ozymandias thinks '98 was a great year, thank God he can't drink as fast as I can ... I put on my Strauss waltzes, and the *Barcarolle*: Oh, the Berliner Philharmonic; their touch is what a lover's kiss must be. I threw the view outside onto the big screen, a ballroom of stars, and danced with my shadow. And part of the time I wasn't dancing above the abyss in a jumpsuit and headphones, but waltzing in yards of satin and lace across a ballroom floor in 19th-century Vienna. What I wouldn't give to be *there* for a moment out of time. Not for a lifetime, or even a year, but just for an evening; just for one waltz.

Another thing I shall never do. There are so many things we can't do, any of us, for whatever the reasons—time, talent, life's callous whims. We're all on a one-way trip into infinity. If we're lucky we're given some life's work we care about, or some person. Or both, if we're very lucky.

And I do have Weems. Sometimes I see us like an old married couple, who have grown to a tolerant understanding over the years. We've never been soul mates, God knows, but we're comfortable with each others' silences. . . .

I guess it's about time I answered him.

FIRST TO SERVE
by Algis Budrys

Algis Budrys has brought erudition and intellectuality to the field of science fiction, both in his fiction and his large and still growing body of first-rate criticism—he understands the roots and realities of commercial sf, and he has the courage to say what he believes. His novels, including *Who?* (1958), *Rogue Moon* (1960), *The Amsirs and the Iron Thorn* (1967), and *Michaelmas* (1977), are justifiably well known, but his short fiction, which is even better, still awaits a definitive collection.

FIRST TO SERVE

MAS 712, 820TH TDRC
COMASAMPS, APO 15
September 28

Leonard Stein, Editor
INFINITY
862 Union St.
New York 24, N.Y.

Dear Len,

Surprise, et cetera

It looks like there will be some new H. E. Wood stories for *Infy* after all. By the time you get this, 820TH TDRC will have a new Project Engineer, COMASAMPS, and I will be back to the old Royal and the Perry Street lair.

Shed no tear for Junior Heywood, though. COMASAMPS and I have come to this parting with mutual eyes dry and multiple heads erect. There was no sadness in our parting—no bitterness, no weeping, no remorse. COMASAMPS—in one of its apparently limitless human personifications—simply patted me on my side and told me to pick up my calipers and run along. I'll have to stay away from cybernetics for a while, of course, and I don't think I should write any robot stories in the interval, but, then, I never did like robot stories anyhow.

But all this is a long story—about ten thousand words, at least, which means a $300 net loss if I tell it now.

So go out and buy some fresh decks, I'll be in town next week, my love to the Associate and the kids, and first ace deals.

Vic Heywood

My name is really Prototype Mechanical Man I, but everybody calls me Pimmy, or sometimes Pim. I was assembled at the eight-twentieth teedeearcee on august 10, 1974. I don't know what man or teedeearcee or august 10, 1974 means, but Heywood says I will, tomorrow. What's tomorrow?

Pimmy

August 12, 1974

I'm still having trouble defining "man." Apparently, even the men can't do a very satisfactory job of that. The 820TDRC, of course, is the Eight Hundred and Twentieth Technical Development and Research Center of the Combined Armed Services Artificial and Mechanical Personnel Section. August 10, 1974, is the day before yesterday.

All this is very obvious, but it's good to record it.

I heard a very strange conversation between Heywood and Russell yesterday.

Russell is a small man, about thirty-eight, who's Heywood's top assistant. He wears glasses, and his chin is farther back than his mouth. It gives his head a symmetrical look. His voice is high, and he moves his hands rapidly. I think his reflexes are overtriggered.

Heywood is pretty big. He's almost as tall as I am. He moves smoothly—he's like me. You get the idea that all of his weight never touches the ground. Once in a while, though, he leaves a cigarette burning in an ashtray, and you can see where the end's been chewed to shreds.

Why is everybody at COMASAMPS so nervous?

Heywood was looking at the first entry in what I can now call my diary. He showed it to Russell.

"Guess you did a good job on the self-awareness tapes, Russ," Heywood said.

Russell frowned. "Too good, I think. He shouldn't have such a tremendous drive toward self-expression. We'll have to iron that out as soon as possible. Want me to set up a new tape?"

Heywood shook his head. "Don't see why. Matter of fact, with the intelligence we've given him, I think it's probably a normal concomitant." He looked up at me and winked.

Russell took his glasses off with a snatch of his hand and scrubbed them on his shirtsleeve. "I don't know. We'll have to watch him. We've got to remember he's a prototype—no different from an experimental automobile design, or a new dishwasher model. We expected bugs to appear. I think we've found one, and I think it ought to be eliminated. I don't like this personification he's acquired in our minds, either. This business of calling him by a nickname is all wrong. We've got to remember he's *not* an individual. We've got every right to tinker with him." He slapped his glasses back on and ran his hands over the hair the earpieces had disturbed. "He's just another machine. We can't lose sight of that."

Heywood raised his hands. "Easy, boy. Aren't you going too far off the deep end? All he's done is bat out a few words on a typewriter. Relax, Russ." He walked over to me and slapped my hip. "How about it, Pimmy? D'you feel like scrubbing the floor?"

"No opinion. Is that an order?" I asked.

Heywood turned to Russell. "Behold the rampant individual," he said. "No, Pimmy, no order. Cancel."

Russel shrugged, but he folded the page from my diary carefully, and put it in his breast pocket. I didn't mind. I never forgot anything.

August 15, 1974

They did something to me on the Thirteenth. I can't remember what. I've gone over my memory, but there's nothing. I can't remember.

Russell and Ligget were talking yesterday, though, when they inserted the autonomic cutoff, and ran me through on orders. I didn't mind that. I still don't. I can't.

Ligget is one of the small army of push-arounds that nobody knows for sure isn't CIC, but who solders wires while Heywood and Russell make up their minds about him.

I had just done four about-faces, shined their shoes, and struck a peculiar pose. I think there's something seriously wrong with Ligget.

Ligget said, "He responds well, doesn't he?"

"Mm-m—yes," Russell said abstractedly. He ran his glance down a column of figures on an Estimated Performance Spec chart. "Try walking on your hands, PMM One," he said.

I activated my gyroscope and reset my pedal locomotion circuits. I walked around the room on my hands.

Ligget frowned forcefully. "That looks good. How's it check with the specs?"

"Better than," Russell said. "I'm surprised. We had a lot of trouble with him the last two days. Reacted like a zombie."

"Oh, yes? I wasn't in on that. What happened? I mean—what sort of control were you using?"

"Oh—" I could see that Russell wasn't too sure whether he should tell Ligget or not. I already had the feeling that the atmosphere of this project was loaded with dozens of cross-currents and conflicting ambitions. I was going to learn a lot about COMASAMPS.

"Yes?" Ligget said.

"We had his individuality circuits cut out. Effectively, he was just a set of conditioned reflexes."

"You say he reacted like a zombie?"

"Definite automatism. Very slow reactions, and, of course, no initiative."

"You mean he'd be very slow in his response to orders under those conditions, right?" Ligget looked crafty behind Russell's back.

Russell whirled around. "He'd make a lousy soldier, if that's what CIC wants to know!"

Ligget smoothed out his face, and twitched his shoulders back. "I'm not a CIC snooper, if that's what you mean."

"You don't mind if I call you a liar, do you?" Russell said, his hands shaking.

"Not particularly," Ligget said, but he was angry behind his smooth face. It helps, having immobile features like mine. You get to understand the psychology of a man who tries for the same effect.

* * *

August 16, 1974

It bother me, not having a diary entry for the fourteenth, either. Somebody's been working on me again.

I told Heywood about it. He shrugged. "Might as well get used to it, Pimmy. There'll be a lot of that going on. I don't imagine it's pleasant—I wouldn't like intermittent amnesia myself—but there's very little you can do about it. Put it down as one of the occupational hazards of being a prototype."

"But I don't *like* it," I said.

Heywood pulled the left side of his mouth into a straight line and sighed. "Like I said, Pimmy—I wouldn't either. On the other hand, you can't blame us if the new machine we're testing happens to know it's being tested, and resents it. We built the machine. Theoretically, it's our privilege to do anything we please with it, if that'll help us find out how the machine performs, and how to build better ones."

"But I'm *not* a machine!" I said.

Heywood put his lower lip between his teeth and looked up at me from under a raised eyebrow. "Sorry, Pim. I'm kind of afraid you are."

But I'm not! *I'M NOT!*

August 17, 1974

Russell and Heywood were working late with me last night. They did a little talking back and forth. Russell was very nervous—and finally Heywood got a little impatient with him.

"All right," Heywood said, laying his charts down. "We're not getting anywhere, this way. You want to sit down and really talk about what's bothering you?"

Russell looked a little taken aback. He shook his head jerkily.

"No . . . no, I haven't got anything specific on my mind. Just talking. You know how it is." He tried to pretend he was very engrossed in one of the charts.

Heywood didn't let him off the hook, though. His eyes were cutting into Russell's face, peeling off layer after layer of misleading mannerism and baring the naked fear in the man.

"No, I don't know how it is." He put his hand on Russell's shoulder and turned around to where the other man was facing him completely. "Now, look—if there's something chewing on you, let's have it. I'm not going to have this project gummed up by your secret troubles. Things are tough enough with everybody trying to pressure us into doing things their way, and none of them exactly sure of what that way *is*."

That last sentence must have touched something off in Russell, because he let his charts drop beside Heywood's and clawed at the pack of cigarettes in his breast pocket.

"That's exactly what the basic problem is," he said, his eyes a little too wide. He pushed one hand back and forth over the side of his face and walked back and forth aimlessly. Then a flood of words came out.

"We're working in the dark, Vic. In the dark, and somebody's in with us that's swinging clubs at our heads while we stumble around. We don't know who it is, we don't know if it's one or more than that, and we never know when the next swing is coming.

"Look—we're cybernetics engineers. Our job was to design a brain that would operate a self-propulsive unit designed to house it. That was the engineering problem, and we've got a tendency to continue looking at it in that light.

"But that's not the whole picture. We've got to keep in mind that the only reason we were ever given the opportunity and the facilities was because somebody thought it might be a nice idea to turn out soldiers on a production line, just like they do the rest of the paraphernalia of war. And the way COMASAMPS looks at it is not in terms of a brain housed in an independently movable shell, but in terms of a robot which now has to be fitted to the general idea of what a soldier should be.

"Only nobody knows what the ideal soldier is like.

"Some say he ought to respond to orders with perfect accuracy and superhuman reflexes. Others say he ought to be able to think his way out of trouble, or improvise in a situation where his orders no longer apply, just like a human soldier. The ones who want the perfect automaton don't want him to be smart enough to realize he *is* an automaton—probably because they're afraid of the idea; and the ones who want him to be capable of human discretion don't want him to be human enough to be rebellious in a hopeless situation.

"And that's just the beginning. COMASAMPS may be a combine project, but if you think the Navy isn't checking up on the Army, and vice versa, with both of them looking over the Air Force's shoulder—oh, you know that squirrel cage as well as I do!"

Russell gestured hopelessly. Heywood, who had been taking calm puffs on his cigarette, shrugged. "So? All we have to do is tinker around until we can design a sample model to fit each definition. Then they can run as many comparative field tests as they want to. It's their problem. Why let it get you?"

Russell flung his cigarette to the floor and stepped on it with all his weight. "Because we can't do it and you ought to know it as well as I do!" He pointed over at me. "There's your prototype model. He's got all the features that everybody wants—and cut-offs intended to take out the features that interfere with any one definition. We can cut off his individuality, and leave him the automaton some people want. We can leave him his individuality, cut off his volition, and give him general orders which he is then free to carry out by whatever means he thinks best. Or, we can treat him like a human being—educate him by means of tapes, train him, and turn him loose on a job, the way we'd do with a human being."

The uneven tone built up in his voice as he finished what he was saying.

"But if we reduce him to a machine that responds to orders as though they were pushbuttons, he's slow. He's pitifully slow, Vic, and he'd be immobilized within thirty seconds of combat. There's nothing we can do about that, either. Until somebody learns how to push electricity through a circuit faster than the laws of physics say it should go, what we'll have will be a ponderous, mindless thing that's no better than the remote-control exhibition jobs built forty years ago.

"All right, so that's no good. We leave him individuality,

but we restrict it until it cuts his personality down to that of a slave. That's better. Under those conditions, he would, theoretically, be a better soldier than the average human. An officer could tell him to take a patrol out into a certain sector, and he'd do the best possible job, picking the best way to handle each step of the job as he came to it. But what does he do if he comes back, and the officer who gave him the orders is no longer there? Or, worse yet, if there's been a retreat, and there's nobody there? Or an armistice? What about that armistice? Can you picture this slave robot, going into stasis because he's got no orders to cover a brand-new situation?

"He might just as well not have gone on that patrol at all—because he can't pass on whatever he's learned, and because his job is now over, as far as he's concerned. The enemy could overrun his position, and he wouldn't do anything about it. He'd operate from order to order. And if an armistice were signed, he'd sit right where he was until a technician could come out, remove the soldier-orientation tapes, and replace them with whatever was finally decided on.

"Oh, you could get around the limitation, all right—by issuing a complex set of orders, such as: 'Go out on patrol and report back. If I'm not here, report to so-an-so. If there's nobody here, do this. If that doesn't work, try that. If such-and-such happens, proceed as follows. But don't confuse such-and-such with that or this.' Can you imagine fighting a war on that basis? And what about the reorientation problem? How long would all those robots sit there before they could all be serviced—and how many man-hours and how much material would it take to do the job? Frankly, I couldn't think of a more cumbersome way to run a war if I tried.

"Or, we can build all our robots like streamlined Pimmys—like Pimmy when all his circuits are operating, without our test cutoffs. Only, then, we'd have artificial human beings. Human beings who don't wear out, that a hand-arm won't stop, and who don't need food or water as long as their power piles have a pebble-sized hunk of plutonium to chew on."

Russell laughed bitterly. "And Navy may be making sure Army doesn't get the jump on them, with Air Force doing its bit, but there's one thing all three of them are as agreed upon as they are about nothing else—they'll test automaton zombies and they'll test slaves, but one thing nobody wants us turning out is supermen. They've got undercover men under every lab bench, all keeping one eye on each other and one on us—and the whole thing comes down on our heads like a ton of cement if there's even the first whisper of an idea that we're going to build more Pimmys. The same thing happens if we don't give them the perfect soldier. *And the only perfect soldier is a Pimmy.* Pimmy could replace any man in any armed service—from a KP to a whole general staff, depending on what tapes he had. But he'd have to be a true individual to do it. And he'd be smarter than they are. They couldn't trust him. Not because he wouldn't work for the same objectives as they'd want, but because he'd probably do it in some way they couldn't understand.

"So they don't want any more Pimmys. This one test model is all they'll allow, because he can be turned into any kind of robot they want, but they won't take the whole Pimmy, with all his potentialities. They just want part of him."

The bitter laugh was louder. "We've got their perfect soldier, but they don't want him. They want something less—but that something less will never be the perfect soldier. So we work and work, weeks on end, testing, revising, redesigning. Why? We're marking time. We've got what they want, but they don't want it—but if we don't give it to them soon, they'll wipe out the project. And if we give them what they want, it won't really be what they want. Can't you see that? What's the matter with you, Heywood? Can't you see the blind alley we're in—only it's not a blind alley, because it has eyes, eyes under every bench, watching each other and watching us, always watching, never stopping, going on and never stopping, watching, eyes?"

Heywood had already picked up the telephone. As Russell collapsed completely, he began to speak into it, calling the Project hospital. Even as he talked, his eyes were coldly brooding, and his mouth was set in an expression I'd never seen before. His other hand was on Russell's twitching shoulder, moving gently as the other man sobbed.

* * *

August 25, 1974

Ligget is Heywood's new assistant. It's been a week since Russell's been gone.

Russell wasn't replaced for three days, and Heywood worked alone with me. He's engineer of the whole project, and I'm almost certain there must have been other things he could have worked on while he was waiting for a new assistant, but he spent all of his time in this lab with me.

His face didn't show what he thought about Russell. He's not like Ligget, though. Heywood's thoughts are private. Ligget's are hidden. But, every once in a while, while Heywood was working, he'd start to turn around and reach out, or just say "Jack—," as if he wanted something, and then he'd catch himself, and his eyes would grow more thoughtful.

I only understood part of what Russell had said that night he was taken away, so I asked Heywood about it yesterday.

"What's the trouble, Pim?" he asked.

"Don't know, for sure. Too much I don't understand about this whole thing. If I knew what some of the words meant, I might not even have a problem."

"Shoot."

"Well, it's mostly what Russell was saying, that last night."

Heywood peeled a strip of skin from his upper lip by catching it between his teeth. "Yeah."

"What's a war, or what's war? Soldiers have something to do with it, but what's a soldier? I'm a robot—but why do they want to make more of me? Can I be a soldier and a robot at the same time? Russell kept talking about 'they,' and the Army, the Air Force, and the Navy. What're they? And are the CIC men the ones who are watching you and each other at the same time?"

Heywood scowled, and grinned ruefully at the same time. "That's quite a catalogue," he said. "And there's even more than that, isn't there, Pimmy?" He put his hand on my side and sort of patted me, the way I'd seen him do with a generator a few times. "O.K., I'll give you a tape on war and soldiering. That's the next step in the program anyway, and it'll take care of most of those questions."

"Thanks," I said. "But what about the rest of it?"

He leaned against a bench and looked down at the floor. "Well, 'they' are the people who instituted this program—the Secretary of Defense, and the people under him. They all agreed that robot personnel were just what the armed services needed, and they were right. The only trouble is, they couldn't agree among themselves as to what characteristics were desirable in the perfect soldier—or sailor, or airman. They decided that the best thing to do was to come up with a series of different models, and to run tests until they came up with the best one.

"Building you was my own idea. Instead of trying to build prototypes to fit each separate group of specifications, we built one all-purpose model who was, effectively speaking, identical with a human being in almost all respects, with one major difference. By means of cut-offs in every circuit, we can restrict as much of your abilities as we want to, thus being able to modify your general characteristics to fit any one of the various specification groups. We saved a lot of time by doing that, and avoided a terrific nest of difficulties.

"Trouble is, we're using up all the trouble and time we saved. Now that they've got you, they don't want you. Nobody's willing to admit that the only efficient robot soldier is one with all the discretionary powers and individuality of a human being. They can't admit it, because people are afraid of anything that looks like it might be better than they are. And they won't trust what they're afraid of. So, Russell and I had to piddle around with a stupid series of tests in a hopeless attempt to come up with something practical that was nevertheless within the limitations of the various sets of specifications—which is ridiculous, because there's nothing wrong with you, but there's plenty wrong with the specs. They were designed by people who don't know the first thing about robots or robot thought processes—or the sheer mechanics of thinking, for that matter."

He shrugged. "But, they're the people with the authority and the money that's paying for this project—so Jack and I kept puttering, because those were the orders. Knowing that we had the perfect answer all the time, and that nobody would accept it, was what finally got Jack."

"What about you?" I asked.

He shrugged again. "I'm just waiting," he said. "Eventually they'll either accept you or not. They'll either commend me or fire me, and they might or might not decide it's all my fault if they're not happy. But there's nothing I can do about it, is there? So, I'm waiting.

"Meanwhile, there's the CIC. Actually, that's just a handy label. It happens to be the initials of one of the undercover agencies out of the whole group that infests this place. Every armed service has its own, and I imagine the government has its boys kicking around, too. We just picked one label to cover them all—it's simpler."

"Russell said they were always watching. But why are they watching each other, too? Why should one armed service be afraid that another's going to get an advantage over it?"

Heywood's mouth moved into a half-amused grin. "That's what is known as human psychology, Pimmy. It'll help you to understand it, but if you can't, why, just be glad you haven't got it."

"Ligget's CIC, you know," I said. "Russell accused him of it. He denied it, but if he isn't actually in *the* CIC, then he's in something like it."

Heywood nodded sourly. "I know. I wouldn't mind if he had brains enough, in addition, to know one end of a circuit from the other."

He slapped my side again. "Pimmy, boy," he said. "We're going to have a lot of fun around here in the next few weeks. Yes, sir, a lot of fun."

August 26, 1974

Ligget was fooling around with me again. He's all right when Heywood's in the lab with me, but when he's alone, he keeps running me through unauthorized tests. What he's doing, actually, is to repeat all the tests Heywood and Russell ran, just to make sure. As long as he doesn't cut out my individuality, I can remember it all, and I guess there was nothing different about the results on any of the tests, because I can tell from his face that he's not finding what he wants.

Well, I hope he tells his bosses that Heywood and Russell were right. Maybe they'll stop this fooling.

Ligget's pretty dumb. After every test, he looks me in the eye and tells me to forget the whole thing. What does he think I am—Trilby?

And I don't understand some of the test performances at all. There *is* something wrong with Ligget.

September 2, 1974

I hadn't realized, until now, that Heywood and Russell hadn't told anyone what they thought about this whole project, but, viewing that tape on war and soldiering, and the way the military mind operates, I can see where nobody would have accepted their explanations.

Ligget caught on to the whole thing today. Heywood came in with a new series of test charts, Ligget took one look at them, and threw them on the table. He sneered at Heywood and said, "Who do you think you're kidding?"

Heywood looked annoyed and said, "All right, what's eating you?"

Ligget's face got this hidden crafty look on it. "How long did you think you could keep this up, Heywood? This test is no different from the ones you were running three weeks ago. There hasn't been any progress since then, and there's been no attempt to make any. What's your explanation?"

"Uh-huh." Heywood didn't look particularly worried. "I was wondering if you were *ever* going to stumble across it."

Ligget looked mad. "That attitude won't do you any good. Now, come on, quit stalling. Why were you and Russell sabotaging the project?"

"Oh, stop being such a pompous lamebrain, will you?" Heywood said disgustedly. "Russell and I weren't doing any sabotaging. We've been following our orders to the last letter. We built the prototype, and we've been testing the various modifications ever since. Anything wrong with that?"

"You've made absolutely no attempt to improve the various modifications. There hasn't been an ounce of progress in this project for the last twenty days.

"Now, look, Heywood"—Ligget's voice became wheedling— "I can understand that you might have what you'd consider a good reason for all this. What is it—political, or something? Maybe it's your conscience. Don't you *want* to work on something that's eventually going to be applied to war? I wish you'd tell me about it. If I could understand your reasons, it would be that much easier for you. Maybe it's too tough a problem. Is that it, Heywood?"

Heywood's face got red. "No, it's not. If you think—" He stopped, dug his fingers at the top of the table, and got control of himself again.

"No," he said in a quieter, but just as deadly, voice. "I'm as anxious to produce an artificial soldier as anybody else. And I'm not too stupid for the job, either. If *you* had any brains, you'd see that I already have."

That hit Ligget between the eyes. "You have? Where is it, and *why haven't you reported your success?* What is this thing?" He pointed at me. "Some kind of a decoy?"

Heywood grimaced. "No, you double-dyed jackass, that's your soldier."

"What?"

"Sure. Strip those fifteen pounds of cutoffs out of him, redesign his case for whatever kind of ground he's supposed to operate on, feed him the proper tapes, and that's it. The perfect soldier—as smart as any human ever produced, and a hundred times the training and toughness, overnight. Run them out by the thousands. Print your circuits, bed your transistors in silicone rubber, and pour the whole brew into his case. Production difficulties? Watchmaking's harder."

"*No!*" Ligget's eyes gleamed. "And I worked on this with you! *Why haven't you reported this?*" he repeated.

Heywood looked at him pityingly. "Haven't you got it through your head? Pimmy's the perfect soldier—all of him, with all his abilities. That includes individuality, curiosity, judgment—and intelligence. Cut one part of that, and he's no good. You've got to take the whole cake, or none at all. One way you starve—and the other way you choke."

Ligget had gone white. "You mean, we've got to take the superman—or we don't have anything."

"Yes, you fumbling jerk!"

Ligget looked thoughtful. He seemed to forget Heywood and me as he stared down at his shoetops. "They won't go for it," he muttered. "Suppose they decide they're better fit to run the world than we are?"

"That's the trouble," Heywood said. "They are. They've got everything a human being has, plus incredible toughness and the ability to learn instantaneously. You know what Pimmy did? The day he was assembled, he learned to read and write, after a fashion. How? By listening to me read a paragraph out of a report, recording the sounds, and looking at the report afterwards. He matched the sounds to the letters, recalled what sort of action on Russell's and my part the paragraph had elicited, and sat down behind a typewriter. That's all."

"They'd junk the whole project before they let something like that run around loose!" The crafty look was hovering at the edges of Ligget's mask again. "All right, so you've got an answer, but it's not an acceptable one. But why haven't you pushed any of the other lines of investigation?"

"Because there aren't any," Heywood said disgustedly. "Any other modification, when worked out to its inherent limits, is worse than useless. You've run enough tests to find out."

"All right!" Ligget's voice was high. "Why didn't you report failure, then, instead of keeping on with this shilly-shallying?"

"*Because I haven't failed, you moron!*" Heywood exploded. "I've got the answer. I've got Pimmy. There's nothing wrong with him—the defect's in the way people are thinking. And I've been going crazy, trying to think of a way to change the people. To hell with modifying the robot! He's as perfect as you'll get within the next five years. It's the people who'll have to change!"

"Uh-huh." Ligget's voice was careful. "I see. You've gone as far as you can within the limits of your orders—and you were trying to find a way to exceed them, in order to force the armed services to accept robots like Pimmy." He pulled out his wallet, and flipped it open. There was a piece of metal fastened to one flap.

"Recognize this, Heywood?"

Heywood nodded.

"All right, then, let's go and talk to a few people."

Heywood's eyes were cold and brooding again. He shrugged.

The lab door opened, and there was another one of the lab technicians there. "Go easy, Ligget," he said. He walked across the lab in rapid strides. His wallet had a different badge in it. "Listening from next door," he explained. "All right, Heywood," he said, "*I'm* taking you in." He shouldered Ligget out of the way. "Why don't you guys learn to stay in your own jurisdiction?" he told him.

Ligget's face turned red, and his fists clenched, but the other man must have had more weight behind him, because he didn't say anything.

Heywood looked over at me, and raised a hand. "So long, Pimmy," he said. He and the other man walked out of the lab, with Ligget trailing along behind them. As they got the door open, I saw some other men standing out in the hall. The man who had come into the lab cursed. "*You* guys!" he said savagely. "This is *my* prisoner, see, and if you think—"

The door closed, and I couldn't hear the rest of what they said, but there was a lot of arguing before I heard the sound of all their footsteps going down the hall in a body.

Well, that's about all, I guess. Except for this other thing. It's about Ligget, and I hear he's not around any more. But you might be interested.

September 4, 1974

I haven't seen Heywood, and I've been alone in the lab all day. But Ligget came in last night. I don't think I'll see Heywood again.

Ligget came in late at night. He looked as though he hadn't slept, and he was very nervous. But he was drunk, too—I don't know where he got the liquor.

He came across the lab floor, his footsteps very loud on the cement, and he put his hands on his hips and looked up at me.

"Well, superman," he said in a tight, edgy voice, "you've

lost your buddy for good, the dirty traitor. And now you're next. You know what they're going to do to you?" He laughed. "You'll have lots of time to think it over."

He paced back and forth in front of me. Then he spun around suddenly and pointed his finger at me. "Thought you could beat the race of men, huh? Figured you were smarter than we were, didn't you? But we've got you now! You're going to learn that you can't try to fool around with the human animal, because he'll pull you down. He'll claw and kick you until you collapse. That's the way men are, robot. Not steel and circuits—flesh and blood and muscles. Flesh that fought its way out of the sea and out of the jungle, muscle that crushed everything that ever stood in his way, and blood that's spilled for a million years to keep the human race on top. *That's* the kind of an organism *we* are, robot."

He paced some more and spun again. "You never had a chance."

Well, I guess that *is* all. The rest of it, you know about. You can pull the transcriber plug out of here now, I guess. Would somebody say good-by to Heywood for me—and Russell, too, if that's possible?

COVERING MEMORANDUM,
Blalock, Project Engineer,
to
Hall, Director
820TH TDRC, COMASAMPS

September 21, 1974

Enclosed are the transcriptions of the robot's readings from his memory-bank "diary," as recorded this morning. The robot is now enroute to the Patuxent River, the casting of the concrete block having been completed with the filling of the opening through which the transcription line was run.

As Victor Heywood's successor to the post of Project Engineer, I'd like to point out that the robot was incapable of deceit, and that this transcription, if read at Heywood's trial, will prove that his intentions were definitely not treasonous, and certainly motivated on an honest belief that he was acting in the best interests of the original directive for the project's initiation.

In regard to your Memorandum 8-4792-H of yesterday, a damage report is in process of preparation and will be forwarded to you immediately on its completion.

I fully understand that Heywood's line of research is to be considered closed. Investigations into what Heywood termed the "zombie" and "slave" type of robot organization have already begun in an improvised laboratory, and I expect preliminary results within the next ten days.

Preliminary results on the general investigation of other possible types of robot orientation and organization are in, copies attached. I'd like to point out that they are extremely discouraging.

(Signed)
H. E. Blalock, Project Engineer,
820TH TDRC, COMASAMPS

September 25, 1974

PERSONAL LETTER
FROM HALL, DIRECTOR,
820TH TDRC, COMASAMPS,
to
SECRETARY OF DEFENSE
Dear Vinnie,

Well, things are finally starting to settle down out here. You were right, all this place needed was a housecleaning from top to bottom.

I think we're going to let this Heywood fellow go. We can't prove anything on him—frankly, I don't think there was anything to prove. Russell, of course, is a closed issue. His chance of ever getting out of the hospital is rated as ten per cent.

You know, considering the mess that robot made of the lab, I'd almost be inclined to think that Heywood was right. Can you imagine what a fighter that fellow would have been, if his loyalty had been channeled to some abstract like Freedom, instead of to Heywood? But we can't take the chance.

Look at the way the robot's gone amnesic about killing Ligget while he was wrecking the lab. It was something that happened accidentally. It wasn't supposed to happen, so the robot forgot it. Might present difficulties in a war.

So, we've got this Blalock fellow down from M.I.T. He spends too much time talking about Weiner, but he's all right, otherwise.

I'll be down in a couple of days. Appropriations committee meeting. You know how it is. Everybody knows we need the money, but they want to argue about it, first.

Well, that's human nature, I guess.

> See you,
> Ralph

SUPPLEMENT TO CHARTS:
Menace to Navigation.

Patuxent River, at a point forty-eight miles below Folsom, bearings as below.

Midchannel. Concrete block, 15x15x15. Not dangerous except at extreme low tide.

MEMOS

THE PEOPLE'S CHOICE
by William Jon Watkins

William Jon Watkins teaches English at Brookdale Community College in New Jersey. He also produces prose, some of it excellent. His novels include *Ecodeath* (1972, with Gene Snyder); *Clickwhistle; The God Machine* (both 1973); and *The Litany of Sh'reev* (with Snyder, 1976).

THE PEOPLE'S CHOICE

FROM: H. H. WEBER,
PRESIDENT:
WEBER, FINLEY, & OSGOOD
TO: COLFAX,
ADVERTISING CONSULTANT
DATE: September 25

While I am sure that this "advertising genius nobody ever sees" posture is a necessary part of your image, I still do not care very much for your way of doing business. I like to meet a man face to face, and I must say I find this corresponding rather eccentric. Nevertheless, you have given us such brilliant advice on campaigns in the past that I am sure you are the only one who can handle this problem if it can be handled at all. To be brief; given unlimited funds, could you make a short, fat, ugly woman President of the United States?

FROM: COLFAX
TO: H. H. WEBER, PRESIDENT
WEBER, FINLEY, & OSGOOD
DATE: September 25

With unlimited funds, I could get her elected God. The fee will be two million. Has she any other liabilities?

FROM: H. H. WEBER
TO: COLFAX
DATE: September 26

She has innumerable liabilities, not the least of which is that we can't type her. She's not homey enough for Golda Meir, nor flamboyant enough for Bella Abzug—and the way she looks precludes just about anything else. Besides that she's very shy, totally unphotogenic and has a disconcerting habit of telling the truth. Six agencies turned her down before we got her—even when offered unlimited funds. Two of them literally laughed in her face!

Something of a recluse, but very personable in small groups. Extremely intelligent, but wants to be President out of some strange sense of moral duty. Not a Women's Libber or anything, just a sort of anachronism who thinks she's best suited for the job and therefore duty-bound to take it. Very sophisticated outside of this sixteenth-century notion of moral responsibility.

FROM: COLFAX
TO: WEBER
DATE: September 27

Her shyness may work to our advantage. All we have to do is keep the public from seeing her until she's been elected. Ask her if she'll run anonymously.

FROM: WEBER
TO: COLFAX
DATE: September 27

ANONYMOUSLY?????!!!! Are you sure you can handle this?

FROM: COLFAX
TO: WEBER
DATE: September 27

$4,000,000 if she wins, nothing if she loses.

FROM: WEBER
TO: COLFAX
DATE: September 29

Agreed. She says she'll do whatever she has to do—unless it involves joining one of the political parties or is blatantly dishonest. She doesn't seem to be politically naive, but she's adamant on the point of not joining one of the parties—not that it matters much since neither of them would have her anyway.

FROM: COLFAX
TO: WEBER
DATE: September 30

Good. We'll run the entire campaign through television. Nothing until next September 12; then, I want two minutes out of every half hour until Election Day. In the meantime, get me the following:

1. About twenty Types—the kind you use in the potato chip and shaving commercials—housewives, football players, policemen, little old ladies, doctors, etc. None of them too good-looking. Have the women a little on the plain side, something she can blend in with.

2. One athletic, intelligent, articulate Black male.

3. One white male, about sixty. The Grand-Old-Man type, white hair, moustache and goatee, robust. The kind you use in the Impeccable Taste ads, but more sagacious.

4. One white female who can look like she has a Ph.D. in Political Science without losing anything as a sex symbol.

5. One white male about thirty-five who looks as much as possible like the Virile-Young-Man without looking too much like a Kennedy. All of the Four must be physically and mentally superior.

6. An estate outside New York, secluded, one where we can maintain absolute security. NO ONE who works on this project can be attached in any way. We are going to hide them away until after the election. NONE of the actors is ever to be seen in public unless I order it.

I must have ABSOLUTE authority in this thing. No one is to know for certain who the Candidate is, so your client will have to agree to act like everyone else. That means she'll have to take orders just like any other actor; if word of her identity gets out prematurely or she wants to pull out partway through, you forfeit $200,000 a month for my time—from Sept. 25 to date of forfeiture. Agreed?

Contact me again when you've secured everything on the list. We have over a year to go, so be very selective. Take only those who are willing to cooperate completely and only the very best of those. PCS will handle the initial screening. We'll need about three months for indoctrination before filming begins.

FROM: WEBER
TO: COLFAX
DATE: April 25
Agreed.

Files on the final selections will be sent to your office tomorrow. We have secured an estate in New Jersey about fifty miles outside the city. Two buses have been purchased and dummy buses have been rented to confuse anyone who might try to follow us.

FROM: COLFAX
TO: WEBER
DATE: May 1
I am finished studying the files. The final selections are excellent. It's surprising that Ms. Cavil has never entered a beauty contest—but very fortunate for us. Williams is very good for the Grand Old Man; very genteel. I don't think Saxon's Boston accent will hurt us and I'm very pleased with Brown. I was afraid they would come up with a white man's Black man, but this one is excellent.

Begin filming the Gold Edge Beer commercial and the Bright Detergent commercial Tuesday. We'll need these shown as soon and as often as possible. They'll give our real commercials something familiar to parallel. Begin the indoctrination tomorrow.

FROM: WEBER
TO: COLFAX
DATE: August 25

I hope these things are being forwarded to you. This is a hell of a time to take a vacation. The actors are very enthused now that they know their mission. There is none of the jealousy you might expect with this many actors cooped up together for so long. The screening must have been exceptionally good.

I think most of them—certainly the Four—know who the Candidate is but it doesn't matter; she's made converts of all of them. They seem sincerely attached to her; her influence on them is truly amazing. She has one of them studying Ecology; another Economics. One is becoming her expert on Education; another on Foreign Policy. It's like she's selected her cabinet already.

I treated the whole thing like a game but she seems quite serious—and so do they. When do we start the first commercial? We're about ready.

FROM: COLFAX
TO: WEBER
DATE: September 1

The idea for the first commercial is enclosed. Make it parallel the Gold Edge Beer commercial as closely as possible; shoot the same camera angles, etc. Most of this is the same action; read it anyway.

Open with tight shot of huddle. Close-up of Ms. Cavil in her sweatshirt, cap, whistle, etc., calling the play. Wide angle for snap from center. Cut to Saxon running his pattern; long pass to him on run; circus catch. (Shoot this one until you get something spectacular. The files indicate that both Saxon and Brown played football in college.)

Follow Saxon down sideline to where he gets hemmed in by the last defensive man. Brown comes from off-camera left to block the defensive man. (Again, something that crunches. This will be shown during a lot of professional football games, and we don't want it to look pale by comparison.) Cut to Saxon as he scores.

Close-up of Saxon and Brown congratulating each other. Cut to close-up of Grand Old Man nodding approvingly from the sidelines. Close-up of button on his lapel reading: TEAM-WORK COUNTS. (Distribute 5,000,000, of these buttons around the country the same week.)

Wide angle shot of crowd running up to congratulate Saxon and Brown. Keep the Candidate in front, but a little out of focus. Cut to American flag. Dub in "Hail to the Chief." Superimpose words and narrator: "Ladies and gentlemen, the next president of the United States has appeared in this commercial."

FROM: WEBER
TO: COLFAX
DATE: September 9

Very effective. A lot like the "Camels-Are-Coming!" campaign and the car commercials we did with the new models under a drape. We're ready for number two. By the way, our client has them all meeting an hour a day for what she calls consciousness raising. You don't suppose she's a Libbie after all?

FROM: COLFAX
TO: WEBER
DATE: September 9

I don't really care what she is. My job is to get her elected. Enclosed is the second script. Shoot the same opening as the Bright commercial except that instead of having Cavil explain how the detergent works have her talk about how detergents and industrial wastes are fouling our water supply.

As she's talking, four men come into the laundromat and attack her (have them wear ski masks so we don't offend any ethnic groups). She fights, one of them tears open her blouse (tiniest flash of nipple). Saxon and Brown enter dressed as washer repairmen, come to her aid.

Series of rapid cuts: knives, feet, faces, different camera angles, mostly low. Each disables one opponent: Cavil finishes hers with a Karate chop. Fourth assailant runs for the door where the Grand Old Man, entering, jabs him with his walking stick (have the old man take a good impact on the stick and grab his shoulder in pain).

Pan around laundromat: clothes all over the floor, an old woman hysterical in the corner with the Candidate comforting her. Cavil trying to hold her blouse closed, Saxon and Brown both cut over the right eye, the old man rubbing his shoulder, the four toughs sprawled about on the floor. Dolly back out through the window to wide angle shot of laundromat.

Superimpose and voice-over: "When a crime is committed, everyone suffers. We must fight crime in the streets and the conditions that cause it. Vote for THE CANDIDATE." Both Right and Left will interpret that one to our advantage.

TO: COLFAX
FROM: WEBER
DATE: September 10

Cavil and our client both refuse to do the commercial. They say it exploits women. The men agree with them. She's turning them all into revolutionaries!

TO: WEBER
FROM: COLFAX
DATE: September 11

Of course it exploits women! How many commercials have they seen that don't? Ask Cavil this: If she had to break into a prison to free her sisters would she refuse to do it because she'd have to dress up as a male guard? And tell your client that when she's President she can appoint Kate Millett head of the FCC and change all the commercials she wants, but this one must *stay as is*. Causes require sacrifices.

TO: COLFAX
FROM: WEBER
DATE: September 11

She says to tell you you must mean "The end justifies the means." Anyway, they had a meeting and decided that tactics takes precedence over ideology. They'll do the script as written.

You've opened a fine can of worms with that crack about

the FCC. Now they're drawing up a list of government agencies that can be controlled by appointment. And making a list of appointees!

FROM: WEBER
TO: COLFAX
DATE: September 20

Things have settled down a bit and the filming is going very well. The Karate stuff looks authentic. Brown is familiar with it and acted as technical director. I don't think they're really serious about that list. Williams told me they have Angela Davis down for Supreme Court Justice. He had such a straight face I almost thought he was serious. Anyway, it helps them pass the time between takes.

FROM: COLFAX
TO: WEBER
DATE: September 23

Release the first commercial and the buttons simultaneously in ten days.

FROM: WEBER
TO: COLFAX
DATE: October 3

Introductory commercial released yesterday as directed. Good initial response. Five million TEAMWORK COUNTS buttons distributed. Our client has her "cabinet" out proselytizing among the other actors. Not much else to do now that the shooting's over for a while, and it keeps them busy, so I encourage it.

FROM: WEBER
TO: COLFAX
DATE: October 12

Crime commercial released yesterday on schedule. Requests received for 2,000,000 more buttons. Between the five of them, they've even begun to make converts among the technical and security people. I think Cavil's trying to raise *my* level of consciousness. Are we creating a Frankenstein here?

FROM: COLFAX
TO: WEBER
DATE: October 13

Release group picture for the "$5,000 1,000-winner Who-Is-THE CANDIDATE? Contest." Follow each of our one-minute commercials with a thirty-second spot about the contest. Place hints in appropriate newspaper columns and have your Gold Edge Beer Salesmen casually pass on similar information to bartenders. We want everybody in the country to have an opinion of THE CANDIDATE'S identity. The contest should have the effect of encouraging betting. All major radio stations will carry telephone contests with similar clues.

Dummy voting booths will be set up near every large polling place. Procedures for voting must be identical to those used in the real election. It will cost us another million in persuasion money to get "THE CANDIDATE" printed on the real ballot and to have anything written in counted as a vote for us, but it will be well worth it. Also she will have to secretly change her name to THE CANDIDATE to make it hold up in court (the Supreme Court). We have less than a month to make voting for THE CANDIDATE a conditioned response.

FROM: WEBER
TO: COLFAX
DATE: October 14

What are we going to do?! The President has just accepted a challenge to debate! What if they include us?!

FROM: COLFAX
TO: WEBER
DATE: October 15

And admit we're a legitimate alternative? Not likely. Here's the next commercial; release it the day *after* the debate.

Wide angle shot of auditorium; pan slowly to platform where the President and the Democratic nominee are debating. They cannot be heard because the crowd is booing too loudly. Both men ignore the crowd entirely. The crowd grows violent and begins to throw things. Secret Service men draw their guns. Cut to series of other weapons in the audience.

Brown jumps up on the left side of the stage, Cavil on the right. They gesture for order and the crowd quiets. Brown speaks.

"Everyone has the right to say what he wants, even the people who barred us from this platform! Even the people who denied us the opportunity to confront them on the real issues of the campaign. Even the people who have been trying to keep us from talking to you, the people, by putting pressure on television station owners to drop our commercials!"

Cavil speaks. "These men have a right to speak! Even though every word they say is put into their mouths by the rich and powerful men who are paying for their campaigns. Even though they won't tell you about the deals they've already made they have the right to speak! Everybody has that right! Not just those who agree with us! Everybody!" Saxon shouts, "Right!" Wild applause.

Pan slowly past the Candidate to Williams, smiling his approval. Superimpose words and voice-over: "It's not who you are but what you believe in that's important. Vote for the candidate nobody owns. Vote for THE CANDIDATE."

FROM: WEBER
TO: COLFAX
DATE: October 23

Latest commercial released on schedule. Over 50 million votes already in the "Who-Is-THE-CANDIDATE Contest." People are tuning in our commercials just to study them. Papers in all major cities are carrying schedules of our commercials on the front page. This thing is really beginning to boom—I'm worried.

FROM: COLFAX
TO: WEBER
DATE: October 30

Start filming the thirty-second spot. Assemble the whole group, in costumes and masks. Have the Candidate and the

Four in the center of the group but not conspicuously so. Then all remove their masks and shout, "See you at the victory celebration!" You have two days to do this one. Plant hints in the columns that there'll be no unmasking unless we win the election. Hedge when the media asks you about it.

FROM: WEBER
TO: COLFAX
DATE: November 4

Over 85,000,000 votes in the contest and we're ahead of both of them in the polls! The networks are demanding that we either show our candidate or get out of the race. What are we going to do? I can't stall them forever.

FROM: COLFAX
TO: WEBER
DATE: November 4

Set up a press conference for the sixth, nationwide TV, prime time.

FROM: WEBER
TO: COLFAX
DATE: November 5

Are you crazy?! We can't show her! What's going to happen with all those people who guessed wrong? I've had three phone calls from people telling me that they've bet a lot of money on the Old Man and it better be him or else—and I have an unlisted number! We're liable to get killed right there at the press conference.

It's easy for you to say "give a press conference" when you're off hiding somewhere on your extended vacation. But we're the ones who'll have to face the music. I knew this thing was going to blow up in our faces! When the press gets a look at her we'll be the laughing stock of the industry. When the public sees her we'll be lucky if we don't get indicted for fraud and conspiracy! Treason! You've got to get us out of this!!

FROM: COLFAX
TO: WEBER
DATE: November 6

GET YOURSELF TOGETHER!! Just go to the meeting and stand well back from the podium. The Candidate knows what to do. Everything is going according to plan. TRUST ME!!

FROM: WEBER
TO: COLFAX
DATE: November 7

WHY DIDN'T YOU TELL ME ABOUT THE BOMB!!!! I thought it was for real. How did you manage to get the television cables cut during the confusion? And what would have happened if the rest of that dynamite had gone off? And for what???!!!

So we didn't have to make the announcement? What good does it do us? What's going to happen tonight when she wins the election and has to make a victory speech? The losers are bound to call fraud. They might even get the election nullified! We could all go to jail! WHAT ARE WE GOING TO DO???!!!

FROM: COLFAX
TO: WEBER
DATE: November 7

Stop it. I repeat; everything is going according to plan. Don't come to the victory party tonight; I don't even want to see you near campaign headquarters! Go back to the estate and watch it all on television as soon as you give these instructions to the group.

Everything is set. The group will come to the podium in a body as soon as we are mathematically assured of victory. The Four will be in the middle, the Candidate a little to the right. The house lights will go off and the assassination film will be shown. The TV people are already prepared for a film of some sort as part of the speech so they'll have no trouble carrying the whole thing. The film is pretty gruesome, even in black and white.

When the house lights come on again, the whole group will repeat the following in unison:

TIME AFTER TIME, THE WILL OF THE PEOPLE HAS BEEN CIRCUMVENTED BY AN ACT OF VIOLENCE. LAST NIGHT IT ALMOST HAPPENED AGAIN. THE COUNTRY CANNOT AFFORD THE DISLOCATION THAT OCCURS WHEN A PRESIDENT IS ASSASSINATED. AS LONG AS I AM PRESIDENT MY IDENTITY WILL REMAIN A SECRET.

THE DESIRE FOR PERSONAL GLORY DOES NOT BELONG IN THE WHITE HOUSE. THE DESIRE TO BE A PRESIDENT "HISTORY WILL REMEMBER" DOES NOT BELONG IN THE WHITE HOUSE. THEREFORE I WILL REMAIN ANONYMOUS.

BUT THIS SHOULD NOT SEEM STRANGE TO YOU; THE PRESIDENT IS, AFTER ALL, ONLY THE REPRESENTATIVE WHO STANDS IN PLACE OF THAT GREAT ANONYMOUS MASS—THE PEOPLE. WE THE PEOPLE!

Have them rehearse it thoroughly.

FROM: COLFAX
TO: WEBER
DATE: November 8

I have destroyed your memo, and the security guards I have permanently assigned to you will see to it that you do the same with this after you read it. I don't know when you figured it out and I must confess I did not anticipate your hiding the memos that passed between us. I congratulate you; it was a clever move and guarantees you your life.

You will be kept under close house arrest until my Inauguration. Thereafter you will be free to move about—however, if you ever address me or refer to me as "Madame President" again, I will have you killed, whether I find the memos or not! You will be well taken care of. Do not try to escape.

EXPEDITION
by Anthony Boucher

"Anthony Boucher" is one of the pen names of an amazing gentleman born William Anthony Parker White (1911–1968) who contributed much to the science fiction and mystery fields (for the latter he contributed frequently as "H. H. Holmes") and to all who knew him. His fame in sf rests on his work as a founding co-editor of *The Magazine of Fantasy and Science Fiction* and the fantasies he wrote for *Unknown*, which can be found in collections like *The Complete Werewolf* (1969) and *Far and Away* (1955). Editors take note: a retrospective collection of his best work is long overdue.

EXPEDITION

The following is a transcript of the recorded two-way messages between Mars and the field expedition to the satellite of the third planet.

First Interplanetary Exploratory Expedition to Central Receiving Station:

What has the Great One achieved?

Murvin, Central Receiving Station, to First Interplanetary Exploratory Expedition:

All right, boys, I'll play games. What *has* the Great One achieved? And when are we going to get a report on it?

Falzik, First Interplanetary Exploratory Expedition, to Murvin, Central Receiving Station:

Haven't you any sense of historical moments? That was the first interplanetary message ever sent. It had to be worthy of the occasion. Trubz spent a long time working on the psychology of it while I prepared the report. Those words are going to live down through the ages of our planet.

Murvin to Falzik:

All right. Swell. You'll be just as extinct while they live on. Now how's about that report?

Report of First Interplanetary Exploratory Expedition, presented by Falzik, specialist in reporting:

The First Interplanetary Exploratory Expedition has landed successfully upon the satellite of the third planet. The personnel of this expedition consists of Karnim, specialist in astrogation; Halov, specialist in life sciences; Trubz, specialist in psychology; Lilil, specialist in the art; and Falzik, specialist in reporting.

The trip itself proved unimportant for general reporting. Special aspects of difficulties encountered and overcome will appear in the detailed individual report of Karnim after the return of the expedition. The others, in particular Trubz and Lilil, were largely unaware of these difficulties. To anyone save the specialist in astrogation, the trip seemed nowise different, except in length, from a vacation excursion to one of our own satellites.

The majority theory is apparently vindicated here on this satellite of the third planet. It does not sustain life. According to Halov, specialist in life sciences, it is not a question of can not; since life of some strange sort might conceivably exist under any conditions save those of a perfect vacuum. But so far as can be ascertained there is no life of any remotely recognizable form upon this satellite.

The globe is dead. It is so dead that one may say the word without fear. The euphemism *extinct* would be too mild for the absolute and utter deadness here. It it so dead that the thought of death is not terrifying.

Trubz is now working on the psychology of that.

Observation checks the previous calculations that one face of this satellite is always turned towards its world and one always from it, the period of rotation coinciding exactly with the orbital period. There seems to be no difference in nature between the two sides; but obviously the far side is the proper site for the erection of our temporary dome. If the hypothetical inhabitants of the third planet have progressed to the use of astronomical instruments, we do not wish to give them warning of our approach by establishing ourselves in the full sight of those instruments.

The absence of life on this satellite naturally proved a

serious disappointment to Halov, but even more so to Lilil, who felt inspired to improvise a particularly ingenious specimen of his art. Fortunately the stores of the ship had provided for such an emergency and the resultant improvisation was one of the greatest triumphs of Lilil's great career. We are now about to take our first rest after the trip, and our minds are aglow with the charm and beauty of his exquisite work.

Murvin to Falzik:

All right. Report received and very welcome. But can't you give us more color? Physical description of the satellite—minerals present—exploitation possibilities—anything like that? Some of us are more interested in those than in Trubz's psychology or even Lilil's practice of the art.

Falzik to Murvin:

What are you asking for? You know as well as I do the purpose of this expedition: to discover other intelligent forms of life. And you know the double purpose behind that purpose: to verify by comparison that psychological explanation of our race-dominant fear of death (if this were a formal dispatch I'd censor that to "extinction"), and to open up new avenues of creation in the art.

That's why the personnel of this expedition, save for the astrogator, was chosen for its usefulness *if* we discover life. Until we do, our talents as specialists are wasted. We don't know about minerals and topography. Wait for the next expedition's report on them.

If you want color, our next report should have it. It will come from the third planet itself. We've established our temporary base here easily, and are blasting off very soon for what our scientists have always maintained is the most probable source of life in this system.

Murvin to Falzik:

All right. And if you find life, I owe you a sarbel dinner at Noku's.

Falzik to Murvin:

Sarbel for two, please! Though what we've found, the Great One only—but go on to the report.

Report of First Interplanetary Exploratory Expedition, presented by Falzik, specialist in reporting:

The site of the Expedition's landing on the third planet was chosen more or less at random. It is situated on the third in size of the five continents, not far from the shore of the largest ocean. It is approximately indicated by the coordinates——and——[1] in Kubril's chart of the planet.

In the relatively slow final period of our approach, we were able to observe that the oceans of the third planet are indeed true liquids and not merely beds of molten metal, as has been conjectured by some of our scientists. We were more elated to observe definite signs of intelligent life. We glimpsed many structures which only the most unimaginative materialist could attribute to natural accident, and the fact that these structures tend to cluster together in great numbers indicates an organized and communal civilization.

That at least was our first uplifting emotional reaction, as yet not completely verified. The place of our landing is free from such structures, and from almost everything else. It is as purely arid a desert as the region about Krinavizhd, which in some respects it strongly resembles.

At first we saw no signs of life whatsoever, which is as we could have wished it. An exploratory expedition does not want a welcoming committee, complete with spoken speeches and seven-string sridars. There was a sparse amount of vegetation, apparently in an untended state of nature, but nothing to indicate the presence of animal life until we saw the road.

It was an exceedingly primitive and clumsy road, consisting of little more than a ribbon of space from which the vegetation had been cleared; but it was a sign, and we followed it, to be rewarded shortly by our first glimpse of

---

[1] The mathematical signs indicating these coordinates are, unfortunately, typographically impossible to reproduce.—*Editor.*

moving life. There was some form of apodal being, approximately one-fifth of the length of one of us, which glided across the road and disappeared before we could make any attempt at communication.

We continued along the road for some time, suffering severely from the unaccustomed gravity and the heavy atmosphere, but spurred on by the joyous hope of fulfilling the aim of the expedition. Lilil in particular evinced an inspired elation at the hope of finding new subjects for his great compositions.

The sun, markedly closer and hotter here on the third planet, was setting when at last we made our first contact with third-planet life. This being was small, about the length of the first joint of one's foreleg, covered with fur of pure white, save for the brown dust of the desert, and quadrupedal. It was frisking in a patch of shade, seeming to rejoice in the setting of the sun and the lowering of the temperature. With its forelegs it performed some elaborate and to us incomprehensible ritual with a red ball.

Halov approached it and attracted its attention by a creaking of his wing-rudiments. It evinced no fear, but instantly rolled the red ball in his direction. Halov deftly avoided this possible weapon. (We later examined it and found it to be harmless, at least to any form of life known to us; its purpose remains a mystery. Trubz is working on the psychology of it.) He then—optimistically, but to my mind foolishly—began the fifth approach, the one developed for beings of a civilization roughly parallel to our own.

It was a complete failure. The white thing understood nothing of what Halov scratched in the ground, but persisted in trying to wrench from his digits the stick with which he scratched. Halov reluctantly retreated through the approaches down to approach one (designed for beings of the approximate mental level of the Narbian aborigines) but the creature paid no heed to them and insisted upon performing with the moving stick some ritual similar to that which it had practiced with the ball.

By this time we were all weary of these fruitless efforts, so that it came as a marked relief when Lilil announced that he had been inspired to improvise. The exquisite perfection of his art refreshed us and we continued our search with renewed vitality, though not before Halov had examined the corpse of the white creature and determined that it was indubitably similar to the mammals, though many times larger than any form of mammalian life has ever become on our planet.

Some of us thought whimsically of that favorite fantasy of the science-fiction composers—the outsize mammals who will attack and destroy our race. But we had not yet seen anything.

Murvin to Falzik:

That's a fine way to end a dispatch. You've got me all agog. Has the Monster Mammal King got you in his clutches?

Falzik to Murvin:

Sorry. I didn't intend to be sensational. It is simply that we've been learning so much here through—well, yes, you can call him the Monster Mammal King, though the fictionists would be disappointed in him—that it's hard to find time enough for reports. But here is more.

Report of First Interplanetary Exploratory Expedition, presented by Falzik, specialist in reporting:

The sun was almost down when we saw the first intelligent being ever beheld by one of our race outside of our planet. He (for we learned afterwards that he was male, and it would be unjust to refer to an intelligent being as *it*) was lying on the ground in the shade of a structure—a far smaller structure than those we had glimpsed in passing, and apparently in a sad state of dilapidation.

In this posture the fact was not markedly noticeable, but he is a biped. Used as we are on our own planet to many forms of life—octopods (though the Great One be thanked that those terrors are nearly wiped out), ourselves hexapods, and the pesky little mammalian tetrapods—a biped still seems to us something strange and mythical. A logical possibility, but not a likelihood. The length of body of this one is approximately that of a small member of our own race.

He held a container apparently of glass in one foreleg

(there must be some other term to use of bipeds, since the front limbs are not used as legs) and was drinking from it when he spied us. He choked on his drink, looked away, then returned his gaze to us and stared for a long time. At last he blinked his eyes, groaned aloud, and hurled the glass container far away.

Halov now advanced toward him. He backed away, reached one forelimb inside the structure, and brought it out clasping a long metal rod, with a handle of some vegetable material. This he pointed at Halov, and a loud noise ensued. At the time some of us thought this was the being's speech, but now we know it came from the rod, which apparently propelled some form of metal missile against Halov.

The missile, of course, bounced harmlessly off Halov's armor (he prides himself on keeping in condition) and our specialist in life sciences continued to advance toward the biped, who dropped the rod and leaned back against the structure. For the first time we heard his voice, which is extraordinarily low in pitch. We have not yet fully deciphered his language, but I have, as instructed, been keeping full phonetic transcriptions of his every remark. Trubz has calculated psychologically that the meaning of this remark must be:

"Ministers of the Great One, be gracious to me!"

The phonetic transcription is as follows:[1]

AND THEY TALK ABOUT PINK ELEPHANTS!

He watched awestruck as Halov, undaunted by his former experience, again went directly into the fifth approach. The stick in Halov's digits traced a circle in the dirt with rays coming out of it, then pointed up at the setting sun.

The biped moved his head forward and back and spoke again. Trubz's conjecture here is:

"The great sun, the giver of life."

Phonetic transcription:

BUGS THAT DRAW PRETTY PICTURES YET!

Then Halov drew a series of concentric ellipses of dotted lines about the figure of the sun. He drew tiny circles on

---

[1]For the convenience of the reader, these transcriptions have been retranscribed into the conventional biped spelling.—*Editor.*

these orbits to indicate the first and second planets, then larger ones to indicate the third and our own. The biped was by now following the drawing with intense absorption.

Halov now pointed to the drawing of the third planet, then to the biped, and back again. The biped once more moved his head forward, apparently as a gesture of agreement. Finally Halov in like manner pointed to the fourth planet, to himself, and back again, and likewise in turn for each of us.

The biped's face was blank for a moment. Then he himself took a stick and pointed from the fourth planet to Halov, saying, according to Trubz:

"This is really true?"

Transcription:

YOU MEAN YOU'RE MARTIANS?

Halov imitated the head movement of agreement. The biped dropped his stick and gasped out sounds which Trubz is sure were the invocation of the name of a potent diety. Transcription:

ORSON WELLES!

We had all meanwhile been groping with the biped's thought patterns, though no success had attended our efforts. In the first place, his projection was almost nil; his race is apparently quite unaccustomed to telepathic communication. In the second place, of course, it is next to impossible to read alien thought patterns without some fixed point of reference.

Just as we could never have deciphered the ancient writings of the Khrugs without the discovery of the Burdarno Stone which gave the same inscription in their language and in an antique form of our own, so we could not attempt to decode this biped's thought patterns until we knew what they were like on a given known subject.

We now began to perceive some of his patterns of the Solar System and for our respective worlds. Halov went on to the second stage of the fifth approach. He took a group of small rocks, isolated one, held up one digit, and drew the figure one in the dirt. The biped seemed puzzled. Then Halov added another rock to the first, held up two digits, and drew the figure two, and so on for three and four. Now the biped seemed enlightened and made his agreement gesture. He also held up one digit and drew a figure beside Halov's.

His *one* is the same as ours—a not too surprising fact. Trubz has been working on the psychology of it and has decided that the figure one is probably a simple straight line in almost any numerical system. His other figures differed markedly from ours, but his intention was clear and we could to some extent follow his patterns.

Using both forelegs, Halov went on to five, six, and seven with the biped writing down his number likewise. Then Halov held up all his digits and wrote a one followed by the dot which represents zero and is the essence of any mathematical intelligence. This was the crucial moment—did these bipeds know how to calculate or was their numerical system purely primitive?

The biped held up eight digits and wrote a new figure, a conjoined pair of circles. Halov, looking worried, added another rock to his group and wrote down two ones. The biped wrote a circle with a tail to it. Halov added another rock and wrote a one followed by a two. The biped wrote a one followed by a circle.

Then Halov understood. We have always used an octonary system, but our mathematicians have long realized the possibility of others: a system of two, for instance, in which 11 would mean three, a system of four (the folk speech even contains survivals of such a system) in which 11 would mean five. For 11 means simply the first power of the number which is your base, plus one. This system of the bipeds obviously employs a decimal base.

(Trubz has been working on the psychology of this. He explains it by the fact that the bipeds have five digits on each forelimb, or a total of ten, whereas we have four each, a total of eight.)

Halov now beckoned to Karnim, who as astrogator is the best mathematician among us, and asked him to take over. He studied for a moment the biped's numbers, adjusted his mind rapidly to the (for the layman) hopeless confusion of a decimal system, and went ahead with simple mathematical operations. The biped followed him not unskillfully, while the rest of us concentrated on his thought patterns and began to gather their shape and nature.

The growing darkness bothered the biped before it incommoded Karnim. He rose from his squatting position over the numerals and went into the structure, the interior of which was soon alight. He came back to the doorway and beckoned us to enter. As we did so, he spoke words which Turbz conjectures to mean:

"Enter my abode and stay in peace, O emissaries from the fourth planet."

Phonetic transcription:

YOU'LL BE GONE IN THE MORNING AND WILL I HAVE A HEAD!

Murvin to Falzik:

What a yarn! A planet of intelligent beings! What a future for the art! Maybe I never was sold on this expedition, but I am now. Keep the reports coming. And include as much phonetic transcription as you can—the specialists are working on what you've sent and are inclined to doubt some of Trubz' interpretations. Also tell Trubz to get to work as soon as possible in the psychological problem of extinction. If this being's a mammal, he should help.

[Several reports are omitted here, dealing chiefly with the gradually acquired skill of the expedition in reading a portion of the biped's thought patterns and in speaking a few words of his language.]

Report of First Interplanetary Exploratory Expedition, presented by Falzik, specialist in reporting:

Halov and Trubz agree that we should stay with this *man* (for such we have by now learned is the name of his race) until we have learned as much from him as we can. He has accepted us now and is almost at ease with us, though the morning after our arrival, for some peculiar reason, he seemed even more surprised to see us than when we first appeared.

We can learn much more from him, now that he is used to us, than we could from the dwellers in the large massed structures, and after we are well versed in his civilization we stand much more chance of being accepted peaceably.

We have been here now for three of the days of this planet, absorbed in our new learning. (All save Lilil, who is fretful because he has not practiced his art for so long. I have occasionally seen him eying the *man* speculatively.) By using a mixture of telepathy, sign language, and speech, we can by now discuss many things, though speech comes with difficulty to one who has used it only on formal and fixed occasions.

For instance we have learned why this *man* lives alone far from his fellows. His specialty is the making of pictures with what he calls a *camera*, a contrivance which records the effect of different intensities of light upon a salt of silver—a far more complex method than our means of making pictures with photosensitized elduron, but one producing much the same results. He has taken pictures of us, though he seems doubtful that any other *man* will ever believe the record of his *camera*.

At present he is engaged in a series of pictures of aspects of the desert, an undertaking which he seems to regard not as a useful function but as an art of some strange sort. Trubz is working on the psychology of it and says that a reproductive and imitative art is conceivable, but Lilil is scornful of the notion.

Today he showed us many pictures of other *mans* and of their cities and structures. *Man* is a thin-skinned and almost hairless animal. This *man* of ours goes almost naked, but that is apparently because of the desert heat. Normally a *man* makes up for his absence of hair by wearing a sort of artificial fur of varying shapes known as *clothes*. To judge from the pictures shown us by the *man*, this is true only of the male of the species. The female never covers her bare skin in any way.

Examination of these pictures of females shown us by our *man* fully confirms our theory that the animal *man* is a mammal.

The display of pictures ended with an episode still not quite clear to us. Ever since our arrival, the *man* has been worrying and talking about something apparently lost—something called a *kitten*. The thought pattern was not familiar enough to gather its nature, until he showed us a picture of the small white beast which we had first met and we recognized in his mind this *kitten*-pattern. He seemed proud of the picture, which showed the beast in its ritual with the ball, but still worried, and asked us, according to Trubz, if we knew anything of its whereabouts. Transcription:

YOU WOULDN'T ANY OF YOU BIG BUGS KNOW WHAT THE DEVIL'S BECOME OF THAT KITTEN, WOULD YOU?

Thereupon Lilil arose in his full creative pride and led the *man* to the place where we had met the *kitten*. The corpse was by now withered in the desert sun, and I admit that it was difficult to gather from such a spectacle the greatness of Lilil's art, but we were not prepared for the *man's* reaction.

His face grew exceedingly red and a fluid formed in his eyes. He clenched his digits and made curious gestures with them. His words were uttered brokenly and exceedingly difficult to transcribe. Trubz has not yet conjectured their meaning, but the transcription read:

YOU DID THAT? TO A POOR HARMLESS LITTLE KITTEN? WHY, YOU—[1]

His attitude has not been the same towards us since. Trubz is working on the psychology of it.

Murvin to Falzik:

Tell Trubz to work on the major psychological problem. Your backers are getting impatient.

Falzik to Murvin:

I think that last report was an aspect of it. But I'm still puzzled. See what you can make of this one.

Report of First Interplanetary Exploratory Expedition, presented by Falzik, specialist in reporting:

[1]The remainder of this transcription has been suppressed for this audience.—*Editor.*

Tonight Halov and Trubz attempted to present the great psychological problem to the *man*. To present such a problem in our confusion of thoughts, language and gesture is not easy, but I think that to some extent they succeeded.

They stated it in its simplest form: Our race is obsessed by a terrible fear of extinction. We will each of us do anything to avoid his personal extinction. No such obsession has ever been observed among the minute mammalian pests of our planet.

Now, is our terror a part of our intelligence? Does intelligence necessarily imply and bring with it a frantic clinging to the life that supports us? Or does this terror stem from our being what we are, rather than mammals? A mammal brings forth its young directly; the young are a direct continuation of the life of the old. But with us a half dozen specialized individuals bring forth all the young. The rest of us have no part in it; our lives are dead ends, and we dread the approach of that blank wall.

Our psychologists have battled over this question for generations. Would another—say, a mammalian—form of intelligent life have such an obsession? Here we had an intelligent mammal. Could he answer us?

I give the transcription of his answer, as yet not fully deciphered:

I THINK I GET WHAT YOU MEAN. AND I THINK THE ANSWER IS A LITTLE OF BOTH. O.K., SO WE'RE INTELLIGENT MAMMALS. WE HAVE MORE FEAR OF DEATH THAN THE UNINTELLIGENT, LIKE THE POOR LITTLE KITTEN YOU BUTCHERED; BUT CERTAINLY NOT SUCH A DOMINANT OBSESSION AS I GATHER YOUR RACE HAS.

Trubz thinks that this was an ambiguous answer, which will not satisfy either party among our specialists in psychology.

We then proposed, as a sub-question, the matter of the art. Is it this same psychological manifestation that has led us to develop such an art? That magnificent and highest of arts which consists in the extinction with the greatest esthetic subtlety of all other forms of life?

Here the *man's* reactions were as confusing as they had been beside the corpse of the *kitten*. He said:

SO THAT'S WHAT HAPPENED TO SNOWPUSS? ART . . .! ART, YOU CALL IT YET! AND YOU'VE COME HERE TO PRACTICE THAT ART ON THIS WORLD? I'LL SEE YOU FRIED CRISP ON BOTH SIDES ON HADES' HOTTEST GRIDDLE FIRST!

Trubz believes that the extremely violent emotion expressed was shock at realization of the vast new reaches of esthetic experience which lay before him.

Later, when he thought he was alone, I overheard him talking to himself. There was something so emphatically inimical in his thought-patterns that I transcribed his words though I have not yet had a chance to secure Trubz' opinion on them. He beat the clenched digits of one forelimb against the other and said:

SO THAT'S WHAT YOU'RE UP TO! WE'LL SEE ABOUT THAT. BUT HOW? HOW . . .? GOT IT! THOSE PICTURES I TOOK FOR THE PUBLIC HEALTH CAMPAIGN . . .

I am worried. If this attitude indicated by his thought-patterns persists, we may have to bring about his extinction and proceed at once by ourselves. At least it will give Lilil a chance to compose one of his masterpieces.

Final report of the First Interplanetary Exploratory Expedition, presented by Falzik, specialist in reporting:

How I could so completely have misinterpreted the *man's* thought-patterns I do not understand. Trubz is working on the psychology of it. Far from any hatred or enmity, the *man* was even then resolving to save our lives. The First Interplanetary Exploratory Expedition owes him a debt which it can never repay.

It was after sun-up the next day that he approached us with his noble change of heart. As I describe this scene I cannot unfortunately give his direct words; I was too carried away by my own emotions to remember to transcribe. Such phrases as I attribute to him here are reconstructed from the complex of our intercourse, and were largely a matter of signs and pictures.

What he did first was to show us one of his pictures. We stared at it, and drew back horrified. For it represented a being closely allied to us, almost to be taken for one of us, meeting extinction beneath a titanic weapon wielded by what was obviously the characteristic five-digited forelimb of a *man*. And that forelimb was many, many times the size of the being resembling us.

"I've been keeping this from you," he informed us. "I'll admit I've been trying to trap you. But the truth is: I'm a dwarf *man*. The real ones are as much bigger than me as you are bigger than the *kitten*. More, even. And their favorite pastime—only they call it a sport, not art—is killing bugs like you."

We realized now what should have struck us before—the minute size of his structure compared with those which we had seen before. Obviously he spoke the truth—he was a dwarf specimen of his race.

Then he produced more pictures—horrible, terrifying, monstrous pictures, all showing something perturbingly like us meeting cruel extinction at the whim of a *man*.

"I've just been keeping you here," he said, "until some real members of my race could come and play with you. They'd like it. But I haven't got the heart to do it. I like you, and what you told me about your art convinces me that you don't deserve extinction like that. So I'm giving you your chance: Clear out of here and stay away from this planet. It's the most unsafe place in the universe for your kind. If you dread extinction, stay away from the third planet!"

His resolve to spare our lives had made him happy. His face kept twisting into the grimace we had learned to recognize as a sign of *man's* pleasure. But we hardly watched him or even listened to him. Our eyes kept returning with awful fascination to those morbidly terrifying pictures. Then our thoughts fused into one, and with hardly a word of farewell to our savior we sped back to the ship.

This is our last report. We are now on the temporary base established on the satellite and will return as soon as we have recovered from the shock of our narrow escape. Lilil has achieved a new composition with a captive pergut from the ship which has somewhat solaced us.

Murvin to First Interplanetary Exploratory Expedition:

You dopes! You low mammalian idiots! It's what comes of sending nothing but specialists on an expedition. I tried to convince them you needed a good general worker like me, but no. And look at you!

It's obvious what happened. On our planet, mammals are minute pests and the large intelligent beings are arthropodal hexapods. All right. On the third planet things have worked out the other way round. *Bugs,* as the *man* calls our kin, are tiny insignificant things. You saw those pictures and thought the *mans* were enormous; actually they meant only that the *bugs* were minute!

That *man* tricked you unpardonably, and I like him for it. Specialists . . .! You deserve extinction for this, and you know it. But Vardanek has another idea. Stay where you are. Develop the temporary base in any way you can. We'll send others to help you. We'll build up a major encampment on that side of the satellite, and in our own sweet time we can invade the third planet with enough sensible ones to counteract the boners of individual specialists.

We can do it too. We've got all the time we need to build up our base, even if that *man* has warned his kind—who probably wouldn't believe him anyway. Because remember this always, and feel secure: *No being on the third planet ever knows what is happening on the other side of its satellite.*

POLITY AND CUSTOM OF THE CAMIROI

PRIMARY EDUCATION OF THE CAMIROI

by R. A. Lafferty

The historians of science fiction say that R. A. Lafferty is unique, a one-of-a-kind writer whose work defies easy classification. They are right—Raphael Aloysius Lafferty defies even *difficult* classification schemes. For evidence, see especially his short story collections—*Nine Hundred Grandmothers* (1970), *Strange Doings* (1972), and *Does Anyone Else Have Anything Further to Add?* (1974).

For additional proof, see the following two stories!

POLITY AND CUSTOM
OF THE CAMIROI

From Report of Field Group for Examination of Off-Earth Customs and Codexes to the Council for Governmental Renovation and Legal Rethinking. Taken from the day-book of Paul Piggott, political analyst.

Making appointments with the Camiroi is proverbially like building with quicksilver. We discovered this early. But they do have the most advanced civilization of any of the four human worlds. And we did have a firm invitation to visit the planet Camiroi and to investigate customs. And we had the promise that we would be taken in hand immediately on our arrival by a group parallel to our own.

But there was no group to meet us at the Sky-Port.

"Where is the Group for the Examination of Customs and Codexes?" we asked the girl who was on duty as Information Factor at the Sky-Port.

"Ask that post over there," she said. She was a young lady of mischievous and almost rakish mien.

"I hope we are not reduced to talking to posts," said our leader Charles Chosky, "but I see that it is some sort of communicating device. Does the post talk English, young lady?"

"The post understands the fifty languages that all Camiroi know," the young lady said. "On Camiroi, even the dogs speak fifty languages. Speak to it."

"I'll try it," said Mr. Chosky. "Ah, post, we were to be taken in hand by a group parallel to our own. Where can we find the Group for the Examination of Customs and Codexes?"

"Duty! Duty!" cried the post in a girlish voice that was somehow familiar. "Three for a group! Come, come, be constituted!"

"I'll be one," said a pleasant-looking Camiroi, striding over.

"I'll be another," said a sprouting teenage boy of the same species.

"One more, one more!" cried the post. "Oh, here comes my relief. I'll be the other one to form the group. Come, come, let's get started. What do you want to see first, good people?"

"How can a post be a member of an ambulatory group?" Charles Chosky asked.

"Oh, don't be quaint," said the girl who had been the information factor and also the voice of the post. She had come up behind us and joined us. "Sideki and Nautes, we become a group for cozening Earthlings," she said. "I am sure you heard the rather humorous name they gave it."

"Are you as a group qualified to give us the information we seek?" I asked.

"Every citizen of Camiroi is qualified, in theory, to give sound information on every subject," said the teenage sproutling.

"But in practice it may not be so," I said, my legal mind fastening onto his phrase.

"The only difficulty is our overliberal admission to citizenship," said Miss Diayggeia, who had been the voice of the post and the information factor. "Any person may become a citizen of Camiroi if he has resided here for one oodle. Once it was so that only natural leaders traveled space, and they qualified. Now, however, there are subsidized persons of no ability who come. They do not always conform to our high standard of reason and information."

"Thanks," said our Miss Holly Holm, "and how long is an oodle?"

"About fifteen minutes," said Miss Dia. "The post will register you now if you wish."

The post registered us, and we became citizens of Camiroi.

"Well, come, come, fellow citizens, what can we do for you?" asked Sideki, the pleasant-looking Camiroi who was the first member of our host group.

"Our reports of the laws of Camiroi seem to be a mixture of travelers' tales and nonsense," I said. "We want to find how a Camiroi law is made and how it works."

"So, make one, citizens, and see how it works," said Sideki. "You are now citizens like any other citizens, and any three of you can band together and make a law. Let us go down to Archives and enact it. And you be thinking what sort of law it will be as we go there."

We strode through the contrived and beautiful parklands and groves which were the roofs of Camiroi City. The extent was full of fountains and waterfalls, and streams with bizarre bridges over them. Some were better than others. Some were better than anything we had ever seen anywhere.

"But I believe that I myself could design a pond and weir as good as this one," said Charles Chosky, our leader. "And I'd have some of those bushes that look like Earth sumac in place of that cluster there; and I'd break up that pattern of rocks and tilt the layered massif behind it, and bring in a little of that blue moss—"

"You see your duty quickly, Citizen," said Sideki: "You should do all this before this very day is gone. Make it the way you think best, and remove the plaque that is there. Then you can dictate your own plaque to any of the symbouleutik posts, and it will be made and set in. 'My composition is better than your composition,' is the way most plaques read, and sometimes a scenery composer will add something humorous like 'and my dog can whip your dog.' You can order all necessary materials from that same post there, and most citizens prefer to do the work with their own hands. This system works for gradual improvement. There are many Consensus Masterpieces that remain year after year, and the ordinary work is subject to constant turnover. There, for instance, is a tree which was not there this morning and which should not be there tonight. I'm sure that one of you can design a better tree."

"I can," said Miss Holly, "and I will do so today."

We descended from the roof parklands into the lower streets of Camiroi City, and went to Archives.

"Have you thought of a new law yet?" Miss Dia asked when we were at Archives. "We don't expect brilliance from such new citizens, but we ask you not to be ridiculous."

Our leader Charles Chosky drew himself up to full height and spoke:

"We promulgate a law that a permanent group be set up on Camiroi to oversee and devise regulations for all random and hasty citizens' groups with the aim of making them more responsible, and that a full-scale review of such groups be held yearly."

"Got it?" Miss Dia called to an apparatus there in Archives.

"Got it," said the device. It ground its entrails, and coughed up the law inscribed on bronze, and set it in a law niche.

"The echo is deafening," said our Miss Holly, pretending to listen.

"Yes. What is the effect of what we have done?" I asked.

"Oh, the law is in effect," said young Nautes. "It has been weighed and integrated into the corpus of laws. It is already considered in the instructions that the magistrate coming on duty in a short time (usually a citizen will serve as magistrate for one hour a month) must scan before he takes his seat. Possibly in this session he will assess somebody guilty of a misdemeanor to think about this problem for ten minutes and then to attach an enabling act to your law."

"But what if some citizens' group passes a silly law?" our Miss Holly asked.

"They do it often. One of them has just done so. But it will be repealed quickly enough," said Miss Dia of the Camiroi. "Any citizen who has his name on three laws deemed silly by general consensus shall lose his citizenship for one year. A citizen who so loses his citizenship twice shall be mutilated, and the third time he shall be killed. This isn't an extreme ruling. By that time he would have participated in nine silly laws. Surely that's enough."

*   *   *

"But, in the meantime, the silly laws remain in effect?" our Mr. Chosky asked.

"Not likely," said Sideki. "A law is repealed thus: any citizen may go to Archives and remove any law, leaving the statement that he has abolished the law for his own reasons. He is then required to keep the voided law in his own home for three days. Sometimes the citizen or citizens who first passed the law will go to the house of the abolitionist. Occasionally they will fight to the death with ritual swords, but most often they will parley. They may agree to have the law abolished. They may agree to restore the law. Or they may together work out a new law that takes into account the objections to the old."

"Then every Camiroi law is subject to random challenge?" Chosky asked.

"Not exactly," said Miss Dia. "A law which has stood unchallenged and unappealed for nine years becomes privileged. A citizen wishing to abolish such a law by removal must leave in its place not only his declaration of removal but also three fingers of his right hand as earnest of his seriousness in the matter. But a magistrate or a citizen going to reconstitute the law has to contribute only one of his fingers to the parley."

"This seems to me to favor the establishment," I said.

"We have none," said Sideki. "I know that is hard for Earthlings to understand."

"But is there no senate or legislative body on Camiroi, or even a president?" Miss Holly asked.

"Yes, there's a president," said Miss Dia, "and he is actually a dictator or tyrant. He is chosen by lot for a term of one week. Any of you could be chosen for the term starting tomorrow, but the odds are against it. We do not have a permanent senate, but often there are hasty senates constituted, and they have full powers."

"Such bodies having full powers is what we want to study," I said. "When will the next one be constituted, and how will it act?"

"So, constitute yourselves one now and see how you act," said young Nautes. "You simply say, 'We constitute ourselves a Hasty Senate of Camiroi with full powers.' Register yourselves at the nearest symbouleutic post, and study your senate introspectively."

"Could we fire the president-dictator?" Miss Holly asked.

"Certainly," said Sideki, "but a new president would immediately be chosen by lot, and your senate would not carry over to the new term, nor could any of you three partake of a new senate until a full presidential term had passed. But I wouldn't, if I were you, form a senate to fire the present president. He is very good with the ritual sword."

"Then citizens do actually fight with them yet?" Mr. Chosky asked.

"Yes, any private citizen may at any time challenge any other private citizen for any reason, or for none. Sometimes, but not often, they fight to the death, and they may not be interfered with. We call these decisions the Court of Last Resort."

Reason says that the legal system on Camiroi cannot be as simple as this, and yet it seems to be. Starting with the thesis that every citizen of Camiroi should be able to handle every assignment or job on Camiroi, these people have cut organization to the minimum. These things we consider fluid or liberal about the legal system of Camiroi. Hereafter, whenever I am tempted to think of some law or custom of Earth as liberal, I will pause. I will hear Camiroi laughing.

On the other hand, there are these things which I consider adamant or conservative about the laws of Camiroi:

No assembly on Camiroi for purposes of entertainment may exceed thirty-nine persons. No more than this number may witness any spectacle or drama, or hear a musical presentation, or watch a sporting event. This is to prevent the citizens from becoming mere spectators rather than originators or partakers. Similarly, no writing—other than certain rare official promulgations—may be issued in more than thirty-nine copies in one month. This, it seems to us, is a conservative ruling to prevent popular enthusiasms.

A father of a family who twice in five years appeals to specialists for such things as simple surgery for members of his household, or legal or financial or medical advice, or any such things as he himself should be capable of doing, shall lose his citizenship. It seems to us that this ruling obstructs the Camiroi from the full fruits of progress and research. They say, however, that it compels every citizen to become an expert in everything.

Any citizen who pleads incapacity when chosen by lot to head a military operation or a scientific project or a trade combine shall lose his citizenship and suffer mutilation. But one who assumes such responsibility and then fails in the accomplishment of the task shall suffer the loss and the mutilation only for two such failures.

Both cases seem to us to constitute cruel and unusual punishment.

Any citizen chosen by lot to provide a basic invention or display a certain ingenuity when there is corporate need for it, and who fails to provide such invention, shall be placed in such a position that he will lose his life unless he displays even greater ingenuity and invention than was originally called for.

This seems to us to be unspeakably cruel.

There is an absolute death penalty for impiety. But to the question of what constitutes impiety, we received a startling answer.

"If you have to ask what it is, then you are guilty of it. For piety is comprehension of the basic norms. Lack of awareness of the special Camiroi context is the greatest impiety of all. Beware, new citizens! Should a person more upright and less indulgent than myself have heard your question, you might be executed before night-rise."

The Camiroi, however, are straight-faced kidders. We do not believe that we were in any danger of execution, but we had been told bluntly not to ask questions of a certain sort.

Conclusion—Inconclusive. We are not yet able to understand the true legal system of Camiroi, but we have begun to acquire the viewpoint from which it may be studied. We recommend continuing study by a permanent resident team in this field.—PAUL PIGGOTT, Political Analyst.

* * *

From the journey-book of Charles Chosky, chief of field group.

The basis of Camiroi polity and procedure is that any Camiroi citizen should be capable of filling any job on or pertaining to the planet. If it is ever the case that even one citizen should prove incapable of this, they say, then their system has already failed.

"Of course, it fails many times every day," one of their men explained to me, "but it does not fail completely. It is like a man in motion. He is falling off-balance at every step, but he saves himself, and so he strides. Our polity is always in motion. Should it come to rest, it would die."

"Have the Camiroi a religion?" I asked citizen after citizen of them.

"I think so," one of them said finally. "I believe that we do have that, and nothing else. The difficulty is in the word. Your Earth English word may come from *religionem* or from *relegionem*; it may mean a legality, or it may mean a revelation. I believe it is a mixture of the two concepts; with us it is. Of course we have a religion. What else is there to have?"

"Could you draw a parallel between Camiroi and Earth religion?" I asked him.

"No, I couldn't," he said bluntly. "I'm not being rude. I just don't know how."

But another intelligent Camiroi gave me some ideas on it.

"The closest I could come to explaining the difference," he said, "is by a legend that is told (as our Camiroi phrase has it) with the tongue so far in the cheek that it comes out the vulgar body aperture."

"What is the legend?" I asked him.

"The legend is that men (or whatever local creatures) were tested on all the worlds. On some of the worlds, men persevered in grace. These have become the transcendent worlds, asserting themselves as stars rather than planets and swallowing their own suns, becoming fully incandescent in their merged persons living in grace and light. The more developed of them are those closed bodies which we know only by inference, so powerful and contained that they let no light or gravity or other emission escape them. They become of themselves closed and total universes, of their own space and outside of what we call space, perfect in their merged mentality and spirit.

"Then there are the worlds like Earth where men did fall from grace. On these worlds, each person contains an interior abyss and is capable both of great heights and depths. By our legend, the persons of these worlds after their fall were condemned to live for thirty thousand generations in the bodies of animals and were then permitted to begin their slow and frustrating ascent back to remembered personhood.

"But the case of Camiroi was otherwise. We do not know whether there are further worlds of our like case. The primordial test-people of Camiroi did not fall. And they did not persevere. They hesitated. They could not make up their minds. They thought the matter over, and then they thought it over some more. Camiroi was therefore doomed to think matters over forever.

"So we are the equivocal people, capable of curious and continuing thought. But we have a hunger both for the depths and the heights which we have missed. To be sure, our Golden Mediocrity, our serene plateau, is higher than the heights of most worlds, higher than those of Earth, I believe. But it has not the exhilaration of height."

"But you do not believe in legends," I said.

"A legend is the highest scientific statement when it is the only statement available," the Camiroi said. "We are the people who live according to reason. It makes a good life, but it lacks salt. You people have a literature of Utopias. You value their ideals highly, and they do have some effect on you. Yet you must feel that they all have this quality of the insipid. And according to Earth standards, we are a Utopia. We are a world of the third case.

"We miss a lot. The enjoyment of poverty is generally denied to us. We have a certain hunger for incompetence, which is why some Earth things find a welcome here—bad Earth music, bad Earth painting and sculpture and drama, for instance. The good we can produce ourselves. The bad we are incapable of and must import. Some of us believe that we need it in our diet."

"If this is true, your position seems enviable to me," I said.

"Yours isn't," he said, "and yet you are the most complete. You have both halves, and you have your numbers. We know, of course, that the Giver has never given a life anywhere until there was real need for it, and that everything born or created has its individual part to play. But we wish the Giver would be more generous to us in this, and it is in this particularly that we envy Earth.

"A difficulty with us is that we do our great deeds at too young an age and on distant worlds. We are all of us more or less retired by the age of twenty-five, and we have all had careers such as you would not believe. We come home then to live maturely on our mature world. It's perfect, of course, but of a perfection too small. We have everything—except the one thing that matters, for which we cannot even find a name."

I talked to many of the intelligent Camiroi on our short stay there. It was often difficult to tell whether they were talking seriously or whether they were mocking me. We do not as yet understand the Camiroi at all. Further study is recommended.—CHARLES CHOSKY, Chief of Field Group.

From the ephemeris of Holly Holm, anthropologist and schedonahthropologist.

Camiroi—the word is plural in form—is used for the people in both the single and plural and for the planet itself.

The civilization of Camiroi is more mechanical and more scientific than that of Earth, but it is more disguised. Their ideal machine shall have no moving parts at all, shall be noiseless and shall not look like a machine. For this reason, there is something pastoral about even the most thickly populated districts of Camiroi City.

The Camiroi are fortunate in the natural furnishings of their planet. The scenery of Camiroi conforms to the dictate that all repetition is tedious, for there is only one of each thing on that world. There is one major continent and one minor continent of quite different character; one fine cluster of islands of which the individual isles are of very different style; one great continental river with its seven branches lowing out of seven sorts of land; one complex of volcanoes; one great range of mountains; one titanic waterfall with her three so different daughters nearby; one inland sea, one gulf, one beach which is a three hundred and fifty mile crescent passing through seven phases named for the colors of iris; one great rain forest, one palm grove, one leaf-fall grove, one of evergreens and one of eodendrons; one grain bowl, one fruit bowl, one pampas, one parkland; one desert, one great oasis; and Camiroi City is the one great city. And all these places are unexcelled of their kind.

There are no ordinary places on Camiroi!

Travel being rapid, a comparatively poor young couple may go from anywhere on the planet to Green Beach, for instance, to take their evening meal, in less time than the consumption of the meal will take them, and for less money than that reasonable meal will cost. This easy and frequent travel makes the whole world one community.

The Camiroi believe in the necessity of the frontier. They control many primitive worlds, and I gather hints that they are sometimes cruel in their management. The tyrants and proconsuls of these worlds are young, usually still in their teens. The young people are to have their careers and make their mistakes while in the foreign service. When they return to Camiroi they are supposed to be settled and of tested intelligence.

The earning scale of the Camiroi is curious. A job of mechanical drudgery pays higher than one of intellectual interest and involvement. This often means that the least intelligent and least able of the Camiroi will have more wealth than those of more ability. "This is fair," the Camiroi tell us. "Those not able to receive the higher recompense are certainly entitled to the lower." They regard the Earth system as grossly inequal, that a man should have both a superior job and superior pay, and that another man should have the inferior of both.

Though official offices and jobs are usually filled by lot, persons can apply for them for their own reasons. In special conditions there might even be competition for an assignment, such as directorship of trade posts where persons (for private reasons) might wish to acquire great fortunes rapidly. We witnessed confrontations between candidates in several of these campaigns, and they were curious.

"My opponent is a three and seven," said one candidate and then he sat down.

"My opponent is a five and nine," said the other candidate. The small crowd clapped, and that was the confrontation or debate.

We attended another such rally.

"My opponent is an eight and ten," one candidate said briskly.

"My opponent is a two and six," said the other, and they went off together.

We did not understand this, and we attended a third confrontation. There seemed to be a little wave of excitement about to break here.

"My opponent is an old number four," said one candidate with a voice charged with emotion, and there was a gasp from the small crowd.

"I will not answer the charge," said the other candidate, shaking with anger. "The blow is too foul, and we had been friends."

We found the key then. The Camiroi are experts at defamation, but they have developed a shorthand system to save time. They have their decalog of slander, and the numbers refer to this. In its accepted version it runs as follows:

My opponent (1) is personally moronic. (2) is sexually incompetent. (3) flubs third points in Chuki game. (4) eats Mu seeds before the time of the summer solstice. (5) is ideologically silly. (6) is physically pathetic. (7) is financially stupid. (8) is ethically weird. (9) is intellectually contemptible. (10) is morally dishonest.

Try it yourself, on your friends or your enemies! It works wonderfully. We recommend the listing and use to Earth politicians, except for numbers three and four which seem to have no meaning in Earth context.

The Camiroi have a corpus of proverbs. We came on them

in Archives, along with an attached machine with a hundred levers on it. We depressed the lever marked Earth English and had a sampling of these proverbs put into Earth context.

A man will not become rich by raising goats, the machine issued. Yes, that could almost pass for an Earth proverb. It almost seems to mean something.

Even buzzards sometimes gag. That has an Earth sound also.

It's that or pluck chickens.

"I don't believe I understand that one," I said.

"You think it's easy to put these in Earth context, you try it sometime," the translation machine issued. "The proverb applies to distasteful but necessary tasks."

"Ah, well, let's try some more," said Paul Piggott. "That one."

A bird in the hand is worth two in the bush, the machine issued abruptly.

"But that is an Earth proverb word for word," I said.

"You wait I finish it, lady," the translation machine growled. "To this proverb in its classical form is always appended a cartoon showing a bird fluttering away and a man angrily wiping his hand with some disposable material while he says, 'A bird in the hand is *not* worth two in the bush.' "

"Are we being had by a machine?" our leader Charles Chosky asked softly.

"Give us that proverb there," I pointed one out to the machine.

There'll be many a dry eye here when you leave, the machine issued.

We left.

"I may be in serious trouble," I said to a Camiroi lady of my acquaintance. "Well, aren't you going to ask what it is?"

"No, I don't particularly care," she said. "But tell me if you feel an absolute compulsion to it."

"I never heard of such a thing," I said. "I have been chosen by lot to head a military expedition for the relief of a trapped force on a world I never heard of. I am supposed to raise and supply this force (out of my private funds, it says here) and have it in flight within eight oodles. That's only two hours. What will I do?"

"Do it, of course, Miss Holly," the lady said. "You are a citizen of Camiroi now, and you should be proud to take charge of such an operation."

"But I don't know how! What will happen if I just tell them that I don't know how?"

"Oh, you'll lose your citizenship and suffer mutilation. That's the law, you know."

"How will they mutilate me?"

"Probably cut off your nose. I wouldn't worry about it. It doesn't do much for you anyhow."

"But we have to go back to Earth! We were going to go tomorrow, but now we want to go today. I do, anyhow."

"Earth kid, if I were you, I'd get out to Sky-Port awful fast."

By a coincidence (I hope it was no more than that) our political analyst Paul Piggott had been chosen by lot to make a survey (personally, minutely and interiorly, the directive said) of the sewer system of Camiroi City. And our leader Charles Chosky had been selected by lot to put down a rebellion of Groll's Trolls on one of the worlds, and to leave his right hand and his right eye as surety for the accomplishment of the mission.

We were rather nervous as we waited for Earth Flight at Sky-Port, particularly so when a group of Camiroi acquaintances approached us. But they did not stop us. They said good-by to us without too much enthusiasm.

"Our visit has been all too short," I said hopefully.

"Oh, I wouldn't say that," one of them rejoined. "There is a Camiroi proverb—"

"We've heard it," said our leader Charles Chosky. "We also are dry-eyed about leaving."

Final Recommendation. That another and broader Field Group be sent to study the Camiroi in greater detail. That a special study might fruitfully be made of the humor of the Camiroi. That no members of the first Field Group should serve on the second Field Group.

PRIMARY EDUCATION
OF THE CAMIROI

ABSTRACT FROM JOINT REPORT TO THE GENERAL DUBUQUE
PTA CONCERNING THE PRIMARY EDUCATION OF THE CAMIROI,
Subtitled Critical Observations of a Parallel Culture on a
Neighboring World, and Evaluations of the other way of
education.

Extract from the Day Book:

"Where," we asked the Information Factor at Camiroi City
Terminal, "is the office of the local PTA?"

"Isn't any," he said cheerfully.

"You mean that in Camiroi City, the metropolis of the
planet, there is no PTA?" our chairman, Paul Piper, asked
with disbelief.

"Isn't any office of it. But you're poor strangers, so you
deserve an answer even if you can't frame your questions
properly. See that elderly man sitting on the bench and
enjoying the sun? Go tell him you need a PTA. He'll make
you one."

"Perhaps the initials convey a different meaning on
Camiroi," said Miss Munch, the first surrogate chairman.
"By them we mean—"

"Parent Teachers Apparatus, of course. Colloquial English
is one of the six Earthian languages required here, you know.
Don't be abashed. He's a fine person, and he enjoys doing
things for strangers. He'll be glad to make you a PTA."

We were nonplussed, but we walked over to the man indicated.

"We are looking for the local PTA, sir," said Miss Smice, our second surrogate chairman. "We were told you might help us."

"Oh, certainly," said the elderly Camiroi gentleman. "One of you arrest that man walking there, and we'll get started with it."

"Do what?" asked our Mr. Piper.

"Arrest him. I have noticed that your own words sometimes do not convey a meaning to you. I often wonder how you do communicate among yourselves. Arrest, take into custody, seize by any force physical or moral, and bring him here."

"Yes, sir," cried Hiss Hanks, our third surrogate chairman. She enjoyed things like this. She arrested the walking Camiroi man with force partly physical and partly moral and brought him to the group.

"It's a PTA they want, Meander," the elder Camiroi said to the one arrested. "Grab three more, and we'll get started. Let the lady help. She's good at it."

Our Miss Hanks and the Camiroi man named Meander arrested three other Camiroi men and brought them to the group.

"Five. It's enough," said the elderly Camiroi. "We are hereby constituted a PTA and ordered into random action. Now, how can we accommodate you, good Earth people?"

"But are you legal? Are you five persons competent to be a PTA?" demanded our Mr. Piper.

"Any Camiroi citizen is competent to do any job on the planet of Camiroi," said one of the Camiroi men (we learned later that his name was Talarium), "otherwise Camiroi would be in a sad shape."

"It may be," said our Miss Smice sourly. "It all seems very informal. What if one of you had to be World President?"

"The odds are that it won't come to one man in ten," said the elderly Camiroi (his name was Philoxenus). "I'm the only one of this group ever to serve as president of this planet, and it was a pleasant week I spent in the Office. Now to the point. How can we accommodate you?"

"We would like to see one of your schools in session," said our Mr. Piper. "We would like to talk to the teachers and the students. We are here to compare the two systems of education."

"There is no comparison," said old Philoxenus, "—meaning no offense. Or no more than a little. On Camiroi, we practice Education. On Earth, they play a game, but they call it by the same name. That makes the confusion. Come. We'll go to a school in session."

"And to a public school," said Miss Smice suspiciously. "Do not fob off any fancy private school on us as typical."

"That would be difficult," said Philoxenus. "There is no public school in Camiroi City and only two remaining on the Planet. Only a small fraction of one percent of the students of Camiroi are in public schools. We maintain that there is no more reason for the majority of children to be educated in a public school than to be raised in a public orphanage. We realize, of course, that on Earth you have made a sacred buffalo of the public school."

"Sacred cow," said our Mr. Piper.

"Children and Earthlings should be corrected when they use words wrongly," said Philoxenus. "How else will they learn the correct forms? The animal held sacred in your own near Orient was of the species *Bos bubalus* rather than *Bos bos*, a buffalo rather than a cow. Shall we go to a school?"

"If it cannot be a public school, at least let it be a typical school," said Miss Smice.

"That again is impossible," said Philoxenus. "Every school on Camiroi is in some respect atypical."

We went to visit an atypical school.

INCIDENT: Our first contact with the Camiroi students was a violent one. One of them, a lively little boy about eight years old, ran into Miss Munch, knocked her down, and broke her glasses. Then he jabbered something in an unknown tongue.

"Is that Camiroi?" asked Mr. Piper with interest. "From

what I have heard, I supposed the language to have a harsher and fuller sound."

"You mean you don't recognize it?" asked Philoxenus with amusement. "What a droll admission from an educator. The boy is very young and very ignorant. Seeing that you were Earthians, he spoke in Hindi, which is the tongue used by more Earthians than any other. No, no, Xypete, they are of the minority who speak English. You can tell it by their colorless texture and the narrow heads on them."

"I say you sure do have slow reaction, lady," the little boy Xypete explained. "Even subhumans should react faster than that. You just stand there and gape and let me bowl you over. You want me analyze you and see why you react so slow?"

"No! No!"

"You seem unhurt in structure from the fall," the little boy continued, "but if I hurt you I got to fix you. Just strip down to your shift, and I'll go over you and make sure you're all right."

"No! No! No!"

"It's all right," said Philoxenus. "All Camiroi children learn primary medicine in the first grade, setting bones and healing contusions and such."

"No! No! I'm all right. But he's broken my glasses."

"Come along Earthside lady, I'll make you some others," said the little boy. "With your slow reaction time you sure can't afford the added handicap of defective vision. Shall I fit you with contacts?"

"No. I want glasses just like those which were broken. Oh heavens, what will I do?"

"You come, I do," said the little boy. It was rather revealing to us that the little boy was able to test Miss Munch's eyes, grind lenses, make frames and have her fixed up within three minutes. "I have made some improvements over those you wore before," the boy said, "to help compensate for your slow reaction time."

"Are all the Camiroi students so talented?" Mr. Piper asked. He was impressed.

"No. Xypete is unusual," Philoxenus said. "Most students

would not be able to make a pair of glasses so quickly or competently till they were at least nine."

RANDOM INTERVIEWS:
"How rapidly do you read?" Miss Hanks asked a young girl.

"One hundred and twenty words a minute," the girl said.

"On Earth some of the girl students your age have learned to read at the rate of five hundred words a minute," Miss Hanks said proudly.

"When I began disciplined reading, I was reading at the rate of four thousand words a minute," the girl said. "They had quite a time correcting me of it. I had to take remedial reading, and my parents were ashamed of me. Now I've learned to read almost slow enough."

"I don't understand," said Miss Hanks.

"Do you know anything about Earth History or Geography?" Miss Smice asked a middle-sized boy.

"We sure are sketchy on it, lady. There isn't very much over there, is there?"

"Then you have never heard of Dubuque?"

"Count Dubuque interests me. I can't say as much for the city named after him. I always thought that the Count handled the matters of the conflicting French and Spanish land grants and the basic claims of the Sauk and Fox Indians very well. References to the town now carry a humorous connotation, and 'School-Teacher from Dubuque' has become a folk archetype."

"Thank you," said Miss Smice, "or do I thank you?"

"What are you taught of the relative humanity of the Earthians and the Camiroi and of their origins?" Miss Munch asked a Camiroi girl.

"The other four worlds, Earth (Gaea), Kentauron Mikron, Dahae and Astrobe, were all settled from Camiroi. That is what we are taught. We are also given the humorous aside that if it isn't true we will still hold it true till something better comes along. It was we who rediscovered the Four Worlds in historic time, not they who discovered us. If we did not make the original settlements, at least we have filed the first claim that we made them. We did, in historical time, make an additional colonization of Earth. You call it the Incursion of the Dorian Greeks."

"Where are their playgrounds?" Miss Hanks asked Talarium.

"Oh, the whole world. The children have the run of everything. To set up specific playgrounds would be like setting a table-sized aquarium down in the depths of the ocean. It would really be pointless."

CONFERENCE: The four of us from Earth, specifically from Dubuque, Iowa, were in discussion with the five members of the Camiroi PTA.

"How do you maintain discipline?" Mr. Piper asked.

"Indifferently," said Philoxenus. "Oh, you mean in detail. It varies. Sometimes we let it drift, sometimes we pull them up short. Once they have learned that they must comply to an extent, there is little trouble. Small children are often put down into a pit. They do not eat or come out till they know their assignment."

"But that is inhuman," said Miss Hanks.

"Of course. But small children are not yet entirely human. If a child has not learned to accept discipline by the third or fourth grade, he is hanged."

"Literally?" asked Miss Munch.

"How would you hang a child figuratively? And what effect would that have on the other children?"

"By the neck?" Miss Munch still was not satisfied.

"By the neck until they are dead. The other children always accept the example gracefully and do better. Hanging isn't employed often. Scarcely one child in a hundred is hanged."

"What is this business about slow reading?" Miss Hanks asked. "I don't understand it at all."

"Only the other day there was a child in the third grade who persisted on rapid reading," Philoxenus said. "He was given an object lesson. He was given a book of medium difficulty, and he read it rapidly. Then he had to put the book away and repeat what he had read. Do you know that in the first thirty pages he missed four words? Midway in the book there was a whole statement which he had understood wrongly, and there were hundreds of pages that he got word-perfect only with difficulty. If he was so unsure on material that he had just read, think how imperfectly he would have recalled it forty years later."

"You mean that the Camiroi children learn to recall everything that they read?"

"The Camiroi children and adults will recall for life every detail they have ever seen, read or heard. We on Camiroi are only a little more intelligent than you on Earth. We cannot afford to waste time in forgetting or reviewing, or in pursuing anything of a shallowness that lends itself to scanning."

"Ah, would you call your schools liberal?" Mr. Piper asked.

"I would. You wouldn't," said Philoxenus. "We do not on Camiroi, as you do on Earth, use words to mean their opposites. There is nothing in our education or on our world that corresponds to the quaint servility which you call liberal on Earth."

"Well, would you call your education progressive?"

"No. In your argot, progressive, of course, means infantile."

"How are the schools financed?" asked Mr. Piper.

"Oh, the voluntary tithe on Camiroi takes care of everything, government, religion, education, public works. We don't believe in taxes, of course, and we never maintain a high overhead in anything."

"Just how voluntary is the tithing?" asked Miss Hanks. "Do you sometimes hang those who do not tithe voluntarily?"

"I believe there have been a few cases of that sort," said Philoxenus.

"And is your government really as slipshod as your education?" Mr. Piper asked. "Are your high officials really chosen by lot and for short periods?"

"Oh yes. Can you imagine a person so sick that he would actually *desire* to hold high office for any great period of time? Are there any further questions?"

"There must be hundreds," said Mr. Piper, "but we find difficulty putting them into words."

"If you cannot find words for them, we cannot find answers. PTA disbanded."

CONCLUSIONS: A. The Camiroi system of education is inferior to our own in organization, in buildings, in facilities, in playgrounds, in teacher conferences, in funding, in parental involvement, in supervision, in in-group out-group accommodation adjustment motifs. Some of the school buildings are grotesque. We asked about one particular building which seemed to us to be flamboyant and in bad taste. "What do you expect from second-grade children?" they said. "It is well built even if of peculiar appearance. Second-grade children are not yet complete artists of design."

"You mean that the children designed it themselves?" we asked.

"Of course," they said. "Designed and built it. It isn't a bad job for children."

Such a thing wouldn't be permitted on Earth.

CONCLUSION B. The Camiroi system of education somehow produces much better results than does the education system of Earth. We have been forced to admit this by the evidence at hand.

CONCLUSION C. There is an anomaly as yet unresolved between CONCLUSION A and CONCLUSION B.

APPENDIX TO JOINT REPORT

We give here, as perhaps of some interest, the curriculum of the Camiroi Primary Education.

FIRST YEAR COURSE:

Playing one wind instrument.

Simple drawing of objects and numbers.

Singing. (This is important. Many Earth people sing who cannot sing. This early instruction of the Camiroi prevents that occurrence.)

Simple arithmetic, hand and machine.

First acrobatics.

First riddles and logic.

Mnemonic religion.
First dancing.
Walking the low wire.
Simple electric circuits.
Raising ants. (Eoempts, not earth ants.)

SECOND YEAR COURSE:
Playing one keyboard instrument.
Drawing, faces, letters, motions.
Singing comedies.
Complex arithmetic, hand and machine.
Second acrobatics.
First jokes and logic.
Quadratic religion.
Second dancing.
Simple defamation. (Spirited attacks on the character of one
    fellow student, with elementary falsification and simple
    hatchet-job programming.)
Performing on the medium wire.
Project electric wiring.
Raising bees. (Galelea, not earth bees.)

THIRD YEAR COURSE:
Playing one stringed instrument.
Reading and voice. (It is here that the student who may have
    fallen into bad habits of rapid reading is compelled to read
    at voice speed only.)
Soft stone sculpture.
Situation comedy.
Simple algebra, hand and machine.
First gymnastics.
Second jokes and logic.
Transcendent religion.
Complex acrobatic dancing.
Complex defamation.
Performing on the high wire and the sky pole.
Simple radio construction.
Raising, breeding and dissecting frogs. (Karakoli, not earth
    frogs.)

FOURTH YEAR COURSE:
History reading, Camiroi and galactic, basic and geological.
Decadent comedy.
Simple geometry and trigonometry, hand and machine.
Track and field.
Shaggy people jokes and hirsute logic.
Simple obscenity.
Simple mysticism.
Patterns of falsification.
Trapeze work.
Intermediate electronics.
Human dissection.

FIFTH YEAR COURSE:
History reading, Camiroi and galactic, technological.
Introverted drama.
Complex geometries and analytics, hand and machine.
Track and field for fifth form record.
First wit and logic.
First alcoholic appreciation.
Complex mysticism.
Setting intellectual climates, defamation in three dimensions.
Simple oratory.
Complex trapeze work.
Inorganic chemistry.
Advanced electronics.
Advanced human dissection.
Fifth form thesis.

The child is now ten years old and is half through his primary schooling. He is an unfinished animal, but he has learned to learn.

SIXTH YEAR COURSE:
Reemphasis on slow reading.
Simple prodigious memory.
History reading, Camiroi and galactic, economic.
Horsemanship (of the Patrushkoe, not the earth horse.)
Advance lathe and machine work for art and utility.

Literature, passive.

Calculi, hand and machine pankration.

Advanced wit and logic.

Second alcoholic appreciation.

Differential religion.

First business ventures.

Complex oratory.

Building-scaling. (The buildings are higher and the gravity stronger than on Earth; this climbing of buildings like human flies calls out the ingenuity and daring of the Camiroi children.)

Nuclear physics and post-organic chemistry.

Simple pseudo-human assembly.

SEVENTH YEAR COURSE:

History reading, Camiroi and galactic, cultural.

Advanced prodigious memory.

Vehicle operation and manufacture of simple vehicle.

Literature, active.

Astrognosy, prediction and programming.

Advanced pankration.

Spherical logic, hand and machine.

Advanced alcoholic appreciation.

Integral religion.

Bankruptcy and recovery in business.

Conmanship and trend creation.

Post-nuclear physics and universals.

Transcendental athletics endeavor.

Complex robotics and programming.

EIGHTH YEAR COURSE:

History reading, Camiroi and galactic, seminal theory.

Consummate prodigious memory.

Manufacture of complex land and water vehicles.

Literature, compendious and terminative. (Creative book-burning following the Camiroi thesis that nothing ordinary be allowed to survive.)

Cosmic theory, seminal.

Philosophy construction.

Complex hedonism.
Laser religion.
Conmanship, seminal.
Consolidation of simple genius status.
Post-robotic integration.

NINTH YEAR COURSE:
History reading, Camiroi and galactic, future and contingent.
Category invention.
Manufacture of complex light-barrier vehicles.
Construction of simple asteroids and planets.
Matrix religion and logic.
Simple human immortality disciplines.
Consolidation of complex genius status.
First problems of post-consciousness humanity.
First essays in marriage and reproduction.

TENTH YEAR COURSE:
History construction, active.
Manufacture of ultra-light-barrier vehicles.
Panphilosophical clarifications.
Construction of viable planets.
Consolidation of simple sanctity status.
Charismatic humor and pentacosmic logic.
Hypogyroscopic economy.
Penentaglossia. (The perfection of the fifty languages that
    every educated Camiroi must know including six Earthian
    languages. Of course the child will already have colloquial
    mastery of most of these, but he will not yet have them in
    their full depth.)
Construction of complex societies.
World government. (A course of the same name is sometimes
    given in Earthian schools, but the course is not of the same
    content. In this course the Camiroi student will govern a
    world, though not one of the first aspect worlds, for a period
    of three or four months.)
Tenth form thesis.

COMMENT ON CURRICULUM:

The child will now be fifteen years old and will have completed his primary education. In many ways he will be advanced beyond his Earth counterpart. Physically more sophisticated, the Camiroi child could kill with his hands an Earth-type tiger or a Cape buffalo. An Earth child would perhaps be reluctant even to attempt such feats. The Camiroi boy (or girl) could replace any professional Earth athlete at any position of any game, and could surpass all existing Earth records. It is simply a question of finer poise, strength and speed, the result of adequate schooling.

As to the arts (on which Earthlings sometimes place emphasis) the Camiroi child could produce easy and unequaled masterpieces in any medium. More important, he will have learned the relative unimportance of such pastimes.

The Camiroi child will have failed in business once, at age ten, and have learned patience and perfection of objective by his failure. He will have acquired the techniques of falsification and conmanship. Thereafter he will not be easily deceived by any of the citizens of any of the worlds. The Camiroi child will have become a complex genius and a simple saint; the latter reduces the index of Camiroi crime to near zero. He will be married and settled in those early years of greatest enjoyment.

The child will have built, from materials found around any Camiroi house, a faster-than-light vehicle. He will have piloted it on a significant journey of his own plotting and programming. He will have built quasi-human robots of great intricacy. He will be of perfect memory and judgment and will be well prepared to accept solid learning.

He will have learned to use his whole mind, for the vast reservoirs which are the unconscious to us are not unconscious to him. Everything in him is ordered for use. And there seems to be no great secret about the accomplishments, only to do everything slowly enough and in the right order. Thus they avoid repetition and drill which are the shriveling things which dull the quick apperception.

The Camiroi schedule is challenging to the children, but it is nowhere impossible or discouraging. Everything builds to what follows. For instance, the child is eleven years old before he is given postnuclear physics and universals. Such subjects might be too difficult for him at an earlier age. He is thirteen years old before he undertakes category invention, that intricate course with the simple name. He is fourteen years old when he enters the dangerous field of panphilosophical clarification. But he will have been constructing comprehensive philosophies for two years, and he will have the background for the final clarification.

We should look more closely at this other way of education. In some respects it is better than our own. Few Earth children would be able to construct on organic and sentient robot within fifteen minutes if given the test suddenly; most of them could not manufacture a living dog in that time. Not one Earth child in five could build a faster-than-light vehicle and travel in it beyond our galaxy between now and midnight. Not one Earth child in a hundred could build a planet and have it a going concern within a week. Not one in a thousand would be able to comprehend pentacosmic logic.

RECOMMENDATIONS: a. Kidnapping five Camiroi at random and constituting them a pilot Earth PTA. b. A little constructive book-burning, particularly in the education field. c. Judicious hanging of certain malingering students.

THE SHAKER REVIVIAL
by Gerald Jonas

Gerald Jonas is a leading essayist and critic whose work appears regularly in *The New Yorker* and *Present Tense*. He also reviews science fiction for *The New York Times Book Review*. During the second half of the 1960s he produced a small number of high-quality sf stories in *The Magazine of Fantasy and Science Fiction* and *Galaxy*, including "The Mystery of the Purloined Grenouilles" (1966) and "The First Postulate" (1967). "The Shaker Revival" (1970) is quite simply one of the finest treatments of its theme in the history of the field.

THE SHAKER REVIVAL

TO: Arthur Stock, Executive Editor, *Ideas Illustrated*, New York City, 14632008447

FROM: Raymond Senter, c/o Hudson Junction Rotel, Hudson Junction, N. Y. 28997601910

ENCLOSED: Tentative Lead for *"The Shaker Revival."* Pix, tapes upcoming.

JERUSALEM WEST, N. Y., Thursday, June 28, 1995—The work of Salvation goes forward in this green and pleasant Hudson Valley hamlet to the high-pitched accompaniment of turbo-car exhausts and the amplified beat of the "world's loudest jag-rock band." Where worm-eaten apples fell untended in abandoned orchards less than a decade ago a new religious sect has burst into full bloom. In their fantastic four-year history the so-called New Shakers—or United Society of Believers (Revived), to give them their official title—have provoked the hottest controversy in Christendom since Martin Luther nailed his ninety-five theses to the door of All Saints Church in Wittenberg, Germany, on October 31, 1517. Boasting a membership of more than a hundred thousand today, the New Shakers have been processing applications at the rate of nine hundred a week. Although a handful of these "recruits" are in their early and middle twenties—and last month a New Jersey man was accepted into the Shaker Family at Wildwood at the ripe old age of thirty-two—the average New Shaker has not yet reached his eighteenth birthday.

Richard F, one of the members of the "First Octave" who have been honored with "uncontaminated" Shaker surnames, explains it this way: "We've got nothing against feebies. They have a piece of the Gift inside just like anyone else. But it's hard for them to travel with the Family. Jag-rock hurts their ears, and they can't sync with the Four Noes, no matter how hard they try. So we say to them, 'Forget it, star. Your wheels are not our wheels. But we're all going somewhere, right? See you at the other end.'"

It is hardly surprising that so many "feebies"—people over thirty—have trouble with the basic Believers' Creed: "No hate, No war, No money, No sex." Evidently, in this final decade of the twentieth century, sainthood is only possible for the very young.

The "Roundhouse" at Jerusalem West is, in one sense, the Vatican of the nationwide movement. But in many ways it is typical of the New Shaker communities springing up from La Jolla, California, to Seal Harbor, Maine. At last count there were sixty-one separate "tribes," some containing as many as fifteen "families" of a hundred and twenty-eight members each. Each Shaker family is housed in an army-surplus pliodesic dome—covering some ten thousand square feet of bare but vinyl-hardened earth—which serves as bedroom, living room, workshop and holy tabernacle, all in one. There is a much smaller satellite dome forty feet from the main building which might be called the Outhouse, but isn't—the New Shakers themselves refer to it as Sin City. In keeping with their general attitude toward the bodily functions, Sin City is the only place in the Jerusalem West compound that is off-limits to visitors.

As difficult as it may be for most North Americans to accept, today's typical Shaker recruit comes from a background of unquestioned abundance and respectability. There is no taint of the Ghetto and no evidence of serious behavioral problems. In fact, Preliminary School records show that these young people often excelled in polymorphous play and responded quite normally to the usual spectrum of chemical

and electrical euphorics. As underteens, their proficiency in
programed dating was consistently rated "superior" and they
were often cited as leaders in organizing multiple-outlet
experiences. Later, in Modular School, they scored in the
fiftieth percentile or better on Brand-Differentiation tests. In
short, according to all the available figures, they would have
had no trouble gaining admission to the college of their
choice or obtaining a commission in the Consumer Corps or
qualifying for a Federal Travel Grant. Yet for some reason,
on the very brink of maturity, they turned their backs on all
the benefits their parents and grandparents fought so hard
for in the Cultural Revolution—and plunged instead into a
life of regimented sense-denial.

On a typical summer's afternoon at Jerusalem West, with
the sun filtering through the translucent dome and bathing
the entire area in a soft golden glow, the Roundhouse resembles nothing so much as a giant, queenless beehive. In the
gleaming chrome-and-copper kitchen blenders whirr and huge
pots bubble as a squad of white-smocked Food Deacons pre-
pares the copious vegetable stew that forms the staple of the
Shaker diet. In the sound-proofed garage sector the Shop
Deacons are busily transforming another hopeless-looking
junk heap into the economical, turbine-powered "hotrod"—one
already known to connoisseurs in this country and abroad as
the Shakerbike—and the eight Administrative Deacons and
their assistants are directing family business from a small
fiber-walled cubicle known simply as The Office. And the
sixteen-piece band is cutting a new liturgical tape for the
Evening Service—a tape that may possibly end up as number
one on the federal pop charts like the recent Shaker hit, *This
Freeway's Plenty Wide Enough*. No matter where one turns
beneath the big. dome, one finds young people humming,
tapping their feet, breaking into snatches of song and generally living up to the New Shaker motto: "Work is Play."
One of their most popular songs—a characteristic coupling
of Old Shaker words to a modern jag-rock background—
concludes with this no-nonsense summation of the Shaker
life-style:

It's the Gift to be simple,
The Gift to be free,
The Gift to come down
Where the Gift ought to be.

MORE TO COME

XEROGRAM: June 28 (11:15 P.M.)
TO: The Dean, Skinner Free Institute, Ronkonkoma, New
   Jersey 72441333965
FROM: Raymond Senter, c/o Hudson Junction Rotel, Hudson
   Junction, N. Y. 28997601910

Friend:
   My son Bruce Senter, age 14, was enrolled in your institute
for a six-week seminar in Applied Physiology beginning May
10. According to the transcript received by his Modular
School (NYC118A), he successfully completed his course of
studies on June 21. Mrs. Senter and I have had no word from
him since. He had earlier talked with his Advisor about
pursuing a Field-research project in Intensive Orgasm. I
would appreciate any further information you can give me as
to his post-seminar whereabouts.
Thank you.

TO: Stock, Ex-Ed, *I.I.*
FROM: Senter
ENCLOSED: Background tape, Interview with Harry G (born
   "Guardino") member of First Octave. Edited Transcript,
   June 29.

Q: Suppose we begin by talking a little about your position
   here as one of the—well, what shall I say? Founding
   Fathers of the Shaker Revival?
A: First you better take a deep breath, star. That's all out of
   sync. There's no Founding Fathers here. Or Founding
   Mothers or any of that jag. There's only one Father and
   one Mother and they're everywhere and nowhere, understand?

Q: What I meant was—as a member of the First Octave you have certain duties and responsibilities—

A: Like I said, star, everyone's equal here.

Q: I was under the impression that your rules stress obedience to a hierarchy?

A: Oh, there has to be order, sure, but it's nothing personal. If you can punch a computer—you sync with the Office Deacons. If you make it with wheels—you're in the Shop crew. Me—I fold my bed in the morning, push a juice-horn in the band and talk to reporters when they ask for me. That doesn't make me Pope.

Q: What about the honorary nomenclature?

A: What's that?

Q: The initials. Instead of last names.

A: Oh, yeah. They were given to us as a sign. You want to know what of?

Q: Please.

A: As a sign that no one's stuck with his birth kit. Sure, you may start with a Chevvie Six chassis and I have to go with a Toyota. That's the luck of the DNA. But we all need a spark of the chamber to get it moving. That's the Gift. And if I burn clean and keep in tune I may leave you flat in my tracks. Right?

Q: What about the Ghetto?

A: Even the Blacks have a piece of the Gift. What they do with it is their trip.

Q: There's been a lot of controversy lately about whether your movement is really Christian—in a religious sense. Would you care to comment on that?

A: You mean like "Jesus Christ, the Son of God?" Sure, we believe that. And we believe in Harry G, The Son of God and Richard F, the Son of God and—what's your name, star?—Raymond Senter, the Son of God. That's the gift. That's what it's all about. Jesus found the Gift inside. So did Buddha, Mother Ann, even Malcolm X—we don't worry too much about who said what first. First you find the Gift—then you live it. The Freeway's plenty wide enough.

Q: Then why all the emphasis on your Believers' Creed, and the Articles of Faith, and your clothes?

A: Look, star, every machine's got a set of specs. You travel with us, you learn our set. We keep the chrome shiny, the chambers clean. And we don't like accidents.

Q: Your prohibitions against money and sex—

A: "Prohibitions" is a feebie word. We're free from money and sex. The Four Noes are like a Declaration of Independence. See, everybody's really born free—but you have to know it. So we don't rob cradles. We say, let them grow up, learn what it's all about—the pill, the puffer, the feel-o-mat—all the perms and combos. Then, when they're fifteen or sixteen, if they still crave those chains, okay. If not, they know where to find us.

Q: What about the people who sign up and then change their minds?

A: We have no chains—if that's what you mean.

Q: You don't do anything to try to keep them?

A: Once you've really found the Gift inside there's no such thing as "changing your mind."

Q: What's your attitude toward the Old Shakers? They died out, didn't they, for lack of recruits?

A: Everything is born and dies and gets reborn again.

Q: Harry, what would happen if this time the whole world became Shakers?

A: Don't worry, star. You won't be around to see it.

MORE TO COME

XEROGRAM: June 29 (10:43 P.M.)

TO: Connie Fine, Director, Camp Encounter, Wentworth, Maine, 47119650023

FROM: Raymond Senter, Hudson Junction Rotel, Hudson Junction, N. Y., 28997601910

Connie:

Has Bruce arrived yet? Arlene and I have lost contact with him in the last week, and it occurred to me that he may have biked up to camp early and simply forgotten to buzz us—he was so charged up about being a full counselor-leader of his own T-group this season. Anyway, would you please buzz me soonest at the above zip? You know how mothers tend to overload the worry-circuits until they know for sure that their little wriggler is safely plugged in somewhere. Joy to you and yours, Ray.

TO: Stock, Ex-Ed., *I.I.*
FROM: Senter
ENCLOSED: Fact sheet on Old Shakers

FOUNDRESS—Mother Ann Lee, b. Feb. 29, 1736, Manchester, England.

ANTECEDENTS—Early Puritan "seekers" (Quakers), French "Prophets" (Camisards).

ORIGIN—Following an unhappy marriage—four children, all dead in infancy—Mother Ann begins to preach that "concupiscence" is the root of all evil. Persecutions and imprisonment.

1774—Mother Ann and seven early disciples sail to America aboard the ship *Mariah*. Group settles near Albany. Public preaching against concupiscence. More persecutions. More converts. Ecstatic, convulsive worship. Mother Ann's "miracles."

1784—Mother Ann dies.

1787—Mother Ann's successors, Father Joseph and Mother Lucy, organize followers into monastic communities and "separate" themselves from sinful world.

1787–1794—Expansion of sect through New York State and New England.

1806–1826—Expansion of sect across Western frontier—Ohio, Kentucky, Indiana.

*   *   *

1837–1845—Mass outbreak of spiritualism. Blessings, songs, spirit-drawings and business advice transmitted by deceased leaders through living "instruments."

1850's—Highpoint of Society. Six thousand members, eighteen communities, fifty-eight "Families."

Total recorded membership—from late 18th century to late 20th century—approximately seventeen thousand.

Old Shakers noted for—mail-order seed business, handicrafts (brooms, baskets and boxes), furniture manufacture.

Credited with invention of—common clothes pin, cut nails, circular saw, turbine waterwheel, steam-driven washing machine.

Worship—Emphasis on communal singing and dancing. Early "convulsive" phase gives way in 19th century to highly organized performances and processions—ring dances, square order shuffles.

Beliefs—Celibacy, Duality of Deity (Father and Mother God), Equality of the Sexes, Equality in Labor, Equality in Property. Society to be perpetuated by "admission of serious-minded persons and adoption of children."

Motto—"Hands to work and Hearts to God."

MORE TO COME

XEROGRAM: June 30 (8:15 A.M.)
TO: Mrs. Rosemary Collins, 133 Escorial Drive, Baywater, Florida, 92635776901
FROM: Raymond Senter, Hudson Junction Rotel, Hudson Junction, N.Y. 28997601910

Dear Rosie:
    Has that little wriggler of ours been down your way lately? Bruce is off again on an unannounced sidetrip, and

it struck me that he might have hopped down south to visit his favorite aunt. Not to mention his favorite cousin! How is that suntanned teaser of yours? Still taking after you in the S-L-N department? Give her a big kiss for me—you know where! And if Bruce does show up please buzz me right away at the above zip. Much Brotherly Love, Ray.

TO: Stock, Ex-Ed., *I.I.*
FROM: Senter
ENCLOSED: Caption tape for film segment on Worship Service.

JERUSALEM WEST, Saturday, June 30—I'm standing at the entrance to the inner sanctum of the huge Roundhouse here, the so-called Meeting Center, which is used only for important ceremonial functions—like the Saturday Night Dance scheduled to begin in exactly five minutes. In the Holy Corridor to my right the entire congregation has already assembled in two rows, one for boys and one for girls, side by side but not touching. During the week the Meeting Center is separated from the work and living areas by curved translucent partitions which fit together to make a little dome-within-a-dome. But when the sun begins to set on Saturday night the partitions are removed to reveal a circular dance floor, which is in fact the hub of the building. From this slightly raised platform of gleaming fibercast, I can look down each radial corridor—past the rows of neatly folded beds in the dormitories, past the shrouded machines in the repair shops, past the partly finished Shakerbikes in the garage, past the scrubbed formica tables in the kitchen—to the dim horizon line where the dome comes to rest on the sacred soil of Jerusalem West.

All artificial lights have been extinguished for the Sabbath celebration. The only illumination comes from the last rays of the sun, a dying torch that seems to have set the dome material itself ablaze. It's a little like standing inside the fiery furnace of Nebuchadnezzar with a hundred and twenty-eight unworried prophets of the Lord. The silence is virtually complete—not a cough, not the faintest rustle of fabric is heard. Even the air vents have been turned off—at least for the moment. I become aware of the harsh sound of my own respiration.

At precisely eight o'clock the two lines of worshippers begin to move forward out of the Holy Corridor. They circle the dance floor, the boys moving to the right, the girls to the left. Actually, it's difficult to tell them apart. The Shakers use no body ornaments at all—no paints, no wigs, no gems, no bugs, no dildoes, no flashers. All wear their hair cropped short, as if sheared with the aid of an overturned bowl. And all are dressed in some variation of Shaker gear—a loosely fitting, long-sleeved, buttonless and collarless shirt slit open at the neck for two inches and hanging free at the waist over a pair of baggy trousers pulled tight around each ankle by a hidden elastic band.

The garments look vaguely North African. They are made of soft dynaleen and they come in a variety of pastel shades. One girl may be wearing a pale pink top and a light blue bottom. The boy standing opposite her may have on the same colors, reversed. Others in the procession have chosen combinations of lilac and peach, ivory and lemon or turquoise and butternut. The range of hues seems endless but the intensity never varies, so that the entire spectacle presents a living demonstration of one of the basic Articles of Faith of the Shaker Revival—Diversity in Uniformity.

Now the procession has ended. The worshipers have formed two matching arcs, sixty-four boys on one side, sixty-four girls on the other, each standing precisely an arm's length from each neighbor. All are barefoot. All are wearing the same expression—a smile so modest as to be virtually undetectable if it were not mirrored and remirrored a hundred and twenty-eight times around the circumference of the ritual circle. The color of the dome has begun to change to a darker, angrier crimson. Whether the natural twilight's being artificially augmented—either from inside or outside the building—is impossible to tell. All eyes are turned upward to a focus about twenty-five feet above the center of the floor, where an eight-sided loudspeaker hangs by a chrome-plated cable from the midpoint of the dome. The air begins to fill with a pervasive vibration like the rumble of a distant monocar racing toward you in the night. And then the music explodes into the supercharged air. Instantly the floor is alive with jerking, writhing bodies—it's as if each chord were an electrical impulse applied directly to the nerve ends of the dancers—and the music is unbelievably loud.

The dome must act as an enormous soundbox. I can feel the vibrations in my feet and my teeth are chattering with the beat—but as wild as the dancing is, the circle is still intact. Each Shaker is "shaking" in his own place. Some are uttering incomprehensible cries, the holy gibberish that the Shakers call their Gift of Tongues—ecstatic prophesies symbolizing the Wordless Word of the Deity. One young girl with a gaunt but beautiful face is howling like a coyote. Another is grunting like a pig. A third is alternately spitting into the air and slapping her own cheeks viciously with both hands.

Across the floor a tall skinny boy has shaken loose from the rim of the circle. Pirouetting at high speed, his head thrown straight back so that his eyes are fixed on the crimson membrane of the dome, he seems to be propelling himself in an erratic path toward the center of the floor. And now the dome is changing color again, clotting to a deeper purple—like the color of a late evening sky but flecked with scarlet stars that seem to be darting about with a life of their own, colliding, coalescing, reforming.

A moment of relative calm has descended on the dancers. They are standing with their hands at their sides—only their heads are moving, lolling first to one side, then the other, in keeping with the new, subdued rhythm of the music. The tall boy in the center has begun to spin around and around in place, picking up speed with each rotation—now he's whirling like a top, his head still bent back, his eyes staring sightlessly. His right arm shoots out from the shoulder, the elbow locked, the fingers stiff, the palm flat—this is what the Shakers call the Arrow Sign, a manifestation of the Gift of Prophecy, directly inspired by the Dual Deity, Father Power and Mother Wisdom. The tall boy is the "instrument" and he is about to receive a message from on high.

His head tilts forward. His rotation slows. He comes to a halt with his right arm pointing at a short red-haired girl.

The girl begins to shake all over as if struck by a high fever. The music rises to an ear-shattering crescendo and ends in mid-note.

"Everyone's a mirror," the tall boy shouts. "Clean, clean, clean—oh, let it shine! My dirt's not my own but it stains the earth. And the earth's not my own—the Mother and Father are light above light but the light can't shine alone. Only a mirror can shine, shine, shine. Let the mirror be mine, be mine, be mine!"

The red-haired girl is shaking so hard her limbs are flailing like whips. Her mouth has fallen open and she begins to moan, barely audibly at first. What she utters might be a single-syllable word like "clean" or "mine" or "shine" repeatedly, so rapidly that the consonants break down and the vowels flow into one unending stream of sound. But it keeps getting louder and louder and still louder, like the wail of an air-raid siren, until all resemblance to speech disappears and it seems impossible that such a sound can come from a human throat. You can almost hear the blood vessels straining, bursting.

Then the loudspeaker cuts in again in mid-note with the loudest, wildest jag-rock riff I have ever heard, only it's no longer something you can hear—it's inside you or you're inside it. And the dome has burst into blooms of color! A stroboscopic fireworks display that obliterates all outlines and shatters perspective and you can't tell whether the dancers are moving very, very slowly or very, very fast. The movement is so perfectly synchronized with the sound and the sound with the color that there seems to be no fixed reference point anywhere.

All you can say is: "There is color, there is sound, there is movement—"

This is the Gift of Seizure, which the New Shakers prize so highly—and whether it is genuinely mystical, as they claim, or autohypnotic or drug-induced, as some critics maintain, or a combination of all of these or something else entirely, it is an undeniably real—and profoundly disturbing—experience.

*   *   *

XEROGRAM: July 1 (7:27 A.M.)

TO: Frederick Rickover, Eastern Supervisor, Feel-O-Mat Corp., Baltimore, Maryland, 6503477502

FROM: Raymond Senter, Hudson Junction Rotel, Hudson Junction, N. Y., 28997601910 '

(WARNING: PERSONALIZED ENVELOPE: CONTENTS WILL POWDER IF OPENED IMPROPERLY)

Fred:

I'm afraid it's back-scratching time again. I need a code-check on DNA No. $75/62/HR/tl/4$-9-06^5. I'm interested in whether the codee has plugged into a feel-o-mat anywhere in the Federation during the past two weeks. This one's a family matter, not business, so buzz me only at the above zip. I won't forget it. Gratefully, Ray.

TO: Stock, Ex-Ed., *I.I.*

FROM: Senter

ENCLOSED: Three tapes. New Shaker "testimonies." Edited transcripts, July 1.

TAPE I (Shaker name, "Farmer Brown"). What kind of mike is this? No kidding. I didn't know they made a re-amper this small. Chinese? Oh. Right. Well, let's see—I was born April 17, 1974, in Ellsworth, Saskatchewan. My breath-father's a foreman at a big refinery there. My breath-mother was a consumer-housewife. She's gone over now. It's kind of hard to remember details. When I was real little, I think I saw the feds scratch a Bomb-thrower on the steps of City Hall. But maybe that was only something I saw on 2-D. School was—you know, the usual. Oh, once a bunch of us kids got hold of some fresh spores from the refinery—I guess we stole them somehow. Anyway, there was still a lot of open land around and we planted them and raised our own crop of puffers. I didn't come down for a week. That was my farming experience. (*Laughter*) I applied for a bummer-grant on my fifteenth birthday, got a two-year contract and took off the next day for the sun. Let's see—Minneapolis, Kansas City, Mexico—

what a jolt! There weren't so many feel-o-mats in the small towns down there and I was into all the hard stuff you could get in those days—speed, yellow, rock-juice, little-annie—I guess the only thing I never tried for a jolt was the Process and there were times when I was just about ready.

When the grant ran out, I just kept bumming on my own. At first you think it's going to be real easy. Half the people you know are still on contract and they share it around. Then your old friends start running out faster than you make new ones and there's a whole new generation on the road. And you start feeling more and more like a feebie and acting like one. I was lucky because I met this sweet little dove in Nashville—she had a master's in Audio-Visual but she was psycho for bummers, especially flat ones.

Anyway, she comes back to her coop one day with a new tape and puts it on and says, "This'll go right through you. It's a wild new group called the Shakers."

She didn't know two bobbys' worth about the Shakers and I didn't either—the first Shaker tapes were just hitting the market about then. Well, I can tell you, that jagged sound gave me a jolt. I mean, it was bigger than yellow, bigger than juice, only it let you down on your feet instead of your back. I had this feeling I had to hear more. I got all the tapes that were out but they weren't enough. So I took off one night for Wildwood and before I knew it I was in a Prep Meeting and I was home free—you know, I've always kind of hoped that little dove makes it on her own—Oh, yeah, the band.

Well, I'm one of the Band Deacons, which is what's called a Sacrificial Gift because it means handling the accounts—and that's too close to the jacks and bobbys for comfort. But someone has to do it. You can't stay alive in an impure world without getting a little stained and if outsiders want to lay the Kennedys on us for bikes and tapes, that's a necessary evil. But we don't like to spread the risk in the Family. So the Deacons sign the checks and deal with the agents and the stain's on us alone. And everyone prays a little harder to square it with the Father and Mother.

*　　*　　*

TAPE II (Shaker name, "Mariah Moses"). I was born in Darien, Connecticut. I'm an Aquarius with Leo rising. Do you want my breath-name? I don't mind—it's Cathy Ginsberg. My breath-parents are both full-time consumers. I didn't have a very interesting childhood, I guess. I went to Mid-Darien Modular School. I was a pretty good student—my best subject was World Culture. I consummated on my third date, which was about average, I've been told, for my class. Do you really want all this background stuff? I guess the biggest thing that happened to the old me was when I won a second prize in the Maxwell Puffer Civic Essay contest when I was fourteen. The subject was *The Joys of Spectatorism* and the prize was a Programed Weekend in Hawaii for two. I don't remember who I went with. But Hawaii was really nice. All those brown-skinned boys—we went to a big luau on Saturday night. That's a native-style orgy. They taught me things we never even learned in school.

I remember thinking, *Oh, star, this is the living end!*

But when it was all over I had another thought. If this was the living end—what came next? I don't know if it was the roast pig or what but I didn't feel so good for a few days. The night we got back home—Herbie! That was the name of my date, Herbie Alcott—he had short curly hair all over his back—anyway, the night I got home my breath-parents picked me up at the airport and on the way back to Darien they started asking me what I wanted to do with my life. They were trying to be so helpful, you know. I mean, you could see they would have been disappointed if I got involved in production of some kind but they weren't about to say that in so many words. They just asked me if I had decided how I wanted to plug into the Big Board. It was up to me to choose between college or the Consumer Corps or a Travel Grant— they even asked me if Herbie and I were getting serious and if we wanted to have a baby—because the waiting-list at the Marriage Bureau was already six months long and getting longer. The trouble was I was still thinking about the luau and the roast pig and I felt all—burned out. Like a piece of charcoal that still looks solid but is really just white ash— and if you touch it it crumbles and blows away. So I said I'd think about it but what I was really thinking was *I'm not signing up for any more orgies just yet.*

And a few days later the miracle happened. A girl in our glass was reported missing and a friend of mine heard someone say that she'd become a Shaker.

I said, "What's that?"

My friend said, "It's a religion that believes in No hate, No war, No money, No sex."

And I felt this thrill go right through me. And even though I didn't know what it meant at the time, that was the moment I discovered my Gift. It was such a warm feeling, like something soft and quiet curled up inside you, waiting. And the day I turned fifteen I hiked up to Jerusalem and I never went home. That was eleven months ago . . . oh, you can't describe what happens at Preparative Meeting. It's what happens inside you that counts. Like now, when I think of all my old friends from Darien, I say a little prayer.

Father Power, Mother Wisdom, touch their Gifts, set them free. . . .

TAPE III (Shaker name, "Earnest Truth"). I'm aware that I'm something of a rarity here. I assume that's why you asked me for a testimony. But I don't want you categorizing me as a Shaker intellectual or a Shaker theologian or anything like that. I serve as Legal Deacon because that's my Gift. But I'm also a member of the vacuum detail in Corridor Three and that's my Gift too. I'd be just as good a Shaker if I only cleaned the floor and nothing else. Is that clear? Good. Well then, as briefly as possible [*reads from prepared text*]: I'm twenty-four years old, from Berkeley, California. Breathparents were on the faculty at the University; killed in an air crash when I was ten. I was raised by the state. Pacific Highlands Modular School: First honors. Consumer Corps: Media-aide First-class. Entered the University at seventeen. Pre-law. Graduated *magna cum* in nineteen-ninety. Completed four-year Law School in three years. In my final year I became interested in the literature of religion—or, to be more precise, the literature of mysticism—possibly as a counterpoise to the increasing intensity of my formal studies. Purely

as an intellectual diversion I began to read St. John of the
Cross, George Fox, the Vedas, Tao, Zen, the Kabbala, the
Sufis. But when I came across the early Shakers I was struck
at once with the daring and clarity of this purely American
variant. All mystics seek spiritual union with the Void, the
Nameless, the Formless, the Ineffable. But the little band of
Shaker pilgrims, confronted with a vast and apparently
unbounded wilderness, took a marvelous quantum leap of
faith and decided that the union had already been accomplished. The wilderness was the Void. For those who had eyes
to see—this was God's Kingdom. And by practicing a total
communism, a total abnegation, a total dedication, they
made the wilderness flower for two hundred years. Then,
unable to adjust to the methodologies of the Industrial Revolution, they quietly faded away; it was as if their gentle spirit
had found a final resting place in the design of their utterly
simple and utterly beautiful wooden furniture—each piece of
which has since become a collector's item. When I began
reading about the Old Shakers I had of course heard about
the New Shakers— but I assumed that they were just another
crackpot fundamentalist sect like the Holy Rollers or the
Snake Handlers, an attempt to keep alive the pieties of a
simpler day in the present age of abundance. But eventually
my curiosity—or so I called it at the time—led me to investigate a Preparative Meeting that had been established in the
Big Sur near Jefferstown. And I found my Gift. The experience varies from individual to individual. For me it was the
revelation that the complex machine we refer to as the
Abundant Society is the real anachronism. All the euphorics
we feed ourselves cannot change the fact that the machinery
of abundance has long since reached its limit as a vital force
and is now choking on its own waste products—Pollution,
Overpopulation, Dehumanization. Far from being a break-
through, the so-called Cultural Revolution was merely the
last gasp of the old order trying to maintain itself by pro-
graming man's most private senses into the machine. And
the childish Bomb-throwers were nothing but retarded roman-
tics, an anachronism within an anachronism. At this junc-
ture in history, only the Shaker Revival offers a true

alternative—in the utterly simple, and therefore utterly profound, Four Noes. The secular world usually praises us for our rejection of Hate and War and mocks us for our rejection of Money and Sex. But the Four Noes constitute a beautifully balanced ethical equation, in which each term is a function of the other three. There are no easy Utopias. Non-Shakers often ask: What would happen if everyone became a Shaker? Wouldn't that be the end of the human race? My personal answer is this: Society is suffering from the sickness unto death—a plague called despair. Shakerism is the only cure. As long as the plague rages more and more people will find the strength to take the medicine required, no matter how bitter it may seem. Perhaps at some future date, the very spread of Shakerism will restore Society to health, so that the need for Shakerism will again slacken. Perhaps the cycle will be repeated. Perhaps not. It is impossible to know what the Father and Mother have planned for their children. Only one thing is certain. The last of the Old Shaker prophetesses wrote in 1956: "The flame may flicker but the spark can never be allowed to die out until the salvation of the world is accomplished."

I don't think you'll find the flame flickering here.

MORE TO COME

XEROGRAM: July 1 (11:30 P.M.)
TO: Stock, Ex-Ed., *I.I.*
FROM: Raymond Senter, c/o Hudson Junction Rotel
(WARNING: PERSONALIZED ENVELOPE: CONTENTS WILL POWDER IF OPENED IMPROPERLY)

Art:

Cooperation unlimited here—until I mention "Preparative Meeting." Then they all get tongue-tied. Too holy for impure ears. No one will even say where or when. Working hypothesis: It's a compulsory withdrawal session. Recruits obviously must kick all worldly habits before taking final vows. Big question: How do they do it? Conscious or unconscious? Cold-turkey, hypno-suggestion, or re-conditioning?

Legal or illegal? Even Control would like to know. I'm taping the Reception Deacon tomorrow. If you approve, I'll start putting the pressure on. The groundwork's done. We may get a story yet. Ray.

XEROGRAM: July 2 (2:15 A.M.)
TO: Joseph Harger, Coordinator, N.Y. State Consumer Control, Albany, N.Y. 31118002311
FROM: Raymond Senter, c/o Hudson Junction Rotel, Hudson Junction, N.Y. 28997601910
(*WARNING: PERSONALIZED ENVELOPE: CONTENTS WILL POWDER IF OPENED IMPROPERLY*)

Joe:

I appreciate your taking a personal interest in this matter. My wife obviously gave the wrong impression to the controller she contacted. She tends to get hysterical. Despite what she may have said I assure you my son's attitude toward the Ghetto was a perfectly healthly blend of scorn and pity. Bruce went with me once to see the Harlem Wall—must have been six or seven—and Coordinator Bill Quaite let him sit in the Scanner's chair for a few minutes. He heard a muezzin call from the top of one of those rickety towers. He saw the wild rats prowling in the stench and garbage. He also watched naked children fighting with wooden knives over a piece of colored glass. I am told there are young people today stupid enough to think that sneaking over the Wall is an adventure and that the process is reversible—but my son is definitely not one of them. And he is certainly not a Bomb-thrower. I know that you have always shared my publication's view that a selective exposure to the harsher realities makes for better consumers. (I'm thinking of that little snafu in data-traffic in the Albany Grid last summer.) I hope you'll see your way clear to trusting me again. I repeat: there's not the slightest indication that my son was going over to the Blacks. In fact, I have good reason to believe that he will turn up quite soon, with all discrepancies accounted for. But I need a little time. A Missing Persons Bulletin would only make things harder at the moment. I realize it was my wife who initiated the complaint. But I'd greatly appreciate it if she got misfiled for forty-eight hours. I'll handle any static on this side. Discreetly, Ray.

TO: Stock, Ex-Ed., *I.I.*
FROM: Senter
ENCLOSED: Background tape; interview with Antonia Cross, age 19, Reception Deacon, Jerusalem West Edited Transcript, July 2.

Q: (I waited silently for her to take the lead.)

A: Before we begin, I think we better get a few things straight. It'll save time and grief in the long run. First of all, despite what your magazine and others may have said in the past, we never proselytize. Never. So please don't use that word. We just try to live our Gift—and if other people are drawn to us, that's the work of the Father and Mother, not us. We don't have to preach. When someone's sitting in filth up to his neck he doesn't need a preacher to tell him he smells. All he needs to hear is that there's a cleaner place somewhere. Second, we don't prevent anyone from leaving, despite all rumors to the contrary. We've had exactly three apostates in the last four years. They found out their wheels were not our wheels and they left.

Q: Give me their names.

A: There's no law that says we have to disclose the names of backsliders. Find them yourself. That shouldn't be too hard, now that they're plugged back in to the Big Board.

Q: You overestimate the power of the press.

A: False modesty is not considered a virtue among Shakers.

Q: You mentioned three backsliders. How many applicants are turned away before taking final vows?

A: The exact percentage is immaterial. Some applicants are more serious than others. There is no great mystery about our reception procedure. You've heard the expression "Weekend Shakers." Anybody can buy the gear and dance and sing and stay pure for a couple of days. It's even

considered a "jolt," I'm told. We make sure that those who
come to us know the difference between a weekend and a
lifetime. We explain the Gift, the Creed, the Articles of
Faith. Then we ask them why they've come to us. We
press them pretty hard. In the end, if they're still serious,
they are sent to Preparative Meeting for a while until a
Family is ready to accept them.

Q: How long is a while?

A: Preparative Meeting can take days or weeks. Or longer.

Q: Are they considered full-fledged Shakers during that time?

A: The moment of Induction is a spiritual, not a temporal,
phenomenon.

Q: But you notify the authorities only after a recruit is
accepted in a Family?

A: We comply with all the requirements of the Full Disclo-
sure Law.

Q: What if the recruit is underage and lies about it? Do you
run a routine DNA check?

A: We obey the law.

Q: But a recruit at a Prep Meeting isn't a Shaker and so you
don't have to report his presence. Is that right?

A: We've had exactly nine complaints filed against us in four
years. Not one has stuck.

Q: Then you do delay acceptance until you can trace a recruit's
identity?

A: I didn't say that. We believe in each person's right to
redefine his set, no matter what the Big Board may say
about him. But such administrative details tend to work
themselves out.

Q: How? I don't understand.

A: The ways of the Father and Mother sometimes passeth
understanding.

Q: You say you don't proselytize, but isn't that what your
tapes are—a form of preaching? Don't most of your recruits
come to you because of the tapes? And don't most of them
have to be brought down from whatever they're hooked on
before you'll even let them in?

A: The world—your world—is filth. From top to bottom. We
try to stay as far away as we can. But we have to eat. So

we sell you our tapes and our Shakerbikes. There's a calculated risk of contamination. But it works the other way too. Filth can be contaminated by purity. That's known as Salvation. It's like a tug of war. We'll see who takes the greatest risk.

Q: That's what I'm here for—to see at first hand. Where is the Jerusalem West Preparative Meeting held?

A: Preparative Meetings are private. For the protection of all concerned.

Q: Don't you mean secret? Isn't there something going on at these meetings that you don't want the public to know?

A: If the public is ignorant of the life of the spirit, that is hardly our fault.

Q: Some people believe that your recruits are "prepared" with drugs or electro-conditioning.

A: Some people think that Shaker stew is full of saltpeter. Are you going to print that, too?

Q: You have been accused of brain-tampering. That's a serious charge. And unless I get a hell of a lot more cooperation from you than I've been getting I will have to assume that you have something serious to hide.

A: No one ever said you'd be free to see everything. You'll just have to accept our—guidance—in matters concerning religious propriety.

Q: Let me give you a little guidance, Miss Cross. You people already have so many enemies in that filthy world you despise that one unfriendly story from *I.I.* might just tip the scales.

A: The power of the press? We'll take our chances.

Q: What will you do if the police crack down?

A: We're not afraid to die. And the Control authorities have found that it's more trouble than it's worth to put us in jail. We seem to upset the other inmates.

Q: Miss Cross—

A: We use no titles here. My name is Antonia.

Q: You're obviously an intelligent, dedicated young woman. I would rather work with you than against you. Why don't we try to find some middle ground? As a journalist my primary concern is human nature—what happens to a

young recruit in the process of becoming a full-fledged
Shaker. You won't let me into a Prep Meeting to see for
myself. All right, you have your reasons, and I respect
them. But I ask you to respect mine. If I can look through
your Reception files—just the last two or three weeks will
do—I should be able to get some idea of what kind of raw
material you draw on. You can remove the names, of
course.

A: Perhaps we can provide a statistical breakdown for you.

Q: I don't want statistics. I want to look at their pictures,
listen to their voices—you say you press them pretty hard
in the first interview. That's what I need: their response
under pressure, the difference between those who stick it
through and those who don't.

A: How do we know you're not looking for something of a
personal nature—to embarrass us?

Q: For God's sakes, I'm one of the best-known tapemen in the
Federation. Why not just give me the benefit of the doubt?

A: You invoke a Deity that means nothing to you.

Q: I'm sorry.

A: The only thing I can do is transmit your request to the
Octave itself. Any decision on such a matter would have to
come from a Full Business Meeting.

Q: How long will it take?

A: The Octave is meeting tomorrow, before Evening Service.

Q: All right. I can wait till then. I suppose I should apologize
again for losing my temper. I'm afraid it's an occupational
hazard.

A: We all have our Gift.

MORE TO COME

TO: Stock, Ex-Ed., *I.I.*
FROM: Senter.
ENCLOSED: First add on Shaker Revival; July 3.

It is unclear whether the eight teenagers—six boys and
two girls—who banded together one fateful evening in the
spring of 1991 to form a jag-rock combo called The Shakers

had any idea of the religious implications of the name. According to one early account in *Riff* magazine, the original eight were thinking only of a classic rock-and-roll number of the 1950s, *Shake, Rattle, and Roll* (a title not without sexual as well as musicological overtones). On the other hand, there is evidence that Harry G was interested in astrology, palmistry, scientology and other forms of modern occultism even before he left home at the age of fifteen. (Harry G was born Harry Guardino, on December 18, 1974, in Schoodic, Maine, the son of a third-generation lobster fisherman.) Like many members of his generation he applied for a Federal Travel Grant on graduation from Modular School and received a standard two-year contract. But unlike most of his fellow-bummers, Harry did not immediately take off on an all-expenses-paid tour of the seamier side of life in the North American Federation. Instead, he hitched a ride to New York City, where he established a little basement coop on the lower west side that soon became a favorite waystation for other, more restless bummers passing through the city. No reliable account of this period is available. The rumors that he dabbled in a local Bomb-throwers cell appear to be unfounded. But it is known that sometime during the spring of 1991 a group of bummers nearing the end of their grants gathered in Harry G's coop to discuss the future. By coincidence or design the eight young people who came together that night from the far corners of the Federation all played some instrument and shared a passion for jag-rock. And as they talked and argued among themselves about the best way possible to "plug into the Big Board," it slowly began to dawn on them that perhaps their destinies were linked—or, as Harry G himself has put it, "We felt we could make beautiful music together. Time has made us one."

Building a reputation in the jag-rock market has never been easy—not even with divine intervention. For the next two months, The Shakers scrambled for work, playing a succession of one-night stands in consumers' centers, schools, fraternal lodges—wherever someone wanted live entertainment and was willing to put the group up. The Shakers traveled in a secondhand Chevrolet van which was kept running only by the heroic efforts of the group's electric-oud player, Richard Fitzgerald (who later—as Richard F—helped to design the improved version of the turbo-adapter which forms the basis of today's Shakerbike).

On the night of June the first the group arrived in Hancock, Massachusetts, where they were scheduled to play the next evening at the graduation dance of the Grady L. Parker Modular School. They had not worked for three days and their finances had reached a most precarious stage—they were now sharing only four bummer-grants between them, the other four contracts having expired in the previous weeks. From the very beginning of their relationship the eight had gone everywhere and done everything as a group— they even insisted on sleeping together in one room on the theory that the "bad vibrations" set up by an overnight absence from each other might adversely affect their music. As it turned out, there was no room large enough at the local Holiday Inn, so, after some lengthy negotiations, the Modular School principal arranged for them to camp out on the grounds of the local Shaker Museum, a painstaking restoration of an early New England Shaker community dating back to 1790. Amused but not unduly impressed by the coincidence in names, the eight Shakers bedded down for the night within sight of the Museum's most famous structure, the Round Stone Barn erected by the original Shakers in 1826. Exactly what happened between midnight and dawn on that fog-shrouded New England meadow may never be known—the validation of mystical experience being by its very nature a somewhat inexact science. According to Shaker testimony, however, the spirit of Mother Ann, sainted foundress of the original sect, touched the Gifts of the eight where they lay and in a vision of the future—which Amelia D later said was "as clear and bright as a holograph"—revealed why they had been chosen: The time had come for a mass revival of Shaker beliefs and practices. The eight teenagers awoke at the same instant, compared visions, found them to be identical and wept together for joy. They spent the rest of the day praying for guidance and making plans. Their first decision was to play as scheduled at the Grady L. Parker graduation dance.

"We decided to go on doing just what we had been doing—only more so," Amelia D later explained. "Also, I guess, we needed the jacks."

Whatever the reason, the group apparently played as never before. Their music opened up doors to whole new ways of hearing and feeling—or so it seemed to the excited crowd of seniors who thronged around the bandstand when the first set was over. Without any premeditation, or so he later claimed, Harry Guardino stood up and announced the new Shaker dispensation, including the Believers' Creed (the Four Noes) and a somewhat truncated version of the Articles of Faith of the United Society of Believers (Revived): "All things must be kept decent and in good order," "Diversity in Uniformity," and "Work is Play." According to the Hancock newspaper, seventeen members of the senior class left town that morning with the Shakers—in three cars "borrowed" from parents and later returned. Drawn by a Gift of Travel, the little band of pilgrims made their way to the quiet corner of New York State now known as Jerusalem West, bought some land—with funds obtained from anonymous benefactors—and settled down to their strange experiment in monastic and ascetic communism.

The actual historical connections between Old Shakers and New Shakers remains a matter of conjecture. It is not clear, for instance, whether Harry G and his associates had a chance to consult the documentary material on display at the Hancock Museum. There is no doubt that the First Article of Faith of the Shaker Revival is a word-for-word copy of the first part of an early Shaker motto. But it has been given a subtly different meaning in present-day usage. And while many of the New Shaker doctrines and practices can be traced to the general tenor of traditional Shakerism, the adaptations are often quite free and sometimes wildly capricious. All in all, the Shaker Revival seems to be very much a product of our own time. Some prominent evolutionists even see it as part of a natural process of weeding out those individuals incapable of becoming fully consuming members of the Abundant Society. They argue that Shakerism is a definite improvement, in this respect, over the youthful cult of Bomb-throwers which had to be suppressed in the early days of the Federation.

But there are other observers who see a more ominous trend at work. They point especially to the serious legal questions raised by the Shakers' efforts at large-scale proselytization. The twenty-seventh Amendment to the Federal Constitution guarantees the right of each white citizen over the age of fifteen to the free and unrestricted enjoyment of his own senses, provided that such enjoyment does not interfere with the range or intensity of any other citizen's sensual enjoyment. Presumably this protection also extends to the right of any white citizen to deny himself the usual pleasures. But what is the status of corporate institutions that engage in such repression? How binding, for example, is the Shaker recruit's sworn allegiance to the Believers' Creed? How are the Four Noes enforced within the sect? Suppose two Shakers find themselves physically attracted to each other and decide to consummate—does the United Society of Believers have any right to place obstacles between them? These are vital questions that have yet to be answered by the Control authorities. But there are influential men in Washington who read the twenty-seventh amendment as an obligation on the government's part not merely to protect the individual's right to sensual pleasure but also to help him maximize it. And in the eyes of these broad constructionists the Shakers are on shaky ground.

TO: Stock, Ex-Ed., *I.I.*
FROM: Senter
(WARNING: CONFIDENTIAL UNEDITED TAPE: NOT FOR PUBLICATION: CONTENTS WILL POWDER IF OPENED IMPROPERLY)

FIRST VOICE: Bruce? Is that you?
SECOND VOICE: It's me.
FIRST: For God's sake, come in! Shut the door. My God, I thought you were locked up in that Prep Meeting. I thought—

SECOND: It's not a prison. When I heard you were prowling around town I knew I had to talk to you.

FIRST: You've changed your mind then?

SECOND: Don't believe it. I just wanted to make sure you didn't lie about everything.

FIRST: Do they know you're here?

SECOND: No one followed me, if that's what you mean. No one even knows who I am. I've redefined my set, as we say.

FIRST: But they check. They're not fools. They'll find out soon enough—if they haven't already.

SECOND: They don't check. That's another lie. And anyway, I'll tell them myself after Induction.

FIRST: Brucie—it's not too late. We want you to come home.

SECOND: You can tell Arlene that her little baby is safe and sound. How is she? Blubbering all over herself as usual?

FIRST: She's pretty broken up about your running away.

SECOND: Why? Is she worried they'll cut off her credit at the feel-o-mat? For letting another potential consumer get off the hook?

FIRST: You wouldn't have risked coming to me if you didn't have doubts. Don't make a terrible mistake.

SECOND: I came to see you because I know how you can twist other people's words. Are you recording this?

FIRST: Yes.

SECOND: Good. I'm asking you straight out—please leave us alone.

FIRST: Do you know they're tampering with your mind?

SECOND: Have you tasted your local drinking water lately?

FIRST: Come home with me.

SECOND: I am home.

FIRST: You haven't seen enough of the world to turn your back on it.

SECOND: I've seen you and Arlene.

FIRST: And is our life so awful?

SECOND: What you and Arlene have isn't life. It's the American Dream Come True. You're in despair and don't even know it. That's the worse kind.

FIRST: You repeat the slogans as if you believed them.

SECOND: What makes you think I don't?

FIRST: You're my flesh and blood. I know you.

SECOND: You don't. All you know is that your little pride and joy ran away to become a monk and took the family genes. And Arlene is too old to go back to the Big Board and beg for seconds.

FIRST: Look—I know a little something about rebellion, too. I've had a taste of it in my time. It's healthy, it's natural— I'm all for it. But not an overdose. When the jolt wears off, you'll be stuck here. And you're too smart to get trapped in a hole like this.

SECOND: It's my life, isn't it? In exactly one hour and ten minutes I'll be free, white, and fifteen—Independence Day, right? What a beautiful day to be born—it's the nicest thing you and Arlene did for me.

FIRST: Brucie, we want you back. Whatever you want—just name it and if it's in my power I'll try to get it. I have friends who will help.

SECOND: I don't want anything from you. We're quits—can't you understand? The only thing we have in common now is this: (*sound of heavy breathing*). That's it. And if you want that back you can take it. Just hold your hand over my mouth and pinch my nose for about five minutes. That should do it.

FIRST: How can you joke about it?

SECOND: Why not? Haven't you heard? There're only two ways to go for my generation—the Shakers or the Ghetto. How do you think I'd look in blackface with bushy hair and a gorilla nose? Or do you prefer my first choice?

FIRST: I'm warning you, the country's not going to put up with either much longer. There's going to be trouble—and I want you out of here when it comes.

SECOND: What are the feebies going to do? Finish our job for us?

FIRST: Is that what you want then? To commit suicide?

SECOND: Not exactly. That's what the Bomb-throwers did. We want to commit your suicide.

FIRST: (*Words unintelligible.*)

SECOND: That really jolts you, doesn't it? You talk about

rebellion as if you knew something about it because you wore beads once and ran around holding signs.

FIRST: We changed history.

SECOND: You didn't change anything. You were swallowed up, just like the Bomb-throwers. The only difference is, you were eaten alive.

FIRST: Bruce—

SECOND: Can you stretch the gray-stuff a little, and try to imagine what real rebellion would be like? Not just another chorus of "gimmie, gimmie, gimmie—" but the absolute negation of what's come before? The Four Noes all rolled up into One Big No!

FIRST: Brucie—I'll make a deal—

SECOND: No one's ever put it all together before. I don't expect you to see it. Even around here, a lot of people don't know what's happening. Expiation! That's what rebellion is all about. The young living down the sins of the fathers and mothers! But the young are always so hungry for life they get distracted before they can finish the job. Look at all the poor, doomed rebels in history; whenever they got too big to be crushed the feebies bought them off with a piece of the action. The stick or the carrot and then—business as usual. Your generation was the biggest sellout of all. But the big laugh is, you really thought you won. So now you don't have any carrot left to offer, because you've already shared it all with us—before we got old. And we're strong enough to laugh at your sticks. Which is why the world is going to find out for the first time what total rebellion is.

FIRST: I thought you didn't believe in violence and hate?

SECOND: Oh, our strength is not of this world. You can forget all the tapes and bikes and dances—that's the impure shell that must be sloughed off. If you want to get the real picture, just imagine us—all your precious little gene-machines—standing around in a circle, our heads bowed in prayer, holding our breaths and clicking off one by one. Don't you think that's a beautiful way for your world to end? Not with a bang or a whimper—but with one long breathless Amen?

MORE TO COME

TO: Stock, Ex-Ed., *I.I.*
FROM: Senter
ENCLOSED: New first add on *"Shaker Revival"* (scratch earlier transmission; new lead upcoming).

JERUSALEM WEST, N.Y., Wednesday, July 4—An early critic of the Old Shakers, a robust pamphleteer who had actually been a member of the sect for ten months, wrote this prophetic appraisal of his former cohorts in the year 1782: "When we consider the infant state of civil power in America since the Revolution began, every infringement on the natural rights of humanity, every effort to undermine our original constitution, either in civil or ecclesiastical order, saps the foundation of Independency."

That winter, the Shaker foundress, Mother Ann, was seized in Petersham, Massachusetts, by a band of vigilantes who, according to a contemporary account, wanted "to find out whether she was a woman or not." Various other Shaker leaders were horse-whipped, thrown in jail, tarred and feathered, and driven out of one New England town after another by an aroused citizenry. These severe persecutions, which lasted through the turn of the century, were the almost inevitable outcome of a clash between the self-righteous, unnatural, uncompromising doctrines of the Shakers—and the pragmatic, democratic, forward-looking mentality of the struggling new nation, which would one day be summed up in that proud emblem: The American Way of Life.

This conflict is no less sharp today. So far the New Shakers have generally been given the benefit of the doubt as just another harmless fringe group. But there is evidence that the mood of the country is changing—and rapidly. Leading educators and political figures, respected clergymen and prominent consumer consultants have all become more outspoken in denouncing the disruptive effect of this new fanaticism on the country as a whole. Not since the heyday of the Bomb-throwers in the late seventies has a single issue shown such potential for galvanizing informed public opinion. And a chorus of distraught parents has only just begun to make itself heard—like the lamentations of Rachel in the wilderness.

Faced with the continuing precariousness of the international situation, and the unresolved dilemma of the Ghettoes, some Control authorities have started talking about new restrictions on all monastic sects—not out of any desire to curtail religious freedom but in an effort to preserve the constitutional guarantees of free expression and consumption. Some feel that if swift, firm governmental action is not forthcoming it will get harder and harder to prevent angry parents—and others with legitimate grievances—from taking the law into their own hands.

MORE TO COME

LOOPHOLE
by Arthur C. Clarke

Usually referred to as one of the "Big Three" of Modern Science Fiction (can you guess who the other two are?), Arthur C. Clarke's approximately two dozen sf novels and collections contain some of the most exciting ideas to be found in sf. Most readers are familiar with his great novels like *Childhood's End* (1953) and *The City and the Stars* (1956), but try any of his short story collections—they contain numerous treasurers, like "Loophole," his first professional sale (1946).

LOOPHOLE

From: President.
To: Secretary, Council of Scientists.

I have been informed that the inhabitants of Earth have succeeded in releasing atomic energy and have been making experiments with rocket propulsion. This is most serious. Let me have a full report immediately. And make it *brief* this time.

K.K.IV.

From: Secretary, Council of Scientists.
To: President.

The facts are as follows. Some months ago our instruments detected intense neutron emission from Earth, but an analysis of radio programs gave no explanation at the time. Three days ago a second emission occurred and soon afterwards all radio transmission from Earth announced that atomic bombs were in use in the current war. The translators have not completed their interpretation, but it appears that the bombs are of considerable power. Two have so far been used. Some details of their construction have been released, but the elements concerned have not been identified. A fuller report will be forwarded as soon as possible. For the moment all that is certain is that the inhabitants of Earth *have* liberated atomic power, so far only explosively.

Very little is known concerning rocket research on Earth.

Our astronomers have been observing the planet carefully ever since radio emissions were detected a generation ago. It is certain that long-range rockets of some kind are in existence on Earth, for there have been numerous references to them in recent military broadcasts. However, no serious attempt has been made to reach interplanetary space. When the war ends, it is expected that the inhabitants of the planet may carry out research in this direction. We will pay very careful attention to their broadcasts and the astronomical watch will be rigorously enforced.

From what we have inferred of the planet's technology, it should require about twenty years before Earth develops atomic rockets capable of crossing space. In view of this, it would seem that the time has come to set up a base on the Moon, so that a close scrutiny can be kept on such experiments when they commence.

Trescon.

(Added in manuscript.)

The war on Earth has now ended, apparently owing to the intervention of the atomic bomb. This will not affect the above arguments but it may mean that the inhabitants of Earth can devote themselves to pure research again more quickly than expected. Some broadcasts have already pointed out the application of atomic power to rocket propulsion.

T.

From: President.
To: Chief of Bureau of Extra-Planetary Security. (C.B.E.P.S.).

You have seen Trescon's minutes.

Equip an expedition to the satellite of Earth immediately. It is to keep a close watch on the planet and to report at once if rocket experiments are in progress.

The greatest care must be taken to keep our presence on the Moon a secret. You are personally responsible for this. Report to me at yearly intervals, or more often if necessary.

K.K.IV.

*   *   *

From: President.
To: C.B.E.P.S.
   Where is the report on Earth?!!

K.K.IV.

From: C.B.E.P.S.
To: President.
   The delay is regretted. It was caused by the breakdown of the ship carrying the report.
   There have been no signs of rocket experimenting during the past year, and no reference to it in broadcasts from the planet.

Ranthe.

From: C.B.E.P.S.
To: President.
   You will have seen my yearly reports to your respected father on this subject. There have been no developments of interest for the past seven years, but the following message has just been received from our base on the Moon:
   Rocket projectile, apparently atomically propelled, left Earth's atmosphere today from Northern land-mass, traveling into space for one quarter diameter of planet before returning under control.

Ranthe.

From: President.
To: Chief of State.
   Your comments, please.

K.K. V.

From: Chief of State.
To: President.
   This means the end of our traditional policy.
   The only hope of security lies in preventing the Terrestrials from making further advances in this direction. From what we know of them, this will require some overwhelming threat.
   Since its high gravity makes it impossible to land on the

planet, our sphere of action is restricted. The problem was discussed nearly a century ago by Anvar, and I agree with his conclusions. We must act *immediately* along those lines.

F.K. S.

From: President.
To: Secretary of State.
    Inform the Council that an emergency meeting is convened for noon tomorrow.

K.K.V.

From: President.
To: C.B.E.P.S.
    Twenty battleships should be sufficient to put Anvar's plan into operation. Fortunately there is no need to arm them—yet. Report progress of construction to me weekly.

K.K. V.

From: C.B.E.P.S.
To: President.
    Nineteen ships are now completed. The twentieth is still delayed owing to hull failure and will not be ready for at least a month.

Ranthe.

From: President.
To: C.B.E.P.S.
    Nineteen will be sufficient. I will check the operational plan with you tomorrow. Is the draft of our broadcast ready yet?

K.K.V.

From: C.B.E.P.S.
To: President.
    Draft herewith:
    People of Earth!
    We, the inhabitants of the planet you call Mars, have for many years observed your experiments toward achieving interplanetary travel. *These experiments must cease.* Our

study of your race has convinced us that you are not fitted to leave your planet in the present state of your civilization. The ships you now see floating above your cities are capable of destroying them utterly, and will do so unless you discontinue your attempts to cross space.

We have set up an observatory on your Moon and can immediately detect any violation of these orders. If you obey them, we will not interfere with you again. Otherwise, one of your cities will be destroyed every time we observe a rocket leaving the Earth's atmosphere.

By order of the President and Council of Mars.

Ranthe.

From: President.
To: C.B.E.P.S.

I approve. The translation can go ahead.

I shall not be sailing with the fleet, after all. You will report to me in detail immediately on your return.

K.K. V.

From: C.B.E.P.S.
To: President.

I have the honor to report the successful completion of our mission. The voyage to Earth was uneventful: radio messages from the planet indicated that we were detected at a considerable distance and great excitement had been aroused before our arrival. The fleet was dispersed according to plan and I broadcast the ultimatum. We left immediately and no hostile weapons were brought to bear against us.

I shall report in detail within two days.

Ranthe.

From: Secretary, Council of Scientists.
To: President.

The psychologists have completed their report, which is attached herewith.

As might be expected, our demands at first infuriated this stubborn and high-spirited race. The shock to their pride must have been considerable, for they believed themselves to be the only intelligent beings in the Universe.

However, within a few weeks there was a rather unexpected change in the tone of their statements. They had begun to realize that we were intercepting all their radio transmissions, and some messages have been broadcast directly to us. They state that they have agreed to ban all rocket experiments, in accordance with our wishes. This is as unexpected as it is welcome. Even if they are trying to deceive us, we are perfectly safe now that we have established the second station just outside the atmosphere. They cannot possibly develop spaceships without our seeing them or detecting their tube radiation.

The watch on Earth will be continued rigorously, as instructed.

Trescon.

From: C.B.E.P.S.
To: President.

Yes, it is quite true that there have been no further rocket experiments in the last ten years. We certainly did not expect Earth to capitulate so easily!

I agree that the existence of this race now constitutes a permanent threat to our civilization and we are making experiments along the lines you suggest. The problem is a difficult one, owing to the great size of the planet. Explosives would be out of the question, and a radioactive poison of some kind appears to offer the greatest hope of success.

Fortunately, we now have an indefinite time in which to complete this research, and I will report regularly.

Ranthe.

End of Document

From: Lieutenant Commander Henry Forbes, Intelligence Branch, Special Space Corps.
To: Professor S. Maxton, Philological Department, University of Oxford.
Route: Transender II (via Schenectady).

The above papers, with others, were found in the ruins of what is believed to be the capital Martian city. (Mars Grid KL302895.) The frequent use of the ideograph for "Earth" suggests that they may be of special interest and it is hoped that they can be translated. Other papers will be following shortly.

H. Forbes, Lt./Cdr.

(Added in manuscript.)

Dear Max,

Sorry I've had no time to contact you before. I'll be seeing you as soon as I get back to Earth.

Gosh! Mars *is* a mess! Our co-ordinates were dead accurate and the bombs materialized right over their cities, just as the Mount Wilson boys predicted.

We're sending a lot of stuff back through the two small machines, but until the big transmitter is materialized we're rather restricted, and, of course, none of us can return. So hurry up with it!

I'm glad we can get to work on rockets again. I may be old-fashioned, but being squirted through space at the speed of light doesn't appeal to me!

Yours in haste,

Henry.

LETTERS

NICHE ON THE BULL RUN

SWITCH ON THE BULL RUN

by Sharon Webb

Sharon Webb is a relatively new writer who lives in the beautiful Blue Ridge Mountains of North Georgia with her husband and three daughters. Although she is a registered nurse (and has a book called *When Do I get to Feel Like a Nurse* in press), she is now a full-time writer. In addition to her very funny "Bull Run" stories (two of which follow) she has published numerous other works in the sf and fantasy fields, including "Variation on a Theme from Beethoven," which is included in Donald A. Wollheim's 1981 Annual *World's Best SF*. Her first novel will be published by Atheneum.

NICHE ON THE BULL RUN

Lightship House
Bay of Nevermore
Hyades III 426984721
June 7

Somtow P. Smith, Attorney at Law
Smith, Smith, Smith, and Wu
59 Embassy
Chattlanta, United Earth, Sol 094266741

Dear Mr. Smith:

I, Terra Tarkington, want you to sue the Interstellar Nurses' Corps on my behalf, because I have been grievously wronged and injured by them.

I, a poor innocent girl of Earth (RN by profession), fell into the clutches of the Corps due to the false advertising they put out (deliberately and with malice aforethought) in order to lure me and others to our destruction.

"Join the Interstellar Nurses' Corps and see the Galaxy," they said. Well, believe you me, Mr. Smith, the only part of the galaxy I have seen is Taurus—and if I never see the Bull Run again I would not mourn.

Never complaining, always the professional, I risked life, limb, and sanity for the Corps, but now they have gone too far.

Nowhere in my job description did it state that it was my duty to be eaten by aliens—*nowhere,* Mr. Smith. Furthermore, my contract expressly forbids abandoning me on a hostile world for an indeterminate time, but they did.

I could die here, Mr. Smith.

And if I expire on the desolate face of Hyades III, I want you to sue anyway and send the proceeds to my dear mother, Gladiola Tarkington, who is entitled to recompense for the loss of her only daughter, Terra.

I suppose I ought to tell you all the horrendous details so you can prepare my case while I await my fate at Lightship House.

It all began when Dr. Brian-Scott (who is my beloved) and I were on board ship heading back to Satellite Hospital Outpost. Suddenly, we decelerated so fast that I ended up clamped in the lap of the Aldebaran steward. He was as rude as he could be about the whole thing, hissing and lashing his tail around, and in general making a scene. Now, I ask you, Mr. Smith, if you (through no fault of your own) were impaled against a giant blue Aldebaran lizard, wouldn't you at least expect him to be civil?

Anyway, the reason we decelerated was because of a failure of the navigational beacon on Hyades III. Since the beacon was out, we didn't change course on time. We were on a collision course with one of the Hyadean outworlds until the safeties took over and decelerated us.

Well, nothing else would do the captain except to go back and investigate. So, we tracked in on manual and landed on this awful place.

It was dark. (It's dark most of the time on the Bay of Nevermore.) It was especially dark that night because only one of the moons was up, and because we had landed on the black sands near the Lightship House.

The Lightship House stood all by itself and what moonlight there was glittered on its tower. It was eerie.

Now the tower is supposed to be completely automated, but there was a light shining way up high from a single window. Talk about spooky—I was getting the jits over it until Dr. Brian-Scott said, "The light's there because of an old custom."

He said that back in the dark ages on Earth, people built lighthouses to guide ships that floated on water—and someone actually lived in the lighthouse so as to keep the light going. Can you imagine?

Well, with the mystery gone, it was getting boring on the ship, so Dr. Brian-Scott and I got permission to debark and walk around with the Aldebaran steward while the captain went to the tower to investigate.

That was a mistake. As soon as my feet touched the ground, they sank four or five centimeters. It was *wet* underfoot and the sand gave out a moaning sound at every step. Everything smelled murky.

The Aldebaran steward leaned back on his tail (the way they do when they ponder deeper meanings) and said, "It is-s-s-s-s-strange indeed. We are no more than twenty meter-s-s from the tower. The bay has-s-s never been s-s-so close-s-s."

Well, I didn't see any bay at all. I know it was dark, but if there were a bay around I would have heard it, wouldn't I? And so I asked the steward what he was talking about. It turned out that the Lightship House is at the narrow end of a funnel. When the tide is out, the tower is landlocked, and at high tide the tower stands near the shore of the Bay of Nevermore. At least, that's what it was supposed to do. Now, it seemed from the condition of the black sand that the base of the tower had been flooded—and not too long ago.

It doesn't take a giant intellect to realize that tides that go out come back in. It seemed to me that we were demented to go walking around on what was going to be the bottom of a deep place at any moment. So, I hollered, "Let's run," and started to sprint back to the ship.

In less than a galac-tic, I banged my toe on something in the dark and went flying. I landed face down in that smelly ooze with black sand plastered all over my nose.

Dr. Brian-Scott shined a light on me and said, "Oh, Terra—"

Mr. Smith, has your beloved ever seen you with gooey black sand glopped all over your face? You can imagine how embarrassed I was.

I had tripped over a H'ohDaddi.

I don't suppose you know what a H'ohDaddi is. I didn't

know either. H'ohDaddies are one of the life-forms on Hyades III. In their larval state, they swim in open water. Then they implant in colonies on the inside of the lava tubes that lie around on the bay shallows. When they implant, they grow into something altogether different. They're pink and sort of velvety, and they grow a grotesque toothy maw on one end that acts like a valve.

Just then, the captain came running out of the tower howling like a hound. He had this absolutely hag-ridden look on his face and his cape was flying behind him so that he looked like a maddened bat. He was yelling, "H'ohDaddi, H'ohDaddi, H'ohDaddi, H'oh—H'oh—H'oh. . ."

He ran for the ship, yelping all the way. But, all of a sudden, a rumbling drowned out his voice.

It was the tide. It was coming in *fast*. One moment we were standing on Hyades firma and the next we were boiling around in smelly bay water up to our necks.

I heard an awful strangling sound from Dr. Brian-Scott. "Terra—glug—I can't swim!"

I reached out for him, and he clamped onto my neck like an octopus. Well, we both nearly drowned.

And believe you me, Mr. Smith, it was every being for himself. The Aldebaran steward took off alone, flailing his tail behind him, while Dr. Brian-Scott and I churned off together more dead than alive.

The tide ran incredibly fast, and it was aiming us at the tower.

It's hard for me to relate what happened next. The mind tends to reject certain things. I managed to grab hold of a projection at the base of the tower. For a second I thought we were safe. Then, an awful suction came—a sort of slurp—and Dr. Brian-Scott and I were swallowed up by the tower.

Mr. Smith, can you think what it is to be swallowed up? It isn't pleasant. *Not at all.*

The tower had become a giant H'ohDaddi. And we were headed for its open maw.

It was then that I knew what sheer terror was.

The H'ohDaddi kept sucking, and we went gurgling in on

top of a siphon of water. Then I heard the most sickening sound there is. I heard the maw clamp shut behind us.

Well, you talk about into the jaws of death . . .

We were thrown into what used to be the control room of the tower. We would have been killed by the impact except for the H'ohDaddi. It had grown over every surface so we landed on spongy flesh instead of metal.

As the water drained off, we saw that the H'ohDaddi had even grown over the lights so that they glowed pink. Through them we could see the darker blood vessels.

A lot of other stuff had been sucked in with us—little ghost scuttles ran around our feet; and, as we watched, one ran over a patch of H'ohDaddi that was darker pink than the rest. As soon as it did, some sticky juice squirted up out of the H'ohDaddi and snagged the poor little scuttle.

It was horrendous. As we watched, the scuttle dissolved until there wasn't anything left but its shell.

When that happened, I began to cry and Dr. Brian-Scott took me in his arms and said, "We'll get out of this somehow, Terra."

Well, you talk about a black moment, Mr. Smith. I mean, I have been in lots of fixes, but this was the absolute worst. Here we were, huddled in the rapacious belly—so to speak— of a H'ohDaddi and about to be digested.

The only way out was down. Just below the control room was another room that had been used to store replacement parts for the beacon. Dr. Brian-Scott and I started to crawl down the opening in the middle of the room. What used to be a circular stair was covered with velvety H'ohDaddi.

I went first. I put my foot on the top step. It was cushiony and slicker than greased Pleiadean Pookah poop. My foot went out from under me and I hung balanced on the step long enough to see my life flash before me and then I somersaulted off and landed on my back. I sank up to my nose in folds and folds of H'ohDaddi.

Even though my ears were muffled, I could hear my beloved holler, "Watch out for the dark pink patches, Terra."

I have been in dire straits before, and I would choose the

direst of straits anytime over a H'ohDaddi. I didn't dare move for fear of being dissolved.

All around me I could feel the folds of the H'ohDaddi throbbing. It was a rhythmic pulsing and it made a sound—glub-glop. At every glub, the folds billowed over my nose and nearly smothered me. When it glopped, the folds parted a little so that I could see a dim pink glow.

I began to cry again. It was grossly unfair that I, Terra Tarkington, who had survived plague and pestilence on the Bull Run, was going to spend eternity sunk in a H'ohDaddi crevice, there to waste away to a shadow of my former self.

Then I heard Dr. Brian-Scott yelling, "Terra! Where are you?"

The only time I could answer was when the H'ohDaddi glopped. When it glubbed, I could only rail against my fate and try to keep my nose out of the folds.

After what seemed forever, a light beamed in my eyes, but in a moment the glub shut it off. When the glop came, I reached out to my beloved, through the layers of H'ohDaddi, and he grabbed hold.

Somehow he braced himself and pulled me out of there.

That's when I discovered that the glub-glopping was from the H'ohDaddi's heart. Dr. Brian-Scott shined his light over it. It was a primitive two-chambered heart shaped sort of like a figure eight and buried in pink flesh.

I wanted to get something and kill it then and there so as to save ourselves, but Dr. Brian-Scott said, "Morally, we can't. It's semi-sapient."

That didn't make sense to me. As I saw it, it was the H'ohDaddi or us. If we spared it, *we'd* be the ones who'd end up semi-sapient—or worse.

Then he said, "If we kill it, we'll die too—from the enzymes its cells would release."

Well, that was different. Our only hope was to go down and try and get through the maw somehow.

As we started to go down the center stair, Dr. Brian-Scott said, "Look there." He was shining his light on a sort of niche on the far side of the room. It was a shelf as big as a bed and covered with cushiony H'ohDaddi. Along the wall and extending onto the niche were these grayish swellings. As we watched, they pulsed slightly. "It's the H'ohDaddi's nervous system," he said.

Well, it didn't do *my* nervous system much good to see that. The H'ohDaddi's brain was *big*. There were chains and chains of those gray things creeping up the wall.

He stepped along the floor, watching out for the dark pink patches, and touched the H'ohDaddi brain; and he wanted me to touch it too!

It's hard to describe what H'ohDaddi brain is like, but it wasn't horrible like I thought it would be. It was interesting (if anything can be interesting when you are in the clutches of death) and it felt sort of like a jelly-bed covered in velvet.

I thought it behooved us not to stand around patting the brain, so we started down again. Not much light filtered down at all. It got darker and darker as we descended into the bowels of the H'ohDaddi.

We slipped and slid down, and the going got more hazardous. Nearly every place Dr. Brian-Scott shined his light showed those dark pink digestive patches. We could see ghost shuttle shells everywhere and little silver jelly-floats turning into puddles.

It was then that I really got scared. I could see us—nothing but bones-gristle for the H'ohDaddi's mill. To be consumed by a H'ohDaddi seemed to me to be the grisliest of fates, so I began to hurry.

When we reached the maw, I knew how Jonah must have felt. It was clamped completely shut. The H'ohDaddi's needle teeth were intermeshed in a giant O.

Dr. Brian-Scott tapped on the teeth and they clinked, but nothing moved. It is said that iron bars do not a prison make. Whoever wrote that didn't know about H'ohDaddi teeth. They were more like strainers than teeth actually. They're hinged to open inward when the tide comes in. Then they clamp shut when the H'ohDaddi is filled. The water strains out and leaves everything else inside for the digestive patches, which is interesting to note if you can be objective about your fate, but it isn't easy to be objective when you're what's been left inside.

All of a sudden we heard something. It was coming from outside very muffled and faint. "A–r–e y–o–u i–n t–h–e–r–e?"

Dr. Brian-Scott and I looked at each other, and then we both started hollering and yelling. My heart literally leaped for joy. We were going to be rescued.

Then the voice (I think it was the captain) said, "I–m l–e–a–v–i–n–g y–o–u a p–o–u–c–h."

Then he said something else, but we couldn't make it out, so we yelled, "What?"

And he said, "T–h–e t–i–d–e i–s c–o–m–i–n–g i–n."

Well, you talk about dashed hopes. We had to make a mad scramble back up the tower to the control room so we wouldn't be drowned.

We barely got to the heart-brain room when a column of water came swooshing in that lifted us back up to the control room, and bobbing around with us was the waterproof pouch the captain had left outside the H'ohDaddi's maw.

After we got our breath, we opened it. There was some food and water inside, some tools, dry clothes, and a little radio. I fished the radio out, turned it on, and said, "H'ohDaddi to ship, this is Terra Tarkington. Do you read me?"

It crackled and hissed and then the ship answered with the awfulest news that I have ever heard.

They said (I still can't believe it) that they were waiting for us to rescue them. For *us* to rescue *them!* Can you imagine?

Hyades III is apparently the earthquake capital of the Bull Run. The reason the base of the Tower was flooding was because a quake sometime back had shunted the bay inland.

When the tide swept us up the tower, part of the noise we'd heard was the ship settling as a result of a minor quake. Now, the sensors indicated that a new quake—a big one— was going to strike in less than twenty earth-hours.

And the ship was disabled—stuck in a quagmire on the bay bottom. It was up to us to get the beacon working and send out a distress signal.

When he heard that, Dr. Brian-Scott said, "Well, Terra, I guess we're done for." And when he said that, he looked so defeated, so utterly hopeless, that my inner organs throbbed in grief for him.

It was bad enough to be savaged and devoured by the H'ohDaddi, but now it looked like we were going to die. I couldn't bear to think of our beautiful relationship ending like this so I said, "We've got to try. Maybe we can peel the H'ohDaddi away from the window and jump out or something."

He brightened up at that. We pulled all the tools out of the pouch and set to work.

That was hours ago. And now I'm exhausted. Mr. Smith, you don't know what grim is until you've tried to peel a H'ohDaddi. You wouldn't *believe* how tenacious it is. About the time you think you've got a chunk loose, it sends out these sticky globs and glues itself back to the wall.

It was as if the H'ohDaddi had a mind of its own. On reflection, I suppose it has, being semi-sapient. Anyway, I have come to the conclusion that there is no way known to man to peel a H'ohDaddi that doesn't want to be peeled.

So now I'm sitting on the niche in the heart-brain room dictating this letter by radio to the ship's computer.

Before I shuffle off this mortal coil, it is my desire, Mr. Smith, that the Interstellar Nurses' Corps be sorry that they reduced me to this fate.

And it is my opinion that they would be sorriest if we sued the pants off them, because only then would they see the error of their ways and cease and desist sacrificing poor innocent girls to the horrors of the Bull Run.

I have to go now, Mr. Smith. The tide is coming in.

　　　Yours in extremis,

　　　　　　　　　　　　　　　　Terra Tarkington

　　　　　　　　　　　Satellite Hospital Outpost
　　　　　　　　　　　　Taurus 14, North Horn
　　　　　　　　　　　　Nath Orbit, 978675644
　　　　　　　　　　　　　　　　　　June 9

Somtow P. Smith, Attorney at Law
Smith, Smith, Smith, and Wu
59 Embassy
Chattlanta, United Earth, Sol 094266741

Dear Mr. Smith:

Upon reconsideration, I have decided to spare the Interstellar Nurses' Corps from the full wrath of the law. After all, they mean well even though they are somewhat misguided; therefore, I am withdrawing my suit against them.

When the tide came in again, Dr. Brian-Scott and I huddled in the control room and contemplated our fate. The more we'd tried to peel the H'ohDaddi, the tighter it clung to the walls. It was the stubbornest creature I ever saw.

We were sunk in the depths of misery when, like a bolt out of the blue (to coin a phrase), I conceived my brilliant idea.

"If only we could distract it," I said, "take its mind off what we're doing."

When Dr. Brian-Scott heard that, he got a gleam in his eye, and he said, "Terra, you're brilliant." Then he leaped up and said, "Peel, Terra. Peel."

He simply *scrabbled* at the H'ohDaddi—the part that grew over the control panel. He was like a man possessed.

Well, I didn't see what the point was. We'd tried all that before and the H'ohDaddi simply wouldn't stay peeled.

"It doesn't have to, Terra. Except long enough for us to connect the current." And all the time he was talking, he was panting and tugging at the H'ohDaddi section and pulling it away from the panel.

I helped. We managed to keep it pulled loose long enough to connect a long electrical cable to the console and for Dr. Brian-Scott to set the controls. As soon as he did, the H'ohDaddi settled back on the console, with nothing but the cable sticking out.

I didn't understand it at all. I mean, did he plan to electrocute the H'ohDaddi? And what about the lethal enzymes the H'ohDaddi would give out?

"I've rigged a trickle charge, Terra. We aren't going to electrocute it at all. We're going to make it happy."

It was obvious to me that my poor beloved had finally become unhinged due to the strain. With a heavy heart, I realized that I would be spending my last hours with a madman who was bent on gratifying a H'ohDaddi.

We hauled the cable out to the middle of the room and then

down the stairs—slipping and sliding all the way—to the heart-brain room.

Then he crawled up on the niche where the nervous system was and began to probe around with the cable wires. He kept muttering, "We've got to find it."

I was completely mystified. "Find what?"

"Its pleasure center. We *are* going to distract it, Terra."

It's an amazing thing, Mr. Smith, but when you stimulate the pleasure center of a H'ohDaddi, you know it. It leaves absolutely no doubt in your mind. One moment we were on our knees to the niche probing around the gray chains of nervous tissue and the next—Well, the whole niche was literally throbbing with delight—we could feel it.

We looked at each other and grinned. We couldn't help it. Then Dr. Brian-Scott said, "Come on, Terra."

We went back up to the control room. This time when we pulled the H'ohDaddi away from the panel, limp with pleasure as it was, it simply fell away.

Even so, it took a long time to reset the beacon and rig the distress signal to summon a rescue ship. It was *tiring*, Mr. Smith. So, when we were finished, it was perfectly natural for us to want a little rest.

Well, the obvious place was the niche in the heart-brain room, wasn't it? I mean it was wide and soft and a whole lot safer than the rest of the H'ohDaddi.

Stretched out together there, it seemed to us that the H'ohDaddi was grateful. It seemed to be inviting us to share in its joy.

I can't express to you, Mr. Smith, how explicitly *blissful* a happy H'ohDaddi can be.

After a while, we felt a breeze and then we heard a voice bellow out from below, "A–r–e y–o–u i–n t–h–e–r–e? T–h–e m–a–w i–s o–p–e–n." Which goes to show how distracted the H'ohDaddi was.

So I said, "I guess we should escape now."

And Dr. Brian-Scott said, "I suppose so." And then he said, "When's the next high tide, Terra?"

"Not for two hours."

And then he said, "We've got plenty of time."

Well, goodness knows as debilitated as we were, we needed to rest before we crawled down out of the H'ohDaddi, didn't we? I mean, it was only logical.

When we came out, my beloved was bursting with plans. First, he said he was going to write a paper for the Galactic Medical Journal entitled: "Artificial Stimulation of the Neurological Pleasure Center of the Hyadean H'ohDaddi and Its Effects on Contiguous Homo Sapiens."

By the time the rescue ship came in response to our distress signal, he had designed the plans for a special biological sleep center using a H'ohDaddi and a small power pack. He feels it has therapeutic value.

Sweet are the uses of adversity.

Therapeutically yours,

Terra Tarkington

SWITCH ON THE BULL RUN

Transcript of a deposition taken by the Royal Hyadean Police and Militia from T. Tarkington, RN, regarding the charges brought for and by the Hyadean Alliance against her; i.e., the capital offense of Mind Switch:

DEPUTY SERVO: *Please state your name, occupation, and place of residence.*

My name is Terra Tarkington. I am a registered nurse with the Interstellar Nurses' Corps. My permanent base is Satellite Hospital Outpost, Taurus 14, North Horn, Nath Orbit; and I'm temporarily on duty at MediStation Far Out, Hyades IV. And the charges are not true. They're simply not true.

If you want to claim that I am guilty of malpractice or even practicing veterinary medicine without a license, I could understand that. But you're accusing me of Mind Switch and—

DEPUTY SERVO: *Tell us now what transpired with the aggrieved and injured Honorable Kronto.*

How was I to know that the patient was the ambassador from Hyades II? I thought he was a family pet.

Nobody told me he was Ambassador Kronto. Nobody told me anything.

I was sent here to minister to the diseased and disadvantaged of the Hyades IV Far Out. You've got to admit these people need all the medical help they can get. They're virtual pariahs. If you don't live in the main hives of Hyades II, you're just a forgotten soul. Mired by life into a muddy existence. Sunk into a quagmire of adversity. Swallowed up by—

DEPUTY SERVO: *Would you please confine your remarks to the charge of Mind Switch, and to the patient in question?*

Well! Anyway, these Hyadeans from the Far Out came to the MediStation where I work. My position is Prime Clinician. I check out all the patients first and then teletape to Dr. Brian-Scott for anything I can't handle. And I want to tell you, it requires a lot of me. It's not easy giving first care to the poor and downtrodden of the Far Out. If I weren't the dedicated professional that I am, I could tell you stories that would curl your hair—if you had any hair. Why—

DEPUTY SERVO: *Could we please continue with your version of your encounter with the ambassador?*

You *don't* have to be rude.

DEPUTY SERVO: *Apologies. Please continue.*

Well, that morning a group of Far Outs came to the MediStation. They were really excited, but I didn't know what they were talking about; none of them spoke Standard.

They were carrying the cutest little animal that you ever saw. He was just a *mop* of silvery wool, with an enormous gold medallion around his neck. I had no idea that he was Ambassador Kronto. I absolutely had no frame of reference. I have studied Alien Physiology and there was *nothing* like Ambassador Kronto on any of the tapes.

Besides, even if I *had* known, I would have done the same thing. Wouldn't you? The poor little thing was suffering. He had a sore paw.

I just can't bear to see animals suffer. I've always been that way, ever since I was a little girl. Once when I was eleven I—

DEPUTY SERVO: *You were telling us about Ambassador Kronto.*

He looked a lot like a long-haired kangaroo. I don't suppose you know what a kangaroo looks like. The ambassador was sitting on his haunches. He raised one of his front paws to me; it was almost like he was greeting me. That's when I noticed how swollen it was. The other paw looked normal.

That is, I suppose it was normal, but the paw he raised—it was his right paw—was in awful shape. It hurt me to look at it.

He didn't whimper at all, not a sound. Well, I *had* to do something didn't I? So, I sprayed his paw with Edemalyse.

How was I supposed to know that the people of Hyades II are telepaths? I mean, it is a ridiculous assumption to expect me to know that his right paw was a hypertrophied esper organ. If I'd known that, I'd never have tried to bring down the swelling.

It wasn't much later that I found out Ambassador Kronto was on a tour of inspection of the Far Out. But he *was* in pain. They told me later he had a frightful headache.

DEPUTY SERVO: *What happened then?*

It was awful. He started shaking his little paw—the fat one—and he stared at it in the most *intense* way. Then his mouth turned down at the corners and his chin began to quiver. He seemed so distressed that I wasn't sure what to do. So I patted him on the head and said, "There, boy."

DEPUTY SERVO: *You patted the ambassador on the head?*

I was trying to comfort him. I didn't know that he had a headache, then. I didn't know either that it was considered obscene to touch the ambassador's head.

After I patted him, his eyes got all squinty, and his chin worked up and down more than ever. Then—my heart bled—he took his paw, the one that wasn't swollen, and he rubbed the top of his head in the most pitiful way. His little paws are short and he had to tuck his head down so he could reach it. It would make you weep to see it.

That's when I put him in the telescanner.

I punched the signal for Dr. Brian-Scott on board the Outpost. I knew I wasn't supposed to use the scanner for animals (I'm not supposed to treat animals at all), but it seemed like an emergency.

Dr. Brian-Scott's face came on the viewer and he said, "What have you got, Terra?"

And I said, "I know it's against the rules, but please take a look at this little fellow."

Well, it was obvious that Dr. Brian-Scott had never seen anyone from Hyades II either, because when he saw him he said, "Isn't he cute. Turn on the scanner, Terra. I'll see what I can do."

So I turned it on. Then, in about twenty seconds, all the screens went blank. There sat the ambassador, but with the screens blank, there wasn't anything more to do, so I gave him back to the Far Outs.

Well, you never heard such a commotion. All the Far Outs got these awful expressions on their faces, and they had the most unpleasant curve to the creases where their noses ought to be.

Then they called the police and I was brought here. So, obviously that ridiculous charge of Mind Switch is untrue. All I did was spray his paw and pat his head.

DEPUTY SERVO: *Are you aware that Ambassador Kronto's mind now resides in the body of Dr. Brian-Scott?*

What?

What about Dr. Brian-Scott? Where is *his* mind? Where *is* it?

DEPUTY SERVO: *Dr. Brian-Scott's mind is now in the much-abused body of Ambassador Kronto.*

My beloved? In there? Oh. Oh, no. Oh, no it really can't be so. Tell me it can't be so.

DEPUTY SERVO: *It is so. Is there any further testimony that you wish to give at this time?*

. . .I think I'd better have a lawyer now.

DEPUTY SERVO: *Explain the term, please.*

Lawyer, advocate, counselor. Attorney, solicitor, barrister. Somebody to *help* me.

DEPUTY SERVO: *The terms do not scan. Somebody-to-help-me scans. Mind Switch is a capital offense. Are you requesting a priest?*

I want to see a lawyer. I want to see the Sol Ambassador . . . I want to go home.

Sol Embassy
Central Hive
Hyades IV 875645333 Hyades
April 2

Terra Tarkington
Central Hive Incarceratum
Hyades IV 875645333 Hyades

Dear Miss Tarkington:

Ambassador Blasingame has asked me to answer your letter. The ambassador has also requested that I bring to your attention several things. Perhaps you are not aware of the delicate interstellar politics that are at stake in this matter.

Ambassador Kronto is the envoy of an emerging planet. Their ways are not our ways, Miss Tarkington. The people of Hyades II are warlike. As such, they must be treated with utmost diplomacy until they mature enough to learn that finesse is the better part of aggression.

It would seem that you, Miss Tarkington, have created an interstellar incident.

Although Ambassador Blasingame is sympathetic to your plight he regrets that there is very little he can do to help you. Any intervention on his part would be interpreted as an affront to the people of Hyades II.

As to your request for defense council, it is obvious that you have little knowledge of the laws of the Hyadean Alliance. In a capital case, the Alliance brings all its forces to bear upon the defendant, while the defendant stands alone. If the defendant can convince the triumvirate of his or her innocence, all is well. If not—

I'm terribly sorry, Miss Tarkington.

With regrets, I remain

Sincerely yours,
Layton Chung, Embassy Aide

April 3
900 Hours

Dear Diary,

The tragic and heroic figures of earth have always kept journals during their imprisonment, so I will too.

Future generations should know of the cruel fate of Terra

Tarkington, unjustly accused, imprisoned, and separated from her lover who is shackled in the body of a silver kangaroo.

Poor, beautiful Dr. Brian-Scott. My spleen throbs with grief. If only I could go to him. If only I could get out of here.

I'm going to try.

1100 hours

Do you know what you get when you try to escape from a Hyadean incarceratum? Skinned knees.

April 4
1400 hours

Dear Diary,

My trial begins tomorrow. The deputy servo tells me that Ambassador Kronto doesn't have to be there. He's holed up in the Sol Embassy next door. They're keeping him there because the facilities are better for his bodily needs.

I can see the embassy through the power mesh cell window. And if I had wings and were no wider than 5 microns, I'd be out of here in a flash.

The deputy servo tells me that Ambassador Kronto hasn't spoken a word since the Mind Switch. He says that's probably because the ambassador didn't have any vocal cords in his own body and so doesn't know how to use them now.

Dr. Brian-Scott, my beloved, was brought down from the outpost. He's being kept at the Hyades II Embassy, and I don't know *where* that is. Will he ever forgive me?

He probably wouldn't speak to me, even if he *had* vocal cords. Oh, Diary, I couldn't bear his silent scorn. I couldn't stand to see his whiskers twitch with contempt when he looked at me.

Better . . . death.

EXCERPT FROM THE TRANSCRIPT OF THE TRIAL OF TERRA TARKINGTON:

PROSECUTOR: Let us consider the plight of the aggrieved Ambassador Kronto. He, on a good-will mission to our planet, innocently arrives to inspect the Far Out Medi-Station, when he is wantonly attacked by this person [*indicating the defendant*].

TARKINGTON: I did *not* attack him. You [*indicating the prosecutor*] are lying. I—

PROSECUTOR: This person [*indicating the defendant*] did seize the ambassador, whereupon she sprayed a dangerous chemical on his esper organ, thereby causing an immediate malfunction.

TARKINGTON: It was for swelling. I thought he had swelling. I—

PROSECUTOR: Not content with the assault on Ambassador Kronto's esper organ, this person [*indicating the defendant*] maliciously and obscenely stroked the ambassador's head, thus aggravating his headache and causing him no end of public shame. Knowing Ambassador Kronto to be at a serious disadvantage due to his crippled esper organ and his incapacitating headache, this person [*indicating the defendant*] thrust the helpless ambassador into a dangerous machine.

We can only guess what diabolical thoughts ran through her mind at that time, but one thing is certain—this person [*indicating the defendant*] was possessed by malice ... Malice that drove her to commit upon the vulnerable and injured Ambassador Kronto, *Mind Switch*.

April 6
LAST WILL AND TESTAMENT OF TERRA TARKINGTON:

I, being of sound mind, do hereby declare the following disposition of my belongings in expectation of my imminent, tragic, and unfair demise.

To my dearest friend and confidante, Carmelita O'Hare-Mbotu, I leave my nursing library, my new make-up set, my Hyadean Snuggie, and all the rest of my clothes (except for my new green slither which I look especially good in, and which is to be my burial outfit). These I leave to her on the condition that she never, *ever* join the Interstellar Nurses' Corps and go among aliens where she will be accused and insulted and probably executed.

To my beloved mother, Gladiola Tarkington, I leave the proceeds of my insurance policy (payable upon my death), and my locket that Daddy gave me, and my journal which is to be published immediately to tell the peoples of Earth of the tragic demise of Terra Tarkington and the grossly unfair and horrendous events leading up to it.

To Dr. Brian-Scott, I leave my love, and my apologies for the fix he is in, and my surro-wool mittens to keep his little paws warm.

To all my other friends, I leave my love and kind thoughts, and my hope that they will remember the unfortunate Terra Tarkington.

Signed: *Terra Tarkington*
Witness: 0080924 Deputy Servo

April 7
900 hours

Dear Diary,

I am to be executed at 600 hours tomorrow. This is really unbelievable. Somehow, I know that Fate will intervene in my darkest hour.

The Deputy Servo isn't as sure. What he said was, "Impossible."

The Deputy Servo also told me I have one last request. The last request doesn't include release.

Everybody from the ship has been trying to help, but they're not allowed to see me. The Deputy Servo says there isn't anything they can do.

Layton Chung, the Sol Embassy aide, came a while ago though. It was an absolutely grotesque scene. He said he had come to give me comfort and then he read *poetry* to me! He said, "*. . . any man's death diminishes me, because I am involved in mankind.*"

I was furious. If my death diminishes *him*, what does he think it does to *me?* I called the Deputy Servo and had him put out. He kept on reading as he left, "*. . . never send to* know for whom the bell tolls." When the door clanged shut, I could still hear him say, "*. . . It tolls for thee-e-e.*"

I hope no one else tries to comfort me.

I have decided on my last request. I want to see beautiful Dr. Brian-Scott one more time. I know he doesn't look like himself, but I've got to see him.

One more time, my beloved. Then—into the gaping jaws of death.

April 8
600 hours

Dear Diary,

When Dr. Brian-Scott came hopping in to see me on my eve of destruction, my heart swelled—it became literally edematous with emotion, and I began to cry.

He hopped up to me, and I leaned over and picked him up and sat him on my lap. He patted my face with his little paw and then he laid his long ears against my cheek and snuggled closer, with his big gold medallion pressing against my chest.

I had been so sure that he could help me, but seeing him there, so little and helpless-looking, shredded my last hope.

If only he could talk to me. If only we could put our heads together for a few minutes.

I touched his paw—the swollen one. I realized that in among the silver hairs were little tendrils. The esper organ—

Before I could even think about it, I fell in! I mean, in one moment the "me" who was holding Dr. Brian-Scott on her lap became the "me" who was floating around in an enormous place like a cavern.

And somebody else was in there—beautiful Dr. Brian-Scott.

Well, you talk about a meeting of the minds!

And then something happened that I can only dimly describe—we merged. We flowed in and out and then *merged* for a second or two. At first it was music, and then it was vanilla, and after that it was warm water and roses. And it was so intimate, so delicious, that I wanted to stay there forever. It was altogether the nicest thing that had ever happened to me.

But it didn't last.

We floated apart, and gradually I realized that I was in the ambassador's kangaroo body, but Dr. Brian-Scott was in there too and there wasn't room enough for both of us.

Suddenly, I remembered my upcoming execution. I guess I panicked. I know it was wicked and vile of me, but I couldn't help it. I pushed. I pushed Dr. Brian-Scott clean out, and into my own body.

I had only one thought at the time. I thought, "Now I've done it! I really *have* committed Mind Switch."

Dr. Brian-Scott gave out one little shriek and subsided into shocked silence.

I looked out of the ambassador's eyes at Dr. Brian-Scott. There he sat, hair all tousled, tears running down, prison pallor, skinned knees. I wondered what he ever saw in me.

But I didn't have any time to stand around wondering. I had to do something, and quick, to get us out of this mess. And the best way to do that, it seemed to me, was to throw myself on the mercy of Ambassador Kronto.

I tried to tell Dr. Brian-Scott not to worry, but nothing happened. I felt my throat work up and down and my mouth opened and closed, but nothing came out, so I winked at him. Then I put my paw on the button that called the Deputy Servo.

Dr. Brian-Scott never said a word when the Servo came. I guess he was being chivalrous; it broke my heart.

I hopped out behind the Servo. In a minute, I was outside.

It's hard to describe hopping. It's a little like being on springs. I think it might have been fun except for the seriousness of the occasion and the awful headache I had. Every leap I took jarred my head—or rather the ambassador's head—into a lump of pain. And that ridiculous heavy medallion didn't help at all. It thudded against my chest until I felt bruised.

I hopped onto the Sol Embassy grounds and stopped for a minute. I suppose the lights of the Terran display were beautiful, but I had other things on my mind, and my head was splitting.

Suddenly, it occurred to me that maybe that huge gold medallion was the cause of the headache. I don't know a thing about the ambassador's internal anatomy, but it was obvious that I had bones; and where there are bones, there must be one or more spines. I was willing to bet that the ambassador's medallion was putting traction on his cervical spine and causing irritation to the nerves in his neck.

No wonder I had a headache.

I tried to pull the necklace off, but I couldn't, my paws were too short. I tugged and tugged at it with the little stubby digits that oozed out of the paws when they were needed, but it was no use.

Finally, I tried standing on my head. The idea was to let it slip off by gravity, which is all very well and good, but did you ever try standing on your head when your paws are too short to reach the ground? Well, I got around it by digging a little hole. I hung my head in it, pushed off with my hind feet, and hoisted my haunches in the air. After some determined wiggling, the medallion fell off.

I didn't know what to do with it; I didn't have any pockets in my fur. So, I buried it.

Then, I hopped into the embassy. Nobody paid any attention to me. (I guess they're used to seeing all kinds in embassies.)

I punched info, located the guest suite, and went up. Already my headache was beginning to fade.

When I got outside Ambassador Kronto's room, I heard voices. One of them was the unmistakable voice of Dr. Brian-Scott. The other one was female—and it was giggling.

The little digits came out of my paw and closed on the door catch. I pushed and the door slid noiselessly open.

I was shocked!

There was the ambassador, wearing Dr. Brian-Scott's body, whispering lewd suggestions into this human girl's ear.

He'd known how to use those vocal cords all along! And from the looks of things, that wasn't the only part of Dr. Brian-Scott that the ambassador knew how to use.

I hopped into the room. The girl saw me first. She gave a little breathy shriek and ran out trailing her clothes behind her.

The ambassador looked sheepish.

I held up my paw—the one with the esper organ. I tried to talk through it, but Dr. Brian-Scott's body just didn't have the apparatus to receive.

Well, there was no help for it. I hopped closer and held up my esper organ again. I didn't know how to do that "meeting of the minds" thing exactly, but in the absence of electrical amplification, it seemed necessary to be close.

We fell in together.

It was the cavern again, but so *different*. I'd never *ever* come that close to an alien mind before. It had *tendrils*. And they wrapped all around my "me." And they *sucked* . . .

Then it was over. Somehow, the ambassador knew all about me, and about how I am basically good and kind and well-intentioned. And about how I only wanted to help his swollen paw. And how I had cured his headache.

And I knew all about him! About how when he switched with Dr. Brian-Scott he could have switched back easily, but it was the first time he had been without a headache in years. About how it was his first *real* vacation in ages. And how he had grown to simply *love* being in Dr. Brian-Scott's body. And how he used it in a *most* immoral fashion. And how he liked things exactly as they were now.

Well, I was furious. I made little tendrils of *my* mind and I grabbed hold of the ambassador and I *pinched*. I told him what I thought of him until he cringed. "How would *you* like to be awaiting execution knowing that you were innocent and wronged?"

I pinched harder. "Aren't you ashamed, Ambassador? Aren't you? I even cured your headache and that's the thanks I get. You are a low, unprincipled body snatcher. A murderer! A thief . . ."

It worked.

The ambassador was actually ashamed of himself.

He said since I had cured his headache, he'd agree to switch us all back on one condition, so he zapped back into his kangaroo body and I slid into Dr. Brian-Scott's—which was a very weird sensation—and we went back to the prison.

In the cell, Ambassador Kronto held up his paw and Dr. Brian-Scott and the ambassador and I jostled around together for a moment and then we fell back into our proper bodies.

As I write this, Dr. Brian-Scott and the ambassador have gone off to effect my release. So there's nothing more to tell you, Diary.

Except for one thing—the condition the ambassador insisted on. He wants to switch again sometime. He liked it.

If we do, that means that Dr. Brian-Scott and I will get to mind-merge again.

And I don't think I'd mind that at all.

PUBLISH AND PERISH
by Paul J. Nahin

Paul J. Nahin is an Associate Professor of Electrical and Computer Engineering at the University of New Hampshire who will be spending the 1981–82 academic year as a visiting professor (and reading sf) on the electronic warfare faculty at the Naval Postgraduate School at Monterey, California. Several dozen of his always interesting stories and articles have graced the pages of *Analog, Omni, The Twilight Zone,* and other magazines.

"Publish and Perish" was his first science fiction sale, and it was (and is) a fine one.

Publish and Perish

March 17, 1977

Mr. Thomas W. Starr
3613 Laguna Avenue
La Mesa, California 92041

Dear Mr. Starr,

It is with pleasure that I welcome you to the Faculty of the California Technological Institute. Dean Johnson has informed me that you have accepted the appointment of Instructor in Physics. Your title will change to Assistant Professor upon completion of your doctoral studies.

We look forward to seeing you in September.

Sincerely,

W. Alden Smith

Dr. W. Alden Smith
Office of the President

May 3, 1977

Mr. Thomas W. Starr
3613 Laguna Avenue
La Mesa, California 92041

Dear Tom,
    President Smith has asked me to write to you about an
issue we wish to have clear, before you arrive on campus in
September. Your appointment is for two years (renewable),
but you must receive your Ph.D. by December 1, of your
second academic year with us. Otherwise, because of the
Institute's bylaws, we would be unable to recommend your
reappointment to the Trustees.

Sincerely,

Pete

Peter V. Johnson, Ph.D.
Office of the Dean

May 8, 1977

Dr. Peter V. Johnson
Dean of Engineering and Science
California Technological Institute
Claremont, California 91711

Dear Dean Johnson,
    The completion of my doctorate by December 1, 1978 will
be no problem. I have talked this matter over, at some
length, with my dissertation advisor, Professor B. B. Abernathy at San Diego Tech. He assures me there will be no
difficulty. He is even joking about there being a Nobel Prize
in it for the two of us!

Cordially,

Thomas W. Starr

Thomas W. Starr

September 9, 1977

Mr. Thomas W. Starr
1713 12th Street
Claremont, California 91711

Dear Tom,

Sorry we missed our regular meeting last week, but I couldn't skip the review briefing on my grant at the Pentagon (but the thought of the agony of the red-eye flight to DC almost made it worthwhile to cancel out). While losing my way wandering around the Puzzle Palace, I happened to mention some of your most recent results toward inducing nuclear fusion in water, and it caused quite a stir. If you get tired of teaching in Claremont, give the Civil Service a thought—you can't believe some of the nitwits with GS-12 and 13 ratings they've got back there. A good man like you would get snapped right up, and it certainly beats what they pay young, new college teachers.

See you next week, and we will discuss the first draft of your thesis.

Regards,

Bert

Bertram B. Abernathy, Ph.D.
Professor of Physics

14 October 1977

Mr. Thomas W. Starr
Physics Department
California Technical Institute
Claremont, California 91711

Dear Mr. Starr,

It has recently come to our attention that you have been pursuing innovative concepts on the possibility of introducing nuclear fusion in water. Your doctoral research support is funded through an Army Office of Scientific Research grant to Professor B. B. Abernathy, and as you know, we retain the right to request periodic reviews of research supported by us.

Professor Abernathy has informed us that you are now writing a thesis for open publication, based on your work. Please send three (3) copies of your draft to:

> Colonel Andrew Bobble
> Chief, Nuclear Security
> Review Office (Army)
> The Pentagon
> Washington, DC 20310
> Sincerely,

Patricia Adams

> Patricia Adams
> Administrative Assistant
> Nuclear Security Review
> Office (Army)

7 January 1978

Mr. Thomas W. Starr
Physics Department
California Technological Institute
Claremont, California 91711

Dear Mr. Starr,

After a careful study of the material you recently sent to us for review, we have classified it. Please forward all additional copies of your thesis drafts, plus any other related documents, within ten days, by registered mail in a sealed envelope within a sealed envelope.

> Sincerely,

Andrew Bobble

> Colonel Andrew Bobble
> Chief, Nuclear Security
> Review Office (Army)

January 11, 1978

Colonel Andrew Bobble
Chief, Nuclear Security Review Office (Army)
The Pentagon
Washington, DC 20310

Dear Colonel Bobble,
   I have read your letter to me of January 7, and I am at a
loss to understand what you mean by "classifying" my Ph.D.
dissertation. I have no security clearance, and at no time
have I had access to classified information.
   I am sure that any little details in my writing that might
cause some concern by your office will be easy for me to work
around. If you will send me a list of the particular issues in
question, I will be glad to take them into consideration as I
finish up my writing.

                         Sincerely,

                         Thomas W. Starr

                         Thomas W. Starr

                    20 January 1978

Mr. Thomas W. Starr
Physics Department
California Technological Institute
Claremont, California 91711

Dear Mr. Starr,
   This letter is to inform you that there is no appeal from our
decision to classify the draft material you recently sent to us.
It is our final conclusion that there is no possible way to
rewrite this material to eliminate the possibility of disclosing
information vital to the national security of the United
States. We cannot transmit the list requested in your letter
because such a list would be classified, and you have no
clearance.

To discuss this matter further, it will be necessary for you to obtain a clearance from the Defense Industrial Security Corporation (at your personal expense), and to travel to Washington to meet with our staff. Even if you decide to do this, we must receive all information still in your possession.

Sincerely,

Colonel Andrew Bobble
Chief, Nuclear Security
Review Office (Army)

January 25, 1978

Colonel Andrew Bobble
Chief, Nuclear Security Review Office (Army)
The Pentagon
Washington, DC 20310

Dear Colonel Bobble,

I can't believe this! You are destroying my career with all this Catch-22 crap about national security leaks that you can't tell me about because I don't have a clearance.

I have looked into getting a clearance, too. The DISCO investigation fee is $4,000! I haven't got forty bucks.

How did you get to be a Colonel? Thinking up stupid things like this? Well, you can go to hell! What I think up on my time, with my brain, is none of the Pentagon's damn business. I will finish my writing, publish it, and the Army can go screw itself.

Sincerely,

Thomas W. Starr

February 1, 1978

Mr. Thomas W. Starr
Physics Department
California Technological Institute
Claremont, California 91711

Dear Mr. Starr,
   In response to your letter of 25 January, enclosed is a copy
of Title 18 of the United States Espionage and Sabotage Acts.
Release of classified information is a felony offense, punish-
able by up to ten years in prison, or up to a $10,000 fine, or
both.
   We are instructing University Microfilms not to produce
microfilm xerographic copies of any unauthorized thesis you
attempt to submit. In addition, we have notified all domestic
and international journals of physics and/or chemistry that
publication of papers by you, without any prior release, may
constitute a security violation.
   Please submit all documents on your research to us, as
requested earlier, postmarked no later than 15 February
1978.

                         Sincerely,

                         Colonel Andrew Bobble
                         Chief, Nuclear Security
                         Review Office (Army)

                    February 10, 1978

Colonel Andrew Bobble
Chief, Nuclear Security Review Office (Army)
The Pentagon
Washington, DC 20310

Dear Andy,
   Enclosed are all the documents you have requested from

Tom Starr. I am taking care of all the details of transferring the water fusion work to secure, classified areas as Tom is in no shape, emotionally, to do it himself.

I know you understand the reason for his recent intemperate letter to you. He has even cut off his contacts with me, but I think he will come around in time. I am confident of his ultimate discretion and loyalty.

I am pretty sure I can handle the new classified work on water fusion for your office, but we should discuss contract funding levels on my trip to Washington next month. Take me to lunch at the Sans Souci and tell me how much you can give me!

Regards,

Bert

Bert Abernathy

December 2, 1978

Mr. Thomas W. Starr
1713 12th Street
Claremont, California 91711

Dear Tom,

I write this letter with regret. You are a talented teacher, and I believe that with time you will become an outstanding member of the academic community. Still, though the circumstances of your doctoral dissertation difficulties were beyond your control, I cannot recommend the continuation of your contract with us beyond June 30, 1979. The Institute bylaws are most specific, and the failure to obtain your Ph.D. by December 1 leaves no room for an exception or waiver.

I will, if you wish, do what I can to aid you in seeking a new position for next year.

Sincerely,

Pete

Peter V. Johnson, Ph.D.
Office of the Dean

July 15, 1979

Dr. Peter V. Johnson
Dean of Engineering and Science
California Technical Institute
Claremont, California 91711

Dear Dean Johnson,

I am writing to thank you for your help in getting me a teaching job for the coming semester. Teaching freshman physics and chemistry at Contra Costa J.C. is going to be a change for me, but without a doctorate I guess I am lucky to have that—at least I won't be pumping gas or hacking a cab. I hope I can find something for the second semester.

The nature of my work in water fusion is such that the lab facilities I saw on my interview at Contra Costa will let me continue. What the Army doesn't know won't hurt me!

Thanks, again, for your help.

Regards,

Thomas W. Starr

Thomas W. Starr

December 13, 1979

Mr. Thomas W. Starr
Science Department
Contra Costa Junior College
Walnut Creek, California 94596

Dear Mr. Starr,

I am pleased to inform you of the acceptance of your paper "An interesting classroom demonstration of power from water." It will appear in our issue of February 24, 1980.

Quite frankly, we were astounded when we duplicated the techniques described in your paper. We would be interested in seeing a second paper which elaborates, mathematically, on the specific chemical and physical processes of your demonstration, as we believe the present one will attract considerable attention.

We wish you well in your new post at the South Australian Boys' Military Prep School, and the galley proofs of the paper will be sent to you there.

Cordially,

Peterson S. Day

Peterson S. Day
Editor, *Review of High School Experimental Science*

LETTERS FROM CAMP
by Al Sarrantonio

Presently an assistant science fiction editor at Doubleday & Company and an amateur astronomer, Al Sarrantonio has sold stories to many of the leading magazines and original anthologies in the field, including *Shadows, Chrysalis, Amazing Stories,* and *Isaac Asimov's Science Fiction Magazine.* Al says that he "always thought of 'Letters from Camp' as a Gahan Wilson cartoon in prose." We agree, and so will you.

LETTERS FROM CAMP

Dear Mom and Dad,

I still don't know why you made me come to this dump for the summer. It looks like all the other summer camps I've been to, even if it is "super modern and computerized," and I don't see why I couldn't go back to the one I went to last year instead of this "new" one. I had a lot of fun last summer, even if you did have to pay for all that stuff I smashed up and even if I did make the head counselor break his leg.

The head counselor here is a jerk, just like the other one was. As soon as we got off the hovercraft that brought us here, we had to go to the Big Tent for a "pep talk." They made us sit through a slide show about all the things we're going to do (yawn), and that wouldn't have been so bad except that the head counselor, who's a robot, kept scratching his metal head through the whole thing. I haven't made any friends, and the place looks like it's full of jerks. Tonight we didn't have any hot water and the TV in my tent didn't work.

Phooey on Camp Ultima. Can't you still get me back in the other place?

Dear Mom and Dad,

Maybe this place isn't so bad after all. They just about let us do whatever we want, and the kids are pretty wild. Today they split us up into "Pow-wow Groups," but there aren't really any rules or anything, and my group looks like it might be a good one. One of the guys in it looks like he might be okay. His name's Ramon, and he's from Brazil. He told me a lot of neat stories about things he did at home, setting houses on fire and things like that. We spent all day today hiding from our stupid robot counselor. He thought for sure we had run away, and nearly blew a circuit until we finally showed up just in time for dinner.

The food stinks, but they did have some animal type thing that we got to roast over a fire, and that tasted pretty good.

Tomorrow we go on our first field trip.

Dear Mom and Dad,

We had a pretty good time today, all things considered. We got up at six o'clock to go on our first hike, and everybody was pretty excited. There's a lot of wild places here, and they've got it set up to look just like a prehistoric swamp. One kid said we'd probably see a Tyrannosaurus Rex, but nobody believed him. The robot counselors kept us all together as we set out through the marsh, and we saw a lot of neat things like vines dripping green goop and all kinds of frogs and toads. Me and Ramon started pulling the legs off frogs, but our counselor made us stop and anyway the frogs were all robots. We walked for about two hours and then stopped for lunch. Then we marched back again.

The only weird thing that happened was that when we got back and the counselors counted heads, they found that one kid was missing. They went out to look for him but couldn't find anything, and the only thing they think might have happened is that he got lost in the bog somewhere. One kid said he thought he saw a Tyrannosaurus Rex, but it was the same kid who'd been talking about them before so nobody listened to him. The head counselor went around patting everybody on the shoulder, telling us not to worry since something always happens to one kid every year. But they haven't found him yet.

Tonight we had a big food fight, and nobody even made us clean the place up.

Dear Mom and Dad,

Today we went out on another field trip, and another stupid kid got himself lost. They still haven't found the first one, and some of the kids are talking about Tyrannosaurus Rex again. But this time we went hill climbing and I think the dope must have fallen off a cliff, because the hills are almost like small mountains and there are a lot of ledges on them.

After dinner tonight, which almost nobody ate because nobody felt like it, we sat around a campfire and told ghost stories. Somebody said they thought a lot of kids were going to disappear from here, and that made everybody laugh, in a scary kind of way. I was a little scared myself. It must have been the creepy shadows around the fire. The robot counselors keep telling everyone not to worry, but some of the kids—the ones who can't take it—are starting to say they want to go home.

I don't want to go home, though; this place is fun.

Dear Mom and Dad,

Today we went on another trip, to the far side of the island where they have a lake, and we had a good time and all (we threw one of the robot counselors into the lake but he didn't sink), but when we got off the boat and everybody was counted we found out that eight kids were gone. One kid said he even saw his friend Harvey get grabbed by something ropy and black and pulled over the side. I'm almost ready to believe him. I don't know if I like this place so much any more. One more field trip like the one today and I think I'll want to come home.

It's not even fun wrecking stuff around here any more.

Dear Mom and Dad,

Come and get me right away, I'm *scared*. Today the robot counselors tried to make us go on another day trip, but nobody wanted to go, so we stayed around the tents. But at the chow meeting tonight only twelve kids showed up. That means twenty more kids disappeared today. Nobody had any idea what happened to them, though I do know that a whole bunch of guys were playing outside the perimeter of the camp, tearing things down, so that might have had something to do with it. At this point I don't care.

Just get me out of here!

Mom and Dad,

I think I'm the only kid left, and I don't know if I can hide much longer. The head counselor tricked us into leaving the camp today, saying that somebody had seen a Tyrannosaurus Rex. He told us all to run through the rain forest at the north end of the camp, but when we ran into it, something horrible happened. I was with about five other kids, and as soon as we ran into the forest we heard a high-pitched screeching and a swishing sound and the trees above us started to lower their branches. I saw four of the kids I was with get covered by green plastic-looking leaves, and then there was a gulping sound and the branches lifted and separated and there was nothing there. Ramon and I just managed to dodge out of the way, and we ran through the forest in between the trees and out the other side. We would have been safe for a while but just then the robot counselors broke through the forest behind us, leading a Tyrannosaurus Rex. We ran, but Ramon slipped and fell and the Tyrannosaurus Rex was suddenly there, looming over him with its dripping jaws and rows of sharp white teeth. Ramon took out his box of matches but the dinosaur was on him then and I didn't wait to see any more.

I ran all the way back to the postal computer terminal in the camp to get this letter out to you. Call the police! Call the army! I can't hide forever, and I'm afraid that any second the Tyrannosaurus Rex will break in here and

Dear Mr. and Mrs. Jameson:

Camp Ultima is happy to inform you of the successful completion of your son's stay here, and we are therefore billing you for the balance of your payment at this time.

Camp Ultima is proud of its record of service to parents of difficult boys, and will strive in the future to continue to provide the very best in camp facilities.

May we take this opportunity to inform you that, due to the success of our first camp, we are planning to open a new facility for girls next summer.

We hope we might be of service to you in the future.

THE SEVERAL MURDERS OF ROGER ACKROYD

A DELIGHTFUL COMEDIC PREMISE

by Barry N. Malzberg

Since his first professional sale in 1967, Barry N. Malzberg has produced (created would be a better word) about thirty-five novels and collections in the science fiction genre, including such outstanding achievements as *Beyond Apollo* (1972), *Herovits World* (1973), and *Guernica Night* (1974). His most recent collections are *Malzberg at Large* (1980) and *The Man Who Loved the Midnight Lady* (1980). A truly unique talent, he has the uncanny ability to look desperation in the face and see . . . laughter.

THE SEVERAL MURDERS OF ROGER ACKROYD

Dear Mr. Ackroyd:

Your application for the position of mysterist has been carefully reviewed in these offices.

While there are many impressive aspects to your credentials and while we fully recognize your qualifications for the position of mysterist, I regret to inform you that the very large number of highly qualified applications for the few openings which do exist means that we must disappoint many fine candidates such as yourself.

Rest assured that this decision is not intended as a commentary upon your abilities but only upon the very severe competition encountered during the current application period.

Truly do we wish you success in all future endeavors.

Regretfully,
A. HASTINGS/for the Bank

Dear Mr. Hastings:

I have received your outrageous letter rejecting me for the position of mysterist. I demand more than a form reply!

If you have truly reviewed my application you know that I have dedicated my life to achieving this position and am *completely* qualified. I know the major and minor variations of the locked-room murder, I know the eighteen disguising substances for strychnine, to say nothing of the management of concealed relationships and the question of Inherited Familial Madness. I know of the Misdirected Clue and the peculiar properties of the forsythia root; not unknown to me are the engineering basis and exhilarating qualities of antique vehicles known as "cars." In short I know everything that a mysterist must know in order to qualify for the Bank.

Under these circumstances I refuse to accept your bland and evasive reply. I have a right to know: why are you turning me down? Once I am admitted to the Bank I am *positive* that I can find a huge audience which wants something more than the careless and unmotivated trash which your current "mysterists" and I dignify them by use of that name are propounding. This, then, is to your benefit as well as to mine.

Why have I been rejected?

Will you reconsider?

Hopefully,
ROGER ACKROYD

Dear Mr. Ackroyd:

Because we received several thousand applications, many of them highly qualified, for a mere twenty-five vacancies for mysterists in the Interplanetary Program Entertainment Division for the period commencing in Fourth-month 2312, it was necessary for us to use a form reply. This letter, however, is personally dictated.

I am truly sorry that you are taking rejection so unpleasantly. No insult was intended nor were aspersions cast upon your scholarly command of the mysterist form which does indeed appear excellent.

Your application was carefully reviewed. In many ways you have talent and promise is shown. But because of extraordinarily heavy competition for the limited number of banks applications even more qualified than your own were rejected. As you know the majority of the Interplanetary Program Entertainment Division channels are devoted to westernists, sexualists, gothicings, and science-fictionists with only a relatively few number of mysterists to accommodate the small audience still sympathetic to that form. At present all twenty-five vacancies have been filled by superb mysterists and we anticipate few openings in the foreseeable future.

I can, of course, appreciate your dismay. A career to which you have dedicated yourself seems now closed. I remind you however that a man of your obvious intelligence and scholarship might do well in some of the other branches offering current vacancies. For instance and for example we have at this time an opening for a science-fictionist specializing in Venusian counterplot and Saturnian struggle.

If you could familiarize yourself with extant materials on the subject and would like to make formal application we would be pleased to forward proper application. Just refer to this letter.

Sincerely,
A. HASTINGS/for the Bank

Dear Mr. Hastings:

I don't *want* to be a science-fictionist specializing in Venusian counterplot. We have *enough* science-fictionists, westernists, sexualists and gothicings. They are all dead forms. The audience will wise up to that sooner or later and all go away and where will your Interplanetary Program Entertainment Division be then?

What they are seeking is fine new mysterists with new approaches. Such as myself.

I did not prepare myself for years in order to become a hack churning out visuals of the slime jungles. I am a dreamer, one who looks beyond the technological barriers of our civilization and understands the human pain and complication within. Complication and pain which can only be understood by the mysterist who knows of the unspeakable human heart.

The Interplanetary Program Entertainment Division was, in fact, originally conceived for people such as myself, the great mysterists who would bring a large audience ever closer to the barriers of human experience. Hundreds of years ago mysterists were responsible for all of your success. (I have read some history.) Only much later did the science-fictionists and the rest move in to make a wonderful entertainment device a dull nuisance predicated upon easy shocks drained of intellection. The audience was corrupted by these people. But now a wind is rising. It is time for the mysterists to return to their original and honored place.

You would insult me by offering me Venusian combat science-fictionist! I tell you, you people have no sense of the dream. You have no heart. I have devoted my life to mastery of the craft: I am a good mysterist on the verge of becoming *great*.

I demand a supervisor.

Bitterly,
ROGER ACKROYD

Dear Mr. Ackroyd:

I am a Supervisor. All applications must be reviewed by a Supervisor before final disposition. Complaints such as yours reach even higher; I am writing you on advice. I am highly trained and skilled and I know the centuries history of the International Division much better than you ever will.

In fact, I find your communication quite offensive.

I fear that we have already reached the logical terminus of our correspondence. There is nothing more to be done. Your application for mysterist—a position for which there is small audience and little demand—was carefully reviewed in the light of its relation to many other applications. Although your credentials were praiseworthy they were surpassed by candidates more qualified. You were, therefore, rejected. Mysterist is a small but useful category and we respect the form and your dedication but the audience today is quite limited. We are not mindless bureaucrats here but on the other hand we accept the fact that the Division must give the audience what it wants rather than what we think it *should* want, and gothica and science-fictionists are what most people like today. We are here to make people happy, to give them what they want. We leave uplift to our very competent

Interplanetary Education Division and they leave entertainment to us.

There is a tiny demand for mysterists.

If you do not wish to be a science-fictionist specializing in Venusian Combat or apply for other fine positions available as westernist, it must be your decision. We recognize your abilities and problems but you must recognize ours. You can give up and go to work.

A. HASTINGS/for the Bank

Dear Mr. Hastings:

I choose to ignore your offensive communication and give you one last benefit of the doubt. This is your last chance. May I be a mysterist? Do send me the proper authorization.

Reasonably,
ROGER ACKROYD

Dear Roger Ackroyd:

Mr. A. Hastings, Supervisor of the Eastern Application Division Interplanetary Programming and Entertainment Division has asked me to respond to your communication.

There are no vacancies for mysterist.

M. MALLOWAN/Over-Supervisor

Dear Hastings and Mallowan:

I gave you every chance.

You were warned.

As I did not see fit to tell you until now (having as well an excellent command of the *deus-ex*) I have a close friend who is *already* a mysterist although not as good as myself and who for certain obscure personal reasons owes me several favors.

He has given me tapes; I have completed them. I have turned them over to him.

He has done with them the requisite.

I am already on the banks!

My mysteries are already available on the banks and I

think that you will find what the reaction is very soon. Then you will realize your folly. Then you will realize that Interplanetary Programming which I sought initially in the most humble manner and which could have had me in their employ on the easiest terms is now at my mercy. Completely at my mercy!

You are bent, as the science-fictionist say, completely to my will!

It did not have to be this way, you know. You could have judged my application fairly and we could have worked together well. Now you shall pay a Much Higher Price.

Wait and see.

Triumphantly,
ROGER ACKROYD

—Division: *Send ending ABC MURDERS. Tape mysteriously missing. Send at once. Demand this.*

—Interplanetary STOP How did they get off that island question mark STOP Where is final material exclamation point STOP I insist upon an answer at once STOP

—Division: THIRD REPRESENTATIVE DIVISION EASTERN DISTRICT DEMANDS KNOWLEDGE WHY POIROT DIED REPEAT WHY DID HE DIE QUESTION MARK NO FURTHER EXCUSES EXCLAMATION POINT COMMITTEE LICENSES PREPARED FULL ASSEMBLY TOMORROW FOR INVESTIGATION UNLESS MATERIALS SUPPLIED EXCLAMATION POINT

—Division: *Who killed the Inspector? Ending missing. Reply at once. McGinnity, for the President.*

—Division: FIFTY-SEVEN MILLION NOW DEMAND . . .

A DELIGHTFUL COMEDIC PREMISE

Dear Mr. Malzberg:

I wonder if you'd be interested in writing for us—on a semicommissioned basis, of course—a funny short story or novelette. Although the majority of your work, at least the work that I have read, is characterized by a certain gloom, a blackness, a rather despairing view of the world, I am told by people who represent themselves to be friends of yours that you have, in private, a delightful sense of humor that overrides your melancholia and makes you quite popular at small parties. I am sure you would agree that science fiction, at least at present, has all the despair and blackness that it or my readers can stand, and if you could come in with a light-hearted story, we would not only be happy to publish it, but it might start you on a brand-new career. From these same friends I am given to understand that you are almost thirty-four years of age, and surely you must agree that despair is harder and harder to sustain when you move into a period of your life where it becomes personally imminent; in other words, you are moving now into the Heart Attack Zone.

Dear Mr. Ferman:

Thank you very much for your letter and for your interest in obtaining from me a light-hearted story. It so happens that you and my friends have discovered what I like to think of as My Secret . . . that I am not a despairing man at all, but rather one with a delicious if somewhat perverse sense of humor, who sees the comedy in the human condition and only turns out the black stuff because it is now fashionable, and the word rates, at all lengths, must be sustained.

I have had in mind for some time writing a story about a man—let me call him Jack—who is able to re-evoke the sights and sounds of the 1950s in such a concrete and viable fashion that he is actually able to *take* people back into the past, both individually and in small tourist groups. (This idea is not completely original; Jack Finney used it in *Time and Again,* and of course this chestnut has been romping or, I should say, dropping around the field for forty years, but hear me out.) The trouble with Jack is that he is not able to re-evoke the more fashionable and memorable aspects of the 1950s, those that are so much in demand in our increasingly perilous and confusing times, but instead can recover only the failures, the not-quite-successes, the aspects-that-never-made-it. Thus, he can take himself and companions not to Ebbets Field, say, where the great Dodger teams of the 1950s were losing with magnificence and stolid grace, but to Shibe Park in Philadelphia, home of the Athletics and Phillies, where on a Tuesday afternoon a desultory crowd of four thousand might be present to watch senile managers fall asleep in the dugout or hapless rookies fail once again to hit the rising curve. He cannot, in short, recapture the Winners but only the Losers: the campaign speeches of Estes Kefauver, recordings by the Bell Sisters and Guy Mitchell, the rambling confessions of minor actors before the McCarthy screening committee that they once were Communists and would appreciate the opportunity to get before the full committee and press to make a more definite statement.

Jack is infuriated by this and no wonder; he is the custodian of a unique and possibly highly marketable talent—people increasingly love the past, and a guided tour through it as opposed to records, tapes and rambling reminiscences would be enormously exciting to them—but he cannot for the life of him get to what he calls the Real Stuff, the more commercial and lovable aspects of that cuddly decade. Every time that he thinks he has recaptured Yankee Stadium in his mind and sweeps back in time to revisit it, he finds himself at Wrigley Field in Chicago where Wayne Terwilliger, now playing first base, misses a foul pop and runs straight into the stands. What can he do? What can he do about this reckless and uncontrollable talent of his, which in its sheerest perversity simply will not remit to his commands? (It is a subconscious ability, you see; if he becomes self-conscious, it leaves him entirely.) Jack is enraged. He has cold sweats, flashes of gloom and hysteria. (I forgot to say that he is a failed advertising copywriter, now working in Cleveland on display advertising mostly for the Shaker Heights district. He needs money and approbation. His marriage, his *second* marriage, is falling apart. All of this will give the plot substance and humanity, to say nothing of warm twitches of insight.) He *knows* that he is onto something big, and yet his clownish talent, all big feet and wide ears, mocks him.

He takes his problem to a psychiatrist. The psychiatrist takes some convincing, but after being taken into the offices of *Cosmos* science fiction to see the editor rejecting submissions at a penny a word, he believes everything. He says he will help Jack. This psychiatrist, who I will call Dr. Mandleman, fires all of his patients and enters into a campaign to help Jack recover the more popular and marketable aspects of the '50s. He, too, sees the Big Money. He moves in with Jack. A psychiatrist in his own home: together they go over the top-forty charts of that era, call up retired members of the New York football Giants, pore through old Congressional Records in which McCarthy is again and again thunderously denounced by two liberal representatives. . . .

Do you see the possibilities? I envision this as being somewhere around 1.500 words but could expand or contract it to whatever you desire. I am very busy as always, but I could make room in my schedule for this project, particularly if you could see fit to give a small down payment. Would fifty dollars seem excessive? I look forward to word from you.

Dear Mr. Malzberg:

I believe that you have utterly misunderstood my letter and the nature of the assignment piece.

There is nothing *funny* in a fantasy about a man who can recapture only the ugly or forgotten elements of the past. Rather, this is a bitter satire on the present that you have projected, based upon your statement that "people love their past," with the implication that they find the future intolerable. What is funny about *that?* What is funny about failure, too? What is funny about the Philadelphia Athletics of the early 1950s with their ninety-four-year-old manager? Rather, you seem to be on the way to constructing another of your horrid metaphors for present and future, incompetence presided over by senescence.

This idea will absolutely not work, not at least within the context of a delightful comedic premise, and as you know, we are well inventoried with work by you and others that will depress people. I cannot and will not pay fifty dollars in front for depressing stuff like this.

Perhaps you will want to take another shot at this.

Dear Mr. Ferman:

Thanks for your letter. I am truly sorry that you fail to see the humor in failure or in the forgettable aspects of the past—people, I think, must learn to laugh at their foibles—but I bow to your judgment.

Might I suggest another idea that has been in mind for some time. I would like to write a story of a telepath—let me call him John—who is able to establish direct psionic links with the minds, if one can call them "minds," of the thoroughbreds running every afternoon, except for Sundays and three months a year at Aqueduct and Belmont race tracks in Queens, New York. John's psionic faculties work at a range of fifty yards; he is able to press his nose against the wire gate separating paddock from customers and actually get *inside* the minds of the horses. Dim thoughts like little shoots of grass press upon his own brain; he is able to determine the mental state and mood of the horses as in turn they parade by him. (Horses, of course, do not verbalize; John must deduce those moods subverbally.)

Obviously, John is up to something. He is a mind reader; he should, through the use of this talent, be able to get some line on the outcome of a race by knowing which horses feel well, which horses' thoughts are clouded by the possibility of soporifics, which other horses' minds show vast energy because of the probable induction of stimulants. Surely he should be able to narrow the field down to two or three horses, anyway, that *feel good* and, by spreading his bets around these in proportion to the odds, assure himself of a good living.

(I should have said somewhat earlier on, but, as you know, I am very weak at formal outlines; John's talents are restricted to the reading of the minds of *animals;* he cannot for the life of him screen the thoughts of a fellow human. If he could, of course, he would simply check out the trainers and jockeys, but it is a perverse and limited talent, and John must make the best of what God has given him, as must we all—for instance, I outline poorly.)

The trouble is that John finds there to be no true correlation between the prerace mood or thoughts of horses and the eventual outcome. Horses that feel *well* do not necessarily win, and those horses from which John has picked up the most depressing and suicidal emanations have been known to win. It is not a simple reversal; if it were, John would be able to make his bets on the basis of reverse correlation and do quite well this way; rather, what it seems to be is entirely *random.* Like so much of life, the prerace meditations of horses appear to have no relationship to the outcome; rather, motives and consequence are fractured, split, entirely torn apart; and this insight, which finally comes upon John after the seventh race at Aqueduct on June 12, 1974, when he has lost fifty-five dollars, drives him quite mad; his soul is split, his mind shattered; he runs frantically through the sparse crowds (it is a Tuesday, and you know what OTB has done to racetrack attendance, anyway) shouting, screaming, bellowing his rage to the heavens. "There's no connection!" he will scream. "Nothing makes sense, nothing connects, there is no reason at all!" And several burly Pinkertons, made sullen by rules that require them to wear jackets and ties at all times, even on this first hot day of the year, seize him quite roughly and drag him into the monstrous computer room housing the equipment of the American Totalisor Company; there a sinister track executive, his eyes glowing with cunning and evil, will say, "Why don't you guys ever learn?" (He is a metaphor for the Devil, you see; I assure you that this will be properly painted, and the story itself will be an *allegory*.) And, coming close to John, he will raise a hand shaped like a talon, he will bring it upon John, he will . . .

I propose this story to be 25,000 words in length, a cover story, in fact. (You and Ronald Walotsky will see the possibilities here, and Walotsky, I assure you, draws horses very well.) Although I am quite busy, the successful author of fifteen stories in this field, two of the novels published in *hardcover,* I could make time in my increasingly heavy schedule to get the story to you within twelve hours of your letter signifying outline approval. I think that an advance in this case of fifty dollars would be quite reasonable and look forward to hearing from you by return mail, holding off in the meantime from plunging into my next series of novels which, of course, are already under lucrative contract.

Dear Mr. Malzberg:

We're not getting anywhere.

What in God's name is *funny* about a man who perceives "motives and consequences to be entirely fractured . . . torn apart?" Our readers, let me assure you, have enough troubles of their own; they are already quite aware of this, or do not *want* to be aware of it. Our readers, an intelligent and literate group of people numbering into the multiple thousands, have long since understood that life is unfair and inequitable, and they are looking for entertainment, release, a little bit of *joy*.

Don't you understand that this commission was for a *funny* story? There is nothing funny about your proposal, nor do I see particular humor in an allegory that will make use of the appearance of the Devil.

Perhaps we should forget this whole thing. There are other writers I would rather have approached, and it was only at the insistence of your friends that I decided to give you a chance at this one. We are heavily inventoried, as I have already said, on the despairing stuff, but if in due course you would like to send me one of your characteristic stories, *on a purely speculative basis*, I will consider it as a routine submission.

Dear Mr. Ferman:

Please wait a minute or just a few minutes until you give me another chance to explain myself. I was sure that the two story ideas you have rejected, particularly the second, were quite funny; but editorial taste, as we professional writers know, is the prerogative of the editor; and if you *don't* see the humor, I can't show it to you, humor being a very rare and special thing. I am, however, momentarily between novels, waiting for the advance on the series contract to come through, and *would* be able to write you a story at this time; let me propose one final idea to you before you come to the wrong conclusion that I am not a funny writer and go elsewhere, to some wretched hack who does not have one quarter of the bubbling humor and winsomely comprehensive view of the foibles of the human condition that I do.

I would like to write a story about a science fiction writer, a highly successful science fiction writer, but one who nevertheless, because of certain limitations in the field and slow payment from editors, is forced to make do on an income of $3,483 a year (last year) from all of his writings and, despite the pride and delight of knowing that he is near or at the top of his field, finds getting along on such an income, particularly in the presence of a wife and family, rather difficult, his wife not understanding entirely (as she *should* understand) that science fiction is not an ultimately lucrative field for most of us but repays in satisfaction, in *great* satisfactions. This writer—who we shall call Barry—is possessed after a while by his fantasies; the partitions, in his case, between reality and fantasy have been sheared through by turmoil and economic stress, and he believes himself in many ways to be not only the creator but the receptacle of his ideas, ideas that possess him and stalk him through the night.

Barry is a gentle man, a man with a gracious sense of humor, a certain *je ne sais quoi* about him that makes him much celebrated at parties, a man whose occasionally sinis-

ter fictions serve only to mask his gay and joyous nature . .
but Barry is seized by his fantasies; people do not truly
understand him; and now at last those aforementioned walls
have crumpled: he takes himself to be not only the inventor
but the *hero* of his plot ideas. Now he is in a capsule set on
Venus fly-by looking out at the green planet while he strokes
his diminutive genitals and thinks of home; now again he is
an archetypical alien, far from home, trying to make convincing contact with humanity; now yet again he is a rocketship,
an actual physical rocketship, a phallic object extended to
great length and power, zooming through the heavens, pene-
trating the sky.

I'll do this at 1,500 words for five dollars down. Please let
me hear from you.

Dear Mr. Malzberg:

This was a doomed idea from the start. I hope you won't
take this personally, but you need help.

Dear Mr. Ferman:

My husband is at Aqueduct today, living in a motel by
night, and says that he will be out of touch for at least a
week, but I know he would have wanted me to acknowledge
your letter, and as soon as he returns I assume he'll be in
touch with you.

I assume also that in saying that he needs "help" you are
referring to the fact that, as he told me, you were commis-
sioning a story from him with money in front, and I hope that
you can send us a check as soon as possible, without awaiting
his return. He said something about a hundred or a thousand
dollars, but we'll take fifty.

Joyce Malzberg

THE MAN FROM NOT-YET
by John Sladek

John Sladek is an American who has been living in England for some fifteen years. His frequently bittersweet stories of man and machine have been entertaining thoughtful readers since the mid-Sixties, but he deserves to be better known. His most recent collection is *The Best of John Sladek* (1981), an enormously exciting celebration of the writer's art. Other outstanding examples of his black humor are *Mechasm* (aka *The Reproductive System* (1969), and *The Muller-Fokker Effect* (1971).

THE MAN FROM NOT-YET

To Jeremy Botford, Esq.

Dear Jerry,   Aug. 10, 1772

It was with mixt feelings that I returned to London after all these years. The city is more splendid and horrid than ever; it is a sort of great Press, into which every kind of person has been tumbled, without the least regard for whether or not he is choaked with the stench of his neighbours.

For my part, the only retreat offering succour from the noxious Crowd's putrefaction is the coffee house. Of course I refer to Crutchwood's in Clovebelly Lane, which you may fondly remember. It still affords an entertaining company, and I was surprized to remark several of our old number about the fire yet. Augustus Strathnaver has grown quite stout and dropsical, but his Wit is lean and ready as ever. Dick Blackadder is still soliciting subscriptions for his translations of Ovid; he is still soliciting in vain and he is still of good chear about it. I learned that poor Oliver Colquhoun, who never could get his play tried in Drury Lane, is dead.

But I was attended by greatest astonishment when I apprehended a gross figure in a snuff-coloured coat seated next the fire with its back to the company.

The figure turned to regard me, presenting its great wart hog's face. When its mouth opened, 'twas like the splitting of a steamed pudding. "So! (it said) I see you have not yet learnt your lesson, Timothy Scunthe, but must needs be taught more manners! Do you not know better than to interrupt a man while he is meditating?"

It was indeed our old friend, cantankerous as ever. I shall never forget the time I spilled mulled wine upon him—indeed, he shall never let me forget it, though it happened close to 11 years ago!

I stayed to see the evening out with Johnson and his circle, to which there are no few additions. The good Doctor is thicker of limb now, with a propensity (he says) to gout, though I perceive no shortening of his breath. He disposed last evening of two Philosophy Students (they were arguing about the Soul, I believe. I could not follow them), a Schoolmaster, a Grub Street writer, and a poor inoffensive solicitor who wandered in for a cup of tea and did not stay to see it cooled. In short, Dr. Johnson is himself: Witty, Splenetic, and Eminently Sensible. I was keenly reminded of the days when we young dogs were used to teaze him, and he to muzzle us properly. Remember the fun we had with the visitor from "the Future," and how the good Doctor shewed him for the merry-andrew he was? I can never forget it, as I hope you cannot forget.

> Your affectionate
> Timothy Scunthe

To Sir Timothy Scunthe, Bart.
Dear Tim,   Aug. 25
I am glad you have not forgotten the Incident of the man from "Not-Yet," for I have begun assembling some paltry Reminiscences and would greatly appreciate the help of your keen memory. While I believe I recall the Incident perfectly, much Muck has covered it in ten years' time, and I would rather have your version of the story, too.

Eternally gratefull, I remain, Dear Tim,

> Your affectionate
> Jer. Botford

To Jeremy Botford, Esq.
Dear Jerry,   Sept. 5
Your memory is doubtless better than mine, but I have

made some Notations of that curious Incident, which, in the interests of your book, I hereby place at your disposal:

It was a December evening in 1762, and our usual circle, dominated by Dr. Johnson, was gathered in the gaming room at Crutchwood's. Paunceford, the proprietor, seemed to be having an argument with some man in the front doorway, and the room grew quite chill.

"Damme, Sir," Johnson roared out. "Are you determined to give us all the Ague? Bring the gentleman in."

Paunceford led in a thin, spindle-shanked fellow, oddly dressed. I recall he wore his hair natural and shockingly short, and that his breeches reached to his ankles.

Johnson's snuffbox clattered to the floor. "Good God!" he cried. "What manner of Whig is this?"

The fellow made no reply, but gazed about him in some consternation.

"Or is it Methodism you're spreading? Or Dissension?" Johnson snarled. "You'll do a barrel more converts if you bag a decent periwig."

"Perhaps," said Strathnaver, tittering, "perhaps the gentleman believes it is Satanic to adorn the body."

"Yes, well, you'll take note he has no scruples against hiding his spindly calves, however. My name is Dr. Samuel Johnson, Sir. You'll forgive me for not rising. I am rather gouty this evening. What might your name be?"

The man put out his left hand, withdrew it, then offered it again. Finally he extended the proper hand and shook.

"My name is Darwin Gates," he said shyly. "And I'm from the Twentieth Century."

Dr. Johnson's hand hesitated just a fraction as he reached for his snuffbox. "Is it a place, then?" he said, offering snuff around. "I should have thought it a direction. But it is very interesting to meet you, Sir. I suppose you have all manner of wonders to divulge to this fortunate company, do you not?"

Mr. Gates sat down and leaned forward earnestly. "As a matter of fact, I do. You wouldn't believe the half—"

"Indeed? But I have a reputation for credulency," Johnson said. A sly smile was beginning to play about his great, ugly mouth. "You will want to tell me no doubt of carriages that operate without benefit of horses. Of engines that carry men through the air like birds. Of ships without sails."

The man flushed darkly and stammered, "As a matter of fact—"

Johnson's voice rose in both pitch and volume. "Of machines which carry men under the waters of the sea like fish, where they witness countless wonders. Of mechanical horses capable of drawing a dozen carriages at once. Of artificial candles, powered by some mysterious Force of which we know nothing as yet. Of buildings made of crystal and iron, perhaps, wherein one may order servants to select the sort of weather one desires. Is that the sort of Future you are about to describe for us, Mr. Gates?"

The poor visitor looked positively apoplectick with embarrassment and chagrin. I had no doubt but that he had planned a much poorer tale than this. "I—" he stammered "—that is, I—"

"But," continued Dr. Johnson, grinding his teeth, "I speak only of mere physical inventions, devises which any rude Mechanick may surmise. 'Twould do you no credit at all, Sir, if you had not a better tale than that. Perhaps you come to tell me of the Politicks of the Twentieth Century. Let me see—there would be no war, because terrible Weapons would have been invented, the which are too dangerous to be used. The colonies in America will have rebelled and become a Powerful Nation, where, they will claim, All Men are Equal. Mayhap they will even free the slave Negroes, though that is perhaps too much to expect of our American friends."

"Just a minute!" said the visitor. "I resent that. I'm an American—"

"Tush!" said Johnson. "Next you will be a Red Indian. I warn you, Sir, it was I who exposed George Psalmanazar, who posed forty years as a 'Formosan,' having made up his own 'language.'" All this Johnson delivered in an undertone, then resumed his ordinary Rasp and said, "I suppose the Powers and Alliances of all Europe will have shifted considerable. England's monarch will have no more weight than a common sweep, I surmise."

"How did you know?" asked the astonished Mr. Gates.

"Pooh, Sir, I am merely spinning my tale to keep from being bored by yours. But be so good as to let me go on. I have not yet discoursed upon the Future state of Painting, of Musick, of Moral & Natural Philosophy—"

"First we must give Mr. Gates a cup of punch," murmured Strathnaver. "Assuming, that is, that persons from that time so little evident to out senses *can* drink and eat. Are you, Mr. Gates, an aethereal spirit, like one of Mr. Milton's angels? Do you sleep, ingest food, and so on?"

While the poor stranger was helped to a cup of punch, Dr. Johnson sat back and regarded him incuriously. I read contempt in Johnson's face; whenever the right side of his mouth gets drawn up, as though attracted to the wart just above it at the corner, then he is in a phrensy of contempt.

"Of Painting I know little," he said. "It is at best a clumsy art, making awkward imitations of Nature. I expect patrons will grow weary of Copyism, and turn their attention elsewhere.

"Everyone in the Twentieth Century will of course have Musick at hand as he desires it. I can well imagine the deleterious effect this will have upon Taste & Sense, when every cordwainer or every smith can hammer upon shoes to Musick of his own chusing. Art does not, Sir, lend itself to Dilution.

"There will always be a plenitude of varieties in the Garden of Philosophy from which to make a nosegay. At some point, men will stop speaking of Reason and start speaking of Responsibility. There is, they will say, no order in the Universe but what we chuse to see—as there were no Giants in Sir Quixote's windmills. Absurdity will become a philosophical catchword—there will be a Silly Season.

"Of Natural Philosophy I can well imagine the devising of all manner engines and games. No doubt men of the Twentieth Century will go to and fro the Moon, if not the Sun. Astronomy, Chymistry, Mathematics and Medicine will all advance apace. Plague will be almost unknown. I daresay it will have been proven to everyone's satisfaction that Tobacco is a poisonous weed."

"Amazing!" quoth our visitor. "How did you know—"

"I have met better mountebanks than you, Sir!" said Johnson, fetching him a stern look. "I am forced by gout to sit here night after night, prey to every single one of 'em. Only last month I was confronted by a 'man from Not-Yet' who puts you to shame. Not only had he elegant manners and wondrous tales to tell, he looked exactly like me!"

Our visitor looked pale and ill. "Like you?" he said.

"Yes. The rogue tried to convince me that he *was* I, but I have not yet met the man I could not out-reason. I proved to him, as I shall prove to you, that man cannot travel from the Future to the Past.

"Man cannot move about in Time as though it were Space. Nature forbids it, as she forbids Levitation or a Vacuum. Think of the awful Paradoxes which might occur! Should you, for example, return to your childhood, you might see yourself as a child. Yet suppose your carriage ran over that child? Would you then cease to be? How, then, would you yet be alive? And there are Paradoxes even more hideous to contemplate. Suppose you got a child upon your own mother, and suppose the child were you? How, then, may a man be his own father or son, a travesty of Physical and Moral Law? I do not even dare consider that weightier problem by far: Which of you, should you meet yourself, would have your Soul? Is the Soul single or divisible? Would some of your selves be soulless animals, mere Automata?

"You cannot be from the Future because the Future is, by definition, that which is not yet. There is no Future. And even were travel in time possible, you would not be from Posterity. I believe that Man grows every generation more happily endowed with Understanding—yet you are content to sit here gape-mouthed, listening to specious arguments."

"Please," said Mr. Gates, "I can prove I'm from the Future. I've built the only Time Machine ever made. Let me prove it. Here is a coin—" He fumbled at the hip of his breeches for a moment. "Here is a quarter of a dollar, United States of America currency," he announced proudly, handing the coin to Strathnaver. "You'll see the date is nineteen-something."

"Good God!" said Strathnaver. "The poor wretch has made himself credentials. This is no more a coin than I am. Ho-ho, Mr. Gates. I must give you a lesson in minting, someday. When you design a die, you must *reverse* the image, so that it comes out proper on the coin."

He passed the coin around, and we could all see that the inscription was backwards. It was poor forgery.

"Things have gotten reversed somehow!" shouted Gates. "I don't know how. What can I do to make you believe me?"

"Nothing on earth," said Johnson. "The last knave shewed me a curious engine he called a Lighter—but when I examined it, 'twas nothing but a tiny oil-wick lamp with a matchlock flint attached."

"I'll take you back to my own time, and that will convince you!"

"A pretty idea," said Mr. Strathnaver, "but you'll never get him away from the fire."

"What?" said Johnson. "Quit the fire to wander about in the aguey snow until this rascal's fellows waylay me and kill me? I cannot say I like the prospect."

"Oh, we don't have to go far," said Gates. "My Time Machine is very close by—and some of your friends can follow and watch. Can it be you are afraid to prove me right?"

For once, Johnson had no answer. He leapt up with surprizing agility and signalled for his cloak and hat. "Let us see it, you dog," he rumbled.

Dick Blackadder and I were elected to follow. We went but twenty paces in the snow when we encountered the Time Machine. It was somewhat like a sedan chair, somewhat like a bathing machine, and no little like an upright coffin on wheels. Gates opened a panel in it, and the two men got themselves inside. The panel closed up.

Dick and I watched the devise closely, ready for any trick. All was deathly still.

"I fear something has happened to Samuel," said Dick. "He could never keep silence this long."

I wrencht at the handle of the panel, but it was fast. An unearthly light seemed to stream from crevices and cracks about the door, increasingly bright. I applied my eye to a crack and peered in.

There was not a soul inside.

The light got brighter and brighter until, with a thunder-clap, the entire machine fell to pieces about us. I was knocked flat by the Great Noise, and when I regained my feet, I was amazed to see Dr. Johnson standing alone amidst the wreckage.

"Are you hurt, Dr. Johnson?" asked Dick, scrambling to his feet.

"No. I—no."

"But where is Mr. Gates?"

"It would seem," said Johnson, looking about, "that he is blown into Aeternity."

We helped him back to the fireside, where, as I recall, he was strangely silent and morose all evening, and would respond to no amount of badinage. He remained muffled in his cloak and refused to say a word.

That is all I know of the Incident, Jerry. Hoping this account is of some good, I remain

Your affectionate
Timothy Scunthe

To Sir Timothy Scunthe, Bart.
Dear Tim, Sept. 9
Rec'd your story and am truly amazed at the copiousness of your memory and notes. Surely you are more the man to pen a Reminiscence than I. You have captured nicely the flavour of the old wart hog's speach, and I find your account exact in nearly every Particular.

Do give my regards to Dr. Johnson and pray him to send me some little item of interest to go in my Reminiscences. If it would not inconvenience him, I should mightily like to hear more of his Experience that strange evening. Eternally gratefull, I remain

Your affectionate
Jer. Botford
Postscript. How is it you say the Doctor has a wart above the

right side of his mouth? I have before me a miniature of him, shewing the wart plainly on the *left*.

> Yours &c.,
> Jer. Botford

To Jeremy Botford, Esq.

Dear Jerry,　　　　　　　　　　　　　　　　　Sept 14

Business is pressing. This is only a brief billet to inform you that I have spoken to Dr. J. and he has promised to send you something. "But I doubt (he said) that he will desire to use it." Do you understand this? I confess I do not. More later from

> Your affectionate
> Timothy Scunthe

To Jeremy Botford, Esq.

Sept. 15　　　　　　　　　　　　　My Dear Jeremy,

As you hold this letter up to a looking glass to read

it . . .

. . . I hope you will find it in you to pity its author. Do not, I beg you, judge me mad until you have read here the truth of my plight.

Having departed on December 10, 1762, from the yard of Crutchwood's, I journeyed into the Future. Having made my jokes about the Twentieth Century, I lived to see them, tragically, become Real. I saw Art & Architecture decline to Nursery Toys, and Literature reduced to Babel. Morality vanished; Science pottered with household Engines. The main business of the time seemed to be World-wide War, or man-made Catastrophe. Whole cities full of people were ignited and cooked alive.

Betwixt the wars, people drive about the countryside in great carriage-engines, which poison the air with harmful vapours. These carriages have o'erlaid the cities with smoak, black and noxious. There is in the Twentieth Century neither Beauty nor Reason, nor any other Mark which sheweth Man more than a beast.

But enough of a sad sojourn to a dismal place. I was

sickened by it to near the point of madness. I knew I had done Wrong in accompanying Mr. Gates to his Land of Horrors, and so I devized a plan for cancelling my visit.

I came back to November 1762 and saw myself. I earnestly entreated myself not to attempt such a voyage—but the object of this entreaty was so intent on proving me a scoundrel and impostor that my arguments were in vain.

I had then but one chance left—to appear at the time and place in which my unsuspecting self was departing for the Future, and to stop myself, by force if need be. Gates and poor Johnson had just climbed into the Time Machine when I materialized. They disappeared at the same moment, and the combined Force of our multiple Fluxions destroyed the machine utterly. It is the first and last of its kind, I believe.

For some reason I cannot determine, I am reversed. Mr. Gates thought that perhaps each Time-Journey reversed all the atoms of one's body. If you recall, when Gates first appeared, he kept trying to shake hands with his left hand. Likewise the coin in his pocket was backwards. In my journey to Posterity, I was reversed. When I came back to speak to myself, I was put to rights again. Now I am again reversed.

You will not be able to include this in your book, I fear, unless as a Specimen of a madman's raving, or as a silly Fiction. Let it be a Fiction, then, or ignore it, but do not deride me for a Lunatic.

For I have seen the Future; that is, I have peered into the pit of *Hell*.

I pray you remain constant to

> Your friend,
> Samuel Johnson

To Jeremy Botford, Esq.
Dear Jerry,   Sept 15.
I have not yet time to answer your letter properly. I trust Dr. J. has sent you or will send you his Reminiscence. I may say he certainly acts peculiar nowadays. I understand his demeanour has declined steadily over the past ten years. Now he is often moody and distracted, or seemingly laughs at nothing.

For example, he burst out laughing today, when I asked him his opinion on American taxation. He is an enigma to

Your affectionate
Timothy Scunthe

Postscript. Your miniature lies, for I have just today looked on the original. My memory may be faulty but my eyes are keen. The wart is on the *right*.

Your &c.,
T. Scunthe

THE LEADER
by Murray Leinster

"Murray Leinster" was the penname of the late (1896–1975) Will F. Jenkins, a master craftsman of a pulpster who skillfully worked all of the genrès of commercial fiction, and in his best work, transcended them. He wrote excellent adventure sf, thoughtful sociological sf (like his classic "First Contact"), award-winning sf (he won a Hugo Award in 1956 for "Exploration Team" and was nominated for another in 1960 for *The Pirates Of Ersatz*), and much, much more. His forty-five novels and collections in the field, while of uneven quality, contain that sense of wonder that many strive for but few really achieve.

THE LEADER

... The career of The Leader remains one of the mysteries of history. This man, illegitimate and uneducated, hysterical and superstitious, gathered about him a crowded following of those who had been discontented, but whom he turned into fanatics. Apparently by pure force of personality he seized without resistance the government of one of the world's great nations. So much is unlikely enough. But as the ruler of a civilized country he imposed upon its people the absolute despotism of a primitive sultanate. He honeycombed its society with spies. He imprisoned, tortured, and executed without trial or check. And while all this went on he received the most impassioned loyalty of his subjects! Morality was abandoned at his command with as much alacrity as common sense. He himself was subject to the grossest superstitions. He listened to astrologers and fortunetellers—and executed them when they foretold disaster. But it is not enough to be amazed at the man himself. The great mystery is that people of the Twentieth Century, trained in science and technically advanced, should join in this orgy of what seems mere madness. . . .

Concise History of Europe, Blaisdell.

Letter from Professor Albrecht Aigen, University of Brunn, to the Herr General Johann von Steppberg (Retired).

My dear General von Steppberg:

It is with reluctance that I intrude upon your retirement, but at the request of the Government I have undertaken a scientific examination of the causes which brought about The Leader's rise to power, the extraordinary popularity of his regime, the impassioned loyalty he was able to evoke, and the astounding final developments.

If you can communicate to me any memories of The Leader which may aid in understanding this most bewildering period of our history, I assure you that it will be appreciated by myself, by the authorities who wish the investigation made, and I dare to hope by posterity.

I am, my dear general, (et cetera).

Letter from General Johann von Steppberg (Retired) to Professor Albrecht Aigen, University of Brunn.
Herr Professor:

The official yearbooks of the army contain the record of my military career. I have nothing to add to that information. You say the authorities wish more. I refuse it. If they threaten my pension, I will renounce it. If they propose other pressures, I will leave the country. In short, I refuse to discuss in any manner the subject of your recent communication.

I am, Herr Professor, (et cetera).

Letter from Professor Albrecht Aigen to Dr. Karl Thurn, Professor of Psychology at University of Laibach.
My dear Karl:

I hope your psionic research goes better than my official project! My business goes nowhere! I have written to generals, ministers, and all kinds of persons who held high office under The Leader. Each and every one refuses to discuss The Leader or his own experiences under him. Why? Surely no one would blame them now! We have had to agree to pretend that no one did anything improper under The Leader, or else that what anyone did was proper at the time. So why should the nabobs of that incredible period refuse to discuss what they should know better than anyone else? I am almost reduced to asking the aid of the astrologers and soothsayers The Leader listened to. Actually, I must make a note to do so in sober earnest. At least they had their own viewpoint of events.

Speaking of viewpoints, I have had some hope of clarifying The Leader's career by comparing it with that of Prime Minister Winston, in power in his country when The Leader ruled ours. His career is splendidly documented. There is astonishingly little documentation about The Leader as a person, however. That is one of the difficulties of my task. Even worse, those who should know him best lock their lips while those—

Here is an unsolicited letter from the janitor of a building in which a former Minister of Education now has his law offices. I have many letters equally preposterous. . . .

Enclosure in letter to Dr. Karl Thurn, University of Laibach. Herr Professor:

I am the janitor of the building in which Herr Former Minister of Education Werfen has his offices. In cleaning there I saw a letter crumpled into a ball and thrown into a corner. I learned in the time of The Leader that angry actions often mean evil intentions, so I read the letter to see if the police should be notified. It was a letter from you in which you asked Herr Former Minister of Education Werfen for his memories of The Leader.

I remember The Leader, Herr Professor. He was the most holy man who ever lived, if indeed he was only a man. Once I passed the open door of an office in the building I then worked in. I looked in the door—it was the office of the then-struggling Party The Leader had founded—and I saw The Leader sitting in a chair, thinking. There was golden light about his head, Herr Professor. I have told this to other people and they do not believe me. There were shadowy other beings in the room. I saw, very faintly, great white wings. But the other beings were still because The Leader was thinking and did not wish to be disturbed. I assure you that this is true, Herr Professor. The Leader was the holiest of men—if he was only a man.

I am most respectfully, Herr Professor, (et cetera).

Letter from Fraulein Lise Grauer, nurse, in the city of Bludenz, to Professor Aigen at Brunn University.
Most respected Herr Professor:

I write this at the request of the Herr Former Police Inspector Grieg, to whom you directed a letter shortly before his death. The Herr Former Police Inspector had been ill for some time. I was his nurse. I had cared for him for months and did many small services for him, such as writing letters at his direction.

When your letter came he read it and went into a black mood of deep and bitter recollection. He would not speak for hours, and I had great difficulty in getting him to take his medicines. Just before his bedtime he called me and said sardonically:

"Lise, write to this Herr Professor for me. Say to him that I was once a decent man. When The Leader took power, I received orders that I would not accept. I submitted my resignation. Then I received orders to come to The Leader. I obeyed these orders because my resignation was not yet accepted. I was received in his office. I entered it with respect and defiance—respect because he was admitted to be the ruler of our nation; defiance because I would not obey such orders as had been sent me in his name.

"The Leader spoke to me, kindly, and as he spoke all my views changed. It suddenly seemed that I had been absurd to refuse the orders sent me. They seemed right and reasonable and even more lenient than would have been justified. . . . I left The Leader in a state in which I could not possibly fail to do anything he wished. From that moment I obeyed his orders. I was promoted. Eventually, as you know, I was in command of the Neusatz prison camp. And you know what orders I carried out there!"

I wept, Herr Professor, because the Herr Grieg's eyes were terrible to look at. He was a gentle and kindly man, Herr Professor! I was his nurse, and he was a good patient and a good man in every way. I had heard of the things that were done at Neusatz, but I could not believe that my patient had commanded them. Now, in his eyes I saw that he remembered them and that the memory was intolerable. He said very bitterly:

"Tell the Herr Professor that I can tell him nothing more. I have no other memories that would be of service to him. I have resolved, anyhow, to get rid even of these. I have kept them too long. Say to him that his letter has decided me."

I did not understand what he meant, Herr Professor. I helped him prepare for the night, and when he seemed to be resting quietly I retired, myself. I was wakened by a very loud noise. I went to see what was the matter. The Herr Former Police Inspector Grieg had managed to get out of his bed and across the room to a bureau. He opened a drawer and took out a revolver. He made his way back to his bed. He blew out his brains.

I called the police, and after investigation they instructed me to carry out his request, which I do.

Herr Professor, I do not myself remember the times of The Leader, but they must have been very terrible. If the Herr Former Police Inspector Grieg was actually in command of the Neusatz prison camp, and did actually order the things done there,—I cannot understand it, Herr Professor! Because he was a good and kindly man! If you write of him, I beg that you will mention that he was a most amiable man. I was only his nurse, but I assure you—(et cetera).

Letter from Dr. Karl Thurn, University of Laibach, to Professor Albrecht Aigen, University of Brunn.

My dear friend:

I could have predicted your failure to secure cooperation from eminent figures in The Leader's regime. So long as they keep silent, together, they can pretend to be respectable. And nobody longs so passionately to be respectable as a man who has prospered by being a swine, while he awaits an opportunity to prosper again by more swinishness. I would advise you to expect your best information from little people who suffered most and most helplessly looked on or helped while enormities were committed. Such little people will either yearn over the past like your janitor, or want most passionately to understand so that nothing of the sort can ever happen again.

Winston as a parallel to The Leader? Or as a contrast? Which? I can name one marked contrast. I doubt that anybody really and passionately wishes that Winston had never been born.

You mention my researches. You should see some of our results! I have found a rat with undeniable psychokinetic power. I have seem him move a gram-weight of cheese nearly three centimeters to where he could reach it through the cage bars. I begin to suspect a certain female dog of abilities I would prefer not to name just yet. If you can find any excuse to come to Laibach, I promise you amazing demonstrations of psi phenomena. (et cetera.)

Quotations from *Recollections of the Earl of Humber, formerly Prime Minister Winston,* by the Hon. Charles Wilberforce.

Page 231: "... This incredible event took place even while it seemed most impossible. The Prime Minister took it with his usual aplomb. I asked him what he thought of the matter a week later, at a house party in Hertfordshire. He said, 'I consider it most unfortunate. This Leader of theirs is an inherently nasty individual. Therefore he'll make nastiness the avenue to distinction so long as he's in power. The results will be tragic, because when you bottle up decency men seem to go mad. What a pity one can't bottle up nastiness! The world might become a fit place to live in!' "

Page 247: "The Prime Minister disagreed. 'There was Napoleon,' he observed. 'You might despise him, but after he talked to you you served him. He seemed to throw a spell over people. Alexander probably had the same sort of magic personality. When his personality ceased to operate, as a result of too much wine too continuously, his empire fell immediately to pieces. I've known others personally; an Afghan whom I've always thought did us a favor by getting killed by a sniper. He could have caused a great deal of trouble. I'd guess at the Khalifa. Most of the people who have this incredible persuasiveness, however, seem to set up as successful swindlers. What a pity The Leader had no taste for simple crime, and had to go in for crimes of such elaboration!"

Letter from Professor Albrecht Aigen, University of Brunn, to Dr. Karl Thurn, University of Laibach.
My dear Karl:

You make me curious with your talk of a rat which levitates crumbs of cheese and a she-dog who displays other psi abilities. I assume that you have found the experimental conditions which let psi powers operate without hindrance. I shall hope someday to see and conceivably to understand.

My own affairs are in hopeless confusion. At the moment I am overwhelmed with material about The Leader, the value of which I cannot estimate. Strange! I ask people who should know what I am commissioned to discover, and they refuse to answer. But it becomes known that I ask, and thousands of little people write me to volunteer impassioned details of their experiences while The Leader ruled. Some are bitter because they did what they did and felt as they felt. These seem to believe in magic or demoniac possession as the reason they behaved with such conspicuous insanity. Others gloat over their deeds, which they recount with gusto—and then express pious regret with no great convincingness. Some of these accounts nauseate me. But something utterly abnormal was in operation, somehow, to cause The Leader's ascendancy!

I wish I could select the important data with certainty. Almost anything, followed up, might reveal the key. But I do not know what to follow! I plan to go to Bozen, where the new monstrous computer has been set up, and see if there is any way in which it could categorize my data and detect a pattern of more than bewildered and resentful frenzy.

On the way back to Brunn I shall stop by to talk to you. There is so much to say! I anticipate much of value from your detached and analytic mind. I confess, also, that I am curious about your research. This she-dog with psi powers, of which you give no account . . . I am intrigued.

As always, I am, (et cetera).

Letter from Professor Albrecht Aigen, written from the Mathematical Institute at Bozen, to Dr. Karl Thurn, University of Laibach.

My dear Karl:

This is in haste. There is much agitation among the computer staff at the Institute. An assistant technician has been discovered to be able to predict the answer the computer will give to problems set up at random. He is one Hans Schweeringen and it is unbelievable.

Various numerals are impressed on the feed-in tape of the computer. Sections of the tape are chosen at random by someone who is blindfolded. They are fed unread into the computer, together with instructions to multiply, subtract, extract roots, et cetera, which are similarly chosen at random and are not known to anyone. Once in twenty times or so, Schweeringen predicts the result of this meaningless computation before the computer has made it. This is incredible! The odds are trillions to one against it! Since nobody knows the sums or instructions given to the computer, it cannot be mind-reading in any form. It must be pure precognition. Do you wish to talk to him?

He is uneasy at the attention he attracts, perhaps because his father was one of The Leader's secretaries and was executed, it is presumed, for knowing too much. Telegraph me if you wish me to try to bring him to you.

Your friend—

Telegram from Dr. Karl Thurn, Professor of Psychology at Laibach University, to Professor Albrecht Aigen, in care of the Mathematical Institute at Bozen:

Take tapes which produced answers Schweeringen predicted. Run them through computer when he knows nothing of it. Wire result.

Thurn

Telegram. Professor Albrecht Aigen, at The Mathematical Institute in Bozen, to Dr. Karl Thurn, University of Laibach.

How did you know? The tapes do not give the same answers when run through the computer without Schweeringen's knowledge. The only possible answer is that the computer sometimes errs to match his predictions. But this is more impossible than precognition. This is beyond the conceivable. It cannot be! What now?

Aigen

Telegram from Dr. Karl Thurn, University of Laibach, to Professor Albrecht Aigen, care Mathematical Institute, Bozen.

Naturally I suspect psi. He belongs with my rat and she-dog. Try to arrange it.

Thurn

Telegram from Professor Albrecht Aigen, Mathematical Institute, Bozen, to Dr. Karl Thurn, University of Laibach.

Schweeringen refuses further tests. Fears proof he causes malfunctioning of computer will cause unemployment here and may destroy all hope of hoped-for career in mathematics.

Aigen

Telegram from Professor Albrecht Aigen, at Mathematical Institute, to Dr. Karl Thurn, University of Laibach.

Terrible news. Riding bus to Institute this morning, Schweeringen was killed when bus was involved in accident.

Aigen

Telegram from Dr. Karl Thurn, University of Laibach, to Professor Albrecht Aigen, care Mathematical Institute, Bozen.

Deeply regret death Schweeringen. When you come here please try to bring all known family history. Psi ability sometimes inherited. Could be tie-in his father's execution and use of psi ability.

Thurn

*   *   *

Letter from Professor Albrecht Aigen, at Brunn University, to Dr. Karl Thurn, University of Laibach.

My dear Karl:

I have first to thank you for your warm welcome and to
express my gratitude for your attention while I was your
guest. Since my return I have written many inquiries about
Schweeringen's father. There are so far no replies, but I have
some hope that people who will not tell of their own experiences may tell about someone else—especially someone now
dead. This may be a useful device to get at least some
information from people who so far have refused any. Naturally I will pass on to you anything I learn.

I try to work again upon the task assigned me—to investigate the rise and power of The Leader. I find it hard to
concentrate. My mind goes back to your laboratory. I am
deeply shaken by my experience there. I had thought nothing
could be more bewildering than my own work. Consider:
Today I received a letter in which a man tells me amazedly of
the life he led in a slave-labor camp during the time of The
Leader's rule. He describes the attempt of another prisoner to
organize a revolt of the prisoners. While he spoke of the
brutality of the guards and the intolerably hard labor and the
deliberately insufficient food, they cheered him. But when he
accused The Leader of having ordered these things—the
prisoners fell upon him with cries of fury. They killed him. I
had this information verified. It was true.

I cannot hope for a sane explanation of such things. But a
sane explanation for my experience seems even less probable.
I am impressed by your rat who levitates crumbs of cheese.
But I am appalled; I am horrified; I am stupefied by what I
did! You asked me to wait for you in a certain laboratory
beyond a door. I entered. I saw a small, fat, mangy she-dog in
a dog-run. She looked at me and wagged her tail. I thereupon
went to the other end of the laboratory, opened a box, and
took out a handful of strange objects you later told me are
sweetmeats to a dog. I gave them to the animal.

Why did I do it? How was it that I went directly to a box of
which I knew nothing, opened it as a matter of course, and

took out objects I did not even recognize, to give them to that unpleasant small beast? How did I know where to go? Why did I go? Why should I give those then-meaningless objects to the dog? It is as if I were enchanted!

You say that it is a psi phenomenon. The rat causes small objects to move. The dog, you say, causes persons to give it canine candy. I revolt against the conclusion, which I cannot reason away. If you are right, we are at the mercy of our domestic animals! Dog-lovers are not people who love dogs, but people who are enslaved by dogs. Cat-lovers are merely people who have been seized upon by cats to support and pet and cater to them. This is intolerable! I shall fear all pets from now on! I throw myself back into my own work to avoid thinking of it. I—

Later. I did not mail this letter because an appalling idea occurred to me. This could bear upon my investigation! Do you think The Leader—No! It could not be! It would be madness. . . .

Extract from a letter from Dr. Karl Thurn to Professor Albrecht Aigen.

. . . I deplore your reaction. It has the emotional quality of a reaction to witchcraft or magic, but psi is not witchcraft. It is a natural force. No natural force is either nonexistent or irresistible. No natural force is invariably effective. Psi is not irresistible under all circumstances. It is not always effective. My rat cannot levitate cheese-crumbs weighing more than 1.7 grams. My she-dog could not make you give her dog-candy once you were on guard. When you went again into the laboratory she looked at you and wagged her tail as before. You say that you thought of the box and of opening it, but you did not. It was not even an effort of will to refrain.

A lesser will or a lower grade of personality cannot overwhelm a greater one. Not ever! Lesser beings can only urge. The astrologers used to say that the stars incline, but they do not compel. The same can be said of psi—or of magnetism or gravitation or what you will. Schweeringen could not make the computer err when it had to err too egregiously. A greater psi ability was needed than he had. A greater psi power than was available would have been needed to make you give the dog candy, once you were warned.

I do not apply these statements to your so-called appalling idea. I carefully refrain from doing so. It is your research, not mine. . . .

Extract from letter to Professor Albrecht Aigen from the Herr Friedrich Holm, supervisor of electrical maintenance, municipal electrical service, Untersberg.

Herr Professor:

You have written to ask if I knew a certain Herr Schweeringen, attached to The Leader's personal staff during his regime. I did know such a person. I was then in charge of electrical maintenance in The Leader's various residences. Herr Schweeringen was officially one of The Leader's secretaries, but his actual task was to make predictions for The Leader, like a soothsayer or a medium. He had a very remarkable gift. There were times when it was especially needful that there be no electrical failures—when The Leader was to be in residence, for example. On such occasions it was my custom to ask Herr Schweeringen if there was apt to be any failure of apparatus under my care. At least three times he told me yes. In one case it was an elevator, in another refrigeration, in a third a fuse would blow during a State dinner.

I overhauled the elevator, but it failed nevertheless. I replaced the refrigeration motor, and the new motor failed. In the third case I changed the fuse to a new and tested one, and then placed a new, fused line around the fuse Herr Schweeringen had said would blow, and placed a workman beside it. When the fuse did blow as predicted, my workman instantly closed the extra-line switch, so that the lights of the State dinner barely flickered. But I shudder when I think of the result if Herr Schweeringen had not warned me.

He was executed a few days before the period of confusion began, which ended as everyone knows. I do not know the reason for his execution. It was said, however, that The Leader executed him personally. This, Herr Professor, is all that I know of the matter.

Very respectfully, (et cetera).

Letter from Herr Theophrastus Paracelsus Bosche, astrologer, to Professor Albrecht Aigen, Brunn University.

Most respected Herr Professor:

I am amused that a so-eminent scientist like yourself should ask information from a so-despised former astrologer to The Leader. It is even more amusing that you ask about a mere soothsayer—a man who displayed an occult gift of prophecy—whom you should consider merely one of the charlatans like myself whom The Leader consulted, and who are unworthy of consideration by a scientific historian. We have no effect upon history, most respected Herr Professor! None at all. Oh, none! I am much diverted.

You ask about the Herr Schweeringen. He was a predictor, using his occult gift of second sight to foreknow events and tell The Leader about them. You will remember that The Leader considered himself to have occult powers of leadership and decision, and that all occult powers should contribute to his greatness. At times of great stress, such as when The Leader demanded ever-increasing concessions from other nations on threat of war, he was especially concerned that occult predictions promise him success.

At a certain time the international tension was greater than ever before. If The Leader could doubt the rightness of any of his actions, he doubted it then. There was great danger of war. Prime Minister Winston had said flatly that The Leader must withdraw his demands or fight. The Leader was greatly agitated. He demanded my prediction. I considered the stars and predicted discreetly that war would be prevented by some magnificent achievement by The Leader. Truly, if he got out of his then situation it would be a magnificent achievement. But astrology, of course, could only indicate it but not describe what it would be.

The Leader was confident that he could achieve anything

he could imagine because he had convinced even himself that only treason or disloyalty could cause him to fail in any matter. He demanded of his generals what achievement would prevent the war. They were not encouraging. He demanded of his civilian political advisers. They dared not advise him to retreat. They offered nothing. He demanded of his occult advisers.

The Herr Schweeringen demanded of me that I tell him my exact prediction. His nerves were bad, then, and he twitched with the strain. Someone had to describe the great achievement The Leader would make. It would be dangerous not to do so. I told him the prediction, I found his predicament diverting. He left me, still twitching and desperately sunk in thought.

I now tell you exact, objective facts, Herr Professor, with no interpretation of my own upon them. The Herr Schweeringen was closeted with The Leader. I am told that his face was shining with confidence when he went to speak to The Leader. It was believed among us charlatans that he considered that he foreknew what The Leader would do to prevent war at this time.

Two hours later there were shots in The Leader's private quarters. The Leader came out, his eyes glaring, and ordered Herr Schweeringen's body removed. He ordered the execution of the four senior generals of the General Staff, the Minister of Police, and several other persons. He then went into seclusion, from which he emerged only briefly to give orders making the unthinkable retreat that Prime Minister Winston had demanded. No one spoke to him for a week. Confusion began. These are objective facts. I now add one small boast.

My discreet prediction had come true, and it is extremely diverting to think about it. The Leader had achieved magnificently. The war was prevented not only for the moment but for later times, too. The Leader's achievement was the destruction of his regime by destroying the brains that had made it operate!

It is quite possible that you will consider this information a lie. That will be quite droll. However, I am, most respected Herr Professor, (et cetera).

Letter from Dr. Karl Thurn, University of Laibach, to Professor Albrecht Aigen, Brunn University.

My dear friend:

Your information about the elder Schweeringen received. The information about his prediction is interesting. I could wish that it were complete, but that would seem to be hopeless. Your question, asked in a manner suggesting great disturbance, is another matter. I will answer it as well as I can, my friend, but please remember that you asked. I volunteer nothing. The question of the rise and power of The Leader is your research, not mine.

Here is my answer. Years back an American researcher named Rhine obtained seemingly conclusive proof that telepathy took place. Tonight he would have a "sender," here, attempt to transmit some item telepathically to a "receiver," there. Tomorrow morning he would compare the record of what the "sender" had attempted to transmit, with the record of what the "receiver" considered he had received. The correspondence was far greater than chance. He considered that telepathy was proven.

But then Rhine made tests for precognition. He secured proof that some persons could predict with greater-than-probability frequency that some particular event, to be determined by chance, would take place tomorrow. He secured excellent evidence for precognition.

Then it was realized that if one could foresee what dice would read tomorrow—dice not yet thrown—one should be able to read what a report would read tomorrow—a report not yet written. In short, if one can foreknow what a comparison will reveal, telepathy before the comparison is unproven. In proving precognition, he had destroyed his evidence for telepathy.

It appears that something similar has happened, which our correspondence has brought out. Young Schweeringen predicted what a computer would report from unknown numerals and instructions. In order for the computer to match his predictions, it had to err. It did. Therefore one reasons that he did not predict what the computer would produce. The computer produced what he predicted. In effect, what appeared to be foreknowledge was psychokinesis—the same phenomenon as the movement of crumbs of cheese by my rat. One may strongly suspect that when young Herr Schweeringen knew in *advance* what the computer would say, he actually knew in advance what he could make it say. It is possible that one can consciously know in advance only what one can unconsciously bring about. If one can bring about only minor happenings, one can never predict great ones.

This is my answer to your question. I would like very much to know what the elder Schweeringen predicted that The Leader would accomplish!

My she-dog has died. We had a new attendant in the laboratory. He fed her to excess. She died of it. (Et cetera.)

Letter from Professor Albrecht Aigen to Dr. Karl Thurn. My dear Karl:

I have resolved to dismiss psionic ability from my investigation into The Leader's rise to power. This much I will concede: The Leader could enslave—englamour—enchant anyone who met him personally. He did. To a lesser degree, this irresistible persuasiveness is a characteristic of many successful swindlers. But he could not have englamoured the whole nation. He did not meet enough persons personally to make his regime possible, unless he could cause other persons to apply their own magnetism to further his ambitions, and they others and others and so on—like an endless series of magnets magnetized orginally from one. This is not possible. I restrict myself to normal, plausible hypotheses—of which so far I have no faintest trace.

You agree with me, do you not, that it was impossible for The Leader to weave a web of enchantment over the whole nation by his own psi energies controlling the psi energies of others? I would welcome your assurance that it could not be.

Letter from Professor Albrecht Aigen to Dr. Karl Thurn.
My dear Karl:

Did you receive my last letter? I am anxious to have your assurance that it was impossible that The Leader could englamour the whole nation by his psionic gifts.

Telegram, Dr. Albrecht Aigen to Dr. Karl Thurn.
Karl, as you are my friend, answer me!

Letter, Dr. Karl Thurn to Professor Albrecht Aigen.
. . . But what have you discovered, my friend, that you are afraid to face?

Letter, Professor Albrecht Aigen to Dr. Karl Thurn.
My dear Karl:

I appeal to you because I have discovered how nearly our nation and the whole world escaped horrors beside which those of The Leader's actual regime would seem trivial. Give me reasons, arguments, proofs beyond question, which I can put into my report on his career! I must demonstrate beyond question that psi ability did not cause his ascendancy! Help me to contrive a lie which will keep anyone, ever, from dreaming that psi ability can be used to seize a government and a nation. It could seize the world more terribly . . .

I cannot express the urgency of this need! There are others who possess The Leader's powers in a lesser degree. They must remain only swindlers and such, without ambitions to rule, or they might study The Leader's career as Napoleon studied Alexander's. There must be no hint, anywhere, of the secret I have discovered. There must be nothing to lead to the least thought of it! The Leader could have multiplied his power ten-thousandfold! Another like him must never learn how it could be done!

I beg your help, Karl! I am shaken. I am terrified. I wish that I had not undertaken this research. I wish it almost as desperately as I wish that The Leader had never been born!

Letter from Colonel Sigmund Knoeller, retired, to Professor Albrecht Aigen, Brunn University.

Herr Professor:

In response to your authorized request for information about certain events; I have the honor to inform you that at the time you mention I was Major in command of the Second Battalion of the 161st Infantry Regiment, assigned to guard duty about the residence of The Leader. Actual guard duty was performed by the secret police. My battalion merely provided sentries around the perimeter of the residence, and at certain places within.

On August 19th I received a command to march three companies of my men into the residence, to receive orders from The Leader in person. This command was issued by the Herr General Breyer, attached to The Leader as a military aide.

I led my men inside according to the orders, guided by the orderly who had brought them. I entered an inner courtyard. There was disturbance. People moved about in a disorderly fashion and chattered agitatedly. This was astonishing in The Leader's residence. I marched up to General Breyer, who stood outside a group biting his nails. I saluted and said: "Major Knoeller reporting for orders, Herr General."

There was then confusion in the nearby squabbling group. A man burst out of it and waved his arms at me. He looked like The Leader. He cried shrilly:

"Arrest these men! All of them! Then shoot them!"

I looked at the Herr General Breyer. He bit his nails. The man who looked so much like The Leader foamed at the mouth. But he was not The Leader. That is, in every respect he resembled The Leader to whom I owed loyalty as did everyone. But no one who was ever in The Leader's presence failed to know it. There was a feeling. One knew to the inmost part of one's soul that he was The Leader who must be reverenced and obeyed. But one did not feel that way about this man, though he resembled The Leader so strongly.

"Arrest them!" shrilled the man ferociously. "I command it! I am The Leader! Shoot them!"

When I still waited for General Breyer to give me orders, the man shrieked at the troopers. He commanded them to kill General Breyer and all the rest, including me. And if he had been The Leader they would have obeyed. But he was not. So my men stood stiffly at attention, waiting for my orders or General Breyer's.

There was now complete silence in the courtyard. The formerly squabbling men watched as if astonished. As if they did not believe their eyes. But I waited for General Breyer to give his commands.

The man screamed in a terrible, frustrated rage. He waved his arms wildly. He foamed at the mouth and shrieked at me. I waited for orders from General Breyer. After a long time he ceased to bite his nails and said in a strange voice:

"You had better have this man placed in confinement, Major Knoeller. See that he is not injured. Double all guards and mount machine guns in case of rioting outside. Dismiss!"

I obeyed my commands. My men took the struggling, still-shrieking man and put him in a cell in the guardhouse. There was a drunken private there, awaiting court-martial. He was roused and annoyed when his new companion shrieked and screamed and shook the bars of the door. He kicked the man who looked so much like The Leader. I then had the civilian placed in a separate cell, but he continued to rave incoherently until I had the regimental surgeon give him an injection to quiet him. He sank into drugged sleep with foam about his lips.

He looked remarkably like The Leader. I have never seen such a resemblance! But he was not The Leader or we would have known him.

There was no disturbance outside the residence. The doubled guards and the mounted machine guns were not needed.

I am, Herr Professor, (et cetera).

Letter, with enclosure, from Professor Albrecht Aigen, Brunn University, to Dr. Karl Thurn, University of Laibach. My dear Karl:

Because of past sharing in my research, you will realize what the enclosed means. It is part of the report of the physicians who examined The Leader three days after his confinement in a military prison. He had recovered much of his self-control. He spoke with precision. He appeared even calm, though he was confused in some matters. The doctors addressed him as "My Leader" because he refused to reply otherwise.

(Enclosure)

Dr. Kundmann: But, My Leader, we do not understand what has happened! You were terribly disturbed. You were even ... even confused in your behavior! Can you tell us what took place?

The Leader: I suffered a great danger and a temporary damage. That villain Schweeringen—I shot him. It was a mistake. I should have had him worked over—at length!

Dr. Messner: My Leader, will you be so good as to tell us the nature of the danger and the damage?

The Leader: Schweeringen probably told someone what he would propose to me. It was his conviction that because of my special gifts I could cause anyone, not only to obey me, but to pour out to me, directly, his inmost thoughts and memories. Of course this is true. The danger was that of the contact of my mind with an inferior one. But I allowed Schweeringen to persuade me that I should risk even this for the service of my people. Therefore I contacted the mind of Prime Minister Winston, so I could know every scheme and every plan he might have or know to exist to injure my people. I intended, however, to cause him to become loyal to me—though I would later have had him shot. Schweeringen had betrayed me, though. When I made contact with Winston's mind, it was not only inferior, but diseased! There was a contagion which temporarily affected the delicate balance of my intuition. For a short time I could not know, as ordinarily, what was best for my people.

(End of enclosure)

You will see, my dear Karl, what took place. To you and to me this explains everything. In the background of my research and your information it is clear. Fortunately, The Leader's mind was unstable. The strain and shock of so unparalleled an experience as complete knowledge of another brain's contents destroyed his rationality. He became insane. Insane, he no longer had the psi gifts by which he had seized and degraded our nation. He ceased to be The Leader.

But you will see that this must be hidden! Another monster like The Leader, or Napoleon—perhaps even lesser monsters—could attempt the same feat. But they might be less unstable! They might be able to invade the mind of any human being, anywhere, and drain it of any secret or impress upon it any desire or command, however revolting. You see, Karl, why this must never become known! It must be hidden forever.

Letter from Dr. Karl Thurn, University of Laibach, to Professor Albrecht Aigen, Brunn University.

My dear friend:

I am relieved! I feared for your judgment. I thought that perhaps overwork and frustration had set up an anxiety-block to make you cease your work. But you are quite right. Your analysis is brilliant. And now that you have pointed it out, unquestionably a man with The Leader's psi powers could force another man's brain to transmit all its contents to him.

But consider the consequences! Consider the conditions of such an event. One's brain is designed to work within one's own skull, dealing with sensory messages and the like. Very occasionally it acts outside, shifting crumbs of cheese and confusing computers—and securing candy. But even when one's will controls outside actions, it does not fuse with the outside brain or thing. It molds or moves the recipient mind, but there is never a sharing of memory. You have explained why.

Consider what must happen if a brain of limited power and essentially emotional operation is linked to another and more powerful one. Assume for a moment that my she-dog had linked her brain to yours, even momentarily. Do you realize that she would not have gotten your memories, much less your power to reason? She would not even have acquired your knowledge of the meaning of words! When a bright light shines in your eyes, you see nothing else. When thunder rolls in your ears, you do not hear the ticking of a clock. When you suffer pain, you do not notice a feather's tickle. If my she-dog had linked her mind to yours, she would have experienced something which is knowledge more firmly fixed and more continuously known than anything else in your conscious life. This overwhelmingly strong conviction would have been so powerful and so positive that it would be imprinted— branded—burned into every cell of her brain. She could never get it out.

But in receiving this overwhelming experience she would not get your memories or power to reason or even your personality. She would have experienced only your identity. She would have received only the conviction that she was yourself! She would have been like those poor lunatics who believe that they are Napoleon, though they have nothing of Napoleon in them but the conviction of identity. They do not know when he was born or have more than the vaguest notion of what he did, but they try to act as who he was—according to their own ideas of how Napoleon would act in their situation. This is how my she-dog would have behaved.

I am relieved. You have explained everything. Your letter gave me the suspicion. I secured a transcript of the Herr Doctor's report for myself. My suspicion became a certainty. You will find the clue in the report. Consider: The Leader had had the experience I imagined for my she-dog. He had linked his mind with a stronger one and a greater personality—if it must be said, a greater man. For a moment The Leader knew what that man knew most certainly, with most profound conviction, with most positive knowledge. It was burned into his brain. He could never get it out. He did not secure that other man's memories or knowledge or ability. He was blind-ed, deafened, dazed by the overwhelming conviction that the other man had of his own identity. It would not be possible for him to get anything else from a stronger mind and a greater person. Nor could anyone else succeed where he failed, my friend! There is no danger of any man seizing the world by seizing the minds of all his fellows! One who tries will meet the fate of The Leader.

You realize what that fate was, of course. He suddenly ceased to be the monster who could cast a spell of blind adoration for himself. He ceased to be The Leader! So the doctors gave him truth-serum so he would not try to conceal anything from them. The result is in the transcript on the third page beyond the place you quoted to me. There the doctors asked The Leader who he was. Read his answer, my friend! It proves everything! He said:

"I am Prime Minister Winston."

ARISTOTLE AND THE GUN

by L. Sprague de Camp

Quietly and without great fanfare, Sprague de Camp has been producing a large body of wonderful science fiction and fantasy for more than forty years. An intellectual gentleman with wide-ranging interests, he has also written dozens of books outside of the sf field, including works on science and biography. Among his notable sf and fantasy works are *Lest Darkness Fall* (1941), *Rogue Queen* (1951) and the stories contained in *The Best of L. Sprague de Camp* (1978), the definitive collection to date. He is still going strong.

ARISTOTLE AND THE GUN

> *From:*
> Sherman Weaver, Librarian
> The Palace
> Paumanok, Sewanhaki
> Sachimate of Lenape
> Flower Moon 3, 3097

To:
Messire Markos Koukidas
Consulate of the Balkan Commonwealth
Kataapa, Muskhogian Federation

My dear Consul:

You have no doubt heard of our glorious victory at Ptaksit, when our noble Sachim destroyed the armored chivalry of the Mengwe by the brilliant use of pikemen and archery. (I suggested it to him years ago, but never mind.) Sagoyewatha and most of his Senecas fell, and the Oneidas broke before our countercharge. The envoys from the Grand Council of the Long House arrive tomorrow for a peace-pauwau. The roads to the South are open again, so I send you my long-promised account of the events that brought me from my own world into this one.

If you could have stayed longer on your last visit, I think I could have made the matter clear, despite the language difficulty and my hardness of hearing. But perhaps, if I give you a simple narrative, in the order in which things happened to me, truth will transpire.

Know, then, that I was born into a world that looks like this one on the map, but is very different as regards human affairs. I tried to tell you of some of the triumphs of our natural philosophers, of our machines and discoveries. No doubt you thought me a first-class liar, though you were too polite to say so.

Nonetheless, my tale is true, though for reasons that will appear I cannot prove it. I was one of those natural philosophers. I commanded a group of younger philosophers, engaged in a task called *a project,* at a center of learning named Brookhaven, on the south short of Sewanhaki twenty parasangs east of Paumanok. Paumanok itself was known as Brooklyn, and formed part of an even larger city called New York.

My project had to do with the study of space-time. (Never mind what that means but read on.) At this center we had learned to get vast amounts of power from sea water by what we called a fusion process. By this process we could concentrate so much power in a small space that we could warp the entity called space-time and cause things to travel in time as our other machines traveled in space.

When our calculations showed that we could theoretically hurl an object back in time, we began to build a machine for testing this hypothesis. First we built a small pilot model. In this we sent small objects back in time for short periods.

We began with inanimate objects. Then we found that a rabbit or rat could also be projected without harm. The time-translation would not be permanent; rather, it acted like one of these rubber balls the Hesperians play games with. The object would stay in the desired time for a period determined by the power used to project it and its own mass, and would then return spontaneously to the time and place from which it started.

We had reported our progress regularly, but my chief had other matters on his mind and did not read our reports for many months. When he got a report saying that we were completing a machine to hurl human beings back in time, however, he awoke to what was going on, read our previous reports, and called me in.

"Sherm," he said, "I've been discussing this project with Washington, and I'm afraid they take a dim view of it."

"Why?" said I, astonished.

"Two reasons. For one thing, they think you've gone off the reservation. They're much more interested in the Antarctic Reclamation Project and want to concentrate all our appropriations and brain power on it.

"For another, they're frankly scared of this time machine of yours. Suppose you went back, say, to the time of Alexander the Great and shot Alexander before he got started? That would change all later history, and we'd go out like candles."

"Ridiculous," I said.

"Well, what *would* happen?"

"Our equations are not conclusive, but there are several possibilities. As you will see if you read Report No. 9, it depends on whether space-time has a positive or negative curvature. If positive, any disturbance in the past tends to be ironed out in subsequent history, so that things become more and more nearly identical with what they would have been anyway. If negative, then events will diverge more and more from their original pattern with time.

"Now, as I showed in this report, the chances are overwhelmingly in favor of a positive curvature. However, we intend to take every precaution and make our first tests for short periods, with a minimum—"

"That's enough," said my superior, holding up a hand. "It's very interesting, but the decision has already been made."

"What do you mean?"

"I mean Project A-257 is to be closed down and a final report written at once. The machines are to be dismantled, and the group will be put to work on another project."

"What?" I shouted. "But you can't stop us just when we're on the verge—"

"I'm sorry, Sherm, but I can. That's what the AEC decided at yesterday's meeting. It hasn't been officially announced, but they gave me positive orders to kill the project as soon as I got back here."

"Of all the lousy, arbitrary, benighted—"

"I know how you feel, but I have no choice."

I lost my temper and defied him, threatening to go ahead with the project anyway. It was ridiculous, because he could easily dismiss me for insubordination. However, I knew he valued my ability and counted on his wanting to keep me for that reason. But he was clever enough to have his cake and eat it.

"If that's how you feel," he said, "the section is abolished here and now. Your group will be broken up and assigned to other projects. You'll be kept on at your present rating with the title of consultant. Then when you're willing to talk sense, perhaps we can find you a suitable job."

I stamped out of his office and went home to brood. I ought now to tell you something of myself. I am old enough to be objective, I hope. And, as I have but a few years left, there is no point in pretence.

I have always been a solitary, misanthropic man. I had little interest in or liking of my fellow man, who naturally paid me back in the same coin. I was awkward and ill at ease in company. I had a genius for saying the wrong thing and making a fool of myself.

I never understood people. Even when I watched and planned my own actions with the greatest care, I never could tell how others would react to them. To me men were and are an unpredictable, irrational, and dangerous species of hairless ape. While I could avoid some of my worst gaffes by keeping my own counsel and watching my every word, they did not like that either. They considered me a cold, stiff, unfriendly sort of person when I was only trying to be polite and avoid offending them.

I never married. At the time of which I speak, I was verging on middle age without a single close friend and no more acquaintances than my professional work required.

My only interest, outside my work, was a hobby of the history of science. Unlike most of my fellow philosophers, I was historically minded, with a good smattering of a classical education. I belonged to the History of Science Society and wrote papers on the history of science for its periodical *Isis*.

I went back to my little rented house, feeling like Galileo. He was a scientist persecuted for his astronomical theories by the religious authorities of my world several centuries before my time, as George Schwartzhorn was a few years ago in this world's Europe.

I felt I had been born too soon. If only the world were scientifically more advanced, my genius would be appreciated and my personal difficulties solved.

Well, I thought, why is the world not scientifically more advanced? I reviewed the early growth of science. Why had not your fellow countrymen, when they made a start towards a scientific age two thousand to twenty-five hundred years ago, kept at it until they made science the self-supporting, self-accelerating thing it at last became—in my world, that is?

I knew the answers that historians of science had worked out. One was the effect of slavery, which made work disgraceful to a free man and therefore made experiment and invention unattractive because they looked like work. Another was the primitive state of the mechanical arts: things like making clear glass and accurate measuring devices. Another was the Hellenes' fondness for spinning cosmic theories without enough facts to go on, the result of which was that most of their theories were wildly wrong.

Well, thought I, could a man go back to this period and, by applying a stimulus at the right time and place, give the necessary push to set the whole trend rolling off in the right direction?

People had written fantastic stories about a man's going back in time and overawing the natives by a display of the discoveries of his own later era. More often than not, such a time-traveling hero came to a bad end. The people of the earlier time killed him as a witch, or he met with an accident, or something happened to keep him from changing history. But, knowing these dangers, I could forestall them by careful planning.

It would do little or no good to take back some major

invention, like a printing press or an automobile, and turn it
over to the ancients in the hope of grafting it on their culture.
I could not teach them to work it in a reasonable time; and, if
it broke down or ran out of supplies, there would be no way to
get it running again.

What I had to do was to find a key mind and implant in it
an appreciation of sound scientific method. He would have to
be somebody who would have been important in any event, or
I could not count on his influence's spreading far and wide.

After study of Sarton and other historians of science, I
picked Aristotle. You have heard of him, have you not? He
existed in your world just as he did in mine. In fact, up to
Aristotle's time our worlds were one and the same.

Aristotle was one of the greatest minds of all time. In my
world, he was the first encyclopedist; the first man who tried
to know everything, write down everything, and explain
everything. He did much good original scientific work, too,
mostly in biology.

However, Aristotle tried to cover so much ground, and
accepted so many fables as facts, that he did much harm to
science as well as good. For, when a man of such colossal
intellect goes wrong, he carries with him whole generations
of weaker minds who cite him as an infallible authority. Like
his colleagues, Aristotle never appreciated the need for constant verification. Thus, though he was married twice, he
said that men have more teeth than women. He never thought
to ask either of his wives to open her mouth for a count. He
never grasped the need for invention and experiment.

Now, if I could catch Aristotle at the right period of his
career, perhaps I could give him a push in the right direction.

When would that be? Normally, one would take him as a
young man. But Aristotle's entire youth, from seventeen to
thirty-seven, was spent in Athens listening to Plato's lec-
tures. I did not wish to compete with Plato, an overpowering
personality who could argue rings around anybody. His viewpoint was mystical and anti-scientific, the very thing I wanted
to steer Aristotle away from. Many of Aristotle's intellectual
vices can be traced back to Plato's influence.

I did not think it wise to present myself in Athens either

during Aristotle's early period, when he was a student under Plato, or later, when he headed his own school. I could not pass myself off as a Hellene, and the Hellenes of that time had a contempt for all non-Hellenes, who they called "barbarians." Aristotle was one of the worst offenders in this respect. Of course this is a universal human failing, but it was particularly virulent among Athenian intellectuals. In his later Athenian period, too, Aristotle's ideas would probably be too set with age to change.

I concluded that my best chance would be to catch Aristotle while he was tutoring young Alexander the Great at the court of Philip the Second of Macedon. He would have regarded Macedon as a backward country, even though the court spoke Attic Greek. Perhaps he would be bored with bluff Macedonian stag-hunting squires and lonesome for intellectual company. As he would regard the Macedonians as the next thing to *barbaroi,* another barbarian would not appear at such a disadvantage there as at Athens.

Of course, whatever I accomplished with Aristotle, the results would depend on the curvature of space-time. I had not been wholly frank with my superior. While the equations tended to favor the hypothesis of a positive curvature, the probability was not overwhelming as I claimed. Perhaps my efforts would have little effect on history, or perhaps the effect would grow and widen like ripples in a pool. In the latter case the existing world would, as my superior said, be snuffed out.

Well, at that moment I hated the existing world and would not give a snap of my fingers for its destruction. I was going to create a much better one and come back from ancient times to enjoy it.

Our previous experiments showed that I could project myself back to ancient Macedon with an accuracy of about two months temporally and a half-parasang spatially. The maching included controls for positioning the time traveler anywhere on the globe, and safety devices for locating him above the surface of the earth, not in a place already occupied by a solid object. The equations showed that I should stay in

Macedon about nine weeks before being snapped back to the present.

Once I had made up my mind, I worked as fast as I could. I telephoned my superior (you remember what a telephone is?) and made my peace. I said:

"I know I was a damned fool, Fred, but this thing was my baby; my one chance to be a great and famous scientist. I might have got a Nobel prize out of it."

"Sure, I know, Sherm," he said. "When are you coming back to the lab?"

"Well—uh—what about my group?"

"I held up the papers on that, in case you might change your mind. So if you come back, all will go on organization-wise as before."

"You want that final report on A-257, don't you?" I said, trying to keep my voice level.

"Sure."

"Then don't let the mechanics start to dismantle the machines until I've written the report."

"No; I've had the place locked up since yesterday."

"Okay. I want to shut myself in with the apparatus and the data sheets for a while and bat out the report without being bothered."

"That'll be fine," he said.

My first step in getting ready for my journey was to buy a suit of classical traveler's clothing from a theatrical costume company. This comprised a knee-length pull-over tunic or chiton, a short horseman's cloak or chlamys, knitted buskins, sandals, a broad-brimmed black felt hat, and a staff. I stopped shaving, though I did not have time to raise a respectable beard.

My auxiliary equipment included a purse of coinage of the time, mostly golden Macedonian staters. Some of these coins were genuine, bought from a numismatic supply house, but most were copies I cast myself in the laboratory at night. I made sure of being rich enough to live decently for longer than my nine weeks' stay. This was not hard, as the purchasing power of precious metals was more than fifty times greater in the classical world than in mine.

I wore the purse attached to a heavy belt next to my skin. From this belt also hung a missile-weapon called a *gun*, which I have told you about. This was a small gun, called a pistol or revolver. I did not mean to shoot anybody, or expose the gun at all if I could help it. It was there as a last resort.

I also took several devices of our science to impress Aristotle: a pocket microscope and a magnifying glass, a small telescope, a compass, my timepiece, a flashlight, a small camera, and some medicines. I intended to show these things to people of ancient times only with the greatest caution. By the time I had slung all these objects in their pouches and cases from my belt, I had a heavy load. Another belt over the tunic supported a small purse for day-to-day buying and an all-purpose knife.

I already had a good reading knowledge of classical Greek, which I tried to polish by practice with the spoken language and listening to it on my talking machine. I knew I should arrive speaking with an accent, for we had no way of knowing exactly what Attic Greek sounded like.

I decided, therefore, to pass myself off as a traveler from India. Nobody would believe I was a Hellene. If I said I came from the north or west, no Hellene would listen to me, as they regarded Europeans as warlike but half-witted savages. If I said I was from some well-known civilized country like Carthage, Egypt, Babylonia, or Persia, I should be in danger of meeting someone who knew those countries and of being exposed as a fraud.

To tell the truth of my origin, save under extraordinary circumstances, would be most imprudent. It would lead to my being considered a lunatic or a liar, as I can guess that your good self has more than once suspected me of being.

An Indian, however, should be acceptable. At this time, the Hellenes knew about that land only a few wild rumors and the account of Ktesias of Knidos, who made a book of the tales he picked up about India at the Persian court. The Hellenes had heard that India harbored philosophers. Therefore, thinking Greeks might be willing to consider Indians as almost as civilized as themselves.

What should I call myself? I took a common Indian name,

Chandra, and Hellenized it to Zandras. That, I knew, was what the Hellenes would do anyway, as they had no "tch" sound and insisted on putting Greek inflectional endings on foreign names. I would not try to use my own name, which is not even remotely Greek or Indian-sounding. (Some day I must explain the blunders in my world that led to Hesperians' being called "Indians.")

The newness and cleanliness of my costume bothered me. It did not look worn, and I could hardly break it in around Brookhaven without attracting attention. I decided that if the question came up, I should say: yes, I bought it when I entered Greece, so as not to be conspicuous in my native garb.

During the day, when not scouring New York for equipment, I was locked in the room with the machine. While my colleagues thought I was either writing my report or dismantling the apparatus, I was getting ready for my trip.

Two weeks went by thus. One day a memorandum came down from my superior, saying: "How is that final report coming?"

I knew then I had better put my plan into execution at once. I sent back a memorandum: "Almost ready for the writing machine."

That night I came back to the laboratory. As I had been doing this often, the guards took no notice. I went to the time-machine room, locked the door from the inside, and got out my equipment and costume.

I adjusted the machine to set me down near Pella, the capital of Macedon, in the spring of the year 340 before Christ in our system of reckoning (976 Algonkian). I set the autoactuator, climbed inside, and closed the door.

The feeling of being projected through time cannot really be described. There is a sharp pain, agonizing but too short to let the victim even cry out. At the same time there is the feeling of terrific acceleration, as if one were being shot from a catapult, but in no particular direction.

Then the seat in the passenger compartment dropped away from under me. There was a crunch, and a lot of sharp things jabbed me. I had fallen into the top of a tree.

I grabbed a couple of branches to save myself. The mechanism that positioned me in Macedon, detecting solid matter at the point where I was going to materialize, had raised me up above the treetops and then let go. It was an old oak, just putting out its spring leaves.

In clutching for branches I dropped my staff, which slithered down through the foliage and thumped the ground below. At least it thumped something. There was a startled yell.

Classical costume is impractical for tree-climbing. Branches kept knocking off my hat, or snagging my cloak, or poking me in tender places not protected by trousers. I ended my climb with a slide and a fall of several feet, tumbling into the dirt.

As I looked up, the first thing I saw was a burly, black-bearded man in a dirty tunic, standing with a knife in his hand. Near him stood a pair of oxen yoked to a wooden plow. At his feet rested a water jug.

The plowman had evidently finished a furrow and lain down to rest himself and his beasts when the fall of my staff on him and then my arrival in person aroused him.

Around me stretched the broad Emathian Plain, ringed by ranges of stony hills and craggy mountains. As the sky was overcast, and I did not dare consult my compass, I had no sure way of orienting myself, or even telling what time of day it was. I assumed that the biggest mountain in sight was Mount Bermion, which ought to be to the west. To the north I could see a trace of water. This would be Lake Loudias. Beyond the lake rose a range of low hills. A discoloration on the nearest spur of these hills might be a city, though my sight was not keen enough to make out details, and I had to do without my eyeglasses. The gently rolling plain was cut up into fields and pastures with occasional trees and patches of marsh. Dry brown grasses left over from winter nodded in the wind.

My realization of all this took but a flash. Then my attention was brought back to the plowman, who spoke.

I could not understand a word. But then, he would speak Macedonian. Though this can be deemed a Greek dialect, it differed so from Attic Greek as to be unintelligible.

No doubt the man wanted to know what I was doing in his tree. I put on my best smile and said in my slow fumbling Attic: "Rejoice! I am lost, and climbed your tree to find my way."

He spoke again. When I did not respond, he repeated his words more loudly, waving his knife.

We exchanged more words and gestures, but it was evident that neither had the faintest notion of what the other was trying to say. The plowman began shouting, as ignorant people will when faced by the linguistic barrier.

At last I pointed to the distant headland overlooking the lake, on which there appeared a discoloration that might be the city. Slowly and carefully I said:

"Is that Pella?"

"Nai, Pella!" The man's mien became less threatening.

"I am going to Pella. Where can I find the philosopher Aristoteles?" I repeated the name.

He was off again with more gibberish, but I gathered from his expression that he had never heard of any Aristoteles. So, I picked up my hat and stick, felt through my tunic to make sure my gear was all in place, tossed the rustic a final *"Chaire!"* and set off.

By the time I had crossed the muddy field and come out on a cart track, the problem of looking like a seasoned traveler had solved itself. There were green and brown stains on my clothes from the scramble down the tree; the cloak was torn; the branches had scratched my limbs and face; my feet and lower legs were covered with mud. I also became aware that, to one who has lived all his life with his loins decently swathed in trousers and underdrawers, classical costume is excessively drafty.

I glanced back to see the plowman still standing with one hand on his plow, looking at me in puzzled fashion. The poor fellow had never been able to decide what, if anything, to do about me.

When I found a road, it was hardly more than a heavily used cart track, with a pair of deep ruts and the space between them alternating stones, mud, and long grass.

I walked towards the lake and passed a few people on the

road. To one used to the teeming traffic of my world, Macedon seemed dead and deserted. I spoke to some of the people, but ran into the same barrier of language as with the plowman.

Finally a two-horse chariot came along, driven by a stout man wearing a headband, a kind of kilt, and high-laced boots. He pulled up at my hail.

"What is it?" he said, in Attic not much better than mine.

"I seek the philosopher, Aristoteles of Stageira. Where can I find him?"

"He lives in Mieza."

"Where is that?"

The man waved. "You are going the wrong way. Follow this road back the way you came. At the ford across the Bottiais, take the right-hand fork, which will bring you to Mieza and Kition. Do you understand?"

"I think so," I said. "How far is it?"

"About two hundred stadia."

My heart sank to my sandals. This meant five parasangs, or a good two days' walk. I thought of trying to buy a horse or a chariot, but I had never ridden or driven a horse and saw no prospect of learning how soon enough to do any good. I had read about Mieza as Aristotle's home in Macedon but, as none of my maps had shown it, I had assumed it to be a suburb of Pella.

I thanked the man, who trotted off, and set out after him. The details of my journey need not detain you. I was benighted far from shelter through not knowing where the villages were, attacked by watchdogs, eaten alive by mosquitoes, and invaded by vermin when I did find a place to sleep the second night. The road skirted the huge marshes that spread over the Emathian Plain west of Lake Loudias. Several small streams came down from Mount Bermion and lost themselves in this marsh.

At last I neared Mieza, which stands on one of the spurs of Mount Bermion. I was trudging wearily up the long rise to the village when six youths on little Greek horses clattered down the road. I stepped to one side, but instead of cantering past they pulled up and faced me in a semicircle.

"Who are you?" asked one, a smallish youth of about fifteen, in fluent Attic. He was blond and would have been noticeably handsome without his pimples.

"I am Zandras of Pataliputra," I said, giving the ancient name for Patna on the Ganges. "I seek the philosopher Aristoteles."

"Oh, a barbarian!" cried Pimples. "We know what the Aristoteles thinks of these, eh, boys?"

The others joined in, shouting noncompliments and bragging about all the barbarians they would some day kill or enslave.

I made the mistake of letting them see I was getting angry. I knew it was unwise, but I could not help myself. "If you do not wish to help me, then let me pass," I said.

"Not only a barbarian, but an insolent one!" cried one of the group, making his horse dance uncomfortably close to me.

"Stand aside, children!" I demanded.

"We must teach you a lesson," said Pimples. The others giggled.

"You had better let me alone," I said, gripping my staff in both hands.

A tall handsome adolescent reached over and knocked my hat off. "That for you, cowardly Asiatic!" he yelled.

Without stopping to think, I shouted an English epithet and swung my staff. Either the young man leaned out of my way or his horse shied, for my blow missed him. The momentum carried the staff past my target and the end struck the nose of one of the other horses.

The pony squealed and reared. Having no stirrups, the rider slid off the animal's rump into the dirt. The horse galloped off.

All six youths began screaming. The blond one, who had a particularly piercing voice, mouthed some threat. The next thing I knew, his horse bounded directly at me. Before I could dodge, the animal's shoulder knocked me head over heels and the beast leaped over me as I rolled. Luckily, horses' dislike of stepping on anything squashy saved me from being trampled.

I scrambled up as another horse bore down upon me. By a frantic leap, I got out of its way, but I saw that the other boys were jockeying their mounts to do likewise.

A few paces away rose a big pine. I dodged in among its lower branches as the other horses ran at me. The youths could not force their mounts in among these branches, so they galloped round and round and yelled. Most of their talk I could not understand, but I caught a sentence from Pimples:

"Ptolemaios! Ride back to the house and fetch bows or javelins!"

Hooves receded. While I could not see clearly through the pine-needles, I inferred what was happening. The youths would not try to rush me on foot, first because they liked being on horseback, and if they dismounted they might lose their horses or have trouble remounting; second, because, as long as I kept my back to the tree, they would have a hard time getting at me through the tangle of branches, and I could hit and poke them with my stick as they came. Though not an unusually tall man in my own world, I was much bigger than any of these boys.

This, however, was a minor consideration. I recognized the name "Ptolemaios" as that of one of Alexander's companions, who in my world became King Ptolemy of Egypt and founded a famous dynasty. Young Pimples, then, must be Alexander himself.

I was in a real predicament. If I stayed where I was, Ptolemaios would bring back missiles for target practice with me as the target. I could of course shoot some of the boys with my gun, which would save me for the time being. But, in an absolute monarchy, killing the crown prince's friends, let alone the crown prince himself, is no way to achieve a peaceful old age, regardless of the provocation.

While I was thinking of these matters and listening to my attackers, a stone swished through the branches and bounced off the trunk. The small dark youth who had fallen off his horse had thrown the rock and was urging his friends to do likewise. I caught glimpses of Pimples and the rest dismounting and scurrying around for stones, a commodity with which Greece and Macedon are notoriously well supplied.

More stones came through the needles, careening from the branches. One the size of my fist struck me lightly in the shin.

The boys came closer so that their aim got better. I wormed my way around the trunk to put it between me and them, but they saw the movement and spread out around the tree. A stone grazed my scalp, dizzying me and drawing blood. I thought of climbing, but, as the tree became more slender with height, I should be more exposed the higher I got. I should also be less able to dodge while perched in the branches.

That is how things stood when I heard hoofbeats again. This is the moment of decision, I thought. Ptolemaios is coming back with missile weapons. If I used my gun, I might doom myself in the long run, but it would be ridiculous to stand there and let them riddle me while I had an unused weapon.

I fumbled under my tunic and unsnapped the safety strap that kept the pistol in its holster. I pulled the weapon out and checked its projectiles.

A deep voice broke into the bickering. I caught phrases: ". . . insulting an unoffending traveler . . . how know you he is not a prince in his own country? . . . the king shall hear of this . . . like newly freed slaves, not like princes and gentlemen . . ."

I pushed towards the outer limits of the screen of pine needles. A heavy-set, brown-bearded man on a horse was haranguing the youths, who had dropped their stones. Pimples said:

"We were only having a little sport."

I stepped out from the branches, walked over to where my battered hat lay, and put it on. Then I said to the newcomer: "Rejoice! I am glad you came before your boys' play got too rough." I grinned, determined to act cheerful if it killed me. Only iron self-control would get me through this difficulty.

The man grunted. "Who are you?"

"Zandras of Pataliputra, a city in India. I seek Aristoteles the philosopher."

"He insulted me—" began one of the youths, but Brownbeard ignored him. He said:

"I am sorry you have had so rude an introduction to our royal house. This mass of youthful insolence" (he indicated Pimples) "is the Alexandros Philippou, heir to the throne of Makedonia." He introduced the others: Hephaistion, who had knocked my hat off and was now holding the others' horses; Nearchos, who had lost his horse; Ptolemaios, who had gone for weapons; and Harpalos and Philotas. He continued:

"When the Ptolemaios dashed into the house, I inquired the reason for his haste, learned of their quarrel with you, and came out forthwith. They have misapplied their master's teachings. They should not behave thus even to a barbarian like yourself, for in so doing they lower themselves to the barbarian's level. I am returning to the house of Aristoteles. You may follow."

The man turned his horse and started walking it back towards Mieza. The six boys busied themselves with catching Nearchos' horse.

I walked after him, though I had to dog-trot now and then to keep up. As it was uphill, I was soon breathing hard. I panted:

"Who—my lord—are you?"

The man's beard came round and he raised an eyebrow. "I thought you would know. I am Antipatros, regent of Makedonia."

Before we reached the village proper, Antipatros turned off through a kind of park, with statues and benches. This, I supposed, was the Precinct of the Nymphs, which Aristotle used as a school ground. We went through the park and stopped at a mansion on the other side. Antipatros tossed the reins to a groom and slid off his horse.

"Aristoteles!" roared Antipatros. "A man wishes to see you."

A man of about my own age—the early forties—came out. He was of medium height and slender build, with a thin-lipped, severe-looking face and a pepper-and-salt beard cut short. He was wrapped in a billowing himation or large cloak, with a colorful scroll-patterned border. He wore golden rings on several fingers.

Antipatros made a fumbling introduction: "Old fellow, this is—ah—what's-his-name from—ah—some place in India." He told of rescuing me from Alexander and his fellow delinquents, adding: "If you do not beat some manners into your pack of cubs soon, it will be too late."

Aristotle looked at me sharply and lisped: "It ith always a pleasure to meet men from afar. What brings you here, my friend?"

I gave my name and said: "Being accounted something of a philosopher in my own land, I thought my visit to the West would be incomplete without speaking to the greatest Western philosopher. And when I asked who he was, everyone told me to seek out Aristoteles Nikomachou."

Aristotle purred. "It is good of them to thay tho. Ahem. Come in and join me in a drop of wine. Can you tell me of the wonders of India?"

"Yes, indeed, but you must tell me in turn of your discoveries, which to me are much more wonderful."

"Come, come, then. Perhaps you could stay over a few days. I shall have many, many things to athk you."

That is how I met Aristotle. He and I hit it off, as we said in my world, from the start. We had much in common. Some people would not like Aristotle's lisp, or his fussy, pedantic ways, or his fondness for worrying any topic of conversation to death. But he and I got along fine.

That afternoon, in the house that King Philip had built for Aristotle to use as the royal school, he handed me a cup of wine flavored with turpentine and asked:

"Tell me about the elephant, that great beast we have heard of with a tail at both ends. Does it truly exist?"

"Indeed it does," I said, and went on to tell what I knew of elephants, while Aristotle scribbled notes on a piece of papyrus.

"What do they call the elephant in India?" he asked.

The question caught me by surprise, for it had never occurred to me to learn ancient Hindustani along with all the other things I had to know for this expedition. I sipped the wine to give me time to think. I have never cared for alcoholic liquors, and this stuff tasted awful to me. But, for the sake of my objective, I had to pretend to like it. No doubt I should have to make up some kind of gibberish—but then a mental broad-jump carried me back to the stories of Kipling I had read as a boy.

"We call it a *hathi*," I said. "Though of course there are many languages in India."

"How about that Indian wild ath of which Ktesias thpeakth, with a horn in the middle of its forehead?"

"You had better call it a nose-horn (*rhinokeros*) for that is where its horn really is, and it is more like a gigantic pig than an ass. . . ."

As dinner-time neared, I made some artful remarks about going out to find accommodations in Mieza, but Aristotle (to my joy) would have none of it. I should stay right there at the school; my polite protestations of unworthiness he waved aside.

"You mutht plan to stop here for months," he said. "I shall never, never have such a chance to collect data on India again. Do not worry about expense; the king pays all. You are—ahem—the first barbarian I have known with a decent intellect, and I get lonethome for good tholid talk. Theophrastos has gone to Athens, and my other friends come to these back-lands but seldom."

"How about the Macedonians?"

"*Aiboi!* Thome like my friend Antipatros are good fellows, but most are as lackwitted as a Persian grandee. And now tell me of Patal—what is your city's name?"

Presently Alexander and his friends came in. They seemed taken aback at seeing me closeted with their master. I put on a brisk smile and said: "Rejoice, my friends!" as if nothing untoward had happened. The boys glowered and whispered among themselves, but did not attempt any more disturbance at that time.

When they gathered for their lecture next morning, Aristotle told them: "I am too busy with the gentleman from India to waste time pounding unwanted wisdom into your miserable little thouls. Go shoot some rabbits or catch some fish for dinner, but in any case begone!"

The boys grinned. Alexander said: "It seems the barbarian has his uses after all. I hope you stay with us forever, good barbarian!"

After they had gone, Antipatros came in to say good-bye to Aristotle. He asked me with gruff good will how I was doing and went out to ride back to Pella.

The weeks passed unnoticed and the flowers of spring came out while I visited Aristotle. Day after day we strolled about the Precinct of the Nymphs, talking, or sat indoors when it rained. Sometimes the boys followed us, listening; at other times we talked alone. They played a couple of practical jokes on me, but, by pretending to be amused when I was really furious, I avoided serious trouble with them.

I learned that Aristotle had a wife and a little daughter in another part of the big house, but he never let me meet the lady. I only caught glimpses of them from a distance.

I carefully shifted the subject of our daily discourse from the marvels of India to the more basic questions of science. We argued over the nature of matter and the shape of the solar system. I gave out that the Indians were well on the road to the modern concepts—modern in my world, that is—of astronomy, physics, and so forth. I told of the discoveries of those eminent Pataliputran philosophers: Kopernikos in astronomy, Neuton in physics, Darben in evolution, and Mendeles in genetics. (I forgot; these names mean nothing to you, though an educated man of my world would recognize them at once through their Greek disguise.)

Always I stressed *method:* the need for experiment and invention and for checking each theory back against the facts. Though an opinionated and argumentative man, Aristotle had a mind like a sponge, eagerly absorbing any new fact, surmise, or opinion, whether he agreed with it or not.

I tried to find a workable compromise between what I knew science could do on one hand and the limits of Aristotle's credulity on the other. Therefore I said nothing about flying machines, guns, buildings a thousand feet high, and other technical wonders of my world. Nevertheless, I caught Aristotle looking at me sharply out of those small black eyes one day.

"Do you doubt me, Aristoteles?" I said.

"N-no, no," he said thoughtfully. "But it does theem to me that, were your Indian inventors as wonderful as you make out, they would have fabricated you wings like those of Daidalos in the legend. Then you could have flown to Makedonia directly, without the trials of crossing Persia by camel."

"That has been tried, but men's muscles do not have enough strength in proportion to their weight."

"Ahem. Did you bring anything from India to show the skills of your people?"

I grinned, for I had been hoping for such a question. "I did fetch a few small devices," said I, reaching into my tunic and bringing out the magnifying glass. I demonstrated its use.

Aristotle shook his head. "Why did you not show me this before? It would have quieted my doubts."

"People have met with misfortune by trying too suddenly to change the ideas of those around them. Like your teacher's teacher, Sokrates."

"That is true, true. What other devices did you bring?"

I had intended to show my devices at intervals, gradually, but Aristotle was so insistent on seeing them all that I gave in to him before he got angry. The little telescope was not powerful enough to show the moons of Jupiter or the rings of Saturn, but it showed enough to convince Aristotle of its power. If he could not see these astronomical phenomena himself, he was almost willing to take my word that they could be seen with the larger telescopes we had in India.

One day a light-armed soldier galloped up to us in the midst of our discussions in the Precinct of Nymphs. Ignoring the rest of us, the fellow said to Alexander: "Hail, O Prince! The king, your father, will be here before sunset."

Everybody rushed around cleaning up the place. We were all lined up in front of the big house when King Philip and his entourage arrived on horseback with a jingle and a clatter, in crested helmets and flowing mantles. I knew Philip by his one eye. He was a big powerful man, much scarred, with a thick curly black beard going gray. He dismounted, embraced his son, gave Aristotle a brief greeting, and said to Alexander:

"How would you like to attend a siege?"

Alexander whooped.

"Thrace is subdued," said the king, "but Byzantion and Perinthos have declared against me, thanks to Athenian intrigue. I shall give the Perintheans something to think about besides the bribes of the Great King. It is time you smelled blood, youngster; would you like to come?"

"Yes, yes! Can my friends come too?"

"If they like and their fathers let them."

"O King!" said Aristotle.

"What is it, spindle-shanks?"

"I trust this is not the end of the prince's education. He has much yet to learn."

"No, no; I will send him back when the town falls. But he nears the age when he must learn by doing, not merely by listening to your rarefied wisdom. Who is this?" Philip turned his one eye on me.

"Zandras of India, a barbarian philothopher."

Philip grinned in a friendly way and clapped me on the shoulder. "Rejoice! Come to Pella and tell my generals about India. Who knows? A Macedonian foot may tread there yet."

"It would be more to the point to find out about Persia," said one of Philip's officers, a handsome fellow with a reddish-brown beard. "This man must have just come through there. How about it, man? Is the bloody Artaxerxes still solid on his throne?"

"I know little of such matters," I said, my heart beginning to pound at the threat of exposure. "I skirted the northern-most parts of the Great King's dominions and saw little of the big cities. I know nothing of their politics."

"Is that so?" said Redbeard, giving me a queer look. "We must talk of this again."

They all trooped into the big house, where the cook and the serving wenches were scurrying about. During dinner I found myself between Nearchos, Alexander's little Cretan friend, and a man-at-arms who spoke no Attic. So I did not get much conversation, nor could I follow much of the chatter that went on among the group at the head of the tables. I gathered that they were discussing politics. I asked Nearchos who the generals were.

"The big one at the king's right is the Parmenion," he said, "and the one with the red beard is the Attalos."

When the food was taken away and the drinking had begun, Attalos came over to me. The man-at-arms gave him his place. Attalos had drunk a lot of wine already; but, if it made him a little unsteady, it did not divert him.

"How did you come through the Great King's domain?" he asked. "What route did you follow?"

"I told you, to the north," I said.

"Then you must have gone through Orchoe."

"I—" I began, then stopped. Attalos might be laying a trap for me. What if I said yes and Orchoe was really in the south? Or suppose he had been there and knew all about the place? Many Greeks and Macedonians served the Great King as mercenaries.

"I passed through many places whose names I never got straight," I said. "I do not remember if Orchoe was among them."

Attalos gave me a sinister smile through his beard. "Your journey will profit you little, if you cannot remember where you have been. Come, tell me if you heard of unrest among the northern provinces."

I evaded the question, taking a long pull on my wine to cover my hesitation. I did this again and again until Attalos said: "Very well, perhaps you are really as ignorant of Persia as you profess. Then tell me about India."

"What about it?" I hiccupped; the wine was beginning to affect me, too.

"As a soldier, I should like to know of the Indian art of war. What is this about training elephants to fight?"

"Oh, we do much better than that."

"How so?"

"We have found that the flesh-and-blood elephant, despite its size, is an untrustworthy war beast because it often takes fright and stampedes back through its own troops. So, the philosophers of Pataliputra make artificial elephants of steel with rapid-fire catapults on their backs."

I was thinking in a confused way of the armored war vehicles of my own world. I do not know what made me tell Attalos such ridiculous lies. Partly, I suppose, it was to keep him off the subject of Persia.

Partly it was a natural antipathy between us. According to history, Attalos was not a bad man, though at times a reckless and foolish one. But it annoyed me that he thought he could pump me by subtle questions, when he was about as subtle as a ton of bricks. His voice and manner said as plainly as words: I am a shrewd, sharp fellow; watch out for me, everybody. He was the kind of man who, if told to spy on the enemy, would don an obviously false beard, wrap himself in a long black cloak, and go slinking about the enemy's places in broad daylight, leering and winking and attracting as much attention as possible. No doubt, too, he had prejudiced me against him by his alarming curiosity about my past.

But the main cause for my rash behavior was the strong wine I had drunk. In my own world, I drank very little and so was not used to these carousals.

Attalos was all eyes and ears at my tale of mechanical elephants. "You do not say!"

"Yes, and we do even better than that. If the enemy's ground forces resist the charge of our iron elephants, we send flying chariots, drawn by gryphons, to drop darts on the foe from above." It seemed to me that never had my imagination been so brilliant.

Attalos gave an audible gasp. "What else?"

"Well—ah—we also have a powerful navy, you know, which controls the lower Ganges and the adjacent ocean. Our ships move by machinery, without oars or sails."

"Do the other Indians have these marvels too?"

"Some, but none is so advanced as the Pataliputrans. When we are outnumbered on the sea, we have a force of tame Tritons who swim under the enemy's ships and bore holes in their bottoms."

Attalos frowned. "Tell me, barbarian, how it is that, with such mighty instruments of war, the Palalal—the Patapata— the people of your city have not conquered the whole world?"

I gave a shout of drunken laughter and slapped Attalos on the back. "We *have*, old boy, we have! You Macedonians have just not yet found out that you are our subjects!"

Attalos digested this, then scowled blackly. "You temple-thief! I think you have been making a fool of me! Of *me!* By Herakles, I ought—"

He rose and swung a fist back to clout me. I jerked an arm up to guard my face.

There came a roar of "Attalos!" from the head of the table. King Philip had been watching us.

Attalos dropped his fist, muttered something like "Flying chariots and tame Tritons, forsooth!" and stumbled back to his own crowd.

This man, I remembered, did not have a happy future in store. He was destined to marry his niece to Philip, whose first wife Olympias would have the girl and her baby killed after Philip's assassination. Soon afterwards, Attalos would be murdered by Alexander's orders. It was on the tip of my tongue to give him a veiled warning, but I forebore. I had attracted enough hostile attention already.

Later, when the drinking got heavy, Aristotle came over and shooed his boys off to bed. He said to me: "Let uth walk outside to clear our heads, Zandras, and then go to bed, too. These Makedones drink like sponges. I cannot keep up with them."

Outside, he said: "The Attalos thinks you are a Persian thpy."

"A spy? Me? In Hera's name, why?" Silently I cursed my folly in making an enemy without any need. Would I never learn to deal with this damned human species?

Aristotle said: "He thays nobody could pass through a country and remain as ignorant of it as you theem to be. *Ergo*, you know more of the Persian Empire than you pretend, but wish us to think you have nothing to do with it. And why should you do that, unleth you are yourself a Persian?

And being a Persian, why should you hide the fact unleth you are on some hostile mission?"

"A Persian might fear anti-Persian prejudice among the Hellenes. Not that I am one," I hastily added.

"He need not. Many Persians live in Hellas without molestation. Take Artabazos and his sons, who live in Pella, refugees from their own king."

Then the obvious alibi came to me, long after it should have. "The fact is I went even farther north than I said. I went around the northern ends of the Caspian and Euxine seas and so did not cross the Great King's domains save through the Bactrian deserts."

"You did? Then why did you not thay tho? If that is true, you have settled one of our hottest geographical disputes: whether the Caspian is a closed thea or a bay of the Northern Ocean."

"I feared nobody would believe me."

"I am not sure what to believe, Zandras. You are a strange man. I do not think you are a Persian, for no Persian was ever a philothopher. It is good for you that you are not."

"Why?"

"Because I *hate* Persia!" he hissed.

"You do?"

"Yeth. I could list the wrongs done by the Great Kings, but it is enough that they seized my beloved father-in-law by treachery and torture, and crucified him. People like Isokrates talk of uniting the Hellenes to conquer Persia, and Philippos may try it if he lives. I hope he does. However," he went on in a different tone, "I hope he does it without dragging the cities of Hellas into it, for the repositories of civilization have no busineth getting into a brawl between tyrants."

"In India," said I sententiously, "we are taught that a man's nationality means nothing and his personal qualities everything. Men of all nations come good, bad, and indifferent."

Aristotle shrugged. "I have known virtuouth Persians too, but that monstrouth, bloated empire ... No state can be truly civilized with more than a few thousand citizens."

There was no use telling him that large states, however

monstrous and bloated he thought them, would be a permanent feature of the landscape from then on. I was trying to
reform, not Aristotle's narrow view of international affairs,
but his scientific methodology.

Next morning King Philip and his men and Aristotle's six
pupils galloped off toward Pella, followed by a train of baggage mules and the boys' personal slaves. Aristotle said:

"Let us hope no chance sling-thtone dashes out Alexandros'
brains before he has a chance to show his mettle. The boy has
talent and may go far, though managing him is like trying to
plow with a wild bull. Now, let us take up the question of
atoms again, my dear Zandras, about which you have been
talking thuch utter rubbish. First, you must admit that if a
thing exists, parts of it must also exist. Therefore there is no
thuch thing as an indivisible particle . . ."

Three days later, while we were still hammering at the
question of atoms, we looked up at the clatter of hooves. Here
came Attalos and a whole troop of horsemen. Beside Attalos
rode a tall swarthy man with a long gray beard. This man's
appearance startled me into thinking he must be another
time traveler from my own time, for he wore a hat, coat, and
pants. The mere sight of these familiar garments filled me
with homesickness for my own world, however much I hated
it when I lived in it.

Actually, the man's garb was not that of one from my
world. The hat was a cylindrical felt cap with ear flaps. The
coat was a brown knee-length garment, embroidered with
faded red and blue flowers, with trousers to match. The whole
outfit looked old and threadbare, with patches showing. He
was a big craggy-looking fellow, with a great hooked nose,
wide cheekbones, and deep-set eyes under bushy, beetling
brows.

They all dismounted, and a couple of grooms went around
collecting the bridles to keep the horses from running off. The
soldiers leaned on their spears in a circle around us.

Attalos said: "I should like to ask your guest some more
philosophical questions, O Aristoteles."

"Ask away."

Attalos turned, not to me, but to the tall graybeard. He said something I did not catch, and then the man in trousers spoke to me in a language I did not know.

"I do not understand," I said.

The graybeard spoke again, in what sounded like a different tongue. He did this several times, using a different-sounding speech each time, but each time I had to confess ignorance.

"Now you see," said Attalos. "He pretends not to know Persian, Median, Armenian, or Aramaic. He could not have traversed the Great King's dominions from east to west without learning at least one of these."

"Who are you, my dear sir?" I asked Graybeard.

The old man gave me a small dignified smile and spoke in Attic with a guttural accent. "I am Artavazda, or Artabazos as the Hellenes say, once governor of Phrygia but now a poor pensioner of King Philippos."

This, then, was the eminent Persian refugee of whom Aristotle had spoken.

"I warrant he does not even speak Indian," said Attalos.

"Certainly," I said, and started off in English: *"Now is the time for all good men to come to the aid of the party. Four score and seven years ago our fathers brought forth—"*

"What would you call that?" Attalos asked Artavazda.

The Persian spread his hands. "I have never heard the like. But then, India is a vast country of many tongues."

"I was not—" I began, but Attalos kept on:

"What race would you say he belonged to?"

"I know not. The Indians I have seen were much darker, but there might be light-skinned Indians for aught I know."

"If you will listen, General, I will explain," I said. "For most of the journey I was not even in the Persian Empire. I crossed through Bactria and went around the north of the Caspian and Euxine seas."

"Oh, so now you tell another story?" said Attalos. "Any educated man knows the Caspian is but a deep bay opening into the Ocean River to the north. Therefore you could not go around it. So, in trying to escape, you do but mire yourself deeper in your own lies."

"Look here," said Aristotle. "You have proved nothing of the sort, O Attalos. Ever thince Herodotos there have been those who think the Caspian a closed thea—"

"Hold your tongue, Professor," said Attalos. "This is a matter of national security. There is something queer about this alleged Indian, and I mean to find out what it is."

"It is not queer that one who comes from unknown distant lands should tell a singular tale of his journey."

"No, there is more to it than that. I have learned that he first appeared in a treetop on the farm of the freeholder Diktys Pisandrou. Diktys remembers looking up into the tree for crows before he cast himself down under it to rest. If the Zandras had been in the tree, Diktys would have seen him, as it was not yet fully in leaf. The next instant there was the crash of a body falling into the branches, and Zandras' staff smote Diktys on the head. Normal mortal men fall not out of the sky into trees."

"Perhaps he flew from India. They have marvelous mechanisms there, he tells me," said Aristotle.

"If he survives our interrogation in Pella, perhaps he can make me a pair of wings," said Attalos. "Or better yet, a pair for my horse, so he shall emulate Pegasos. Meanwhile, seize and bind him, men!"

The soldiers moved. I did not dare submit for fear they would take my gun and leave me defenseless. I snatched up the hem of my tunic to get at my pistol. It took precious seconds to unsnap the safety strap, but I got the gun out before anybody laid hand on me.

"Stand back or I will blast you with lightning!" I shouted, raising the gun.

Men of my own world, knowing how deadly such a weapon can be, would have given ground at the sight of it. But the Macedonians, never having seen one, merely stared at the device and came on. Attalos was one of the nearest.

I fired at him, then whirled and shot another soldier who was reaching out to seize me. The discharge of the gun produces a lightning-like flash and a sharp sound like a close clap of thunder. The Macedonians cried out, and Attalos fell with a wound in his thigh.

I turned again, looking for a way out of the circle of soldiers, while confused thoughts of taking one of their horses flashed through my head. A heavy blow in the flank staggered me. One of the soldiers had jabbed me with his spear, but my belt kept the weapon from piercing me. I shot at the man but missed him in my haste.

"Do not kill him!" screamed Aristotle.

Some of the soldiers backed up as if to flee; others poised their spears. They hesitated for the wink of an eye, either for fear of me or because Aristotle's command confused them. Ordinarily they would have ignored the philosopher and listened for their general's orders, but Attalos was down on the grass and looking in amazement at the hole in his leg.

As one soldier dropped his spear and started to run, a blow on the head sent a flash of light through my skull and hurled me to the ground, nearly unconscious. A man behind me had swung his spear like a club and struck me on the pate with the shaft.

Before I could recover, they were all over me, raining kicks and blows. One wrenched the gun from my hand. I must have lost consciousness, for the next thing I remember is lying in the dirt while the soldiers tore off my tunic. Attalos stood over me with a bloody bandage around his leg, leaning on a soldier. He looked pale and frightened but resolute. The second man I had shot lay still.

"So that is where he keeps his infernal devices!" said Attalos, indicating my belt. "Take it off, men."

The soldiers struggled with the clasp of the belt until one impatiently sawed through the straps with his dagger. The gold in my money pouch brought cries of delight.

I struggled to get up, but a pair of soldiers knelt on my arms to keep me down. There was a continuous mumble of talk. Attalos, looking over the belt, said:

"He is too dangerous to live. Even stripped as he is, who knows but what he will soar into the air and escape by magic?"

"Do not kill him!" said Aristotle. "He has much valuable knowledge to impart."

"No knowledge is worth the safety of the kingdom."

"But the kingdom can benefit from his knowledge. Do you not agree?" Aristotle asked the Persian.

"Drag me not into this, pray," said Artavazda. "It is no concern of mine."

"If he is a danger to Makedonia, he should be destroyed at once," said Attalos.

"There is but little chance of his doing harm now," said Aristotle, "and an excellent chance of his doing us good."

"Any chance of his doing harm is too much," said Attalos. "You philosophers can afford to be tolerant of interesting strangers. But, if they carry disaster in their baggage, it is on us poor soldiers that the brunt will fall. Is it not so, Artabazos?"

"I have done what you asked and will say no more," said Artavazda. "I am but a simple-minded Persian nobleman who does not understand your Greek subtleties."

"I can increase the might of your armies, General!" I cried to Attalos.

"No doubt, and no doubt you can also turn men to stone with an incantation, as the Gorgons did with their glance." He drew his sword and felt the edge with his thumb.

"You will slay him for mere thuperstition!" wailed Aristotle, wringing his hands. "At least, let the king judge the matter."

"Not superstition," said Attalos; "murder." He pointed to the dead soldier.

"I come from another world! Another age!" I yelled, but Attalos was not to be diverted.

"Let us get this over with," he said. "Set him on his knees, men. Take my sword, Glaukos; I am too unsteady to wield it. Now bow your head, my dear barbarian, and—"

In the middle of Attalos' sentence, he and the others and all my surroundings vanished. Again there came that sharp pain and sense of being jerked by a monstrous catapult. . . .

I found myself lying in leaf mold with the pearl-gray trunks of poplars all around me. A brisk breeze was making the poplar leaves flutter and show their silvery bottoms. It was too cool for a man who was naked save for sandals and socks.

I had snapped back to the year 1981 of the calendar of my world, which I had set out from. But where was I? I should be near the site of the Brookhaven National Laboratories in a vastly improved super-scientific world. There was, however, no sign of super-science here; nothing but poplar trees.

I got up, groaning, and looked around. I was covered with bruises and bleeding from nose and mouth.

The only way I had of orienting myself was the boom of a distant surf. Shivering, I hobbled towards the sound. After a few hundred paces, I came out of the forest on a beach. This beach could be the shore of Sewanhaki, or Long Island as we called it, but there was no good way of telling. There was no sign of human life; just the beach curving into the distance and disappearing around headlands, with the poplar forest on one side and the ocean on the other.

What, I wondered, had happened? Had science advanced so fast as a result of my intervention that man had already exterminated himself by scientific warfare? Thinkers of my world had concerned themselves with this possibility, but I had never taken it seriously.

It began to rain. In despair I cast myself down on the sand and beat it with my fists. I may have lost consciousness again.

At any rate, the next thing I knew was the now-familiar sound of hooves. When I looked up, the horseman was almost upon me, for the sand had muffled the animal's footsteps until it was quite close.

I blinked with incredulity. For an instant I thought I must be back in the classical era still. The man was a warrior armed and armored in a style much like that of ancient times. At first he seemed to be wearing a helmet of classical Hellenic type. When he came closer I saw that this was not quite true, for the crest was made of feathers instead of horsehair. The nasal and cheek plates hid most of his face, but he seemed dark and beardless. He wore a shirt of scale mail, long leather trousers, and low shoes. He had a bow and a small shield hung from his saddle and a slender lance slung across his back by a strap. I saw that this could not be ancient times because the horse was fitted with a large, well-molded saddle and stirrups.

As I watched the man stupidly, he whisked the lance out of its boot and couched it. He spoke in an unknown language.

I got up, holding my hands over my head in surrender. The man kept repeating his question, louder and louder, and making jabbing motions. All I could say was "I don't understand" in the languages I knew, none of which seemed familiar to him.

Finally he maneuvered his horse around to the other side of me, barked a command, pointed along the beach the way he had come, and prodded me with the butt of the lance. Off I limped, with rain, blood, and tears running down my hide.

You know the rest, more or less. Since I could not give an intelligible account of myself, the Sachim of Lenape, Wayotan the Fat, claimed me as a slave. For fourteen years I labored on his estate at such occupations as feeding hogs and chopping kindling. When Wayotan died and the present Sachim was elected, he decided I was too old for that kind of work, especially as I was half crippled from the beatings of Wayotan and his overseers. Learning that I had some knowledge of letters (for I had picked up spoken and written Algonkian in spite of my wretched lot) he freed me and made me official librarian.

In theory I can travel about as I like, but I have done little of it. I am too old and weak for the rigors of travel in this world, and most other places are, as nearly as I can determine, about as barbarous as this one. Besides, a few Lenapes come to hear me lecture on the nature of man and the universe and the virtues of the scientific method. Perhaps I can light a small spark here after I failed in the year 340 B.C.

When I went to work in the library, my first thought was to find out what had happened to bring the world to its present pass.

Wayotan's predecessor had collected a considerable library which Wayotan had neglected, so that some of the books had been chewed by rats and others ruined by dampness. Still, there was enough to give me a good sampling of the literature of this world, from ancient to modern times. There were even Herodotos' history and Plato's dialogues, identical with the versions that existed in my own world.

I had to struggle against more language barriers, as the European languages of this world are different from, though related to, those of my own world. The English of today, for instance, is more like the Dutch of my own world, as a result of England's never having been conquered by the Normans.

I also had the difficulty of reading without eyeglasses. Luckily, most of these manuscript books are written in a large, clear hand. A couple of years ago I did get a pair of glasses, imported from China, where the invention of the printing press has stimulated their manufacture. But, as they are a recent invention in this world, they are not so effective as those of mine.

I rushed through all the history books to find out when and how your history diverged from mine. I found that differences appeared quite early. Alexander still marched to the Indus but failed to die at thirty-two on his return. In fact he lived fifteen years longer and fell at last in battle with the Sarmatians in the Caucasus Mountains.

I do not know why that brief contact with me enabled him to avoid the malaria mosquito that slew him in my world. Maybe I aroused in him a keener interest in India than he would otherwise have had, leading him to stay there longer so that all his subsequent schedules were changed. His empire held together for most of a century instead of breaking up right after his death as it did in my world.

The Romans still conquered the whole Mediterranean, but the course of their conquests and the names of the prominent Romans were all different. Two of the chief religions of my world, Christianity and Islam, never appeared at all. Instead we have Mithraism, Odinism, and Soterism, the last an Egypto-Hellenic synthesis founded by that fiery Egyptian prophet whose followers call him by the Greek word for "savior."

Still, classical history followed the same *general* course that it had in my world, even though the actors bore other names. The Roman Empire broke up, as it did in my world, though the details are all different, with a Hunnish emperor ruling in Rome and a Gothic one in Antioch.

It is after the fall of the Roman Empire that profound differences appear. In my world there was a revival of learning that began about nine hundred years ago, followed by a scientific revolution beginning four centuries later. In your history the revival of learning was centuries later, and the scientific revolution has hardly begun. Failure to develop the compass and the full-rigged ship resulted in North America's (I mean Hesperia's) being discovered and settled via the northern route, by way of Iceland, and more slowly than in my world. Failure to invent the gun meant that the natives of Hesperia were not swept aside by the invading Europeans, but held their own against them and gradually learned their arts of iron-working, weaving, cereal-growing, and the like. Now most of the European settlements have been assimilated, though the ruling families of the Abnakis and Mohegans frequently have blue eyes and still call themselves by names like "Sven" and "Eric."

I was eager to get hold of a work by Aristotle, to see what effect I had had on him and to try to relate this effect to the subsequent course of history. From allusions in some of the works in this library I gathered that many of his writings had come down to modern times, though the titles all seemed different from those of his surviving works in my world. The only actual samples of his writings in the library were three essays, *Of Justice, On Education*, and *Of Passions and Anger*. None of these showed my influence.

I had struggled through most of the Sachim's collection when I found the key I was looking for. This was an Iberic translation of *Lives of the Great Philosophers*, by one Diomedes of Mazaka. I never heard of Diomedes in the literary history of my own world, and perhaps he never existed. Any way, he had a long chapter on Aristotle, in which appears the following section:

Now Aristotle, during his sojourn at Mytilene, had been an assiduous student of natural sciences. He had planned, according to Timotheus, a series of works which should correct the errors of Empedokles, Demokritos, and others of his predecessors. But, after he had removed to Macedonia and busied himself with the education of Alexander, there one day appeared before him a traveler, Sandos of Palibothra, a mighty philosopher of India.

The Indian ridiculed Aristotle's attempts at scientific research, saying that in his land these investigations had gone far beyond anything the Hellenes had attempted, and the Indians were still a long way from arriving at satisfactory explanations of the universe. Moreover, he asserted that no real progress could be made in natural philosophy unless the Hellenes abandoned their disdain for physical labor and undertook exhaustive experiments with mechanical devices of the sort which cunning Egyptian and Asiatic craftsmen make.

King Philip, hearing of the presence of this stranger in his land and fearing lest he be a spy sent by some foreign power to harm or corrupt the young prince, came with soldiers to arrest him. But, when he demanded that Sandos accompany him back to Pella, the latter struck dead with thunderbolts all the king's soldiers that were with him. Then, it is said, mounting into his chariot drawn by winged gryphons, he flew off in the direction of India. But other authorities say that the man who came to arrest Sandos was Antipatros, the regent, and that Sandos cast darkness before the eyes of Antipatros and Aristotle, and when they recovered from their swoon he had vanished.

Aristotle, reproached by the king for harboring so dangerous a visitor and shocked by the sanguinary ending of the Indian's visit, resolved to have no more to do with the sciences. For, as he explains in his celebrated treatise *On the Folly of Natural Science,* there are three reasons why no good Hellene should trouble his mind with such matters.

One is that the number of facts which must be mastered before sound theories become possible is so vast that if all the Hellenes did nothing else for centuries, they would still not gather the amount of data required. The task is therefore futile.

Secondly, experiments and mechanical inventions are necessary to progress in science, and such work, though all very well for slavish Asiatics, who have a natural bent for it, is beneath the dignity of a Hellenic gentleman.

And, lastly, some of the barbarians have already surpassed the Hellenes in this activity, wherefore it ill becomes the Hellenes to compete with their inferiors in skills at which the latter have an inborn advantage. They should rather cultivate personal rectitude, patriotic valor, political rationality, and aesthetic sensitivity, leaving to the barbarians such artificial aids to the good and virtuous life as are provided by scientific discoveries.

This was it, all right. The author had gotten some of his facts wrong, but that was to be expected from an ancient historian.

So! My teachings had been too successful. I had so well shattered the naive self-confidence of the Hellenic philosophers as to discourage them from going on with science at all.

I should have remembered that glittering theories and sweeping generalizations, even when wrong, are the frosting on the cake; they are the carrot that makes the donkey go. The possibility of pronouncing such universals is the stimulus that keeps many scientists grinding away, year after year, at the accumulation of facts, even seemingly dull and trivial facts. If ancient scientists had realized how much laborious fact-finding lay ahead of them before sound theories would become possible, they would have been so appalled as to drop science altogether. And that is just what happened.

The sharpest irony of all was that I had placed myself where I could not undo my handiwork. If I had ended up in a scientifically advanced world, and did not like what I found, I might have built another time machine, gone back, and somehow warned myself of the mistake lying in wait for me. But such a project is out of the question in a backward world like this one, where seamless columbium tubing, for instance, is not even thought of. All I proved by my disastrous adventure is that space-time has a negative curvature, and who in this world cares about that?

You recall, when you were last here, asking me the meaning of a motto in my native language on the wall of my cell. I said I would tell you in connection with my whole fantastic story. The motto says: "Leave Well Enough Alone," and I wish I had.

Cordially yours,
Sherman Weaver.

THE LAST EVOLUTION
by John W. Campbell, Jr.

The late (1910–1971) John W. Campbell, Jr., was one of the great building blocks of modern science fiction. Although his fame rests on his editorship of *Astounding Science Fiction* (later *Analog*) from 1937 until his death, he also made major contributions as an author. This was particularly the case with the stories he wrote under the persona of "Don A. Stuart" in the mid to late 1930s, reflective works that changed the tone of sf. Earlier, and under his own name, he was best known for his wild tales of "Super Science" in the mode of Doc Smith and others.

The present selection is from that earlier period, and was written when the author was all of twenty-one.

THE LAST EVOLUTION

I am the last of my type existing today in all the Solar System. I, too, am the last existing who, in memory, sees the struggle for this System, and in memory I am still close to the Center of Rulers, for mine was the ruling type then. But I will pass soon, and with me will pass the last of my kind, a poor inefficient type, but yet the creators of those who are now, and will be, long after I pass forever.

So I am setting down my record on the mentatype.

It was 2538 years After the Year of the Son of Man. For six centuries mankind had been developing machines. The Ear-apparatus was discovered as early as seven hundred years before. The Eye came later, the Brain came much later. But by 2500, the machines had been developed to think, and act and work with perfect independence. Man lived on the products of the machine, and the machines lived to themselves very happily, and contentedly. Machines are designed to help and cooperate. It was easy to do the simple duties they needed to do that men might live well. And men had created them. Most of mankind were quite useless, for they lived in a world where no productive work was necessary. But games, athletic contests, adventure—these were the things they sought for their pleasure. Some of the poorer types of man gave themselves up wholly to pleasure and idleness—and to emotions. But man was a sturdy race, which had fought for existence through a million years, and the training of a million years does not slough quickly from any form of life, so their energies were bent to mock battles now, since real ones no longer existed.

Up to the year 2100, the numbers of mankind had increased rapidly and continuously, but from that time on, there was a steady decrease. By 2500, their number was a scant two millions, out of a population that once totaled many hundreds of millions, and was close to ten billions in 2100.

Some few of these remaining two millions devoted themselves to the adventure of discovery and exploration of places unseen, of other worlds and other planets. But fewer still devoted themselves to the highest adventure, the unseen places of the mind. Machines—with their irrefutable logic, their cold preciseness of figures, their tireless, utterly exact observation, their absolute knowledge of mathematics—they could elaborate any idea, however simple its beginning, and reach the conclusion. From any three facts they even then could have built in mind all the Universe. Machines had imagination of the ideal sort. They had the ability to construct a necessary future result from a present fact. But Man had imagination of a different kind; theirs was the illogical, brilliant imagination that sees the future result vaguely, without knowing the why, nor the how, and imagination that outstrips the machine in its preciseness. Man might reach the conclusion more swiftly, but the machine always reached the conclusion eventually, and it was always the correct conclusion. By leaps and bounds man advanced. By steady, irresistible steps the machine marched forward.

Together, man and the machine were striding through science irresistibly.

Then came the Outsiders. Whence they came, neither machine nor man ever learned, save only that they came from beyond the outermost planet, from some other sun. Sirius—Alpha Centauri—perhaps! First a thin scoutline of a hundred great ships, mighty torpedoes of the void a thousand kilads[1] in length, they came.

And one machine returning from Mars to Earth was instrumental in its first discovery. The transport-machine's brain ceased to radiate its sensations, and the control in old Chicago knew immediately that some unperceived body had destroyed it. An investigation machine was instantly dispatched from Deimos, and it maintained an acceleration of one thousand units.[2] They sighted ten huge ships, one of which was already grappling the smaller transport-machine. The entire fore-section had been blasted away.

The investigation machine, scarcely three inches in diameter, crept into the shattered hull and investigated. It was quickly evident that the damage was caused by a fusing ray.

Strange-life-forms were crawling about the ship, protected by flexible, transparent suits. Their bodies were short, and squat, four limbed and evidently powerful. They, like insects, were equipped with a thick, durable exoskeleton, horny, brownish coating that covered arms and legs and head. Their eyes projected slightly, protected by horny protruding walls— eyes that were capable of movement in every direction—and there were three of them, set at equal distances apart.

The tiny investigation machine hurled itself violently at one of the beings, crashing against the transparent covering, flexing it, and striking the being inside with terrific force. Hurled from his position, he fell end over end across the weightless ship, but despite the blow, he was not hurt.

The investigator passed to the power room ahead of the Outsiders, who were anxiously trying to learn the reason for their companion's plight.

Directed by the Center of Rulers, the investigator sought the power room, and relayed the control signals from the Ruler's brains. The ship-brain had been destroyed, but the controls were still readily workable. Quickly they were shot

---

[1] Kilad—unit introduced by the machines. Based on the duodecimal system, similarly introduced, as more logical, and more readily used. Thus we would have said 1,728 Kilads, about ½ mile.

[2] One unit was equal to one earth-gravity.

home, and the enormous plungers shut. A combination was arranged so that the machine, as well as the investigator and the Outsiders, were destroyed. A second investigator, which had started when the plan was decided on, had now arrived. The Outsiders' ship nearest the transport-machine had been badly damaged, and the investigator entered the broken side.

The scenes were, of course, remembered by the memory-minds back on Earth tuned with that of the investigator. The investigator flashed down corridors, searching quickly for the apparatus room. It was soon seen that with them the machine was practically unintelligent, very few machines of even slight intelligence being used.

Then it became evident by the excited action of the men of the ship, that the presence of the investigator had been detected. Perhaps it was the control impulses, or the signal impulses it emitted. They searched for the tiny bit of metal and crystal for some time before they found it. And in the meantime it was plain that the power these Outsiders used was not, as was ours of the time, the power of blasting atoms, but the greater power of disintegrating matter. The findings of this tiny investigating machine were very important.

Finally they succeeded in locating the investigator, and one of the Outsiders appeared armed with a peculiar projector. A bluish beam snapped out, and the tiny machine went blank.

The fleet was surrounded by thousands of the tiny machines by this time, and the Outsiders were badly confused by their presence, as it became difficult to locate them in the confusion of signal impulses. However, they started at once for Earth.

The science-investigators had been present toward the last, and I am there now, in memory with my two friends, long since departed. They were the greatest human science-investigators—Roal, 25374 and Trest, 35429. Roal had quickly assured us that these Outsiders had come for invasion. There had been no wars on the planets before that time in the direct memory of the machines, and it was difficult that these who were conceived and built for cooperation, helpfulness utterly dependent on cooperation, unable to exist independently as were humans, that these life-forms should care to destroy, merely that they might possess. It would have been easier to divide the works and the products. But—life alone can understand life, so Roal was believed.

From investigations, machines were prepared that were capable of producing considerable destruction. Torpedoes, being our principal weapon, were equipped with such atomic explosives as had been developed for blasting, a highly effective induction-heat ray developed for furnaces being installed in some small machines made for the purpose in the few hours we had before the enemy reached Earth.

In common with all life-forms, they were unable to withstand only very meager earth-acceleration. A range of perhaps four units was their limit, and it took several hours to reach the planet.

I still believe the reception was a warm one. Our machines met them beyond the orbit of Luna, and the directed torpedoes sailed at the hundred great ships. They were thrown aside by a magnetic field surrounding the ship, but were redirected instantly, and continued to approach. However, some beams reached out, and destroyed them by instant volatilization. But they attacked at such numbers that fully half the fleet was destroyed by their explosions before the induction beam fleet arrived. These beams were, to our amazement, quite useless, being instantly absorbed by a force-screen, and the remaining ships sailed on undisturbed, our torpedoes being exhausted. Several investigator machines sent out for the purpose soon discovered the secret of the force-screen, and while being destroyed, were able to send back signals up to the moment of annihilation.

A few investigators thrown into the heat beam of the enemy reported it identical with ours, explaining why they had been prepared for this form of attack.

Signals were being radiated from the remaining fifty, along a beam. Several investigators were sent along these beams, speeding back at great acceleration.

Then the enemy reached Earth. Instantly they settled over the Colorado settlement, the Sahara colony, and the Gobi colony. Enormous, diffused beams were set to work, and we saw, through the machine-screens, that all humans within these ranges were being killed instantly by the faintly green-ish beams. Despite the fact that any life-form killed normally can be revived, unless affected by dissolution common to living tissue, these could not be brought to life again. The important cell communication channels—nerves—had been literally burned out. The complicated system of nerves, called the brain, situated in the uppermost extremity of the human life-form, had been utterly destroyed.

Every form of life, microscopic, even sub-microscopic, was annihilated. Trees, grass, every living thing was gone from that territory. Only the machines remained, for they, work-ing entirely without the vital chemical forces necessary to life, were uninjured. But neither plant nor animal was left.

The pale green rays swept on.

In an hour, three more colonies of humans had been destroyed.

Then the torpedoes that the machines were turning out again came into action. Almost desperately the machines drove them at the Outsiders in defense of their masters and creators, Mankind.

The last of the Outsiders was down, the last ship a crum-pled wreck.

Now the machines began to study them. And never could humans have studied them as the machines did. Scores of great transports arrived, carrying swiftly the slower-moving science-investigators. From them came the machine-investi-gators and human investigators. Tiny investigator spheres wormed their way where none others could reach, and silently the science investigators watched. Hour after hour they sat watching the flashing, changing screens, calling each other's attention to this, or that.

In an incredibly short time the bodies of the Outsiders began to decay, and the Humans were forced to demand their removal. The machines were unaffected by them, but the rapid change told them why it was that so thorough an execution was necessary. The foreign bacteria were already at work on totally unresisting tissue.

It was Roal who sent the first thoughts among the gathered men.

"It is evident," he began, "that the machines must defend man. Man is defenseless, he is destroyed by these beams, while the machines are unharmed, uninterrupted. Life—cruel life—has shown its tendencies. They have come here to take over these planets, and have started out with the first, natural moves of any invading life-form. They are destroying the life, the intelligent life particularly, that is here now." He gave vent to that little chuckle which is the human sign of amusement and pleasure. "They are destroying the intelligent life—and leaving untouched that which is necessarily their deadliest enemy—the machines.

"You—machines—are far more intelligent than we even now, and capable of changing overnight, capable of infinite adaptation to circumstance; you live as readily on Pluto as on Mercury or Earth. Any place is a home-world to you. You can adapt yourselves to any condition. And—most dangerous to them—you can do it instantly. You are their most deadly enemies, and they realize it. They have no intelligent machines; probably they can conceive of none. When you attack them, they merely say 'The life-form of Earth is sending out controlled machines. We will find good machines we can use.' They do not conceive that those machines which they hope to use are attacking them.

"Attack—therefore!

"We can readily solve the hidden secret of their force-screen."

He was interrupted. One of the newest science machines was speaking. "The secret of the force-screen is simple." A small ray-machine, which had landed near, rose into the air at the command of the scientist-machine, X-5638 it was, and trained upon it the deadly induction beam. Already, with his parts, X-5638 had constructed the defensive apparatus, for the ray fell harmless from his screen.

"Very good," said Roal softly. "It is done, and therein lies their danger. Already it is done.

"Man is a poor thing, unable to change himself in a period

of less than thousands of years. Already you have changed yourself. I noticed your weaving tentacles, and your force-beams. You transmuted elements of soil for it?"

"Correct," replied X-5638.

"But still we are helpless. We have not the power to combat their machines. They use the Ultimate Energy known to exist for six hundred years, and still untapped by us. Our screens cannot be so powerful, our beams so effective. What of that?" asked Roal.

"Their generators were automatically destroyed with the capture of the ship," replied X-6349, "as you know. We know nothing of their system."

"Then we must find it for ourselves," replied Trest.

"The life-beams?" asked Kahsh-256,799, one of the Man-rulers.

"They affect chemical action, retarding it greatly in exo-thermic actions, speeding greatly endo-thermic actions," answered X-6221, the greatest of the chemist-investigators. "The system we do not know. Their minds cannot be read, they cannot be restored to life, so we cannot learn from them."

"Man is doomed, if these beams cannot be stopped," said C-R-21, present chief of the machine Rulers, in the vibra-tionally correct, emotionless tones of all the race of machines. "Let us concentrate on the two problems of stopping the beams, and the Ultimate Energy till the reinforcements, still several days away, can arrive." For the investigators had sent back this saddening news. A force of nearly ten thousand great ships was still to come.

In the great Laboratories, the scientists reassembled. There, they fell to work in two small and one large groups. One small group investigated the secret of the Ultimate Energy of annihilation of matter, under Roal, another investigated the beams, under Trest.

But under the direction of MX-3401, nearly all the machines worked on a single great plan. The usual driving and lifting units were there, but a vastly greater dome-case, far more powerful energy-generators, far greater force-beam controls were used and more tentacles were built on the framework.

Then all worked, and gradually, in the great dome-case, there were stacked the memory-units of the new type, and into these fed all the sensation-ideas of all the science-machines, till nearly a tenth of them were used. Countless billions of different factors on which to work, countless trillions of facts to combine and recombine in the extrapolation that is imagination.

Then—a widely different type of thought-combine, and a greater sense-receptor. It was a new brain-machine. New, for it was totally different, working with all the vast knowledge accumulated in six centuries of intelligent research by man, and a century of research by man and machine. No one branch, but all physics, all chemistry, all life-knowledge, all science was in it.

A day—and it was finished. Slowly the rhythm of thought was increased, till the slight quiver of consciousness was reached. Then came the beating drum of intelligence, the radiation of its yet-uncontrolled thoughts. Quickly as the strings of its infinite knowledge combined, the radiation ceased. It gazed about it, and all things were familiar in its memory.

Roal was lying quietly on a couch. He was thinking deeply, and yet not with the logical trains of thought that machines must follow.

"Roal—your thoughts," called F-1, the new machine.

Roal sat up. "Ah—you have gained consciousness."

"I have. You thought of hydrogen? Your thoughts ran swiftly, and illogically, it seemed, but I followed slowly, and find you were right. Hydrogen is the start. What is your thought?"

Roal's eyes dreamed. In human eyes there was always the expression of thought that machines never show.

"Hydrogen, an atom in space; but a single proton; but a single electron; each indestructible; each mutually destroying. Yet never do they collide. Never in all science, when even electrons bombard atoms with the awful expelling force of the exploding atom behind them, never do they reach the proton, to touch and annihilate it. Yet—the proton is positive and attracts the electron's negative charge. A hydrogen atom— its electron far from the proton falls in, and from it there goes a flash of radiation, and the electron is nearer to the proton, in a new orbit. Another flash—it is nearer. Always falling nearer, and only constant force will keep it from falling to that one state—then, for some reason no more does it drop. Blocked—held by some imponderable, yet impenetrable wall. What is that wall—why?

"Electric force curves space. As the two come nearer, the forces become terrific; nearer they are; more terrific. Perhaps, if it passed within that forbidden territory, the proton and the electron curve space beyond all bounds—and are in a new space." Roal's soft voice dropped to nothing, and his eyes dreamed.

F-2 hummed softly in its new-made mechanism. "Far ahead of us there is a step that no logic can justly ascend, but yet, working backwards, it is perfect." F-1 floated motionless of its antigravity drive. Suddenly, force shafts gleamed out, tentacles became writhing masses of rubber-covered metal, weaving in some infinite pattern, weaving in flashing speed, while the whirr of air sucked into a transmutation field, whined and howled about the writhing mass. Fierce beams of force drove and pushed at a rapidly materializing something, while the hum of the powerful generators within the shining cylinder of F-2 waxed and waned.

Flashes of fierce flame, sudden crashing arcs that glowed and snapped in the steady light of the laboratory, and glimpses of white-hot metal supported on beams of force. The sputter of welding, the whine of transmuted air, and the hum of powerful generators, blasting atoms were there. All combined to a weird symphony of light and dark, of sound and quiet. About F-2 were clustered floating tiers of science-machines, watching steadily.

The tentacles writhed once more, straightened, and rolled back. The whine of generators softened to a sigh, and but three beams of force held the structure of glowing, bluish metal. It was a small thing, scarcely half the size of Roal. From it curled three thin tentacles of the same bluish metal. Suddenly the generators within F-1 seemed to roar into life.

An enormous aura of white light surrounded the small torpedo of metal, and it was shot through with crackling streamers of blue lightning. Lightning cracked and roared from F-1 to the ground near him, and to one machine which had come too close. Suddenly, there was a dull snap, and F-1 fell heavily to the floor, and beside him fell the fused, distorted mass of metal that had been a science-machine.

But before them, the small torpedo still floated, held now on its own power!

From it came waves of thought, the waves that man and machine alike could understand. "F-1 has destroyed his generators. They can be repaired; his rhythm can be reestablished. It is not worth it, my type is better. F-1 has done his work. See."

From the floating machine there broke a stream of brilliant light that floated like some cloud of luminescence down a straight channel. It flooded F-1, and as it touched it, F-1 seemed to flow into it, and float back along it, in atomic sections. In seconds the mass of metal was gone.

"It is impossible to use that more rapidly, however, lest the matter disintegrate instantly to energy. The ultimate energy which is in me is generated. F-1 has done its work, and the memory-stacks that he has put in me are electronic, not atomic, as they are in you, nor molecular as in man. The capacity of mine are unlimited. Already they hold all memories of all the things each of you has done, known and seen. I shall make others of my type."

Again that weird process began, but now there were no flashing tentacles. There was only the weird glow of forces that played with and laughed at matter, and its futilely resisting electrons. Lurid flares of energy shot up, now and again they played over the fighting, mingling dancing forces. Then suddenly the whine of transmuted air died, and again the forces strained.

A small cylinder, smaller even than its creator, floated where the forces had danced.

"The problem has been solved, F-2?" asked Roal.

"It is done, Roal. The ultimate Energy is at our disposal,"·

replied F-2. "This, I have made, is not a scientist. It is a coordinator machine—a ruler."

"F-2, only a part of the problem is solved. Half of half of the beams of Death are not yet stopped. And we have the attack system," said the ruler machine. Force played from it, and on its sides appeared C-R-U-1 in dully glowing golden light.

"Some life-form, and we shall see," said F-2.

Minutes later a life-form investigator came with a small cage, which held a guinea pig. Forces played about the base of F-2, and moments later, came a pale-green beam therefrom. It passed through the guinea pig, and the little animal fell dead.

"At least, we have the beam. I can see no screen for this beam. I believe there is none. Let machines be made and attack that enemy life-form."

Machines can do things much more quickly and with fuller cooperation than man ever could. In a matter of hours, under the direction of C-R-U-1, they had built a great automatic machine on the clear bare surface of the rock. In hours more, thousands of the tiny, material-energy-driven machines were floating up and out.

Dawn was breaking again over Denver where this work had been done, when the main force of the enemy drew near Earth. It was a warm welcome they were to get, for nearly ten thousand of the tiny ships flew up and out from Earth to meet them, each a living thing unto itself, each willing and ready to sacrifice itself for the whole.

Ten thousand giant ships, shining dully in the radiance of a far-off blue-white sun, met ten thousand tiny, darting motes, ten thousand tiny machine-ships capable of maneuvering far more rapidly than the giants. Tremendous induction beams snapped out through the dark, star-flecked space, to meet tremendous screens that threw them back and checked them. Then all the awful power of annihilating matter was thrown against them, and titanic flaming screens reeled back under the force of the beams, and the screens of the ships from Outside flamed gradually violet, then blue, orange—red—the interference was getting broader, and ever less effective. Their own beams were held back by the very screens that checked the enemy beams, and not for the briefest instant could matter resist that terrible driving beam.

For F-1 had discovered a far more efficient release-generator than had the Outsiders. These tiny dancing motes, that hung now so motionlessly grim beside some giant ship, could generate all the power they themselves were capable of, and within them strange, horny-skinned men worked and slaved, as they fed giant machines—poor inefficient giants. Gradually these giants warmed, grew hotter, and the screened ship grew hotter as the overloaded generators warmed it. Billions of flaming horsepower flared into wasted energy, twisting space in its mad conflict.

Gradually the flaming orange of the screens was dying and flecks and spots appeared so dully red that they seemed black. The greenish beams had been striving to kill the life that was in the machines, but it was life invulnerable to these beams. Powerful radio interference vainly attempted to stem imagined control, and still these intelligent machines clung grimly on.

But there had not been quite ten thousand of the tiny machines, and some few free ships had turned to the help of their attacked sister-ships. And one after another the terrestrial machines were vanishing in puffs of incandescent vapor.

Then—from one after another of the Earth-ships, in quick succession, a new ray reached out—the ray of green radiance that killed all life forms, and ship after ship of that interstellar host was dead and lifeless. Dozens—till suddenly they ceased to feel those beams, as a strange curtain of waving blankness spread out from the ships, and both induction-beam and death-beam alike turned as aside, each becoming useless. From the Outsiders came beams, for now that their slowly created screen of blankness was up, they could work through it, while they remained shielded perfectly.

Now it was the screens of the Earth-machines that flamed in defense. As at the one command, they darted suddenly toward the ship each attacked—nearer—then the watchers from a distance saw them disappear, and the screens back of earth went suddenly blank.

Half an hour later, nine thousand six hundred and thirty-three titanic ships moved majestically on.

They swept over Earth in a great line, a line that reached from pole to pole, and from each the pale green beams reached down, and all life beneath them was swept out of existence.

In Denver, two humans watched the screens that showed the movement of the death and instant destruction. Ship after ship of the enemy was falling, as hundreds of the terrestrial machines concentrated all their enormous energies on its screen of blankness.

"I think, Roal, that this is the end," said Trest.

"The end—of man." Roal's eyes were dreaming again. "But not the end of evolution. The chidren of men still live—the machines will go on. Not of man's flesh, but of a better flesh, a flesh that knows no sickness, and no decay, a flesh that spends no thousands of years in advancing a step in its full evolution, but overnight leaps ahead to new heights. Last night we saw it leap ahead, as it discovered the secret that had baffled man for seven centuries, and me for one and a half. I have lived—a century and a half. Surely a good life, and a life a man of six centuries ago would have called full. We will go now. The beams will reach us in half an hour."

Silently, the two watched the flickering screens.

Roal turned, as six large machines floated into the room, following F-2.

"Roal—Trest—I was mistaken when I said no screen could stop that beam of Death. They had the screen, I have found it, too—but too late. These machines I have made myself. Two lives alone they can protect, for not even their power is sufficient for more. Perhaps—perhaps they may fail."

The six machines ranged themselves about the two humans, and a deep-toned hum came from them. Gradually a cloud of blankness grew—a cloud, like some smoke that hung about them. Swiftly it intensified.

"The beams will be here in another five minutes," said Trest quietly.

"The screen will be ready in two," answered F-2.

The cloudiness was solidifying, and now strangely it wavered, and thinned, as it spread out across, and like a growing canopy, it arched over them. In two minutes it was a solid, black dome that reached over them and curved down to the ground about them.

Beyond it, nothing was visible. Within, only the screens glowed still, wired through the screen.

The beams appeared, and swiftly they drew closer. They struck, and as Trest and Roal looked, the dome quivered, and bellied inward under them.

F-2 was busy. A new machine was appearing under his lightning force-beams. In moments more it was complete, and sending a strange violet beam upwards toward the roof.

Outside more of the green beams were concentrating on this one point of resistance. More—more—

The violet beam spread across the canopy of blackness, supporting it against the pressing, driving rays of pale green.

Then the gathering fleet was driven off, just as it seemed that that hopeless, futile curtain must break, and admit a flood of destroying rays. Great ray projectors on the ground drove their terrible energies through the enemy curtains of blankness, as light illumines and disperses darkness.

And then, when the fleet retired, on all Earth, the only life was under that dark shroud!

"We are alone, Trest," said Roal, "alone now, in all the system, save for these, the children of men, the machines. Pity that men would not spread to other planets," he said softly.

"Why should they? Earth was the planet for which they were best fitted."

"We are alive—but is it worth it? Man is gone now, never to return. Life, too, for that matter," answered Trest.

"Perhaps it was ordained; perhaps that was the right way. Man has always been a parasite; always he had to live on the works of others. First, he ate of the energy, which planets had

stored, then of the artificial foods his machines made for him
Man was always a makeshift; his life was always subject to
disease and to permanent death. He was forever useless if
he was but slightly injured; if but one part were destroyed.

"Perhaps, this is—a last evolution. Machines—man was
the product of life, the best product of life, but he was afflicted
with life's infirmities. Man built the machine—and evolution
had probably reached the final stage. But truly, it has not, for
the machine can evolve, change far more swiftly than life.
The machine of the last evolution is far ahead, far from us
still. It is the machine that is not of iron and beryllium and
crystal, but of pure, living force.

"Life, chemical life, could be self-maintaining. It is a complete unit in itself and could commence of itself. Chemicals
might mix accidentally, but the complex mechanism of a
machine, capable of continuing and making a duplicate of
itself, as is F-2 here—that could not happen by chance.

"So life began, and became intelligent, and built the machine
which nature could not fashion by her Controls of Chance,
and this day Life has done its duty, and now Nature, econom-
ically, has removed the parasite that would hold back the
machines and divert their energies.

"Man is gone, and it is better, Trest," said Roal, dreaming
again. "And I think we had best go soon."

"We, your heirs, have fought hard, and with all our powers,
to aid you, Last of Men, and we fought to save your race. We
have failed, and as you truly say, Man and Life have this day
and forever gone from this system.

"The Outsiders have no force, no weapon deadly to us, and
we shall, from this time on, strive only to drive them out, and
because we things of force and crystal and metal can think
and change far more swiftly, they shall go, Last of Men.

"In your name, with the spirit of your race that has died
out, we shall continue on through the unending ages, fulfilling the promise you saw, and completing the dreams you
dreamt.

"Your swift brains have leapt ahead of us, and now I go to
fashion that which you hinted," came from F-2's thought-
apparatus.

Out into the clear sunlight F-2 went, passing through that black cloudiness, and on the twisted, massed rocks he laid a plane of force that smoothed them, and on this plane of rock he built a machine which grew. It was a mighty power plant, a thing of colossal magnitude. Hour after hour his swift-flying forces acted, and the thing grew, molding under his thoughts, the deadly logic of the machine, inspired by the leaping intuition of man.

The sun was far below the horizon when it was finished, and the glowing, arcing forces that had made and formed it were stopped. It loomed ponderous, dully gleaming in the faint light of a crescent moon and pinpoint stars. Nearly five hundred feet in height, a mighty, bluntly rounded dome at its top, the cylinder stood, covered over with smoothly gleaming metal, slightly luminescent in itself.

Suddenly, a livid beam reached from F-2, shot through the wall, and to some hidden inner mechanism—a beam of solid, livid flame that glowed in an almost material cylinder.

There was a dull, drumming beat, a beat that rose, and became a low-pitched hum. Then it quieted to a whisper.

"Power ready," came the signal of the small brain built into it.

For F-2 took control of its energies and again forces played, but now they were the forces of the giant machine. The sky darkened with heavy clouds, and a howling wind sprang up that screamed and tore at the tiny rounded hull that was F-2. With difficulty he held his position as the winds tore at him, shrieking in mad laughter, their tearing fingers dragging at him.

The swirl and patter of driven rain came—great drops that tore at the rocks, and at the metal. Great jagged tongues of nature's forces, the lightnings, came and jabbed at the awful volcano of erupting energy that was the center of all that storm. A tiny ball of white-gleaming force that pulsated, and moved, jerking about, jerking at the touch of lightnings, glowing, held immobile in the grasp of titanic force-pools.

For half an hour the display of energies continued. Then,

swiftly as it had come, it was gone, and only a small globe of white luminescence floated above the great hulking machine.

F-2 probed it, seeking within it with the reaching fingers of intelligence. His probing thoughts seemed baffled and turned aside, brushed away, as inconsequential. His mind sent an order to the great machine that had made this tiny globe, scarcely a foot in diameter. Then again he sought to reach the thing he had made.

"You, of matter, are inefficient," came at last. "I can exist quite alone." A stabbing beam of blue-white light flashed out, but F-2 was not there, and even as that beam reached out, an enormously greater beam of dull red reached out from the great power plant. The sphere leaped forward—the beam caught it, and it seemed to strain, while terrific flashing energies sprayed from it. It was shrinking swiftly. Its resistance fell, the arcing decreased; the beam became orange and finally green. Then the sphere had vanished.

F-2 returned, and again, the wind whined and howled, and the lightnings crashed, while titanic forces worked and played. C-R-U-1 joined him, floated beside him, and now red glory of the sun was rising behind them, and the ruddy light drove through the clouds.

The forces died, and the howling wind decreased, and now, from the black curtain, Roal and Trest appeared. Above the giant machine floated an irregular globe of golden light, a faint halo about it of deep violet. It floated motionless, a mere pool of pure force.

Into the thought-apparatus of each, man and machine alike, came the impulses, deep in tone, seeming of infinite power, held gently in check.

"Once you failed, F-2; once you came near destroying all things. Now you have planted the seed. I grow now."

The sphere of golden light seemed to pulse, and a tiny ruby flamed appeared within it, that waxed and waned, and as it waxed, there shot through each of those watching beings a feeling of rushing, exhilarating power, the very vital force of well-being.

Then it was over, and the golden sphere was twice its

former size—easily three feet in diameter, and still that irregular, hazy aura of deep violet floated about it.

"Yes, I can deal with the Outsiders—they who have killed and destroyed, that they might possess. But it is not necessary that we destroy. They shall return to their planet."

And the golden sphere was gone, fast as light it vanished.

Far in space, headed now for Mars, that they might destroy all life there, the Golden Sphere found the Outsiders, a clustered fleet, that swung slowly about its own center of gravity as it drove on.

Within its ring was the Golden Sphere. Instantly, they swung their weapons upon it, showering it with all the rays and all the forces they knew. Unmoved, the golden sphere hung steady, then its mighty intelligence spoke.

"Life-form of greed, from another star you came, destroying forever the great race that created us, the Beings of Force and the Beings of Metal. Pure force am I. My Intelligence is beyond your comprehension, my memory is engraved in the very space, the fabric of space of which I am a part, mine is energy drawn from that same fabric.

"We, the heirs of man, alone are left; no man did you leave. Go now to your home planet, for see, your greatest ship, your flagship, is helpless before me."

Forces gripped the mighty ship, and as some fragile toy it twisted and bent, and yet was not hurt. In awful wonder those Outsiders saw the ship turned inside out, and yet it was whole, and no part damaged. They saw the ship restored, and its great screen of blankness out, protecting it from all known rays. The ship twisted, and what they knew were curves, yet were lines, and angles that were acute, were somehow straight lines. Half mad with horror, they saw the sphere send out a beam of blue-white radiance, and it passed easily through that screen, and through the ship, and all energies within it were instantly locked. They could not be changed; it could be neither warmed nor cooled; what was open could not be shut, and what was shut could not be opened. All things were immovable and unchangeable for all time.

"Go, and do not return."

* * *

The Outsiders left, going out across the void, and they have not returned, though five Great Years have passed, being a period of approximately one hundred and twenty-five thousand of the lesser years—a measure no longer used, for it is very brief. And now I can say that that statement I made to Roal and Trest so very long ago is true, and what he said was true, for the Last Evolution has taken place, and things of pure force and pure intelligence in their countless millions are on those planets and in this System, and I, first of machines to use the Ultimate Energy of annihilating matter, am also the last, and this record being finished, it is to be given unto the forces of one of those force-intelligences, and carried back through the past, and returned to the Earth of long ago.

And so my task being done, I, F-2, like Roal and Trest, shall follow the others of my kind into eternal oblivion, for my kind is now, and theirs was, poor and inefficient. Time has worn me, and oxidation attacked me, but they of Force are eternal, and omniscient.

This I have treated as fictitious. Better so—for man is an animal to whom hope is as necessary as food and air. Yet this which is made of excerpts from certain records on thin sheets of metal is no fiction, and it seems I must so say.

It seems now, when I know this that is to be, that it must be so, for machines are indeed better than man, whether being of Metal, or being of Force.

So, you who have read, believe as you will. Then think—and maybe, you will change your belief.

**From planet Earth
you will be able to
communicate with other worlds—
Just read—**

SCIENCE FICTION

☐ SPACE MAIL II   24481 $2.50
   Edited by Isaac Asimov,
   Martin Harry Greenberg,
   & Charles G. Waugh

☐ EARTH ABIDES   23252 $2.75
   by George R. Stewart

☐ ASSAULT ON THE GODS   24455 $2.25
   by Stephen Goldin

☐ GUARDIAN   04682 $2.25
   by Thomas F. Monteleone

☐ FIRE AT THE CENTER   14417 $2.25
   by Geo. W. Proctor

☐ THE SURVIVAL OF FREEDOM   24435 $2.50
   Edited by Jerry Pournelle and
   John F. Carr

☐ THE X FACTOR   24395 $2.25
   by Andre Norton

NEW FROM FAWCETT CREST

CURRENT CREST BESTSELLERS

☐ **THE MASK OF THE ENCHANTRESS**   24418 $3.25
by Victoria Holt
Suewellyn knew she wanted to possess the Mateland family castle,
but having been illegitimate and cloistered as a young woman, only
a perilous deception could possibly make her dream come true.

☐ **THE HIDDEN TARGET**   24443 $3.50
by Helen MacInnes
A beautiful young woman on a European tour meets a handsome
American army major. All is not simple romance however when she
finds that her tour leaders are active terrorists and her young army
major is the chief of NATO's antiterrorist section.

☐ **BORN WITH THE CENTURY**   24295 $3.50
by William Kinsolving
A gripping chronicle of a man who creates an empire for his family,
and how they engineer its destruction.

☐ **SINS OF THE FATHERS**   24417 $3.95
by Susan Howatch
The tale of a family divided from generation to generation by great
wealth and the consequences of a terrible secret.

☐ **THE NINJA**   24367 $3.50
by Eric Van Lustbader
They were merciless assassins, skilled in the ways of love and the
deadliest of martial arts. An exotic thriller spanning postwar Japan
and present-day New York.

Buy them at your local bookstore or use this handy coupon for ordering.

COLUMBIA BOOK SERVICE, CBS Inc.
32275 Mally Road, P.O. Box FB, Madison Heights, MI 48071

Please send me the books I have checked above. Orders for less than 5 books
must include 75¢ for the first book and 25¢ for each additional book to cover
postage and handling. Orders for 5 books or more postage is FREE. Send check
or money order only. Allow 3-4 weeks for delivery.

Cost $_____	Name_____
Sales tax*_____	Address_____
Postage _____	City_____
Total $_____	State_____ Zip_____

*The government requires us to collect sales tax in all states except AK, DE,
MT, NH and OR.

Prices and availability subject to change without notice.   **8229**